CANCER'S CURSE

BOOK 4 OF THE ZODIAC

PAUL SATING

Editor: Cindy Niespodzianski

Cover Design: Jake at jcalebdesign.com

ISBN-13: 978-1-7322617-7-8

To Jon Grilz, your kindness knows no bounds, and if the rest of the world cared about others as you do for strangers, it would be a wonderful place to be.

THREE FREE BOOKS

THE ZODIAC SERIES

UNDERWORLD, FIFTH CIRCLE

ONE YEAR AFTER GEMINI

BLESS IT, it was hot.

Yes, I know you mortals have this general perception of Hell being all about Hellfire and brimstone, and it is. Well, sort of. But the Underworld—or Hell, as I prefer to call it because it's simply so much easier to say—is much more than trite stereotypes.

We have the Hellfire—it's blue, by the way—and brimstone—which is all our streets seem to be made of—but we also have oceans, lakes, prairies, cities, city parks, old towns, new towns, dancing and bar districts, and even walking trails and coffee shops for all the old demons to do old demon things in and around.

When you boil—get it?—it all down, Hell is a lot like the human world. I should know; I've been there twice and consider myself an expert in my circles, though my circles extend to just two other incubi, my boss, and my parents.

My point is, Hell is similar to the Overworld and, today, here in the Fifth Circle, it was hot.

Like, suffocatingly hot.

Though that might have something to do with me

standing in the middle of a pack of demons in the height of the day, smack-dab in the center of the Samhain carnival.

Bless it, today was hot.

The one difference I guess I would have to recognize if I'm being honest, is that Hell doesn't have seasons. As I learned from my time in the Overworld, those are common for mortals. Here, not so much. Not at all, actually.

There are no seasons because—axial tilt aside—the Hell-fire, our version of your sun, misses the mark. We get our light and sense of passing time from it, when the Grand Chamber is opened and closed each day. Callers, magical purple creatures, ensure the Underworld's residents who do not live near clock towers start their days on-time, even before the blue light escapes. Life here is a well-oiled machine. Day-in and day-out, each one is the same as the previous, identical to the next.

Don't feel for us; it's our reality, our truth. The vast majority of demons don't know any better. I like the predictability of life here. To most demons it's one less thing to worry ourselves about, one less distraction from serving Lucifer and His grand plan. At least for typical demons—which I am not.

The only thing I was serving right now was my face. With corn dogs, cotton candy, and deep-fried hamburgers.

"Wipe your face," Ralrek said, flicking a finger at the corner of my mouth. "You're wearing more food than you're eating."

Placing the crook of my elbow against my mouth, I watched his face twist in disgust before yanking my sleeve across and away. "Better?"

He looked away. "You're gross."

Bilba, my best friend, laughed at the observation, covering his much-slimmer stomach with both hands, decorated with his typical black fingernail polish.

"But my mouth is clean."

Bilba laughed harder, the tips of his ears turning pink.

My argument game was solid. Ralrek didn't bother to argue. Such was the newfound healthy status of our relationship.

The only time I now saw the pair was on social occasions like this. I still had my job at The Book Abyss, working for that slave-driver Dialphio, but in the past year, none of us had received any work from Lucifer's Third Council. That lack of work deprived us of those moments of intensity that usually led to us fighting or getting at each other's throats. Things were much more peaceful now, so I had to antagonize him somehow. Can't have life becoming boring now, can we?

"Which one do you want to ride next?" Bilba was in front, leading the way through the crowd of demons hanging around gaming booths, standing in ridiculously lengthy lines for a ride, those waiting to lose coin in one of the rip-off schemes otherwise known as carnival games.

It was the opening night of Samhain, the annual carnival celebrating our liberation from Yahweh's reign of terror. Now, now; don't get offended until you've walked a mile in our shoes. None of us were there at the beginning and we can't be sure what went down between the two behemoths that control the fates of immortal and mortal alike—well, I used to think that until Dialphio educated me on One, but that story is for another time. For now, it was about Lucifer and his escape from Yahweh; the Fall according to angels and any mortals who believed them. It's a very festive time for us.

I love Samhain. Not only is it our biggest holiday, it is also the most lavish and most revered. Literally everything except the Hellfire factories and retail outlets—because demons just cannot imagine a shopping-less day—close for a few days before and after Samhain. So revered is it that we fill hours of our free time with conversations about the stories of how mortals have blasphemed our holiday by culturally appropriating it, dressing their kids up in costumes to "scare off evil."

Mortal ignorance can hurt sometimes.

But we don't let it dampen our festive season, keeping those chats restricted to nights, when demons have finished a day of celebrating, overeating, and spending time with family. It's in those times, at night, when the implings are in bed, and exhausted parents are trying to catch their breath, that the childless and more liberated sit around, sharing drinks and other pleasures of the imbibing type, along with opinions of what mortals have done to our most sacred period. Outside that, Samhain is all about the celebration of demonhood.

And the holiday's high point is the carnival. A time for unadulterated fun. Which was exactly what the three of us were doing now, with Bilba leading the way.

"I swear, every year, you turn into an impling," Ralrek said at Bilba's back, because Bilba slowed for no one when it came to fitting in as many rides as possible on a day ticket.

"We've only been on twenty-two rides!" he replied without looking over his shoulder. "And it's getting late."

Ralrek and I shared a look. "It's early. There's plenty of time," I said. "You're going to trample a little one."

"Then they need to stay out of my way," Bilba laughed. I didn't think he was joking.

I grabbed for his shirt, which was a feat. Bilba moved through the crowd with a ride-inspired grace completely unbecoming of him and his typical abilities. It was adorable. But annoying. His newfound sprite came from dropping some seriously unhealthy weight he carried for thousands of years while he was in the Eighth Circle trying to force his truant mother to love him. Though he wasn't fit by our health department standards, he was getting healthier every day and gaining some agility, which would be great in a fight, not so great when we were packed in clump of bodies at the Samhain celebration.

"Slow down," I said after missing my swipe at his shirt.

"Seriously. This is supposed to be fun and, in case you hadn't heard, sweating is not fun."

Bilba finally pulled up, glancing around.

"What are you looking for?"

"A clock tower," he said, his eyes never finding mine. "I need to know what time it is."

"Why?"

"Zeke, we haven't broken even yet." His tone was flat, uninterested in carrying on a conversation that would hinder him reaching his goals.

Bilba had this principle of frugality. It came from being raised in a single-income home since his mother abandoned their family half a lifetime ago. He'd always been cheap, but that personality quirk was exasperated by her absence, even after he started working for the Council and getting fat paydays every time we'd finished a job. Being cheap meant managing his coin carefully and one way he did that was to calculate how much a ticket cost per ride ridden. The standard was variable—I never bothered asking why—depending on his mood, but each year he let us know what an acceptable rate was. This year's rate was three coppers, a higher-than-normal-Bilba-rate, and we were currently averaging nearly double that. All that meant we had serious riding ahead of us before he allowed us to slow.

The things you do for friends.

"We're not implings," I countered. "We can stay out all night until they close for cleanup if we want to."

"Can't take that chance," Bilba said, turning to dash through the crowd.

"When we catch him, I'm going to kill him," Ralrek said, bringing a hand up to his perfect oil-black hair and smoothing one side that didn't need to be smoothed.

"I would too, but I feel bad for him." I mirrored Ralrek's hair-fixing, tussling my shaggy cut. He didn't notice the subtle jibe.

"Why? He's the dumbass that blew everything he'd earned."

Ralrek and I never had the healthiest of relationships. In fact, it wasn't until we were forced to work together by the Council that we spoke more than a sentence or two whenever we had the distinct displeasure of crossing each other's paths. That changed, slowly, after our first mission to the Overworld to capture an ancient demon called Aries the First. Ralrek teamed with Beelzebub and Bilba to kill him instead, and our relationship suffered as a consequence. During our last mission I discovered his secret, one he'd only recently shared with Bilba, that he was into mortals. By sheer luck, I earned Ralrek's trust enough that I could now chastise him for his insensitivity without setting off a round of verbal sparring. But only after I earned his trust enough to believe that he was not the one who stole and burned *The Histories of the Balance*, only the most important book in my world, in the middle of our Gemini adventure.

In the year since, we'd grown enough that I considered him a friend.

"Don't give him crap about that, okay? He finally found her and wanted to help because, be honest, you've both earned a lot of coin from the Council. How was he supposed to guess that it would dry up so quickly, especially after he spent it all trying to help his mother's stupid flower shop stay open?"

If any comment was coming, Ralrek bit it off, which was nice. The old Ralrek would have loosed it, regardless of the pain it would have caused. The improved version of this tall, handsome demon at least considered the cost of being an ass before proving himself so. It was refreshing, even if I was still skeptical of its viability.

We caught up with Bilba at the end of the line to the most popular roller coaster called *Heaven's Gate*, the scariest ride at the carnival. White beams of steel twisted and turned in waves and loops, arcing high into the Hellfire blue sky. Just as we joined him, a cart carrying a dozen screaming demons corkscrewed over our heads, thrusting them into a tunnel of blinding white light.

"I love this one," Bilba said once the cart passed and we could hear again. Another cranked up the long climb, about ready to release another screaming torrent of pleased passengers. I swallowed. He laughed. "What's the problem, Zeke? Not ready for this?"

"Since when did I like roller coasters?" The beams rattled above us as the cart had completed its climb and was loosed, the momentum sending it spiraling down. The memory of the last time I felt that drop was immediate, and I felt myself dropping along with the actual occupants of the cart racing toward the first loop.

"You've done more dangerous things than this," Bilba said, turning to watch the new cart carry its occupants up and around. "This should be nothing."

"Well, it *is* something, and it's something I don't like," I said, pointing as the cart shot out of the massive loop, jettisoning into the first of a series of corkscrew turns. "There is no control when you're trapped in those blessed things. Honestly, I don't understand how more demons don't die on them every year."

"Physics," Ralrek answered. "But seriously, Zeke. It's just a roller coaster." He moved closer, lowering his voice. "You've faced scarier things before. This is nothing. Plus, you can cast some freaking amazing spells now. Just magic yourself out of any trouble."

Wagging my finger at Ralrek, I looked around, making sure no one was listening, not that we could be heard over the rumble of the cart racing around the coaster even as another one was cranking its way up the initial climb. The crowd of excited demons in front and behind us appeared to be more fascinated by their impending death at the hands of this mechanism than our conversation. "I have control, well, sort of, over the things I have faced. At least how I responded to them. That, I don't." My finger found the speeding cart zipping over our heads, filled with petrified faces, distracting me from thinking about my new Abilities, thanks to the ancient halberd. "If I could use Creed's power, which I control, on that coaster, I would. If nothing else, it would make me feel a little better about this."

"Well, I'm glad you can't, because you have no control over your new Abilities," Bilba said.

"They're not new," I countered. "It's been a year."

"Ohhhh, an entire year," Ralrek said, Bilba joining him in laughing at my infantile skills.

When you're thousands of years old, a single year is hardly impressive. But when those years were lived as the only demon in Hell's history without magical Abilities, a year of possessing them was significant no matter how it was sliced. I just tried to ignore the fact that sometimes Creed seemed to have a mind of its own, altering spells even as I was in mid-conjure. If the weapon was sentient, I'd swear it was screwing with me.

The coaster line inched forward. Just like mortal males act when they're together, incubi don't like holding long conversations. Any situation that forces us to talk about things that don't involve movies, sports, or succubi aren't enjoyable. It was only a matter of time before someone said something stupid. Thankfully, it wasn't me.

"Do you think we're actually being punished?" Bilba broke the silence between the three of us.

"Punished? For what?" Ralrek said while I tried to ignore the conversation as the roller coaster's disembarking passengers taunted me with their smiles and yelps of joy. Liars, all of them.

Bilba sighed. It was heavy and a little too dramatic for a carnival atmosphere. "For what happened with Gemini." He turned away from looking forward to address the cyclops in the room we'd avoided for the past year.

Neither Ralrek nor I wanted to dive back into that piece of history. It was behind us and had been for a year. The memories of that entire situation, however, were as fresh as if it happened yesterday. With only the slight prompt from Bilba, the brightness of the Angelfire attack that killed hundreds of demons at Gemini's execution ceremony flashed through my mind. The burned air, the death cries. All of it, raw, simply from Bilba mentioning Gemini's name. For me, there was no mystery why this particular cyclops went ignored.

"We didn't do anything wrong," I finally answered Bilba.

"I didn't say you did," Bilba said, sounding hurt. "What I meant was, if you look at the facts, the Council has ignored us since they absolved you and Ralrek of any wrongdoing. A year, and ever since that incident, how many assignments have you gotten, Ralrek?"

He shrugged. "None."

"Zeke?"

"Zilch."

Bilba rolled his hands as if our answers proved his point. "See?"

"No."

"No," I echoed Ralrek. "And I'm in no big hurry to either," I said, dipping my head and giving Bilba that look. You know, the one that tells your friend he should know better than to tread on soft hearts.

He knew the story, knew that Ralrek and I had been arrested for a crime we did not commit and that we likely would have been executed right after Gemini had angels not attacked to save their own. He knew, because I often ranted about it, that I was not interested in ever seeing the Council or their paychecks again.

Bilba sighed, his shoulders dropping. "All that stuff went down with Gemini. Angels killing hundreds to rescue him.

And in the past year, what has happened? Nothing. That's what. They haven't retracted anything they said about you guys and sure as heaven didn't apologize to you for what they did, did they?"

We shook our heads simultaneously.

"Not that I'd take a coin from them, of course," Bilba said with a sour expression before looking at us from the corner of his eyes. "When was the last time anyone on the Council reached out to check on us?"

Ralrek grunted. "Lucifer's Council is a little busy for that."

"Zeke? What about you? After all, you're the one who started this. The Council recruited *you*. Ralrek and I are just your support team, but you're the one they wanted in the first place and you have always had an interesting relationship with them. Have any of them come to you?"

I didn't have to think about it. "No."

Bilba was silent for a few short roller-coaster shuffles forward. A weight pressed heavily, I could tell.

"What is it?" I asked.

He opened his mouth before snapping it shut again and half-spinning to face the front of the line.

Life was better without the Council in it. I guess that comes from wasting away in a prison cell with Ralrek. Bilba would understand if he'd been sitting on that damp floor, chained to a wall, waiting to face fate. He was trying to; I knew that, but because he did not live through it, he would never fully understand what it was like.

"Aren't you guys … don't you feel, I don't know … rejected … from time to time," he said. His voice was lacking any conviction, and I felt pained for him. His had been a unique experience to ours. And his sense of rejection was coming from some place deep, as deep or worse than the rejection being labeled Hell's Segregate used to have on me. Bilba's pain came in the shape of a middle-aged succubus who owned a flower shop in the Eighth Circle and forgot to love her son.

Mine was just a label that meant far less to me today than it did a year ago, thanks to an angel, the mortal enemy.

Man, I did not want to think about Cassie again.

"I mean, I think about it from time to time," Ralrek said, interrupting my thoughts of the cocoa haired angel, "but I'm not addicted to it. There's enough other stuff to deal with."

"I … I've been having a hard time with finding work and without their assignments, my confidence is sort of shaken. I think that's, in part, why I wonder why the Council is shunning us? To me, what's more important?"

"Torlan," Ralrek said in a way that sounded like a slip.

"Who?" I said, turning fully on him. There was something in his voice and the way he bit the corner of his lip that made me smile. "A boyfriend? You hellhound."

Ralrek smirked as I punched him in the shoulder.

"How long?"

"A few weeks," Ralrek dipped his head toward his raised shoulder.

"And why haven't we met him yet?" I said, narrowing my eyes.

Weird how quickly things change. A year and a half ago, I wouldn't have cared who was involved in Ralrek's lonely life. Now, being the first to learn of his secret, things had changed drastically. Behind that off-putting tall and handsome exterior hid a nice demon who had a personality and was actually vulnerable.

"I'm not sure I'm ready for that," Ralrek said, his eyes flickering at Bilba. "But at least this one is an immortal creature."

Subtle clues rarely get my attention, but this time I noticed Bilba hadn't said anything. He stood in our small circle, unresponsive, his face unreadable. The awkwardness was palpable.

I coughed, drawing Ralrek's whitening face in my direction. "Well, when you are, I'll be excited to meet him."

"Thanks, Zeke," Ralrek said. "That means a lot."

Another cart rattled overhead, reminding me I was standing in line to be voluntarily strapped into a death trap. My rising panic must have been obvious because Ralrek laughed and Bilba snorted through his nose before covering it and trying to play it off like he hadn't. Nothing like having good friends.

Underneath the fading roar of the cart disappearing into the tunnel of light, came the chattering of excited demons all around me, sounding like a cluster of annoying fairies—sorry, they're annoying, the way they flit about, mess with you by putting bugs in your hair and flying away before you can swat them, and the such. The air of excitement changed in seconds, moving away from the light-hearted and carefree feeling to one edged with anxiety. More demons chattered, the noise grew to more than an irritant as they engaged in the mysterious conversation rippling down the line. Incubi slapped each other's shoulders and made dumb faces. Succubi put hands to mouths or rubbed their loved one's arms.

"What's going on?" Bilba said, facing forward and craning to see down the line. He had a better chance of doing that then I did. There were implings who were taller than my sixty-seven inches.

Ralrek stretched to look over the heads in the crowd.

This was more than fairies chattering. This was the intangible nervous excitement that raced through crowds whenever something was happening that fell outside the scope of daily life.

A lump formed in my throat as I risked stepping out of line to catch a clue. "Not sure, but be ready," I said, my hand slipping to Creed's knob as I extended my senses outward. In addition to now being super sensitive to noises and the visual bombardment of life in Hell, the past year, me and the magical halberd bounded more than ever before. Not only could I call it from greater distances, but Creed had somehow hooked me into my surroundings. Now, everything was brighter, louder, and more aromatic than ever before. It was a wonderful skill to have picked up and developed, at home, in the relative silence of my Old Towne apartment. But here, surrounded by thousands of Fivers—my Fifth Circle neighbors—it was a little much. Whatever energy surged through the crowd, it irritated my senses, sort of like the fizzle of a firework, just without the bang, boom, awww.

Suddenly, I wasn't as confident about my level of control, which rivaled adolescent implings and their nocturnal emissions when dreaming of pleasurable things.

"Is something happening, Zeke?" Ralrek moved closer to whisper. Proximity was another outcome of our shared challenge with the Council last year, reluctant as it still was. At least he appreciated my talents for a change.

I shook my head. "No one's conjuring."

"Then what's going on? Everyone is jittery. I'm jittery," Bilba asked, his eyes growing wider, the tips of his big ears turning pink.

"You're always jittery," Ralrek quipped, but his expression was lax, unfocused on picking on our friend and more on picking up clues to the pockets of conversation that were swelling amongst the waiting ride-goers.

I put my finger to my lips. "Listen, instead of blabbing over top of everyone and we might just learn."

Slow but undeterred, the ripple of excitement waved from group to group, carrying the ominousness typical of big news. As the news traveled back, the roller coaster became less interesting.

"Humans," an old demon said, shaking his balding head.

"Overworld." A young succubus with a bad complexion cupped her hands around her mouth, shouting the message back, filling the role of the informed expert.

"I'm not shocked." This irritated response came from a short, stout mother who placed her hand on the top of the young red-headed impling clinging to her leg. "What do you expect from them?"

"Full-blown?" A thin incubus, brown skin cracking with age, grimaced.

"That's what they're saying," the know-it-all with the bad complexion nodded her head aggressively.

"When?" a succubus who appeared too young to be an adult but too old to be an impling held her hand to her mouth.

Word of whatever event everyone was talking about was getting closer, but I didn't feel like waiting. The group in front of us was making me nervous with their fidgeting to hear. Leaning closer to the incubus in front of me, I asked, "What's everyone talking about?"

"I don't know," he said with a sneer, pulling away from me. "Talk about minding your own business." He finished with a laugh to his friends, who looked at me as if I was the oddball.

Further ahead, someone shouted, "Oh, my Lucifer! Not again!"

"When will they learn? You'd think they'd be tired of fighting after the last one." The old, gray-haired demon shook his head again, like it was his own children making awful decisions.

"Wasn't the last one supposed to be the end of it?" another asked.

"The war to end all wars?" The gray-haired demon's wife laughed bitterly.

"Nah, there was another big one after that, remember?"

"Can't keep 'em straight. Dumb humans."

"Best hope we don't get involved," gray-hair said.

I couldn't take it anymore. Stepping out of line, ignoring Ralrek's tug on my sleeve and Bilba's questioning look, I walked a few groupings forward to where gray-hair was holding council.

"What's everyone talking about?" I said, interrupting the small group who looked me up and down in yo-yoing flicks of eyes. Patience was for those who had the privilege of peaceful lives.

Noone answered immediately.

"The humans," know-it-all said, leaning into the conversation.

I welcomed her desire to be the center of attention. "What about them?"

"Supposedly they've started another war," she replied in a prideful tone. Her eyes widened as if she expected me to understand some implied message.

The older male piped in. "Bet the Council will be convening to recruit soldiers."

"Soldiers?"

Know-it-all's eyes scrunched and her head jerked back. "Yes, soldiers," she cackled, like I was the idiot here. "Just like every time. To join the mortal armies?"

I knew that. Everyone did. Just a few decades ago we went through something similar when it seemed like the entire mortal realm wanted to destroy itself. When the dung hit the fan up there, we got called to arms. But I refused to intensify these localized conversations. When I didn't revel in her drama-weaving she turned her back. I returned to Bilba and Ralrek, neither of whom looked calm.

"War, Zeke," Bilba said. "Can you believe it?"

"How did you know?"

"We told him," the incubus who told me to bugger off said without making eye contact. "Wasn't as nosy as you. Seems like a nice lad."

Of course.

"They said there might be a draft. The old incubus up

there said there's already talk of recruiting demons for the human armies," Ralrek said.

"I wonder what they pay," Bilba said.

I noticed he was wringing his hands. "The human army?"

He nodded. "Guys," he paused, looking around, "I'm short on coin. Like, bad. If the humans are at war and the Council needs volunteers ... well, would you volunteer if we could?"

"Volunteer? You're serious?" Ralrek said with a scoffing laugh, looking around at the groups in line around us as if he couldn't believe the question. His smile dropped when he faced Bilba again. "You are, aren't you?"

Bilba didn't look humored. He squared on me. "Zeke?"

My love and respect for him drove the truth; well, that and the fact we didn't have anything to worry about because we were speaking in the hypothetical. "You bet, bud. Plus, I could use the coin too."

"You're not getting enough hours at Dialphio's shop?" Ralrek asked. "You're always there, or at least, that's what you claim when we've invited you out to the clubs for some dancing."

I shook my head. Ralrek knew I hated clubs. And dancing. And dancing in clubs. But that wasn't it. "No, she's been great. But I'm still renting the Old Towne apartment and, with the hours I'm getting, I'm saving up to get my own place. I can't rent forever."

"Don't tell me you burned through everything the Council gave you?" Ralrek's eyes narrowed.

"First, don't forget, they didn't pay me for the Aries mission," I said with the wag of a finger. "And they don't 'give' us anything. We earn it."

Ralrek threw his head back. "Don't start. I know. I know. Yield. I yield already. That's not what I meant."

"Are you sure? A prison term might not have been enough for you to see the light. You're pretty thick sometimes," I said with a grin and wink.

"I'm confident you're not as dumb as I used to think you were." Ralrek shrugged. "If it wasn't for them giving us the assignments they have, I wouldn't have what I do. My situation isn't like yours. I don't have a family; well, not in the sense you both do. Your mother is an issue, Bilba, but at least you have your father. And Zeke, yours is a dick, but your mother is awesome. Until Torlan, the only hope I had for a different tomorrow came because of what the Council gave me."

"So he's got potential to be a serious thing?" Bilba asked.

"Yes, if I keep him around," Ralrek answered nonchalantly. "We aren't even close to thinking about that type of stuff yet. Heavens, we're not even exclusive yet."

I blew a huge exhale out, letting my lips flap as I looked up at the next coaster cart about to plummet toward the surface. "Well, it doesn't matter what any of us would do, because it's not going to happen. We don't even know if there *is* a war in the Overworld. It's all just hearsay from a bunch of carnival goers."

"Hey, I'm more than a 'goer,' I'm a carnival lover," Bilba protested good-naturedly. "And, why would so many demons be talking about it if it wasn't true?"

I gestured at know-it-all, who was still reveling in the Hellfire-light of attention. "Because demons feed off gossip." I put my hands up in playful surrender. "Look, let's just enjoy this death trap and get in enough rides so you break even. Tomorrow, we'll see what the news says. But tonight, let's have fun." I paused as another cart rocketed overhead, shooting into the open mouth of the tunnel at irresponsible speeds. I swallowed that stupid lump in my throat again. "As much as we can."

Watching the full cart of screamers disappear into that frightening white tunnel, I wondered if it was possible for any of us to do that now, for different reasons.

2

UNDERWORLD, FIFTH CIRCLE

THE FINAL NIGHT of Samhain would be spent the way it always was: with a family dinner. As an impling, I used to enjoy the occasion. Back then, it was all about great food—unless Mother and Father hosted—and fun. Whichever house hosted was filled with Mother and Father, grandparents, aunts and uncles and associated cousins. There were board games, yard games, stories, terrible jokes and everything that made the annual gathering the type of event created by unfiltered trust and love. Now, it wasn't the same. Everyone was a few thousand years older. Many in the family moved across the Fifth, too far away to make it practical to travel, or had families of their own, leaving the fun feeling scripted.

I let out a long, slow breath.

"What's wrong?" Dialphio said, not taking her eyes from the report on her desk. A hand in her auburn hair, my boss looked exhausted, though her robust liveliness still sparkled in her emerald eyes.

We had closed the store, and she set about doing the administrative things she did every night while I cleaned and straightened up for the next day. Heading to my desk to collect my jacket and Creed, the thought of going to my parents' instead of my own home hit me, causing the reaction that drew her somewhat-dedicated attention.

"I'm headed to my parents' tonight for Samhain dinner," I said, trying to blot out the scratching of her quill.

Dialphio's mouth moved as she crunched numbers from the sales receipts. Her daily penance—sitting there, each day at the close of business, in front of piles of curled paper and coppers—some silvers, but not many—ensuring everything was accounted for. Not only boring and tedious, but confusing, if you asked me. Math and accounting never made friends with me.

Disrupting her nightly duties was a crappy thing to do, not that she seemed bothered. The Book Abyss was her only family and thinking about spending the last night of Samhain alone probably wasn't something she wanted to have on her mind.

I fixed that. "I'm sorry, Dialphio. I wasn't thinking. But I have an idea. Would you like to come to dinner with me? My mother … *cooks*." I couldn't call Mother a 'cook,' not with a straight face, I respected Dialphio too much for that.

She set her quill down, pulling the red-rimmed glasses she started using over the past year for reading from her eyes and taking me in. "That's very sweet of you Zeke, but I couldn't intrude on your family like that. Plus," she said, waving her glasses at the chaotic pile of receipts, "I've got to get through the rest of these."

"They'll be there after dinner, I promise," I said with a friendly smile. My heart twitched at the thought of her spending tonight in the bookstore. "Come on, I need backup."

She laughed. It sounded like a small bird's chirp. "So you want me to get wrapped up in your family drama? No thanks, I've got enough of my own."

My boss knew so much about my personal life. Maybe too much. I shrugged. "Not to wrap you in my family drama, but because you love me?" I offered, my voice rising with each word.

"Not that much," she said with a smile that evaporated instantly. "No family is free of drama, mine included. I ... I don't do well around it. Can't keep my trap shut."

"That's why you never talk about yours?"

Dialphio bit the end of her glasses' arm. "It's not any fun when a family gets to that point. Not healthy. The thing is, Lucifer may have His plan, but it's not etched in brimstone. We get to choose the demons we spend our time with, Ezekial. We're not immortal, not truly, regardless of what the humans think, so we should carefully consider how we live during the time we have. My family? That's one reason I work so hard, to be sure that I never have to return to what I was. You have that choice too."

"It doesn't feel like it." I cast my eyes down at Creed, rubbing the knob of the hilt.

There was a *tunk* as she dropped her glasses on the pile of receipts and stood, approaching me. Grabbing my hand—Dialphio was a hand holder—she said, "It rarely does until you decide that it is so. I'll tell you what," she followed up when I flinched, "I'll go with you. I don't need to stay here all night staring at numbers. I can get that done tomorrow if you'll take care of the front of the store for me."

"Are you sure?" I asked. If her going meant she would have a late night, I wouldn't ask that of her.

"Yes, I'm sure or I wouldn't do it, Ezekial." Her tone was light. "Let me clean this up and I'll be ready."

I hugged her. "Thank you, Dialphio. I'm glad you're coming."

She squeezed. "You're welcome. Now, let me finish. I'm starving. I cannot wait to try your mother's cooking."

"Don't count your curses too early," I smirked.

"THERE IT IS," I SAID, POINTING AT THE MASSIVE ANGEL OAK tree that my parents owned.

Dialphio whistled. "Who knew you came from money."

"Money? Hardly," I laughed. "They're old and bought it when the market was good, I guess."

"Aren't they about my age?" She gave me a sidelong glance.

I answered carefully because she was right. "Well, it's not like it was that long ago. But you get my point. Things are more expensive now. They had to rent out the top half of it to an incubus who works somewhere in the Fifth's tech department. He told me once, but I don't remember. He's not the most social incubus in Hell, that's for sure. A bachelor."

"Oh, is he attractive?"

"He's my age," I answered flatly, which only made Dialphio's chirping laugh raise an octave.

"But he's in tech, so he's got money," she said, batting her eyelids that were touched with green eye shadow.

I pulled up short, crossing my arms. "I didn't realize you were so fixated with coin."

"Business owners have to be or we aren't business owners for long. Especially bookstores. It's not easy, surviving, that is. Not in a world where most demons seem allergic to reading. A young incubus with coin sounds like an interesting way for me to spend the Samhain feast."

I barked a laugh. "Ulseil won't be joining us. Father put that stairwell in before they even rented out the top half so he wouldn't have to interact with renters. After twenty years of him renting from my parents, I think I've seen him a handful of times."

"Techies," she said with a playful smirk.

"Techies," I chuckled.

"Such a shame," she said. "Very well. I guess I'll just enjoy the dinner with your family and save my romantic interests for another time."

"Thanks for your sacrifice."

I held the gate open for Dialphio and took my time walking to the door and ringing the bell. It was weird, after spending thousands of years in the tree house to not walk straight into the home. But acting as if it was still my home was equally weird. How many years would pass before this awkward transitory period ended? Or was home a place you simply could never return to?

"Ezekial! Why didn't you just come in?" My mother shouted with joy after pulling the door open. She threw her arms open and hugged me before pulling back and forming her intimidating square jaw into a smiling one. "And who is this?"

Strong jawline aside, my mother was a warm succubus who covered her caring nature with hard eyes and a no-frills haircut that made her look five thousand years younger.

I wanted to tell her that she wouldn't have to ask if she'd bothered to stop by the bookstore in the year and a half I'd worked there, but I'd already heard their excuses and wasn't buying any of them.

"Mother, this is Dialphio, my boss. Dialphio, my mother, Lilith."

They exchanged polite introductions, each almost racing the other to their obligatory hug. Formalities out of the way, we stepped inside—but only after I drew a deep breath before facing my father. I stripped my shoes off as my cousin ran over and hugged my leg. I reached down and rubbed her blond hair, tussling it. "Hey Ursela, how are you? How's school?"

Ursela was barely over a thousand years old and in elementary school. But my aunt, Xarpa, and her husband Lal were professionals, focused on their careers for as long as I could remember, delaying any desire for children well past their due date.

"It's great!" she exclaimed, still squeezing my leg. "We

have been working on cellular structure this month. It's so interesting! Inside the cytoplasm are hundreds, maybe even thousands of things called organelles? They—"

"Wow, that's awesome! They've got you working on cells already?" The last time I saw Ursela she was taking humanology and learning about the entire history of humankind, which she dutifully recounted in its entirety for me at a family gathering. No one rescued me, my aunt and uncle preferring to dump parental responsibilities on me so they could get a break during the visit. After that incident, I understood why they needed a break, and I'd also learned how to counteract Ursela's adorable but exhausting passion for learning. "We need to talk about that during dinner."

Ungrateful looks snapped in my direction from the table around which the older demons gathered and chatted. I smiled at them. There was no way in Heaven I was going through that alone.

"Ezekial." My father's lukewarm welcome broke up Ursela's latest debrief on her progressing education.

I straightened to my full height, still far short of his, and plastered on a fake smile, acutely aware that Dialphio had moved closer. "Hi," I said, my throat tightening around the word as if it wanted to prevent me from giving him any more than he deserved.

"I'm glad you were able to make it," he said, his face unreadable until his eyes moved to his new guest. Reaching to extend his hand to Dialphio, he introduced himself with a warmth I hadn't felt since the first time I left for the Overworld. The prick. "I'm Kanthor, Ezekial's father. Nice to meet you and welcome."

Dialphio grasped has hand in her chubby pair, but only after checking me with a glance. "So nice to meet you, Kanthor. I'm Dialphio. Ezekial has told me so much about you. It's nice to put a face to those stories."

"Has he?" my father answered, arcing his back just a little straight.

I tucked away the joy rising at Dialphio's double entendre. Father didn't appear to pick up on it, making this even more enjoyable. Heavens, he wouldn't think anything negative could be said about him or that his perspective on anything wasn't *the* perspective. Mother almost always agreed with him, and when she disagreed, he conceded. But she was the only one I had ever seen get that allowance from him. Four or five hundred years ago, Kanthor had a drinking buddy, Maximus Truse, who was experiencing one of those personal growth moments you secretly hope all demons with outdated perspectives go through. Intolerant to a fault, Father accepted his friend and even agreed with him on a lot of things I found repulsive, like personal freedoms—or the lack thereof—the Council should restrict. But during a poker night out at our house, Maximus told the small gathering of incubi he had changed his mind on a few things, and one of those things was the restrictions on inter-Circle travel. Temperatures rose as the debate continued until Maximus stood, slapped his cards on the table, and ranted for five minutes about the restrictions being a totalitarian measure by a government with something to hide. Father did not take that well, they shouted, they screamed, they had to be pulled apart, and they probably would have come to blows if it hadn't been for Mother stomping into the room and giving my father 'the look,' which calmed the beast. The night ruined, the poker gathering ended, the incubi went home, Maximus and father never spoke again, and my eyes were opened about inter-Circle traveling. Father never conceded, never reached out to his old friend, and never entertained the possibility that he might not be absolutely correct. Maximus aside, I don't know if Father ever met someone who outright told him he was wrong about something and accepted that alternate opinion. Dialphio wouldn't be that individual because of her allegiance to me, not out of fear of making him angry, but it was fun to imagine.

"Yep." I lifted my chin. "All the quality stuff."

"Glad to hear it," he said carefully, before replacing his placid expression with something warmer, only reserved for her. "I'm so glad you could join us for the Samhain feast. Let's finish introducing you to everybody."

Dialphio let herself be dragged away to the table where introductions were made. I followed. It was pleasant, and a side-bar conversation between my parents and my boss gave me a chance to catch up with my aunt and uncle in peace, without Father's influence or disapproving comments.

Peace was not something that existed in this home for me recently. Besides the atrocity where hundreds of demons were killed at the failed execution of the angel Gemini, a cloud that still hung over Hell, that fateful day left small, less significant but still impactful personal ramifications lingering. Namely, the increased tensions between myself and my father. Throughout my life, they had suffered the indignity of my status as the Segregate—Hell's only demon to never have magic. The status disqualified me for academic and job opportunities, caused me to be bullied throughout my child-hood, and even cost my parents a number of friends. The cost of having a freak for a son. A label that had every succubi rejecting my advances, and every incubus wanting to fight me. I was not one of the tribe. It was a label many insisted I still wear. If they only knew what I could do now. How things had changed, right under the noses of the Fivers who shunned and ostracized me for thousands of years.

But even owning the awesome halberd did not bring that sense of peace. When the Council saw fit to hand me more assignments, the tension between me and my father started evaporating. Slowly. Agonizingly slow. We were on the road to recovery until Gemini and my imprisonment. Attending the execution in chains shamed my father, and that was the final straw in his humiliation. Our relationship had not been the same since, and a year later, it was still difficult to have cordial conversations. Whenever we were together, we pretended that was all. Pretended to get along. Pretended to be father and son.

Tonight was destined to be an uneasy event. For weeks I struggled with how to decline the invitation to the feast. Never finding a believable excuse, I'd accepted the invite and faced the doom of disapproving parents. Not until Dialphio accepted to come along did I see this as something I could survive. Now that she had my father distracted, I could at least get a little enjoyment out of the evening.

"Zeke, you must tell us about your adventures," Uncle Lal said. "Your mother talks about you all the time. Says you're doing incredible things for the Council."

I looked away because lying is hard. "Did she now? Well, I have done a few things for them, but I haven't worked for them in almost a year, so I don't have anything new to talk about."

From the corner of my eyes, I noticed my parents and Dialphio halt in mid-conversation. I did my best to ignore them.

"Is it true that you've actually gone to the Overworld?" Aunt Xarpa asked.

"Of course, it's true. Why would anyone lie about that?" Uncle Lal said, refilling his wine.

Wine was a favorite drink of the Samhain feast. Bottles would fill trash cans by the morning all around the neighborhood. A recipe for disaster anytime family got together. Especially families with unresolved tension. Demons under the influence of Lucifer's rich wines didn't always make for the best conversations, sending millions of Samhain feasts spirally in dangerous directions over the course of our history, I'm sure.

"Oh, because demons lie all the time?" Aunt Xarpa replied

with a sideways wink at me. I think she sometimes forgets how old I am, though I may always be an impling in her eyes.

Uncle Lal nodded. "Demons lie, yes. But the Council doesn't. That's why I asked him. No harm in that."

I drew a deep breath, trying to keep it hidden by dipping my head and tucking my chin against my chest. It sounded like Uncle Lal was drinking from the same batch of Council–infused wine as my father. Encouraged that my aunt didn't take things like my donkey ride humiliation after I refused to help fight Aries at face value, I answered. "Yes, I did. Twice, in fact."

Aunt Xarpa sucked in a breath, excited. "What was it like? Is it as horrible as rumors say? Are the mortals truly as foul as I've heard? Tell me everything."

I shook my head. "No, in fact they're quite a lot like us, believe it or not. Pretty diverse too. They have towering struc-tures and motorized vehicles and their skies are filled with flying vehicles called planes. You've probably seen them in mortal movies, but they're bigger in real life. Mortals have a terrible reputation amongst us, I'd say. They have struggles, they screw things up; they're fallible. But aren't we all?"

"Listen to him, a demon of the world," Uncle Lal slapped his leg. In my head, the sound was more like a pop of a rifle. "Never, in a million years would I have thought the Council would select a Sunstone to do anything, but especially to be lifted up. You've made us proud, boy."

"Thanks, Uncle Lal," I said with a smile. And then the smart ass in me slipped out. "It's nice to know some demons understand and appreciate what they have made me do."

Both my aunt and uncle cast glances in my father's direc-tion. I didn't bother to gauge his thoughts on the matter. Those were already firmly established. In my time working for Hell's rulers my father had excused away my humiliation, accepted my lack of autonomy, and ignored my frustrations at being forced into morally grotesque events.

My aunt lifted her head, a smile splitting her face. "Well, I for one am very proud of everything you've done, for Lucifer, the Council, and us. The Sunstone's, a family that has served the Council." She shook her head. "I can't believe it's true, even now."

"When are you going back?" Uncle Lal said.

"No idea."

"The boy isn't getting any more work from them after what happened last year," said father, taking a long drink of his wine while eyeing me.

From the kitchen, my mother tsk'ed. "We're not going to talk about that, remember?" Her tone was light, but anyone who knew her could pick out the hidden threat buried in her message.

I wasn't surprised. She still hadn't come to terms with the fact that I'd been arrested and imprisoned. Being barred from seeing me thanks to that scheming snake of a Founder, Apopis, for months afterward wasn't helpful. And because we weren't able to have an open and honest conversation about the truth, my parents still had no idea of the extent to which the Council went to protect themselves. Even sacrificing two young demons who'd been in their employ. The shame, the confusion and turmoil, and the heightened tense attention from the Council was too much for even her, I guess. We still had so much to talk about and clear up.

Ursela jumped in the chair next to me. "Father says you did something very, very bad. Is that true?"

Aunt Xarpa flinched, her cheeks darkening. Uncle Lal gave his daughter an eye roll. "Now, now. Let's not be telling tales. Okay, darling?"

"But," Ursela protested, "that's what you said. You said that Ezekial was bad, and he had to go to jail." She turned to me, excited in her innocence. "Is that true? What's it like? Is it as scary as it seems?"

I don't know what made me happier, the unadulterated

beauty of honesty—even if it came from the youngest demon at the table—or the absolute discomfort of everyone else seated around me.

I tussled Ursela's blond mop of hair. She giggled. Before I answered, I reminded myself that she was still an impling, unaware of how deceitful adults could be. It wasn't my role or responsibility to shatter her innocence. Her parents and the Underworld would do that soon enough, just as it had for me. Just as it had for any observant and insightful demon.

"It is true," I said in a low voice as if she and I shared a conspiracy. "I went to jail."

Her eyes grew large. "What did you do? Were you as naughty as father said?"

I looked at my uncle, who distracted himself in the bottom of his wine glass. I couldn't really fault him since the only information he had came from the Council and my parents. His ignorance was only partially his fault. "Actually, no. I wasn't naughty at all."

"Then what happened?"

"That's a very long story. A very boring one, I promise."

Ursela thrust her shoulders up and then down again, tucking her hands into her arms and jutting out her bottom lip. "No one will tell me anything."

The comment drew a round of uneasy laughter from around the table.

"That's because it really is like Ezekial said," Mother said. "It is a boring story, one we don't need to discuss."

"But I want to know."

"That's enough now," Uncle Lal said in a firm tone, waving his wineglass around at the attendees of the feast. "We're all here for a wonderful Samhain feast your aunt has been fever-ishly working on for hours. Let's enjoy the food and the family while we can. We don't have these times often enough."

"That's true," my father finally contributed.

"Who would like to say the invocation?" Mother offered.

"I will," Ursela said excitedly. And she did. She thanked Lucifer for the food—she hadn't eaten my mother's cooking yet or that might have been retracted—for the family, for the family time, that I wasn't in jail for being 'bad' anymore, for her devildog Sparky. She thanked Lucifer for the Hellfire, for her favorite doll Jezabel, that her mommy and daddy loved each other. She thanked Him for more things than a succubus ten times her age should be thankful for as I watched Mother's interesting meal cool on the table. I almost quipped that the youngest demon at the feast should throw in a kind word to the big man that I wasn't Abandoned in the Overworld, stripped of my demonhood, as punishment for my supposed screwups. The occasion did not need anymore tension between me and my father. Plus, Ursela had it right. Being thankful for all life's good things instead of bitching about its bad things, like the tall white-haired incubus across the table from her did, was the healthier way to live life. The last thing I would do would be to contribute to throwing her off-course.

As the conversation turned back toward less awkward topics, Dialphio stared at me, unwavering. Her head swiveled from demon to demon as everyone transitioned from an awkward assessment of my life to Ursela's innocent rambling chat with the king of Hell. After a moment, she spoke up.

"Are you really not going to tell them, Zeke?" Dialphio said. My chest clenched. The problem with having good demons on your side is that they want the best for you no matter the circumstances. And the really good ones defend you even when you won't defend yourself.

"Tell us what?" Mother said with an air of caution, holding a spoonful of mashed—but lumpy—potatoes over her plate.

Dialphio's emerald eyes widened as she jutted her head forward. "Well?"

My boss knew my family only through my stories, of which I had shared many during my time working for her. I could defend myself until the mysterious One, creator of everything, destroyed their work in a hissy fit and it wouldn't matter. Mother would listen, comfort, and advise, but nothing would change. Father? Well, that was as pointless as Lucifer and Yahweh sitting down to hash out a permanent peace treaty. I swallowed the apprehension in my throat. She was as stoic as the figures in Hell's most famous painting, The Obscene Chapel—a panel painting of three heroes of Hell's past, long annulled—deceased, in demon language—offering themselves to the dominant hand of Lucifer. A piece of art that always made me feel slightly uncomfortable, its depiction of our ultimate purpose, to sacrifice even ourselves for Lucifer's cause, was held as an icon of our species. A sharp talking to was definitely in my future during my next shift.

"It's okay," I replied without meeting her eyes.

"Are we sharing secrets," Ursela clapped her hands and bounced on her knees.

"Secrets aren't nice," Uncle Lal said, again in a firm voice.

Dialphio leaned over the table, toward the young succubus. "Honey, Ezekial didn't do anything bad. Don't believe anyone who says that. In fact, he was doing something very brave."

"He was?" the little one gasped.

Dialphio nodded. Around the table, everyone sat up a little straighter and found something interesting on their plate to examine. Except my father. Of course, Kanthor Sunstone would sit rigidly, listening to my boss provide a counter story to the popular tales of the adventures of Zeke. "He was very brave. He went to the Overworld and helped Lucifer find someone He missed dearly. Ezekial even brought that demon back so Lucifer could see His old friend again. Wasn't that nice?"

Ursela nodded, an air of fascination in her eyes. "That was a nice thing to do, Ezekial."

"Thanks," I said, not able to accept praise even when delivered to defend me against those I shouldn't have to defend myself against.

"You're our guest, and you are free to speak, but do so with caution," my father said stiffly.

If he thought that would intimidate Dialphio, he was truly clueless. But, then again, Kanthor was accustomed to demons complying with his edicts. My boss, in no uncertain terms, laid down her own marker with her response.

"I didn't see any caution being exercised when everyone seemed fine making the claim that Ezekial had committed a crime. So I apologize if it feels I'm being reckless, but wouldn't it be better, for her and him, to tell the truth?"

I shifted in my seat. I wasn't the only one.

"The truth is that Ezekial was arrested," father said, looking at Ursela with no kindness reaching his eyes. "He did something that wasn't authorized. But," he said, adjusting his collar by wrenching his neck like he was mad at himself, "he was punished and served his time. It's over as far as I'm concerned."

That was news to me. "Is it?"

All heads turned in my direction. I was pretty sure no one breathed.

"From what I've been able to tell, it's not. Not at all," I said in a follow-up.

Tears formed in my mother's eyes. "Now isn't the time to have this conversation."

As hurt as I was from their rejection, it was still painful to see her react like this. But it was equally painful to know she was okay with Father perpetuating a lie, even if only by asking to delay the conversation we still had not been able to have. Whatever Apopis threatened my parents with after the attack in the square after Gemini's failed execution, it had changed my mother. She didn't flinch every time something clanged on the floor or someone said 'boo,' but she was not the same Lilith Sunstone who could dress down Lucifer with a look. I missed the old her.

Dialphio watched me, her jaw set firm and her emerald eyes piercing, encouraging me on.

My chest swelled as I drew in the shaking breath. "It's true, Ursela. Everyone. The Council lied about what happened. I was sent to the Overworld to find Gemini. He was a spy for Yahweh. The Council didn't know he was a double-agent."

My aunt held a hand to her chest. "So it's true then? You brought an angel into the Underworld? You put us all at risk?"

I shook my head. "None of us knew what he was. Not even the Founders, who had employed him for years."

"Are angels as ugly as everyone says they are?" Ursela asked.

In the tension of adults readying themselves to combat rumors, my niece was ignored until Xarpa patted her hand. Still physically connected to her daughter, she looked at me, her eyes begging the question. "How could the leaders Lucifer selected not know that?"

"The Council doesn't know everything."

Father jerked back from the table. Dialphio gave me one, sharp nod of her head. I sought out my mother. Her expression was flat, unreadable, the type of look of someone trying to hold their shit together.

"Son, you can't be saying things like that," Uncle Lal mumbled, shaking his lowered head.

"Ezekial," my mother's raspy voice told me how stressed she was.

But I'd had enough. Whether it was through Dialphio's encouragement or not, a year of not being given the chance to tell my side pushed me on. For millennia, Ursela might not understand the gift she'd given me. "It's the truth, and everyone needs to face it. The Council makes mistakes. A lot of them. It *can't* know everything. They tell us they do, but it's not true. They had no idea Gemini was an angel who could infiltrate Hell. Ralrek and I were just scapegoats to cover for the Council's failure. We did nothing wrong, and we were arrested, jailed, and humiliated. Who knows what would have happened had the attack not killed hundreds. That kept them from bothering us for a long time and they only freed us because they knew it would shut us up. When the alternative is to rot in a prison cell for eternity, you keep your trap shut. I'm not proud of it, but it's not like I have the power to change anything. You can trust me or not, but none of you have walked in my shoes. You have no idea what it's really like, but I guarantee you, the Council isn't half as benign or just as they want you to believe."

A heavy silence fell over the table. My mother looked down at her lap, adjusted her napkin, pulled it up and refolded it before replacing it. Only the slight sway of her shoulder length hair gave away the fact she was shaking her head. Collecting herself, she raised her head again and looked at me and I saw the thousands of years of indoctrination fighting rationality for control of her mind. Her square jaw quivered.

My father was rigid. He straightened, casting uneasy glances between my aunt and uncle, who themselves appeared ready to catch the first carriage back to their sector.

"Why is everyone quiet?" Ursela rotated her head. The corners of her eyes turned down in adolescent fright. "Did I say something bad?"

"It's okay. I just told them a story that wasn't very entertaining. That's all," I smiled at her, though I felt a distinct sadness wash over me at my family's reactions.

Her wide, innocent eyes shot back and forth between mine. She leaned in and whispered, "They look scared."

In unison, we turned our heads to examine the adults at the table and then looked back at each other; me mimicking her giggle, which only made her giggle more. It was infectious. "They do, don't they?"

I grinned and tickled her. Ursela squirmed in her seat, giggling with the levity of life only implings can manage. The result was immediate. The air around the dinner table lightened now that the youngest demon gifted everyone a way out of the awkwardness.

Until my uncle spoke.

"Heard there's a war in the Overworld," he said.

Father nodded. "Supposedly ramping up too."

Aunt Xarpa frowned, reclaiming Ursela's hand. "Such a shame, that species. Always fighting."

I wondered if she had listened to what I said. Apparently, demons only heard what they wanted to hear.

"Escalating quickly from the rumors I've been hearing." Uncle Lal dug into the stew bowl being passed around. The wooden spoon scraped the bottom of the bowl, making my teeth tingle. The smell emanating from it was reminiscent of Eve's Sanctuary, the garden where I often sparred with Bilba, after a rainstorm. I was not sure what Mother crammed into the concoction, but it promised to be an interesting culinary adventure. "Something like twenty nations already involved."

"Twenty?" Mother said in surprise.

"Yep," Uncle Lal nodded. "I don't keep up with mortal politics, but I guess it started under some desire for democracy or the such, but then oilfields got bombed and that's when these other nations got involved. Guess once one did, the others quickly followed."

"The mortals and their oil," Aunt Xarpa shook her head. "Not only are they happy to kill their planet, but they're happy to kill each other for the right to kill it."

There was a shared laughter at the comment, the type by those personally not affected by the poor choices of others. Only me and Dialphio refrained, along with Ursela who had no idea what the adults were talking about if her stunted giggle was any indication. The odoriferous stew bowl made its way around to me and provided an excuse to disengage and hide my disgust. Maybe it was because I'd been to the Overworld and among mortals, or maybe it was because I was a better demon, but I didn't see how the mortal's escalating conflict was casual dinnertime conversation, especially during the season of Samhain when we were celebrating our own liberation. Plus, I expected everyone to be more considerate of what war actually was, considering only a year had passed since hundreds died in the Angelfire attacks in the First Circle.

"I heard we might even get involved," Uncle Lal reignited the conversation.

Great Satan almighty, would he not talk about something fun, like the recent spate of exorcisms in the Overworld, a result of—yet another—rogue demon having too much fun with the mortals. Too bad the Council acted like petulant children and refused to hire us to help them with the problem. If they had hired a crew to deal with the demon, that team was taking its time. Who knew? Maybe Bilba, Ralrek, and I would be appreciated a little more.

"Again?" Mother said with a stiff shake of her head, her one–length hair waving in a single movement. "It's only been a few years since we last had to rescue them."

"And that one was bad, remember?" Uncle Lal added with the wag of his finger.

I did. I don't think any demon alive didn't remember what it was like just over a hundred years ago when forty–odd nations of the mortal world did everything they could do to destroy their species in a war that lasted four years.

Father's head dipped toward the table. "I think everyone lost a dear friend or family member during that period." He inhaled a long breath through his nose, lifting his head again. "But it is our duty to the Council, to Lucifer. If He decides that we're to serve, then we serve. Simple as that."

"Right on," Uncle Lal gestured with a fist pump.

"Mommy, are you and Daddy going away?" Ursela said, no longer bouncing on her knees.

Aunt Xarpa patted her hand. "No. No, honey, we won't. We're too old for Lucifer's Army," she finished with an uneasy laugh.

"But what about Ezekial? He's not old."

The weight of attention shifted back to me. Everyone wanted to hear my answer. I did too. "No idea. But, if they call me to go, I don't imagine I'll have much of a choice."

Tension released like gas being passed after Taco Tuesday —just without the smell, but almost as awkward. Mother's shoulders drooped as she spooned a healthy portion of buttered green beans onto her plate. Aunt Xarpa gave a flickering smile while her husband nodded sharply. My father was the only one to not react. I didn't like seeing the sad smile on Dialphio's face.

"With the human military finally evolving and including women in combat, if he goes, maybe he'll find himself a wife. It's about time he settled down," Aunt Xarpa said through a smile that tried to rub heat off her statement.

"Praise Lucifer for that," my mother joked.

"He'll need to get a real job before settling," my father said, stabbing a chunk of mysterious stew meat and shoving it in his mouth while he continued to analyze my personal life. "Can't support a wife and implings on any salary from that bookstore. No offense, Dialphio. But he needs to be a career man first."

Dialphio looked ready to deliver a rollicking when I jumped in, the need to defend her irresistible. "Like slaving away in the Hellfire pits?" The comment was out before I processed it and realize how antagonistic it was. Just because I was tired of his cheap shots didn't mean I needed to stoop to his level. But I had anyway.

Mother tilted her head and narrowed her eyes, jutting her jaw out.

My father stopped chewing and stared at me. His head over his plate, he said, "The Hellfire paid for everything you enjoyed while growing up. Plus," he smiled at my uncle like they shared a secret, waving his fork in the air, "I don't think you could handle the Hellfire. It's tough work. Hard work. But maybe you could make amends with the Council and start working for them on a more regular basis."

"Even something permanent," Uncle Lal added his encouragement.

I shook my head. "Sorry to disappoint everybody, but that's not going to happen."

"Well," my father huffed, "let's hope that changes, for your sake."

"I have to agree," my mother said, blowing a wayward strand of hair out of her eyes. "If you land yourself something permanent, maybe it will keep you away from being drafted into Lucifer's Army. I don't want you fighting in this ridiculous mortal war. We should just stop getting involved in those." She said that last part as more of a mumble to herself.

"That's the truth," Aunt Xarpa nodded. "It's so absolutely ridiculous that we constantly keep sending our incubi to fight in these skirmishes, putting their lives on the line. Too many of them have died over the years for mortal nonsense."

Uncle Lal waved a spoonful of potatoes at her. "It's not nonsense. If we don't get involved, we lose."

"How so?" his wife replied in a biting tone, her neck blotching with red heat.

Lucifer, I really hate Samhain feasts.

He spread his hands. "If this thing kicks off, the angels will get involved. Do you really want a mortal war where angels get to dictate what happens?"

Aunt Xarpa huffed. "They should stay out of it too."

Everyone at the table nodded, knowing that wasn't reality.

In my six thousand years of life, I'd lost count of how many skirmishes, battles, and wars the mortals waged against each other. And there seemed to be no end in sight. You humans evolved quickly; not that long ago you were throwing scorching oil down on each other's heads and tossing corpses inside castle walls. Overnight, those gave way to atomic and nuclear bombs. Demonkind tried to help stop the ravages, but mortals have been poisoned against us and ignored our whispers.

My father looked like he wanted to chew through his fork. "They won't stay out of anything they can get their dirty hands on. Look at how conniving and destructive they are. We should never forget the square."

"Never forget," my Aunt and Uncle murmured, Mother nodded in agreement, and even Dialphio lowered her head.

The square would never be forgotten by anyone in Hell, of that, I was sure. Lucifer knew I never would. Some of the horrific images from that day were permanently burned into my brain.

Silent somberness blanketed the table at the memory of those lost. Regardless of their intentions, the faceless angels who attacked us to rescue Gemini had forever etched a stain on their reputation among Hell's residents. If I'm being honest, I'm still not okay with what they did, our cruelty to Gemini aside.

Sometimes, there just wasn't a right and wrong in a situation. From all angles, crap was crap. Angels attacking the Underworld or our involvement in mortal clashes. Crap. If a full-blown war erupted in the Overworld, demons would be part of it because angels would be involved.

Sometimes, it was as simple as that.

3

UNDERWORLD, FIFTH CIRCLE

WE CLINKED OUR GLASSES TOGETHER. Just one more sound in a club full of them.

"Thank Lucifer Samhain is over," I said in a toast to Bilba and Ralrek.

"That's what's wrong with you, Zeke," Bilba said, toasting me with a dip of his glass before downing the bourbon. He winced and looked like he might cough the entire drink back up. The loose skin under his chin wobbled. "You have no holiday spirit."

"Oh, he has plenty; it's just all negative," Ralrek laughed.

I looked up at the handsome devil of a jerk. "Holidays wear me out. You two are lucky I even came out tonight."

And that was the truth. I didn't want to go out, but the guys wanted to grab drinks. We hadn't gotten together since I defied death via roller coaster. If I'm being honest, we needed time together for fun conversation—incubi talk—and alcohol. So I went, reluctantly. The price of friendship.

We were in *El Diablo*—which used to be called Angelfire Lounge until the mass murder of three hundred demons in the Gemini attack—the trendiest nightclub in the Fifth Circle. So trendy that incubi needed to show up early if they wanted in, due to the club giving succubi priority entry. Succubi always got in, no matter the hour or how overcrowded the place was. Incubi? Not so much. But since when was Hell interested in equal rights?

The real fun didn't start until around eleven, so we showed up four hours early, right after the Callers announced the official end of the day, and were pleasantly surprised at getting in. Even the heroes of Hell, at least Bilba still was, didn't enjoy the privilege of entry without showing up before the Hellfire faded.

At this hour, the nightclub was packed. Demons filled every vacant space except for the narrow alleys carved between clumps of bodies to and from the bar and dance floor. Any other spot in the club anyone wanted to visit would have to be reached only after picking your way through intoxicated, horny demons. Even the archway that led to the bathrooms was occupied by a couple who seemed more interested in exploring each other's esophaguses with their tongues than allowing demons with aching bladders to pass to relieve themselves. Our early arrival was the sole reason we nabbed a place at the bar and had done our best to ensure that it remained ours throughout the evening, even taking shifts for restroom breaks. Dancing wasn't an issue; Bilba can't, I abhor it, and Ralrek just didn't seem interested, meaning we didn't have to work out the logistics of navigating the dance floor in search of a future mate. Bilba and I were consistent at a few things, like being excellent video game players, goofballs, dorks about pop culture, and striking out with succubi. Tonight was no different, even in a club where two out of three demons was one. The only time we got attention from a succubus was when the dozens of them flirted with us for access to the bar only to ignore us after they got their drinks. I didn't expect many, if any, opportunities to have a conversation with one. Bilba hoped. I'll let you guess which one of us was the more disappointed.

Someone shoved me from the side, not hard, but forcibly. I turned to face my assaulter and stared into the eyes of a beauty. She was shorter than me by a few inches, meaning she was a good foot shorter than Ralrek, with almond eyes and long, flowing blond hair—bleached—that fell past her shoulders. She smelled of vanilla. She had full lips and dressed to draw attention. She definitely had mine.

"Oh, excuse me," the stunner said with a wide smile that showed three-fourths of her teeth. Those pearly whites sparkled. Everything about her was perfect.

"Was I in your way?" I said, trying to be charming. Bilba and Ralrek smiled behind their glasses, angling themselves away just enough to make it appear they weren't listening. I knew better; I would have done it to either of them.

She rocked her head back and forth as if indecisive. "Oh, you know how it is. Trying to get a drink in this place is an absolute nightmare."

I nodded, trying to ignore my heart kick-starting a gallop. "That, it can be. Here," I said, sliding into Bilba and Ralrek's space, "let me give you some room."

"Hey!" Bilba protested when I almost bumped him.

I shot him a glance that told him to be quiet, returning my attention to the succubus who deserved it. My mouth was suddenly very dry. "Do you come here often?"

She smiled and pulled her hair behind her ear. The room grew hotter until the bartender interrupted my reverie by taking her order. "I enjoy coming out here," she said when he moved away, "but it's so hard to get to. I live across the Circle, so it takes most of the night."

"That would be tough," I responded as if I knew what I was talking about. "Well, I'm glad you made it out."

She adjusted, leaning her elbow on the bar and facing me. "Oh yeah? Why's that?"

Careful, Zeke, my rational self shouted, knowing I was approaching dangerous territory where I typically make a banal comment ... or accidentally said something inappropriate.

I didn't let myself down. "I just meant that ... well, that everyone needs time to relax and get out. You look like you could use it. I mean, not that you look exhausted or anything, just that ... oh, Lucifer."

The stunner threw her head back and laughed. "Wow, you really are terrible at this."

Just then, the bartender was back, smiling flirtatiously and sliding her drink across the waxed wood bar. Apparently, serving her was a priority. She took it and gave him a slow wink that nearly stopped my heart; how that incubus remained standing was beyond me. "Thank you, Erebos," she said before turning away and returning to her life without even saying farewell to me.

This time it was Ralrek who shoved me. "For Lucifer's sake, Zeke, are you trying to check off some list of every way possible to bore succubi?"

I shrugged. Rejection was a staple of my dating diet. "At least I succeeded at something."

"That you did. That you did." Bilba turned to the bartender who hadn't moved too far away and ordered another round of drinks. "That exquisite failure deserves to be celebrated."

And we drank to my inability to know how to talk to the female persuasion. Six thousand years and still no clue.

"But this is it for me, guys. I can't afford another drink after this," Bilba said with a grimace.

Ralrek and I glanced at each other, me warning him to not preach right now.

"Flat broke?" Ralrek asked carefully.

Bilba rolled his thick bottom lip over his top. "Yep. But hey, my father said I can stay as long as I need, so that'll help cut down on expenses. Now I need to sell my stuff."

"Really? Is it that bad?" Bilba's money troubles weren't a

secret. For him to sell his personal things showed the precariousness of his situation. Bilba never had money growing up in a single parent household, so when he was hired by the Council and received their bounty, he'd enjoyed his earnings. Nothing lavish by any means. Coin burned holes in his purse because he expected the Council jobs to continue and had a soft heart for his frigid mother. Still, a creeping thought pestered me; if I hadn't been so confrontational with the Council, maybe we'd have received a few assignments and my best friend would not be in this predicament. "I'm so sorry, Bilba."

"It's okay guys, it really is," he said. It wasn't. "It's just junk I don't need, anyway. My fault for buying it in the first place. Sort of got carried away with those nice paydays." Bilba said it in the way demons do when they're checking to see if others thought they were insane or not. He wasn't. Deprived of the luxury of financial security throughout his life, seeing his father struggle daily, desperately trying to buy a mother's love, his behaviors were understandable. Reckless, but understandable.

"And it's not like I was smart with the rest of my money," Bilba continued as if he needed to fill the silence. "Most of it went to my mother."

"How so?" Ralrek asked.

I pulled Bilba out of the way before three university-aged demons stumbled through us to the bar, shouting at each other with bravado only young incubi can create. One apologized, but I was less interested in that physical disruption than how they stemmed the flow of our conversation.

"Didn't see them. Thanks, Zeke," my friend said, eyes locked on his glass.

"No worries, I'm all over it," I replied, more worried about him than trying to stem the flow of stimulus in the room. Bilba had looked on the verge of sharing his troubles until the invasion of the drunk idiots gave him second thoughts.

Rough scratching raced down my arms. Fire magic being conjured drew my attention to our tall friend. "Plus, it stopped him from starting a fight." I pointed at Ralrek, whose fingers burned with small flames.

The flames blinked out when we caught him. "What? It was only going to be a small spell. Just to light their asses on fire for a second, nothing major."

"I don't think I need to see their asses," Bilba chuckled.

We were getting off topic. "Come on. Open up." I jerked a thumb toward Ralrek. "We're your friends. That means we're supposed to be here for you, for each other. But we can't help you if you don't give us an idea of what's going on."

Bilba looked apprehensive, blinking shyly.

"Zeke is wrong about a lot, but he's right about that," Ralrek said, throwing an toned arm around Bilba, who didn't move away. "We're your friends and if you can't open up and let us help, who can you open up to?"

Bilba shrugged. Even in the strobing violet nightclub light, I could see the tips of Bilba's ears darken with blood flood. Moving myself next to him, I wrapped my arm around the opposite shoulder, sandwiching Bilba.

He smiled at the group love. "Thanks guys. It's just been a little scary, you know? We were doing so well with the Council and I thought it would be a long-term thing. Who expected them to leave us out like this because ..." He paused and gave us an apologetic shrug, which I promptly waved away. Of anyone, Bilba had nothing to apologize for. His voice lowered, undiscernible under the thumping bass of the nightclub music. He was still shouting, just shouting at the quietest level possible. "Things got bad for her."

"Your mom?" Ralrek interjected.

Bilba gave a stiff, cautious nod. "Yeah, the flower shop ... it started going downhill when there was a rift of crimes in the neighborhood. You all know what the Eighth is like."

Ralrek and I agreed. That Circle, where Bilba tripped

across his mother while we were on a Council mission, was notorious for distrust, dishonesty, and general scummery of our species. It's a gross place full of gross demons. Bilba's mother owned a flower shop, which seemed to be healthy, as healthy as any business in the Circle, when we met her.

"I tried to help, I really did," he said, casting his eyes at his empty glass. "At first she didn't appreciate me coming around, but then, when I started helping with getting things for the shop, she slowly opened up."

I'll bet she did. I kept that thought to myself.

Bilba turned his glass counterclockwise in his open palm. "It was stupid, I know. But I figured if I could just get her to open up, she would. And she did ... but not until things started getting worse in the neighborhood." His head suddenly snapped up. "Did I tell you guys that I had to install a security system in my apartment? Fully furnished, so I only had a few things there, but that's where I kept my coin and it was getting so bad around the building, even inside, that I paid way too much to get a system installed to protect the little I had. Crazy stuff."

"What happened?" Ralrek pulled back, crossing his arms, the sinews flexing like thin snakes rippled underneath his skin. And he didn't even have to work out to look like that, the jerk.

"I don't know if it was gang activity or what, but it was like a wave. Crime crept closer and closer all the time. My mother said she knew it would always hit the neighborhood, you'd have to be blind to miss it. She hoped the authorities would do something before it swept through the sector. That didn't happen. Whoever runs the Eighth now that Taurus is ... gone, they didn't care. Or, if they did, they didn't bother stopping it. The robberies started a few weeks after you left. And once those dirtbags knew how vulnerable she was, they kept coming back. Over and over."

"Couldn't you do anything? I mean, you're a heaven of a

caster," Ralrek said. The comment was supposed to be encouraging.

"That's the thing," Bilba shook his head, his thoughts shifting back to that horrible place, "they hit at random times. Not always when we were in the shop. I don't know if they thought we kept coin there overnight or not. It didn't seem to matter. Every few days, they'd conduct these random break-ins and robberies. At first, she tried to keep up with the repairs. But profit margins in a flower shop aren't that high, and having to replace windows and locks all the time exhausted her funds."

"And that's where you came in," I said, filling in the remaining detail. I knew this; we had talked about it a few days after he returned. The first time was over drinks and it was short, scant details. The next time was at my Old Towne apartment over pizza and video games. The distraction of competition on the screen was always a safe way for us to open up to each other, and it had been for Bilba then. I'd known for a long time he had rescued her shop, or at least tried to, I just did not realize how drained the experience left him.

Bilba confirmed that with another stiff head nod.

I wasn't going to kick him when he was down, even though that was standard protocol for our small group. Good-natured and loving as it might be intended, it wouldn't be helpful. "Everything? All of your coin is gone?"

The humiliation was plain on his face. Red blotches sprang on his puffy cheeks. "Everything. Every last coin."

"I'm sorry. I knew you were struggling, but I had no idea it was that bad."

The corners of Bilba's mouth curled up in a flat, disconsolate smirk. "Not something I exactly wanted to share, if you know what I mean. It's embarrassing. Especially since she was done with me as soon as the coin was gone."

Fellia Ravenous was officially a dirt-bag in my book. If I

could make a covert trip to the Eighth Circle, I would stop by Fellia's Flowers, or whatever was left of it, and ask Creed to torch it—okay, I wouldn't really do that, but I was pissed off for my best friend, probably because he looked too heart-broken to be pissed off for himself.

Without a word, Ralrek and I moved in on him, squeezing him in our bro-sandwich. It was subtle and over as fast as it started, but it was enough to convey that we cared and he wasn't alone.

"There's got to be something we can do?" Ralrek said.

"I appreciate it guys, but this is my struggle to face. It was my decisions that got me into it in the first place. So it's my responsibility to get myself out of it."

I shook my head. "Nonsense. We can come up with something."

"No, no. I already have a plan."

"What?" Ralrek and I said simultaneously.

"I'm considering volunteering," Bilba said, a slight frown wiped away his faux smile.

"For what?" I asked.

"Lucifer's Army," he answered.

I snickered. "I don't think it'd have you, buddy. No offense."

"Why?"

I poked his belly, still squishy, but nearly flat. Bilba was fitter now than in any of his previous six thousand years, but he abused himself for too long to be army-healthy after a single year of taking care of himself.

"I can work on that," he said defensively, looking to Ralrek for support. "You'd help me work out, right?"

I slapped his shoulder. "Hey, why didn't you ask me? I'm in great shape and Ralrek hasn't seen the gym since they fired that one personal trainer. What was his name?"

"Oh, Asdar," Ralrek bobbed his head. "Man, he was smoking. That ass. No reason to go back after that. When he used to spot me on the bench press—"

"Oh, Lucifer," I interrupted, trying to blot the visual out. "My point was, I could help too."

"Yeah, but you're not in Ralrek-type shape."

"Ouch."

"I would," Ralrek broke up the fun. "But I'm sure you can't just volunteer for the Army. There's a whole process you have to go through."

"I know. I'm not a complete idiot."

"Even if they accepted you, why would you volunteer?" It was a fair question. Military service wasn't a big draw for most demons because it was a tough, unrewarding life, attractive to only the most gung–ho of thrill seekers who couldn't get enough danger. In fairness, when you live as long as we do, life can get extremely boring. Still, I didn't see the sense in rushing along one's own demise, especially since volunteering often led demons into service in the Overworld, where we are physically susceptible to actual death.

Bilba held up his empty glass. "Because I'm tired of not going out with you guys and being able to afford drinks ... or lying about being able to pay for them. The Army pays decently. Better than nothing, and it's consistent. I could serve for a few years and at least get back on my feet, financially."

"If you don't die first." I didn't like making a habit of raining on his parade, but Bilba was my responsibility as much is anyone's and I wasn't about to let him make foolhardy decisions.

"Well, we might not have a choice, so I'd rather volunteer first instead of being drafted. I heard they take it easier on you if you're a volunteer."

Ralrek turned to the bartender, lifting three fingers and shrugging. Before his gesture reminded me that Bilba had ordered another round, Erebos was sliding the three drinks to my tall friend. Ah, the privilege of beautiful demons. We snagged our glasses from the bar. This moment called for male bonding through alcohol consumption.

Drinks in hand, we raised a toast.

"To Bilba, Lucifer's next general!" Ralrek shouted, drawing the attention of a group of succubi. Sadly, for them and me and Bilba, their eyes fell on the tall, dark, and handsome incubus who never gave a second glance to any of their sex.

We laughed and toasted.

"To Bilba!"

"To me!"

After wincing from the burning traveling down my throat, I said through a grimace, "Fat chance of there being a draft, buddy. Are you sure you want to do this?"

Bilba looked between us. "You guys haven't heard?"

"Heard what?"

"Wow, I thought everybody had. Bet it's why half these demons are in here drinking their brains away. Everyone has been talking about it for hours. Haven't you been watching the news?"

"Some of us were busy at our jobs." When Bilba frowned, accompanied by Ralrek, I added with a smirk, "Too soon?"

"Besides Zeke being an asshole, I was out with Torlan today. We didn't get back to my place until just before I needed to leave to head here. He was being so clingy. Anyway, what did I miss?"

"The mortal war," Bilba said in a serious tone. "It's escalating. Getting bad from the way I understand it. Lucifer's Army *has* been activated, and they announced a ramping up of troop recruitment by twenty thousand just next month!"

Ralrek whistled.

I groaned. "You can't be serious."

"I am. It's all over the news. I've been thinking about it all afternoon and evening. If they're recruiting that many, what's the chances we can avoid being drafted? We're the prime demographic."

Ralrek squinted and smirked. "Well, I am. I'm not so sure about you."

Bilba smiled because he always did when Ralrek picked on him. I used to think it was because he was intimidated or bullied by our tall friend, but ever since our trip to the Overworld to find Gemini, I realized Ralrek had a deeper story that explained why he was brash with almost everyone he encountered. Bilba had simply seen that side of the tall incubus long before I did.

"I'm being serious, guys. And you should be too. At least think about it. I would hate to see you drafted and sent into the infantry or something."

"Oh, I'm not going into the military. No way." I shook my head for added emphasis.

"Ralrek?" Bilba pleaded.

His gaze drifted toward the ceiling, far away in thought. "Hmmm, interesting. Being drafted sounds unappealing and I don't have much going on. My job sucks. Torlan is alright, but we're not serious or anything. Seeing what the military is like could be interesting. If nothing else, it would get us out of the Fifth for a little while. And," he said, smirking and leaning down to whisper, "I heard there are a lot of hot incubi in the service. Talk about an effective recruitment policy."

I had leaned in too, thinking Ralrek was going to share some inside word he'd somehow received. At his flippant comment, I shot straight, duped. "You're disgusting," I said between laughs.

"Please, like you wouldn't if it was an all-female force."

I dipped my empty glass to him, conceding the point. "Well played, sir. Well played." Then I turned serious. "You'd actually think about this?"

"Yeah, why not?"

I threw my hands up, almost sending the shot glass skyward. "Because you're in a relationship and serving in the Army would end that."

Ralrek cocked his head, one corner of his mouth curling up while he winked. "It's not like we've been together that long, and we're definitely not that serious." He read our quiet reactions. "Come on, guys. Torlan and I just started dating. We're not even freaking exclusive. I like him; he's a good incubus. But he's not my life. Heavens, I don't even know yet if he has the potential to be. And like Bilba said, we could be drafted. If that's my decision point, to risk being drafted for an incubus who may or may not be in my life next week, it makes things a little simpler. I might do it."

I looked at both of them, not believing this conversation was happening. "You guys can't be serious?"

"I am," Bilba said firmly enough. "I have to be."

"Think about it," Ralrek said. "If this is happening, would you want to be drafted? None of us have served in any of their wars. How many chances do you think you'll get to volunteer, Zeke? The Army will look at those who haven't served first, before they draft those who already have. Are you willing to take that chance?"

Ralrek had a point. Within the last hundred years, humans had fought two mammoth conflicts that spread across half the blessed planet. Both times there were rumors that the Army would be recruiting, and ultimately they did. Both times they instituted a draft. And both times my number hadn't come up. Neither had Bilba's or Ralrek's. We'd been lucky, especially with the First World War. So many died in those short years; nearly ten thousand never came home. Was the third time the charm? If they drafted me and put me in the most dangerous job, I'd never forgive myself and neither would my mother. My boss would kick my ass.

But could I really do it? If I joined and was sent to the Overworld, it would only be a couple of years. Four, in fact. What was four years when you lived tens of thousands? I mean, I would never get excited by suffocating daily structure, early mornings, and all the screaming and shouting, but, if I would have to serve anyway, shouldn't it be on my terms?

I ran a hand through my messy hair.

Bilba laughed. "I won't ask you to do anything you didn't want to do, Zeke. But I think you're making this out to be more than what it is. If we volunteer, we might get great administrative jobs far away from the fighting."

"And if we don't ..." Ralrek said. "Something each one of us better think about."

I pulled my hand away from my hair. Not that it mattered. None of the hundred succubi had looked my way the entire night. Maybe if I was a combat veteran, I'd have enough credibility to be worth five seconds of their time? "You guys are ridiculous."

Both of them wore stupid smiles.

"Why's that?" Bilba asked.

"Because," I said with a big sigh, "I'll do it. I'll volunteer for Lucifer's stupid Army."

4

UNDERWORLD, FIFTH/SEVENTH CIRCLE

A PIECE of advice for you mortals. The thing about making difficult decisions is that you have to make them as soon as you have enough information to be confident, at least if you want a favorable outcome. Don't linger and pontificate endlessly, since doing so may cost you. Take it from me, Hell's recovering reject, learner of life's tough lessons.

A week passed since our nightclub conversation. In that time, I may or may not have been distracted by life. Work was going well, and I was getting plenty of hours, meaning more coin stashed away. My parents were still absent since the Samhain feast, so there was little in the way of family stress. Succubi were still uninterested in me on a romantic level and only Gigi at the Chilly Willy's coffee stand had a conversation with me that lasted more than five minutes. This should have been a perfect opportunity for me to do some thinking about my future. As fate would have it—true, I don't believe in fate, but blaming a concept is easier than admitting to laziness—I didn't give a second thought to the conversation at El Diablo about volunteering for the Army.

We get comfortable and then we get lazy, right? Use the demands of life to convince yourself you'll get around to that nagging need as soon as you can? Immortal or mortal, we're all guilty. The fact is, I wasn't the only one who dawdled.

How do I know that? Because, like I said, a week had passed since the nightclub conversation and now Bilba and Ralrek were pounding on my door.

Half asleep on the couch after a long day of taking inventory at the bookstore, their racket snatched me from a enjoying what promised to be a wonderful slumber. My heart didn't stop hammering until long after I reached the door, throwing it open and shouting, "What the heaven to you want?"

Bilba pulled back, his face whiter-than-normal.

Ralrek's laugh was timid. His face, not whiter-than-normal, was still handsome—of course—but strained. "Invite us in," he said. "We have news you'll want to hear."

Demons have an adage that there is no good way to deliver bad news. Best to throw it out on the table and deal with it than spending energy softening the oncoming blow.

And that's what my friends were doing at this very moment. Together in my living room, Bilba by my side, we read the letter he'd received. It was identical to the one Ralrek also held, only the personal identification information differed. Before they stopped by, I had a small pile of unopened mail precariously stacked on my kitchen counter— I hate opening mail unless I absolutely have to because it's usually a company demanding money for a service I probably didn't need but was too lazy to cancel.

With Bilba and Ralrek's sudden visit, I struggled to determine if I was happy to have not opened my mail earlier as I held my own letter in shaking hands.

"I'm sorry, buddy." Bilba rubbed my shoulder.

I swayed back and forth, feeling like I was about to fall over. My eyes traveled to the subject line for what had to be the thirtieth time.

Subject: Notification Of Draft Selection

"And you guys got one?" I said without pulling my eyes away.

Bilba nodded. "I heard hundreds did, just in our zone. There are probably thousands who did across the Circles."

"At least," Ralrek said in a voice devoid of its usual confidence.

"Drafted." I said the word again. It sounded foreign in my head. "I can't be drafted into the Army."

Bilba looked off into the distance. "I never wanted this either, but there's nothing we can do about it."

I thrust the letter at Ralrek. Disgusted. "Can you do something about that? I don't want to see it anymore."

An instant of skin scratching passed as he cast a small flame and torched the notification letter. Smoke drifted up as it burned down to his fingers. Nothing had every smelled sweeter—well, except for the Overworld's chicken wings, but who could think of food at a time like this?

I groaned. "There has to be someone we can talk to! This isn't right."

"It is what it is," Ralrek said as he leaned back in a chair, his hands drooping over the arms as he stretched his long legs out.

"What the heaven is that supposed to mean? This isn't a joke. They've drafted us. Freaking drafted us. And you're just going to take it?" I said with far more heat than was fair for the oil-black haired incubus. Would Ralrek feel the same when he realized what this development would mean for his wonderfully thick locks?

"What else can we do?" Ralrek's tone was soft, defeated, but kind. He'd given up, just as Bilba had.

How quickly did these two capitulate? Minutes? *Seconds*? They couldn't have received the notifications that much earlier than I did, and in the time it took them to find each other and come check on me, they'd decided they were at peace with this?

"We can ask for a waiver or something," I said. "There has to be a way to get out of this. Let's just say we're conscientious objectors. The mortals have movies about that, and it gets them out of service all the time. Well, at least the rich ones."

"But we're not human or rich," Ralrek offered, unhelpful as ever. "So we have to accept this."

"Yep," huffed Bilba.

"Come on, guys. Don't give up on me now."

Bilba patted my leg in a grandfatherly way. "We're going to have to do this, Zeke. Look at the date. There isn't much time."

"And we need to use that time to get everything situated," Ralrek added, standing. "Look at it this way, at least you're not in trouble with the Council or being Abandoned in the Overworld. A nice head shave and few years in uniform is a lot better than that, isn't it?"

This was moving too fast. There was too much to do. Too many things to get settled, and I didn't even know if I could rely on my parents to help with the life I was leaving behind.

The world spiraled. Control was slipping. Who could help settle it?

DIALPHIO HUGGED ME. HER NECK WAS BLOTCHY. "I'M SO SORRY. I know this is the last thing in the world you wanted. And I can't believe you're leaving so soon."

I looked around The Book Abyss, the narrow bookstore that was my home, with its shelves crammed with titles no matter how hard I worked to counter-act Dialphio's love of buying more and more books. "Trust me, neither can I. I don't know what I'm going to do. There's so much to take care of and so many things I don't know."

She waved with a chubby hand. "Don't you dare worry about that. You have enough going on."

"I feel bad asking you to do this."

Dialphio leaned to look around me at the shop. It was quiet, even though we were a few hours into the day. "In case you haven't noticed, this is a bookstore where we sell ... books." She paused to chirp a half-hearted laugh. "Things don't get so crazy that I can't handle it. I don't want you worrying about a single thing. Take care of what you need to and I'll watch over your life back here until you come home."

I swept in and wrapped my arms around her, squeezing tight. "I don't know what I would do without you."

"I hear that so often that I must be doing something right. Maybe you should be the one paying me?"

"Seriously, Dialphio, you are so kind. I wish I had more demons like you in my life."

"There's no one like me, Ezekial." She winked, the blotches in her neck beginning to fade as the mood of our conversation lightened. "Plus, give it time and things will turn around. If anything comes out of this military service, demons might appreciate you a little more. You deserve that."

"Thank you." My voice croaked.

Dialphio moved to her desk in the back corner of the bookstore behind the half-wall and the stacks of books atop it that blocked off our 'office' area from the customer area. Her desk drawer was pulled open slowly, as if she didn't want me to notice. I did. "You already said that. Now get back to work. This is your last day; I need to get all the labor out of you that I can."

And we did just that, spending the rest of the day together, mostly silent. When I first met Dialphio, she tried to play the tough gal boss role. That lasted for about as long as ice in Hell outside freezers. My mother was an amazing succubus, but Dialphio was on-par with her, and my boss had no blood relation to motivate her. She cared because that's who she was. She looked out for me better than I looked out for myself, and that was something I would miss with this upcoming military service. *If* I didn't flunk out first, which was always a possibility, especially if I put enough effort toward it.

It was probably the fastest any workday had ever passed, this last day at The Book Abyss, and walking out the front door held an unnerving finality. I lingered, halfway in and halfway out, taking in the space which had become my second home. I was going to miss it, and being a realist, the possibility that I might never see it again was my new companion. These things happened.

If Dialphio noticed my delay, which I'm sure she did because nothing got past her, she said nothing, choosing to remain in the office. As I was about to close the door, I swore I heard sniffling from her hiding spot. Half my heart tugged me back into the store, encouraging me to ease her pain, but my rational side realized doing so would only delay the inevitable. Separation brought pain, even if it was temporary. My ambiguous return was much, much worse. Attempts to comfort her would only extend the discomfort for both of us. So I stepped out of the shop and clicked the door closed, sending a message to Lucifer, asking Him to be kind enough to give Dialphio a rush of customers that would keep her busy for the next few days. The empty shopping zone, however, laughed at my desperation.

I STOOD IN MY LIVING ROOM, TWO SUITCASES BY THE FRONT DOOR. I was alone and considering the immensity of what was about to happen. This was a simple moment of reflection and appreciation for everything in the apartment. My lamps, the first I ever bought. The nightstands in the bedroom, acquired from an old succubus down the street who held a garage sale to get rid of her old junk. The gaming console that helped me pass thousands of lonely hours. The stove where I made my first dinners—horrible, but still able to rival my mother's. The single picture in the hall, a housewarming gift from that very same terrible cook. The apartment, sparse, but all mine. And I was about to leave it, possibly for the last time.

I should have been downstairs already, making my way to the gateway, but I delayed. Once I dragged my suitcases downstairs, loaded them into the hired carriage, and headed to the collection point, my future would become all too real.

Collection point.

Such a wonderful term.

I'm not sure how long I stood there, mourning the loss of the things I took for granted. All the wasted hours playing games, sleeping, or exploring bottoms of vodka bottles. I could have done better. I should have. Now, it was too late.

Letting loose a stunted growl, my shoulders dropped, I grabbed my bags and pulled open the door before I changed my mind to hide from the Army until they came to arrest me for desertion.

The open square where we stood waiting for someone to tell us to do something was quiet. The houses that surrounded us watched silently, as if they understood the gravity of the event. The Fifth, my home, was not about to intervene on my behalf.

My suitcases were light and small. The Army was kind enough to send along a recommended packing list with their letter informing me I was to be a slave. That stopped me from over-packing. Light and simple was the way to go—though I still had a problem with the whole 'going' part.

When I arrived at the gateway, I learned that even my slim packing was still over-packing. A crowd of forty other recruits stood in the vicinity, and each one of them had a single bag or suitcase at their feet. One. Not two. My double bag approach garnered odd looks—which was great, because I really feared this fresh start on life would deny me from being the oddball again—that's sarcasm, by the way.

I had hoped that Bilba and Ralrek would already be here. They weren't though, so I tried to strike up a conversation with the incubus closest to me.

"Hey," I said awkwardly to a short, stout demon with a spotty complexion and long, unkempt hair. Rumor was, the Army loved making examples of anyone who went to boot camp with long hair because they saw it as an affront to tradition. By his expression, this incubus wasn't worried. Better him than me.

He nodded and returned his focus to the gateway.

Nervous anticipation stifled the area. Few spoke, and those who did only did so in reserved tones. The air itself seemed wound with tension, spruced with a bit of apprehension.

No one representing the Army was here yet, but I was still early. I busied myself watching the other draftees and fiddling with my suitcases, wishing I'd brought a single bag like the rest of them. I double, triple, and quadrupled checked their contents.

A familiar smell hit my nose. I spun. "Mother? What are you doing here?"

She blinked, surprised, at my sudden recognition of her presence. "Hello, Ezekial," Lilith said in a shaking voice before she embraced me. Locked in a mother's grip, I was reserved in my return of affection. We hadn't spoken since the Samhain feast, though I had sent a merlin to tell her the Army drafted me and when I was scheduled to leave.

As my mother held me, I struggled to find the right words to say.

She pulled back, but kept both hands wrapped around my triceps. "I'm so sorry this is happening." She made a snorting sound, a mixture of a bitter laugh and a choked sob. "It's the last thing any of us wanted. But you'll get through this. I know you will. You're an amazing incubus, and you're going to do wonderful things while you're gone."

"I wish I had your faith, Mother. I don't." I looked around to make sure no one was listening. From what I heard, the Army favored those who ratted out troublemakers, and I didn't need to start on the same foot as that long–hair.

She rubbed my arm. Her square jaw tightened as if she was trying to suppress tears or harsh words. "You've always been short on faith, Ezekial. But maybe that's what will come out of this? After you return home, we can talk about all of this and what it means for you; will mean for you. But I don't care about that right now. I just wanted to say bye to my baby boy."

"Where's Father?"

Sorrow deepened in her expression.

"He's not coming, is he?" I concluded so she didn't have to. "It's okay."

She scanned the sparse crowd of future soldiers of Lucifer, most of whom had lovers or parents, sometimes both, waiting along with them. I swear, the five hundred-year-old impling in me wailed when her voice quivered. "You two should have made up before this."

"We will, when I come back," I said, honestly not sure if I meant it.

"Please do, Ezekial. Please do." Her eyes filled with tears, again flittering from mine to the other incubi. "Sometimes we don't get the chance to say goodbye to demons we care about. Don't let that become our story. Please."

We fell silent, ignoring the meek awkwardness in the middle of a cluster of demons about to have their lives changed. Time, though, didn't relieve the tension as we stood and waited for something to happen. The minutes ticked away agonizingly slow, each edged more than the previous.

"You should head home," I said, finally breaking the strained silence. "There's no reason to hang out here. Nothing's happening until it does."

She shook her head, her dark hair swaying as one piece. "Absolutely not. I'm not leaving you alone."

One corner of my mouth curled in a sad smile. "You don't need to protect me anymore. I can handle this. I have to, remember? Plus, this is torture, standing around, waiting for the inevitable. Everyone has to move on with their lives while I go through this, so why not start now?"

She looked away. "Because it doesn't feel right." Her voice was soft, as if it required all her energy to hide the shaking from me.

I wrapped my arm around her shoulder, pulling her into me. Together, we surveyed the recruits slowly growing by a trickle as demons arrived. Each of us, I noticed, had the same wide eyes, recording every movement and sound, trying to pick up every subtle clue to what the next hours held. Each new arrival carried a single bag.

My chest swelled with anxiety and pressure. I gave her one more squeeze and stepped away. "I need you to go. This is too difficult."

She faced me, her square jaw set, and brown eyes hardening. She crossed her arms. I knew what she was thinking.

"It's okay. I need to focus, and I can't have you worried about me like this. Please?"

She sighed, slight but apparent. The corners of her eyes leaked her turmoil. Her lips quivered. Right now, she was trying to hold herself together. "It's impossible to walk away, Ezekial."

I rubbed the back of her arm. "Just take the first step then. That's where every journey starts."

The corners of her mouth flickered up and down in a smile that wouldn't hold. "I know. I raised you, remember? But just because I get it doesn't mean I have to like it."

I shook my head. "No, you don't. But I need this. I love you, Mother." I leaned in for a hug.

Her crossed arms unlatched, and she fell into me, crying. Demons in the clumps nearest us turned, and then spun away.

I broke contact, pulling away but not before kissing her cheek.

Her hands lingered on my arms a little longer and then she, too, turned and walked away, looking over her shoulder once. Her shoulders shook as she broke down. Swallowing was impossible and the sight of her so distraught unbearable. I turned away, listening as her footsteps quickened, carrying her through the growing layers of Army recruits.

I stood alone for a while. At one point, my neighbor attempted to start a conversation about his excitement at this opportunity. After a few questions, he realized I wasn't interested and found a more accommodating partner.

Bilba arrived shortly after that, his father Akimon accompanying him, and Ralrek a few minutes behind him. Both wore long expressions, like sleep was slow in visiting everyone last night. Only Akimon dared smile.

"He's proud of me," Bilba said, excusing away his father's joy and drawing a slow breath. "Are you ready for this?"

My gaze found the gateway. "No. And I never will be."

WE STEPPED THROUGH THE GATEWAY AND INTO A LARGE, OPEN room crowded with demon recruits, most looking as frightened as the others. Demons propped themselves along the long walls. The few standing milled around in the fragmented spaces in the middle of the room. One, a lanky redhead, dragged his bag behind like it contained a dead chimera. Imagine my relief when, in a room of fifty incubi, I spotted a few who also made the same mistake of bringing multiple bags. If ass-chewings were going to be handed out over the issue, at least I wouldn't be the only one receiving one.

The room was as quiet as a library. We all knew what was coming. The explosion. Stories of drill instructors were stuff of legend. They were, purportedly, as angry as angels— though I struggled with that image ever since meeting Cassie —and twice as nasty. The smart ones among us kept our mouths closed. The dummies who spoke were at least smart enough to only whisper.

Along with the absence of words was a complete void of military personnel. That the Army trusted us enough to congregate without a soldier overlord was a revelation. Did they not think us capable of burning down the waiting room, all alone and unsupervised as we were?

We tried to find an open spot along the wall.

"What do you think is going on?" Bilba asked, moving to a sliver of space next to a sleeping incubus with a towering high top fade hairstyle, setting his bag down and fiddling with the zipper.

"No idea. Maybe this is where the torture begins?"

Ralrek snorted, and slumped against the wall until he was laid out, his head rested on his bag. "Who knows what it takes to run something like this. I imagine it's a logistical nightmare; one I wouldn't want to deal with. I'm sure we'll find out soon enough. Probably should get some rest before then."

And with that, he unchecked and passed the time sleeping while everyone who remained conscious paced, bit finger nails, zipped and unzipped bags or did whatever they could to relieve the building tension.

"For Lucifer's sake! Will they just get on with it already?" Bilba huffed so time later, the tips of his ears growing a deeper shade of pink.

His sudden, but tiny, outburst surprised me, forcing me to ignore a rhythmic clicking on the other side of the room.

Though he hadn't shouted across the expanse of the room, he might as well have as quiet as everyone was. "Whoa there, buddy. How about we keep that attitude under wraps? Don't need you starting off on the wrong foot."

He leaned in, quieter this time. "I'm tired of waiting, Zeke. This isn't right. It's torture."

The thin and unremarkable demon seated next to Bilba pressed himself against the wall so forcefully I thought he was trying to back his way through it.

"What's torture?" a new voice asked in a low but menacing growl.

Bilba's head jerked up. Mine was slower, but just as nervous.

Above us, a demon in Army fatigues planted two fists on his hips in a broad stance. He was tall and thin; from my vantage point squatting next to Bilba, he looked taller than Ralrek. Debatable height aside, the soldier could not have more than three percent body fat. I wondered if he'd ever eaten an ounce of stale chocolate or chewy Underworld meat in his entire life. His uniform was pressed and perfect, not a wrinkle anywhere. A wide-brimmed circular hat hid any hair he might have, exposing the shaved sides of his skull.

His jaw flexed as he spoke. "Because I'm curious how you consider this torture. If this is, well, you've lived a very lucky life." His unhappy smile turned into a sneer. "Now, get on your feet."

Bilba lips trembled.

The tall Army incubus thrust his hand out, palm forward. "Best you don't say a thing because, I guarantee you, the next words you do say will determine how painful this experience will be."

I noticed he didn't give us a range of possibilities, leaving the threat open for interpretation. I wondered if Bilba picked up on that. Ralrek was likely just as clueless because he'd woken from his sleep at the first barking syllable.

Bilba's lips continued quivering.

The soldier nodded with a jerk, his green eyes hard and piercing. "Get on your feet," he ordered before spinning on the rest of the recruits, watching apprehensively. "All of you! Get on your feet and pick up your bags! Now, move, scum!"

I didn't feel like scum, nor did I appreciate being called it, but I followed his orders begrudgingly.

And he was in my face before I knew it. "I said now, recruit! Is that too difficult for you to understand, or do you not speak the Lord's language?"

"No, I do. And I did as you said."

On the surface, there was nothing wrong with my tone or the words I chose, but his nose flared, eyes raged like I'd just called his mother a goose-necked sow's tongue. I swear he was on the verge of bursting a blood vessel in his eye.

"You're in Lucifer's Army now, scum. You call me 'sir.' You call every single blessed Army person you ever see from this day forward 'sir.' You call your drill instructors 'sir.' You call the carriage drivers 'sir.' You call the cooks 'sir.' And so help me, Lucifer, as long as you're in my army, you call your blessed mother 'sir.' Got it?" Spit flew from his mouth as he shouted, his eyes drawn down to Creed. Fire burned in his gaze as if the halberd's presence offended him. For a second, I was convinced he was going to try to toss it back through the gateway. Part of me wanted to see him try.

My face flushed as hundreds of eyeballs watched us. The room faded into the background as he screamed. I'd even lost track of Bilba and Ralrek. For all I knew, they might have slunk home through the gateway. I couldn't blame them; I would have abandoned me too if I wasn't me.

The tall soldier spun on the room, making the standing demons take a step back and the ones pressed against the wall sink further against it. "What are all of you looking at? You don't have anything better to do, like getting your asses in line?" He stabbed a finger toward the front of the room. It was the first time I noticed three other military personnel, all fierce and fit, watching us from the open arch like an ember cat eyes a rat. Behind them was what looked like a large foyer. "Line up on each one of those men. Now!"

Demons grabbed their bags, sometimes accidentally picking up their neighbors in the scramble, and raced to form lines.

My face still burning, I picked up my possessions and stepped off to join the growing lines, before being yanked back and almost falling over. I turned to see what I got caught on and noticed the soldier held the arm of one suitcase. His smile was purely angelic.

"Let me do you a favor, scum," he said with a snarl that promised torture. "You've got about three seconds to get your act together before your life turns uncomfortable. I recommend you leave whatever attitude you have in this room. Once you join that line and we march your sorry asses out of here, you'll have heaven to pay for thirteen weeks if you aren't smart enough to straighten up. *If* you make it that long."

With his threat finished, he shoved my suitcase away, which kicked up and hit me in the shin. I instinctively yanked my leg up and hopped on a single foot.

"Stop screwing around!" he shouted, making more demons near me scramble even faster.

I joined the line and before we knew it, we were marched into a broader terminal. The glass ceiling rose fifty feet, exposing the now–darkened evening. Along the long terminal were other rooms like the one they had penned us in. Each held demons; some only held a handful, while others were as crowded as where we'd been.

I turned to ask Bilba if he thought those were more recruits as well, but as soon as I did a new Army guy, this one barely old enough to shave, shoved his dark face into mine. His breath smelled like old cheese and he, too, spit when he shouted. It must be something they teach in the Army.

"What is so interesting behind you that you can't follow simple orders and keep your pathetic eyes looking forward?"

I jerked back, my suitcase swinging out and catching the leg of the recruit marching to my right. He tripped over it and managed one of the slowest, ugliest falls you're ever likely to see, hitting the linoleum floor with a loud 'ooof,' and dumping his bag, which burst open. The floor was littered with chocolate bars, a few too many bottles of skin lotion, and about a dozen succubi magazines, one flopping open and revealing the centerfold to every nearby eyeball.

The recruit behind chocolate-porn guy tripped over him. The third barely dodged going down. Five seconds in the military and I'd already made a mess and made at least one enemy.

"Halt! Lucifer bless it, halt!" Our new tyrant shouted from the front of the three marching columns. "That means to stop fucking walking, morons!"

Everyone did. The recruits in front of me turned around to see what the commotion was while two more Army personnel strode back toward us.

"What the fuck is going on, recruit?" A freckle-faced soldier screamed in my face.

"I was—"

The first soldier to start this mess back in the large room stepped up in latest in the Beat Down Zeke Round Robin tournament. "Who in the heaven gave you permission to talk? Do you think you're our equals? That you can talk to us like we're you're Lucifer-blessed buddies?"

In fact, I did think I was their equal because all demons are, but something told me they weren't interested in hearing my opinions on equality, or anything else for that matter. My mouth remained shut.

"You were asked a question," the dark-skinned soldier

who'd made me trip screamed. "When you get asked a question, you answer it. From now on, every single time your weak mouth opens, you better start your sentence with 'sir, permission to speak?' Understood?"

I nodded. "Sir, permission to speak?"

"What, scum?"

If he called me scum one more time I might introduce him to the blue heat of a Creed spell—though it was the halberd who usually decided which spell it was going to cast.

"It was an accident," I said, raising my arm to point at Bilba, but before I could get my arm fully extended, the skinny soldier swatted it down.

"I don't know where you got the idea that you are free to do what you want, when you want," he spat. "But you're part of Lucifer's Army now. You do what we say, when we say, and how we say it. And you do it without thinking. Now pick up your shit. Since you seem to think you're more important than the rest of the recruits because you need two bags, you can show us how important you are. Out in front. Now! Move!"

I scrambled forward, feeling every incubus's eyes on me as I took the lead in the column. I don't think I swallowed as we were marched out of the building to open-top train wagons waiting outside. We stayed in line, no one daring to speak, as we loaded.

"Cram in, you idiots!" A female soldier screamed as we filled the benches. She was at the end of the line of recruits, ushering them forward faster than they could fill the seats. A few rows in front of where I sat, she stopped to lean into the face of a frightened looking demon with a dark complexion that was lightening toward pale. He kept rolling his lips into his mouth, making his cheeks dimple. "You better get over your intimacy issues and squeeze in. Make room."

"But my bag, I need space," he started.

"I don't care what you need!" she predictably screamed.

"The Army doesn't care what you need. Lucifer doesn't care what you need. Move your ass over until his leg asks yours out for a date!"

The recruit mumbled something but scooted over just the same.

I'd lost my friends in the suitcase debacle but did not dare turn around to look for them. I was squeezed between two demons bigger than me, like everyone else. The demon to my left must have preferred a more bohemian lifestyle, embracing the elegance of natural fragrances. Unfortunately for me, his funk was overwhelming, forcing me to spend the entire ride breathing through my mouth. Whatever our destination, we couldn't get there soon enough.

I'd regret that thought when we finally arrived.

We pulled up to the base gate, whispers and groans spread down the length of the wagon. The night was so dark, and full of chaotic distraction, I never even got a good look at the part of the Seventh Circle we sped through before arriving at the base. Heads turned toward the buildings we passed, each identical in shape and color. Street lamps cast a blue glow in fuzzy pockets of space along the sidewalk and under the overhangs of each building. Nothing moved, as if this place had been abandoned.

All heaven broke out when we pulled up to a square building three stories tall. Out of nowhere, a pair of soldiers rushed the wagon, pressing us off from the front and back. Another small squad directed us underneath the overhang where four more Army personnel waited. They were spaced out evenly along the wall of the building, hands clasped behind their backs, unmoving.

"Line up on us scumbags!" A male demon on the left shouted.

Recruits looked at each other. The dimmer among the recruits rushed up to the soldiers, only to be screamed at so aggressively they scurried away. Someone, I wasn't sure who, definitely one of the recruits, begged us to line up in four different lines, so we did.

Columns formed, one to each instructor, they moved up and down their respective line of recruits, each at least thirty deep. So much shouting and screaming made it difficult to make out which instructor was responsible for our line. From my spot toward the back of the line, I could only sense his presence by his echoing shouts to pick up our bags, followed by an angrier shout to put them back down again. I thought the dismembered voice was joking until he repeated the command. We complied. So did the recruits in the lines on either side of me.

"Quicker!" the angry voice shouted. He repeated his order so often my shoulders burned out before his voice did.

Over and over, we repeated the cruel and tedious game. And each time, he demanded we get quicker, faster, with more snap. No matter how fast we were, at times almost anticipating his command, it wasn't good enough. Having grown tired of the game, I started counting the number of repetitions. We did it another forty times before he lost his patience.

"Lucifer bless it!" The tall, dark-skinned soldier screamed, striding into my sight, his shoes clicking on the concrete. He kicked a recruit's bag. Glass shattered, and I winced.

The soldier spun on the recruit, who looked like someone had just stolen his devildog. The round, wide-brimmed hat obscured most of the soldier's face. He shoved the brim in the recruit's face. I could only make out the thick lips of the soldier's wide mouth, cracked in a sadistic smile. "Don't worry. Whatever that was, you won't need it." Lack of remorse and empathy expressed, he marched to the front of the line. "I'm Sergeant Kelem, and I'm officially your worst nightmare."

I already didn't disagree with that.

Sergeant Kelem stood to the side of the line, exposing

himself clearly for the first time. He was a sturdy demon, with a narrow waist and broad, rounded shoulders. When he yelled, I could see the strain of his vocal cords against his dark skin, which was almost as black as the night. The round hat hid the top of his shaven head—and probably a blessed halo.

He yo-yo'ed up and down the line, growling as he did. "In approximately twenty-three seconds, we're going to march through that door there." He thrust out an arm toward a dark green door in the corner of the building. Faded blue light emanated from behind it. His head swiveled to examine the line of exhausted and frightened recruits. His face scrunched in a scowl. "What the heaven are you waiting for? Move!"

In a scramble of arms and legs and dulled brains, we ran. In our collective buzz of urgency, we broke our single column formation. Too scared or exhausted, no one seemed to register the screaming voice of Sergeant Kelem—a name I would never forget—chastising us from behind for being, and I quote, "absolute fucking morons."

My nightmare was just beginning.

5

UNDERWORLD - SEVENTH CIRCLE

I DIDN'T KNOW what time it was. The narrow windows pinched at the corner where the ceiling met the wall revealed darkness outside. The floor was cold on my feet, even through my socks, and its chill raked my skin as I jumped out of bed. My brain was slow to recognize the strange surroundings and just why in the heaven someone was creating a raucous clanging philharmonic. The yelling only made it all the more painful of a wake-up.

The demon next to me fell out of his bunk onto the cold tile. I rubbed my eyes clear. What nightmare was this?

Boot camp. Oh, my Lucifer. I was in boot camp.

As the cacophony rose, starting the first day of what would surely be a living nightmare, my fellow recruits looked as disoriented as me. Heads swiveled the length of the room, bunk neighbors looked at each other dumbly. The brave stood and fumbled with their bunks, trying to look busy. Then the air changed as three instructors strode into the bay and down the aisle between the rows of bunks, awake and raising heaven.

Sergeant Kelem led the way, his boot taps clicking on the

tile. He occasionally reached down to shake a bunk and scream at a slow-moving recruit. Behind him, his two cohorts revealed themselves as those who woke us. One smashed together a pair of steel garbage can lids, and the other beat on the bottom of the can with a thick black flashlight.

"Get the heaven out of your bunks," Sergeant Kelem screamed, his face distorted. Who could be this angry so early in the morning?

Recruits were on their feet now, unsteady and looking unsure about what they were supposed to be doing. I was no better. I just stood still by my bunk and watched the hostile procession.

"Get dressed, scum," he howled. "I don't need to see your pasty asses and tighty whities!"

I jumped to the end of my bed and snagged the shirt and pants I'd draped there, donning them. Some incubus went to the front of their bunks, some to their lockers, and others were already dressed and hastily making their beds.

The entire time, Sergeant Kelem and his garbage can posse stalked up the aisle, giving us no clue whether he was pleased or not. His sidekicks dropped their noisemakers in the middle of the aisle and watched us like hungry hellions. Kelem marched past his recruits, his hands clamped into fists, casting disapproving glares at everyone all at once.

Finished covering tidy whities with pants and slipping on their shirts, demons began making their beds. I hadn't thought that task would be so important, but I also noticed that none of the soldiers bothered the recruits who were working on theirs, so I figured it would keep me out of trouble to follow suit. I moved to the end of my bunk and tucked in my sheet, straightened my pillow, and pulled the wool blanket up, taking a second to make sure everything appeared orderly.

By the time I finished, most others already stood at the

sides of their bunks at the edge of the aisle. Sergeant Kelem's two partners took positions at either end of the long bay and he stood in the middle, slowly turning in a circle. I took my position near the aisle at the side of my bunk, sweating from the turbulent first moments of my first day of boot camp and wondering how some of these incubi seemed to know what to do.

Sergeant Kelem looked back and forth at his two assistants, nodding. Then, in a coordinated attack, all three began tossing bunks. My mouth dropped open as I watched the two soldiers move from both ends of the bay toward the center, while Kelem raised Abel in the middle. They flipped mattresses, threw pillows, tossed sheets and green wool blankets, sometimes in the face of the demons who'd made them. Some recruits jumped out of the way as if the pillows would hurt, one yelped at the assault, but most stood their ground and waited. A couple recruits did the unwise thing and tried to stop the surgeons of destruction from ruining their hard work.

A demon grabbed the arm of the skinnier sergeant. Time flashed. The sergeant grabbed the recruit's arm, spinning the recruit and pinning his arm behind his back in a bolt of movement. Subdued, the demon was marched face-first toward his locker. I knew what was coming, but it was so aggressive, so fast, my dulled brain didn't want to believe it, even as the sergeant slammed the incubus against the metal.

Sergeant Kelem wore an angelic smile as he marched past the two columns of beds, panting. I stopped breathing when he neared me. "Who in the heaven gave you permission to make your beds? Huh?" He stopped in front of one recruit who hadn't done a thing and hadn't even moved from the end of his bed yet. The demon flinched as if he expected to be struck. Sergeant Kelem's head moved in a slow, methodical manner, up and down the recruit. His jaw jutted from underneath that wide-brimmed hat. "You're not worth my time, scum." Then he turned on all of us. "None of you are. You're all worthless and weak. And guess what the Army doesn't want in its soldiers?"

Ten demons down from me, a redheaded, freckle-faced demon raised his hand. I think there was a collective wince around the room. "Sir, permission to speak?"

Sergeant Kelem moved with the speed of an athlete, getting in the face of the brave redhead. "You're too stupid to speak. So shut your mouth." Moving away from freckle-face, Kelem screamed, "All of you are too stupid to have anything worth hearing. For the next few weeks of your life, the only thing you need to worry about is doing what I want you to do and doing it perfectly. Every detail, every effort, every corner of a fold, ever polished millimeter of your boots, and every blessed step you take. Your life is now ruled by me. As far as you're concerned, I'm your Lucifer now."

A collective gasp took the air out of the room at his blasphemy. I'm not a staunch fundamentalist by any stretch of the imagination, but his comment surprised even me. A sergeant in Lucifer's Army, I expected a little more reverence. But hey, I'm all about nonconformity, so our drill instructor just raised himself a few notches in my book—not that he would care, I'm sure.

"Now, since you all are too stupid to follow orders, and none of you can make a bunk worth a damn, Sergeant Panzer here will show you how to do it correctly. Gather your sorry asses around and pay attention. And if even one of you thinks about using your Abilities, to get yours done or to help another scum, forget it. Abilities are a thing of the past, until you leave Lucifer's Army."

No one was allowed to use Abilities? The Army had my attention now.

You wouldn't think it was possible to squeeze thirty

demons around a single bunk. But with the proper motivation and level of fear, it was. What I also didn't think was possible was that there was so much detail and work involved in making a bed, or that it required nearly forty minutes to show us how to do it properly. First impression of the Army? Details mattered.

Toward the end of the lesson, my stomach reminded me it hadn't received any attention, growling loudly. Unfortunately for it, me, and anyone suffering the same predicament, Sergeant Kelem noticed.

"You can forget about eating, scum," he snapped, not even making eye contact. "You'll eat after you make your bed like a big boy."

No one was allowed to talk, so they couldn't advise me on why my corners were loose enough to ripple like sails in the wind. By the twenty-fifth time flipping over my mattress, I couldn't ignore their growing frustration at each failure. Whenever they thought the sergeants weren't looking they pointed and gesticulated, sometimes jabbing their fingers at critical points in the sheet I needed to pinch to get the proper fold. Trying to fix my corner, I took my hand off the fold and placed it against my stomach, releasing the sheet, sending it all crumbling apart.

I was sure my fellow recruits were seconds away from stuffing me inside my mattress.

Before they killed me, I finally got the fold—though I think Sergeant Kelem let it slip because they had other things they needed us to accomplish—and they marched us out into the early morning.

Rare—never on purpose and often because I was sick or hungover—was it for me to be up and outside before the Hellfire rose. And it was miserable. Standing underneath an overhang, a stiff breeze taunted us, picking up speed and blowing through the space shared by our platoon and two others. Its consistent assault cut through my jeans and shirt.

Sergeant Kelem monitored us, shouting at anyone he saw shivering.

We were waiting for access to the mess hall, and the anticipation of eating overrode my discomfort at the cold. Sergeant Kelem passed by me more often and, after a while, he hovered near. His eyes flickered toward Creed each time he neared, but he would only scowl.

Our platoon was called to enter the hall, and I breathed a sigh of relief. Cold and hungry, both would be satiated now.

At breakfast, we sat at large round tables, eight demons to each, and ate silently while Sergeant Kelem and his peers patrolled to ensure silence. It was the most awkward meal I was ever appreciative to have in my entire six-thousand-year life.

And it was enjoyable—even though it was barely better than my mother's cooking—until I gestured to the demon seated two chairs away from me. "Mind passing the salt?"

Apparently, that's not a good idea in boot camp. The recruit's eyes shot open as he looked beyond me. I turned to see four instructors moving in my direction. Trouble was coming, and I was its target. How had I not felt them behind me? Usually, my sensitivity would have picked up on their presence. Man, I was exhausted.

"Who in the heaven are you talking to, recruit?" a sergeant with a scar down his left cheek shouted.

"This one thinks he deserves salt!" a round-faced sergeant laughed as he unscrewed the saltshaker and dumped its entire contents over my breakfast. Demons tend to use a lot of salt for listless foods, but I only wanted a sprinkling to flavor my chimera eggs. Now, it was more like I was going to have eggs with my salt.

"Maybe he likes being the center of attention?" the sole female sergeant proposed with a smirk. My stomach no longer desired this concoction that passed as a meal.

"Then let's make him the center of attention," the scar-faced sergeant said.

They agreed, a little too excitedly I might add. The female sergeant slid behind me. "Sit forward, recruit," she ordered, and as soon as I complied, she kicked my chair out from underneath me. I fell to the floor as it clattered away, drawing hundreds of eyes from across the mess hall.

"On your feet, scum," the round-faced sergeant hovered over me, grabbing and twisting my shirt in his meaty fist and yanking me to my feet.

The female retrieved the chair and set it in an open pathway between tables, tapping the back of it. "Come on celebrity, let's take the stage."

I could not ignore the feeling that this situation was barreling toward Heaven in a handbasket.

Meaty-hands shoved me forward. I stumbled before regaining my balance, looking over my shoulder. "What am I supposed to do?" It wasn't until I asked that I realized I hadn't started my inquiry with the required stupid permission to speak.

Meaty-hands shook his shaved head. "This one will require a lot of work. Who's your drill instructor, scum?"

"Sergeant Kelem."

Meaty's eyes squinted. "Sir," he said through clenched teeth. "End every single one of your Lucifer-blessed sentences with 'sir.' Understand?"

I didn't have the heart—you may call it courage—to tell him that those instructions had already been given but also forgotten.

From behind, the female sergeant slapped the back of the plastic chair. She must have been wearing a ring because it was a sharp whack. She spoke in a low growl. "Get your sorry ass up on this chair now."

I did, rising above the seated crowd of fellow recruits. Scanning and not finding the friendly faces of Bilba or Ralrek,

I looked over everyone's heads, trying to focus on the serving line on the far wall of the mess hall, where the employees were busy with the constant traffic of hungry recruits. Focusing on them helped the hundreds of faces watching me blend into obscurity.

"Attention. Attention," the female sergeant shouted with mock levity. "Recruits, put down your utensils. Stop eating. One of you believes he is so important he deserves to take mealtime away from you. Since that is the case, we're going to give him his due. None of you will be allowed to eat until this recruit is done getting your attention, so if you end up missing out on the rest of your meal period, you have him to thank for it."

I swallowed as pairs of eyes flared, lips were pulled back in scowls, and fists were clenched.

"Since this demon is in such need of attention, we're going to give it to him, because Lucifer's mantra is all about 'one team, one fight,'" she continued mocking. She pointed at a side wall where a vertical forest green banner hung. "You see that, recruit? That's the Army's Oath of Excellence. You're going to recite it for everyone."

"Yes sir," I answered through my constricted throat.

Her growl promised pain. "Oh, so I'm a sir, am I? All right then, wise ass. Not only are you going to recite the Oath, but you're going to do it to your favorite song. Would you all like that?" she asked the captive audience.

The cooling food on their plates taunted them as viciously as the drill instructors carrying out this farce. How many enemies had I made now?

"I asked if you would like that," the female shouted.

"Yes, ma'am!" the hall erupted with roars filled with vigor.

She turned to me, crossing her arms. "Your audience awaits, wise ass. Start singing. And don't skip any lines. All Army personnel know the Oath by heart, so you'll pay if you try to play us for stupid."

"Ma'am, permission to speak?" See? I am teachable.

Her eyes squinted. "Permission granted. But make it quick."

"To what tune should I sing? I don't know the melody." Regardless, even if I did, it would be a horrendous experience for everyone. A singer, I am not.

Her hands dropped to her side, and she leaned to look around me to her meaty-handed peer. "Can you believe this one?"

"Kelem has his hands full," meaty-hands laughed. "They'll probably put him in for promotion after this one cycles through."

"*If* this one does," she replied with her own laugh at my expense. "What's your favorite song, wise ass?"

It was such an odd question in the middle of the mess hall on my first morning of boot camp that I couldn't think of a single blessed song. The heat of pressure scrambled my brain further as a dozen sergeants and hundreds of recruits waited. I searched through my mental library, all songs blending into one another. Just when I was about to ask the sergeant for a recommendation, one finally came. The title fell out of my mouth before I analyzed its appropriateness.

"I guess it would be 'Save a Chimera, Ride a Hellboy'," I finally answered.

"Oh, good," she said, throwing her hands up and slowly spinning for the entire mess hall. "Not only is he a wise ass, but he's got horrible taste in music. I can't wait to hear this, wise ass. Start singing."

So I did. My voice was creaky and shook, but I was doing what they wanted. Maybe, just maybe, they would leave me alone after this, and my fellow recruits wouldn't have the chance to burn the image of my face in their minds.

"*Across the seas, And on the shores,*" I started. Meaty-hands interrupted me by kicking the chair. I wobbled but didn't fall. That only seemed to piss him off more.

"Louder. Like a man, scum," he snarled.

I cleared my throat and began again, louder.

> *"Across the seas,*
> *And on the shores,*
> *We fight and win, fight and win.*
> *In the trenches,*
> *We struggle on,*
> *Never defeated, we fight and win.*
> *For one, for all,*
> *All as one,*
> *We fight and win, fight and win.*
> *Near and far,*
> *Through dark and cold,*
> *We fight and win, fight and win.*
> *All for one, one for all,*
> *By our brothers, we never fall,*
> *Fight and win, we fight and win.*
> *The old me is dead,*
> *I am a soldier now,*
> *To fight and win, to kill again.*
> *For His name,*
> *I will give my all,*
> *To fight and win, to fight and win.*
> *Until I fall,*
> *Excellence in all,*
> *I'll die to fight and win."*

My chest thumped from my speeding heart.

A single hand clap sounded from somewhere toward the back of the mess hall. Bilba? The female sergeant spun. "Don't you dare clap for him! None of you. Why in Heaven would you clap for someone who just cost you ten minutes of your breakfast?"

Too many faces twisted at the realization the sergeant was serious.

A bell rang from the top corner of the mess hall.

"In fact," the female sergeant shouted over the ringing, pointing to the bell, "that is your signal. Mealtime is over. Pick up your trays and take them to the cleaning reservoir. You're done. Don't any of you think about grabbing a nibble of food remaining on your plate. I want you to remember that face." She pointed at me. "When you're hungry until your next mealtime. Let this be a lesson. None of you is more important than the other. Don't forget that, because this is what happens when you think you are. Your brothers suffer. Now, move!"

Incubi jumped from their chairs, grabbing their trays and drinks and forming a line at the reservoir. It moved with an efficiency of a long-perfected system; the only thing that slowed progress was us bumbling through it as we scraped food from plates, rinsed glasses, and deposited them in bins.

I was nearly the last in line because of the time it took to get off the chair and move it back to my original seat.

The last to join the line came from the other side of the mess hall. I felt their hateful eyes on me as they made their way closer. When they finally joined us, the demon behind me pressed his tray against my lower back, pushing in. I shuffled forward a few inches. Then the tray was there again, with greater pressure. I shuffled forward a few more inches, and it came back. A clear signal.

I twitched when hot breath coated the back of my neck. The incubus growled. "I'm going to fucking kill you if you ever do that again."

I swallowed the lump in my throat and focused on getting out of the mess hall in one piece.

I did, and I even made it through having my head shaved. Bilba looked even dumber and Ralrek, of course, had a perfectly symmetrical head. Uniform disbursement followed and our first experience on the drill field where we learned to march followed that. At least I didn't screw that up—I actually picked up quickly.

As we headed off the drill field, my stomach knotted in protest. I willed it to shut up, celebrating my drill performance and the fact I wasn't an absolute failure at everything.

6

UNDERWORLD, SEVENTH CIRCLE

"Not too bad, Zeke," Bilba smiled, nodding at the boot in my hands.

Two weeks on from my mess hall humiliation, we'd gotten into a rhythm of boot camp life. I still wasn't enjoying it. There was nothing fun about the military—though no one ever promised that there would be—but the distinct flow of daily life helped gather momentum. No longer was I struggling to adjust to the Army's demands. I'd even learned to not call female drill instructors 'sir' in that time. Everyone in the platoon was regrowing their hair—though I still couldn't look in the mirror at my stubble-covered misshapen head and take myself seriously.

Since we'd hit our training targets and performed to Sergeant Kelem's expectations, we were given time to ourselves. There were no days off for recruits, just for the full-time staff, but the sense of freedom that came with not having to worry about a drill instructor tossing your bed or having you stand at attention for an hour was a joyous occasion all the same.

Today was about perfecting uniforms. Done with starching and ironing mine until it felt like it would cut skin with its sharp creases, I tended to my black leather boots, trying to get a semblance of a shine out of the toes. Bilba was done with his, so was Ralrek—because he flirted his way into getting help. Mine were pathetic. I willed the tip of the boot to take a shine. It refused. Creed would be useful if it could channel a spell that shined boots—not that we were allowed to use our Abilities—but the halberd had no recommendations.

I dropped the boot to the floor, so tired of looking at the dull leather toe.

"Hand it over," Bilba said with a light laugh. "I'll finish it for you."

Determined, I shook my head, never lifting my face, and picked it up. "No, I've got it. I can't have you saving me on everything."

"You can't fail the uniform inspection. Just let me help you, I'm done with everything else."

"No, I've got it," I said, my elbow burning from rubbing small circles of blackened wax onto the toe for far longer than any demon should have to, even if they had an eternity of free time.

Bilba sighed, stopping me.

"What?" I asked.

"I don't want you to fail inspection. How many times have you?"

"Failed?"

He nodded. "Twice. And you know what can happen if you do again."

I did because Sergeant Kelem set clear expectations at every opportunity, as if he took pleasure in threatening us with the promise of making those who failed too often restart boot camp, something they elegantly called 'washing out.'

Bilba pointed at the tip of my boot. "That's half your problem, right there."

"What?"

"You're rubbing that wax in as if you're trying to remove a stain. Relax, Zeke. Light touches. Oh, and more cold water. The bin has been sitting out so long it is room temperature. That won't help."

I stopped rubbing, resting the cotton ball on the leather. "How am I supposed to keep water cold for that long? We live in the blessed Underworld, we're in boot camp, and no one is allowed to use their Abilities even if one of us has blessed Water magic."

My cursing drew a few snickers from the demons near us, the strangers who became friends over these past weeks. Amazing how it happened, really, without me being sacrificed in a hazing ritual. Half a month ago, I was the focus of their frustration when I deprived them of that first meal in the mess hall. Now we were a team who helped each other out of binds. Everyone had strengths and weaknesses—mine seemed to be centered on everything and anything the Army needed me to learn—and we'd learned what each of those were for the other. My boot camp experience would have been rebooted a few times already if it weren't for the other twenty-eight incubi sharing this open living space with me. I say twenty-eight because we lost a recruit a few nights before.

One night we heard him yelling in the bathroom after lights out, wrenching us from our sleep. His outburst drew the attention of the on-call drill instructor, who entered the bathroom and immediately ran back out, shouting at us to stay in our bunks. We found out the recruit had put his fist through a mirror and was talking to himself in the corner when the instructor found him.

I don't know if they kept him around or if they sent him home, but I wasn't going to wash out and take my chances of running across someone like that in a new platoon.

"I've got to learn how to get this right on my own, Bilba. You guys can't always save me."

He looked away, a sure signal that he was about to be

dishonest. "We're not saving you."

I raised an eyebrow. "Are you really going to try to say that with a straight face? To me, of all demons?"

"We haven't been."

"Yes, you have." I countered.

Bilba returned his focus to his own tasks. How could he deny the truth? He had saved me numerous times. Ralrek too, in his charming way. So had many others. Too many. I needed to get this boot right if for no other reason than to prove to myself I actually could.

I followed my friend's advice, refreshing my water bin and returning to my bunk. I resumed buffing the toe, careful to rub tenderly with the wax-covered cotton ball. I don't know how long I buffed, dipping the cotton ball in water and switching to new ones whenever I'd abused an old one, but I got lost in the task when I started seeing progress. Slowly, an unmistakable sheen began spreading across the tip of the boot.

"Keep going," Bilba encouraged, moving on to study for a test coming up later in the week, getting ahead as I fell further behind.

"Nice work, Zeke," Kayden Lancer fist pumped.

Momentum was gathering. This wasn't just platitudes, this was real. The boot was starting to shine. The cotton ball was gliding over the wax now, instead of fighting the microscopic grains in the leather surface. Their encouragement pushed me through the sweat and tedium.

"Nice work, Sunstone," a gruff voice said above me.

I looked up … into Sergeant Kelem's face. I hadn't heard him come in—this was supposed to be his day off—and no one had announced his arrival, or if they did, I missed it, as focused as I was.

Immediately dropping my boot, I shot to my feet and stood at the position of attention. "Thank you sir," I said, forgoing the formal permission to speak garbage they made us do weeks ago. Once we learned to follow orders well enough, he stopped requiring it.

The sergeant bent and retrieved my boot, holding it up for examination in my line of sight. His eyes traveled its dimensions like a horny incubus consuming a racy magazine. I squirmed. My lack of situational awareness at not recognizing the bay being called to attention would cost me after this impromptu boot inspection.

He turned it, examining every inch of black leather that had just started holding a feeble shine. Rubbing the flat of his thumb across the boot, he huffed. I tried to hide my wince. The oil from his skin would screw with the wax layers. I'd have to repair that area. Great. As if I wasn't far enough behind.

His eyes flicked to mine. To Creed. Back to me. Without a doubt, he was watching to see if I would slip back into civilian mode at his antagonistic action. What he couldn't comprehend was that part of me was gone, at least temporarily. The military was effective in destroying the demon inside. Old Zeke was dead, for now, surrounded by magicless incubi just like him. One of the tribe.

Instead of chastising me or ridiculing my hard work, Sergeant Kelem leaned closer, and without a smile, said, "Not bad, Sunstone. It appears you might not be a complete fuck-up after all. Just don't let it go to your head." Without waiting for me to respond or even give him a cursory thank you, our drill instructor started away toward the center of the aisle, addressing everyone. "Meeting in the day room in five. Move your sorry asses."

Something was different in our drill instructor's tone, something that made all of us check with each other when he walked out of the room, leaving us to our own devices and imagination. The nervous glances we shot at each other told me I wasn't the only one interested in hearing what he had to say.

"What do you think this is about?" Bilba asked as he finished folding his physical training uniform into a perfect square and putting it away in his orderly drawer.

"No idea," I said, rolling my shirt and tucking it in my dirty laundry bag.

Bilba watched, shaking his head. "How many uniforms are you actually wearing?"

I opened my locker door further so he could see the nearly-full set of duty and physical training uniforms hanging inside. My smile was irresistible as Bilba did the math.

He looked shocked, his ears rimmed with pink. "You've gotten through boot camp rotating out two uniforms?"

"Don't hate me because I'm smarter than you."

"You're not smarter," he laughed. "You're disgusting. No wonder the bay stinks."

"It stinks," I countered, "because there's almost thirty incubi spending eighteen hours a day in it and they feed us gruel full of additives. That's just asking for it, if you ask me."

He still shook his head, unimpressed by my effective uniform rotation system that saved me untold time, and finished cleaning his area as the stream of demons moving toward the day room increased. I hurried and joined them, leaving Bilba behind because his need to have the perfect locker and desire to follow every stupid rule only reminded me of how many I consistently broke.

"Hurry up, slowpoke," I teased.

The platoon crammed into the dayroom, sitting on the floor in cross-legged positions so we could all fit. The room held no furniture except a simple gray metal desk and chair, both of which belonged to Sergeant Kelem. A demon we called Charlie, even though his real name was Valsiri, volunteered for the position of Administrative Assistant on Day Two, and touted his accomplishment like a conquering hero. Tall, lanky, and with a bottom lip three times the size of his top, Charlie was covering for something, I just had not had the time or interest to uncover what it was. Part of his duties called for him to ensure no one had the gall to sit at the sergeant's desk, and definitely not on it. He stood by the desk, guarding it as if his life depended on it.

"Hey, Charlie," I said, walking as close as possible to watch him twitch.

"Don't touch the—" he started.

"I know. I know." I said, extending my pointer finger toward it. "But let me just clean this speck of dust from—"

"I've got it!" Charlie dove to prevent me from cleaning the nonexistent dust. I turned away as he caught his thigh on the edge of the desk, releasing an *oooof!* and cursing me.

I was still laughing as I found an open spot on the floor. The tile was cool, the chill creeping up through my physical training shorts, the uniform they now allowed us to wear when we weren't in our military fatigues. It was a privilege of being at this part of our training, having survived the early indoctrination.

Small clumps of demons spoke in hushed tones. I remained sitting at attention—yes, we have a seated position of attention in Lucifer's Army—because I didn't want Sergeant Kelem walking in and catching me slacking. Improved boots or not, the last thing I'd do is give him any reason to scold me or mark me down. When I left for boot camp, I planned to figure out a way to flunk out so I could get home. Only after our training kicked off did I discover there was no flunking out, just endless cycles of retraining until I got it. Now, it was all about getting through boot camp on the first shot. I'm not a masochist. No way would I hand him ammunition to wash me out and make me start this heaven over again, especially since I had enough marks against me to be borderline. Imagining Day One all over again was what would keep me up at night if I was not always so exhausted. We weren't technically allowed to talk when gathered together without our drill instructor's permission, and everyone knew that. Sometimes Sergeant Kelem overlooked that if we were performing well. Sometimes not. The criteria were as inconsistent as my father's love. None of us knew for sure when he'd have a problem with sneaky conversations, so it wasn't a risk worth taking. Not for me.

Bilba joined us, and Ralrek finally moseyed in like he had more important things occupying him. He squeezed in behind us, leaning forward and wrapping his arms around our necks and pulling us backwards, almost toppling me.

"Something's happening guys," he said excitedly.

I pulled away, removing his arm and sitting at attention again. Ralrek, cool as ever, didn't appear bothered by my shunning.

"I know. The thing I can't figure out is why you're excited. It's never good news when they have unscheduled talks," I whispered as I pulled on my training shorts to straighten them again.

"I'm ready for a change," Bilba said, the blotches on his cheeks just now clearing from the exertion of hurrying.

I snickered. "We haven't even been here for a month. How in the world are you already ready for a change? I thought you wanted this?"

"It's too stressful."

"It's designed to be," I said, my eyes on the door and my ears focused down the hall for any sign that our drill instructor was on his way.

"Well, I can't wait to hear what it is," Ralrek said before sitting back.

Everyone turned toward the door at the clicking of Sergeant Kelem's taps striking the tile floor. Silence was immediate, already so well trained, compliant. Official lapdogs of the Army—probably my greatest accomplishment if anyone asked my father.

Anxiety lanced the air as the clicking approached. The

demon performing sentry duty performed a right face and called to the room, "Platoon, ten–hut!"

The precise moment Sergeant Kelem stomped into the room, I knew something had changed. His face was drawn, lacking any of the sadistic joy all drill instructors seemed to have perpetually staining their expressions.

"At ease. Take your seats, boys," he said in a flat tone.

Usually, I would relax slightly when he gave us that permission, but I couldn't this time. This was so unlike him.

"We've got a few things to go over," he said, spreading notes in front of him at his desk before looking up at Charlie. "What are you doing hanging around my desk, scum? Go take your blessed seat."

Charlie jumped as if someone had pinched his ass. A smile flickered on my face, and I wasn't alone.

"Not sure why so many of you are happy. The Army doesn't want happy soldiers. Anyway," Sergeant Kelem growled as if we were to blame for what he was about to share. "I haven't had nearly the time I need with you scum. But things beyond my control dictate our actions. Those things are namely being the human war. It has escalated."

The room chilled. We had been cut off from the outside Underworld and any news about the mortal conflict. Everything was news to us, even down to the daily reports on the health of the Hellfire. The last thing anyone talked about was the human war. From the sharp edges to Kelem's narrowed eyes and the way his jaw jutted, things had to be bad.

"Sir, permission to speak?" I found myself asking.

Sergeant Kelem nodded. "Go ahead, Sunstone."

"How bad has it gotten, sir? And what does it have to do with us?"

As one, all heads moved from our drill instructor to me.

"Bad enough that we've cut your training time in more than half." The news made his face look like he had just eaten an entire lemon with the peel intact.

This time, no one could hold back a gasp. A dozen hands shot into the air.

Sergeant Kelem closed his eyes and drew a deep breath. "Listen boys, I'm going to get real with you. You're seeing the real Sergeant Kelem now. We need to spin you up and make you into Army troops as quickly as possible. That means I don't have time to entertain every question. We've got too much to do and no time to do it."

He ran a hand over the top of his close cropped, tightly curled black hair. "Gotta be honest with you boys. This will suck for everyone. You think you've had long days? You haven't seen shit yet. The only time you're going to stop is when you're sleeping. It will be that busy. In fact, I'm moving into the office in the bay and staying with you so we can train on as much as possible before you graduate."

Bilba and Ralrek and I shared looks, validating that we'd heard accurately.

Even though he clenched his jaw, his eyes seemed to be looking at something a thousand yards away. "In fact, we need to start this accelerated training within the hour; and we have a long march ahead. Get your shit put away because we need to hit chow before we set out."

I raised my hand again—hey, if things were this bad I wouldn't have to worry about washing out, so why not see how far I could push the rules?

He closed his eyes and shook his head, but there was a hint of a smile on his lips. "And before any of you dumbasses ask; we're going out to the firing range. Today, I'll make sharpshooters out of you sorry scum."

WHEN YOU SPEND YOUR ENTIRE LIFE AS THE ONLY DEMON IN THE history of a species to not have magic, being restricted from using it isn't necessarily a big deal. So when we were informed on Day One that it was strictly prohibited to access our Abilities, I coped much better than the rest of my platoon mates. For the first time in my life, I was normal, and it felt glorious—even in the context of early wake-ups, tons of marching, crappy food, and a complete lack of autonomy.

Our purpose in boot camp was to be prepared to covertly join the human army, seamlessly blending in with the mortals to fight the enemy. Who their enemies were, I had no idea—I didn't keep up on the mortal's politics—but I knew we would join whatever side was the opposing force to the side angels were joining. Angels and demons, in the Overworld, ostensibly fighting a mortal war for mortal reasons. The real reason we were going, and I imagine the angels were being sent, was to maintain the Balance, the middle ground in the eternal tug-of-war between Hell and Heaven. So it made sense to ban all Abilities. In the Overworld, we would look and act just like the typical human soldier. To restrict our training to a magic-less one gave us a life dependent on a different law of physics and mechanics. I can't lie, I was stoked that everyone had a further taste of what it was like to live as the Segregate for six thousand years. When all was said and done, maybe I would return to the Fifth being given a little more respect?

But it was still strange to march to the firing range to learn how to operate rifles. I'd only ever seen them in the movies and always thought they looked so cool. But so did driving cars on empty streets, or doing dangerous maneuvers during speeding chases, and I never saw anyone doing that during my two trips to the Overworld, including the trip to Germany where supposedly everyone drove too fast to be safe.

At the range, the staff walked us through the functionality of our M-16 rifles and forced us to tear them down and put them back together a dozen times. Hours of breaking down and rebuilding rifles made the room smell of oil and grime. By the time we perfected that portion of our training, we were ready for chow.

Sergeant Kelem had been honest with us about the truth behind our fast-paced training. Though it was ambiguous and frightening, I was a fan of this condensed schedule. The longer days meant we completed more training, meaning we'd finish boot camp quicker. Once we joined the mortal Army, we would have some semblance of a normal life and a taste of freedom again. Plus, the Overworld had chicken wings. Enough said.

Smiles and quiet cheers spread across the platoon when we discovered we would not have to march to the mess hall for our late lunch. Instead, our drill sergeant had organized a delivery of meals–ready–to–eat. So we got to stay where we were and have boxed meals brought to us. Of course, it behooved Sergeant Kelem's schedule as well, since he could keep us with the arms masters, tearing down our rifles and putting them back together again, but I didn't care. Less marching was always a good thing.

After lunch we went to the range and were walked through the safety procedures. About an hour later, the arms master, one Sergeant Halcion, a gruff, older noncommissioned officer who was still somehow serving Lucifer's Army, informed us that we would be firing.

"Today?" asked one recruit with a gleam in his eye that made me question if he should have a gun at all.

The arms master, who didn't care about the formalities of our boot camp training, gave a stiff nod. "Right now."

We weren't even given the chance to entertain the thought that Sergeant Halcion was screwing with us. As soon as he gave the command, his two younger instructors spread down the line, setting small buckets at each station. When they finished, one of the pair moved to a chain on the side wall and gave it a series of yanks. A hidden mechanism above him began grinding, and the corrugated metal wall in front of the stations slowly rose, exposing the firing range. It didn't look nearly as neat and tidy as the ones in mortal movies. Instead of cool gray concrete walls and automatic trolleys that pulled targets toward shooters at the push of a button, ours was black brimstone floor and wall, with a slanted wall of crumbled brown sandstone at the far end. The range had no roof, so the elements would affect our shots. Paper targets in the shape of armless torsos swayed on cardboard in the breeze.

"What did they just do, sir?" Bilba asked, nodding at the assistants.

Sergeant Halcion growled. "Laying out rounds."

A storm of high-fives, fist bumping, and other various manifestations of male bravado mixed with childish excitement sprang up around the platoon.

"You boys know the rules, but we're going to go over them again before we begin and then in between each round," Sergeant Halcion shouted over top of the fervor, drawing our eyes back to him. "This is real, boys, not fun and games and not some contest to see which of you has the biggest balls. It's not about earning bragging points. What you do today will prepare you, the best we can, for survival in the Overworld with the human army. Don't take this lightly. Pay attention to everything we say. Don't unlock the safety unless we say so. Don't look downrange if we don't say so. Don't *blink* if we don't say so. And, I swear to Lucifer, if one of you even thinks to put your finger on the trigger before we say so, I'll wrap my knuckles around your lungs."

"But lungs are internal organs, sir," Charlie said while raising his hand, his thick bottom lip falling open.

"Exactly." Sergeant Halcion grinned without humor, stepping off the platform. Another, younger instructor replaced him. "Listen to Sergeant Pythan, boys. He's got your station assignments."

Sergeant Pythan, all one hundred and thirty pounds of him, commanded attention by withholding the information we needed to hear.

"Make a hole," Sergeant Halcion ordered without stopping, splitting our group. We reformed when he passed. Sergeant Pythan began reading names and station numbers and released us once all assignments were given out.

Mine was smack in the middle of the line. "Hmmm," I moaned noncommittally.

"What's up?" Ralrek asked.

I waved my arm from side to side. "Stuck in the middle."

"So?"

"I'm not going to be able to concentrate." An ugly but true admission.

Much had changed in my life since being gifted Creed. Subtle changes I hadn't recognized until after the failed execution attempt on the angel spy Gemini. My ability to focus on a single point, item, or demon began to slip. I didn't make the connections when we were sent to steal the Horn of Taurus. The first signs crept up during our second trip to the Overworld in Kaiserslautern, Germany. But even those were too subtle, and I excused my culpability by focusing on the stress and turmoil of our mission and the Council's betrayal.

What began as an inherent hypersensitivity to conjuring was exacerbated by Creed's power and I'd normalized it for far too long. In the past year since Gemini, though, I couldn't. The influence of the powerful halberd extended to my core, making me more observant than those around me, as if the water tap to my brain was constantly open and it was being flooded. In that time, I hadn't yet figured out how to deal with the volume.

Everything, every fractional aspect of life, registered in my brain now. When walking through Eve's Sanctuary, I noticed the vibrant colors, heard the whisper of the wind and the rhythmic beat of insect wings. When in Old Towne, a million conversations pierced my brain, making every shopping excursion a living heaven. Working in The Book Abyss was a curse in disguise as I noticed each book misplaced by a customer who'd changed their mind. Samhain carnivals were simply overwhelming. All the demons, the shouts of joy, the rattling of death trap roller coasters, was a tsunami of sights and sounds. The nightclubs—oh, don't get me started on the nightclubs. It didn't matter where I was, Creed had plugged me into life intimately.

Dealing with the inflow of sensory information was an incremental daily journey, and I'd become decent at hiding my discomfort and adept at faking it. Even the time in boot camp didn't reveal my struggle to process so much stimuli, impressive considering being constantly surrounded by twenty-eight other demons every minute of the day, plus a perpetually enraged drill instructor. But this, everyone firing M-16s? This might be a stretch in the best of circumstances. One I didn't expect Ralrek, or anyone, to understand—yes, yes, hard for them to since I wasn't exactly open about this developing skill, I know. Even I wouldn't know how bad this was going to be until we started firing.

Ralrek gave me an all-knowing grin that said he didn't believe me. "You've got this. Plus, I'm sure you'll have plenty of chances to shoot again after you fuck it up."

He patted me on the arm and walked away to take his station. I stood in front of mine and looked down range, not feeling any better.

Sergeant Halcion and his two assistants spread down the line, each taking a third and walking us through the safety steps before having us lay prone. Step-by-excruciating-step, they led us through the tedium of eye and ear protection, loading rounds into the magazine, and inserting the magazine. Then came the time for magic—not literally, of course. We aimed our rifles at the black, armless targets.

"Alright boys," the arms master shouted, "flip your safety switch off."

My thumb found the ribbed metal of the safety switch. The internal spring, tight, protested at my command to flip the switch off. It lost. The switch clicked open. I had a live rifle in my hands and the same fair shot at this task as my as fellow platoon members. No magic. No folding stupid uniforms or polishing boots or making the tightest bunk. This was about demon against physics, and this time no one got to cheat with their Abilities.

The sergeant's shout jerked me out of my thoughts. "On the horn, you have thirty seconds to fire your ten rounds."

I swallowed the apprehension. Shit was about to get real.

The seconds hung in the air like a spotlighted cross in the middle of Lucifer's living room. My breath filled my ears inside the hearing protection.

The horn sounded, and I forgot every instruction, like my mind had been blown clean by the blast. I scrambled to remember not only what I was supposed to do, but how I was supposed to do it.

Pop!

I jumped, flinching backward as the first trainee fired from somewhere down the line. His quick action encouraged everyone else as the covered gallery exploded into violent life, spraying death toward the paper torsos in the open range.

My heart thudded. I ran through the checklist before firing. Sight the target. Curl the first knuckle around the trigger. Breathe, breathe, hold breath. Squeeze.

But the noise was too much, even with the hearing protection. My finger didn't cooperate. I reminded myself that it had to be a slow, steady squeeze, but found myself counting the seconds. Thirty. Twenty. Eighteen. I still had not fired a single round. Soon I would have to fire one every second and a half.

Part of me wondered if the instructors would laugh at the wild spray pattern I was about to decorate the target with. Even the two by four foot target seemed to shrink from existence just thirty feet away, dangling from the clip on the guideline. Taunting. Mocking. Just like every Fiver had over the past six thousand years.

I closed my eyes, drew a deep breath, and sought calmness, something I'd been practicing for a few months now. The M-16, heavy even though I was prone, grounded me. The cold steel, aluminum alloy, and plastic rubber was just an extension of me. My hands, me, one with it. The distraction of hundreds of rounds being fired by my platooon mates dulled.

My fear squeezed, my knuckle no longer feeling like a foreign object between my brain and the weapon.

Pop!

The rifle kicked back, surprising me. I had expected something like a firehorse kick, but the rifle's recoil felt more like a punch from a pissed off impling. Still, the force dislodged the butt of the rifle from the socket in my shoulder I'd tucked it against. Remembering that Sergeant Halcion warned us against that, I readjusted, feeling the pressure of the seconds ticking away and the fact I still had nine more shots to get off. I had to be close to the end of the allotted time now.

Butt replaced in my shoulder socket, I adjusted my trigger finger once more, sighted the middle of the target and popped off three quick rounds. They felt good. Six more to go, and the air horn signaling the end of shooting hadn't sounded yet.

I drew a deep breath, slowing my heartbeat, and pressed my knuckle joint against the smooth, curved metal of the trigger even as I found the center of the target again. It looked much larger than it had only a minute ago. And I knocked out my last six rounds. Within a second of getting off my last shot, the air horn sounded.

"Cease-fire!" Sergeant Halcion's voice was thin and metallic as it came through the megaphone. "Cease-fire!"

Deep breaths of released anxiety filled my ears. Every other sound of the world finally faded away behind my hearing protection as I remained prone, waiting for the arms masters to finish checking each recruit. Only after they'd insured the safety of the line did they allow us to rest the muzzles of our rifles in a wooden brace just to the side of our positions, still pointed downrange. I ensured my safety was engaged again, even though it had just been checked, and set my rifle in the brace. Standing, I smiled like I remembered having done the first time I saw a pair of breasts in a succubi magazine.

I'd never felt power like that except in Creed. The mortal weapon was different from my halberd—less powerful, but the newness was exhilarating. The few times I used Creed's magic felt like a slow burn of energy that surged long before I needed it and well after I'd dispelled its magic. Shooting this rifle was more like a powerful punch, short and obvious. The rest of the day promised fun.

The Private First Class went downrange to score the targets, coming back as he tallied and made notes on his scoresheet. The staff analyzed the data before working with each of us to adjust our rifle's sites. When Sergeant Halcion got to me, he did a quick glance at the rifle that seemed more procedural than necessary, set it back down and gave me a stiff nod.

"Nice work," he said before moving on to the next recruit.

I stood in my position, unsure what to do next. Sergeant Halcion nor his staff adjusted my rifle, though they were doing so with every other platoon member. When they finished re-sighting weapons, he returned to the megaphone and ordered us to load a new magazine. This time we were shooting fifteen rounds. As everyone prepared, a metallic clanking clicked away to the side of the line. The targets collectively moved away from us. I don't think anyone else noticed.

"We'll be shooting at thirty yards now," Sergeant Halcion announced.

Now heads went up to the targets I'd already spotted moving further down the range.

Thirty yards. The black shape of a head and torso was

smaller. We repeated the same processes, each step identical. They allotted forty seconds this time. When the air horn sounded, I spent the first few seconds calming my breathing and focusing on the target, pushing out the distractions of popping rifles, the spent rounds falling to the concrete all around us, and the thumping of bullets slamming into the sandstone barrier. This time I didn't take nearly as long to get off my shots. Ten seconds of peaceful assessment lay between my last shot and the air horn.

The air was thick with sharp, acrid gunpowder.

The scoring and analysis went much more quickly now. When he got to me for the post-round feedback, Sergeant Halcion nodded without making eye contact and moved on to the next recruit. He hadn't stopped to inspect my rifle.

Ready for the next round, he announced that we were about to start the official qualification rounds. Now, every shot counted. This was it—the test. Sixty rounds total, broken into four stages of fifteen–round magazines at different distances. The next distance was fifty yards.

A few recruits grumbled at that.

The targets clanked backwards, the black form shrinking. The horn sounded. I forced the world out. Again, I emptied my magazine well before the round ended.

We were ordered to load another magazine and a new round began. The recruit next to me shot me a nervous glance, as if the staff's neglect to re-sight our weapons and check in was the most shocking thing he'd ever experienced. I gave him a reassuring smile—I was feeling good—but he didn't look any more confident.

"On one knee, boys. Rest the muzzle of your weapon on the stanchion to your side."

I took the position even as I stole glances up and down the line to ensure I was doing it correctly. The two assistants corrected those who had taken an improper stance. It was awkward, kneeling like this, less steady than the prone position, but when I spread my legs further apart, I found I had a good foundation.

"Here we go, boys," the metallic voice of the sergeant called through the megaphone.

Even before the air horn sounded, the world fell into my forced silence and, when it did blow to signal the start, I rattled off fifteen rounds.

And waited. And waited. Finally, everyone else finished.

The third stage of qualification had us standing, with the muzzle braced against a thick four by four vertical beam on the side of our station. The targets moved away.

"I wish they would stop doing that," Ralrek's muffled voice announced to my side.

I smiled down range, almost unable to pull my eyes away from the target no longer taunting me.

Seventy-five yards this time. This stance was the least secure of all, requiring me to use the first few seconds of the round to make minuscule adjustments. Soon enough, I found a position I could tolerate and knocked out my rounds.

"This is it," Sergeant Halcion announced. "The last round. Take whichever of those positions we just used you feel most comfortable with."

I figured we would do most of our shooting prone in the Overworld, and I wasn't a fan of thinking about standing when real bullets were flying the other way. So my chest met the concrete once more.

The horn commanded us to fire.

I exhausted my magazine with twenty seconds to spare, even though the targets seemed like nothing more than blurry shapes at the far end of the range.

When everyone was finished, the two assistants went downrange and counted holes punched through the targets. Tallying duties completed, they collected the targets to bring back.

Sergeant Halcion called out each individual's name as

the assistants handed out their target when they came forward. When he called me, the assistant smiled and gave me a nod. I didn't understand why until I looked at what I held.

The cardboard backing was shredded. A tight grouping of punctures in the center of the target attested to my comfort with the human weapon. In the top left, the Private First Class had written: '40/40'.

Murmurs grew as recruits saw their scores and compared them with others. Ralrek carried his target over, with Bilba joining us shortly thereafter, his face drawn in shadow.

"Did everyone qualify?" I asked.

"Barely," Ralrek said with a half–laugh.

Bilba was silent.

"And you?" I prodded.

He turned his target. The top left corner filled in the information his expression hadn't already conveyed. Emblazoned in red ink was his score. '28/40', it read. The minimum requirement was thirty target strikes.

"You are so close. Don't worry about it. I'm sure we're going to shoot a few more times."

Bilba didn't seem reassured at all. "I should have done better."

I wrapped my arm around his shoulder. "Don't do that to yourself, bud. This is the first time we've ever done this."

He flicked my target with a finger. "Easy for you to say. You have a perfect score."

"Luck."

"Missing two or three is luck. A perfect score isn't."

"Don't sweat it, Bilba," Ralrek said. "You'll do fine next time."

"Next time it might be for real." Bilba's voice shook.

I got it. I'd dealt with humiliation my entire life. Being the Segregate meant the rest of the Fifth thought I deserved to be humiliated. "The sting goes away in a little while."

Bilba pursed his lips and scrunched his eyes. "You don't get it, Zeke."

I patted him on the shoulder.

"All right, boys," Sergeant Halcion shouted, "get your weapons and let's head back to the training room. Before we leave, though. We've got clean-up. Collect the shells in your area. I want this place looking as clean as it did when you found it."

Two hours later we finished cleaning the range and our weapons well enough to pass inspection—and when I say 'us' I mean me; I was the last one done, having failed the weapon inspection over and over. The staff finally stepped in to help me—they called it 'training'—by overlooking a problem with a spring. I blamed the spring.

"Go join your platoon, recruit," Sergeant Pythan smirked. "You're hopeless."

Obviously, a perfect range score doesn't count for much in boot camp.

I rejoined my platoon outside. By the time we marched to our barracks, my stomach was angry at me for neglecting it for so long—again.

"Chow will have to wait," Sergeant Kelem told us when we stepped into our bay, and was even kind enough to ignore our whining. "Put your shit away and get in the day room."

Maybe this whole accelerated training wasn't a good thing after all?

We did as ordered.

"I'm so hungry," Bilba groaned.

I gave him an understanding smile. "Me too, bud."

Spurred by hunger, we raced each other to the day room, joined shortly by the rest of the platoon. Once seated, Charlie went to inform Sergeant Kelem that we were ready.

"Have fun at the range?" he asked as he stomped into the room.

"Yes sir!" we shouted in unison. It was the only answer to

give.

"Good, now calm down. I hope you learned enough to help you survive in the Overworld. You'll need it. The war escalated again today, a major capital was bombed in Saudi Arabia. Looks like this accelerated training needs to do as much as it can in the time we have left. Learn as much as you can. Ask questions if you've got them. You've got to be ready, boys." Sergeant Kelem paused and glanced up at the narrow window. "The crew at the range had good things to say about your weapons training. Well done, boys. You've earned your dinner tonight, so go get ready."

"Yes sir!" A collective shout rattled around the room. Nothing struck the heart of an army recruit like the proposition of a meal well earned. We snapped to attention when he departed.

As we prepared to head out for formation, I wondered what this meant for us. I was walking back to my bunk, past Sergeant Kelem's office, when he called out to me. "Sunstone."

I halted. "Yes, sir?"

"Get your ass in here and close my office door."

I did, wondering what I had done wrong at the firing range. Was it possible to get in trouble for shooting too well while being a complete ignoramus in weapon cleaning?

"Sir?"

Sergeant Kelem wore u–shapes of dark circles under his eyes. He gestured to the chair. "Take a seat."

"Sir, if I did anything wrong, I apologize. I didn't think I—"

His hand karate chopped the air. "You didn't do anything, Sunstone. I wanted to talk to you about your performance today. Be honest with me. Did you use mortal weapons when you went to the Overworld?"

I sat up straighter. Of all the questions he could have asked, I hadn't expected this one. I don't know why, but I didn't expect him to know I'd been lifted up.

"No sir, I didn't."

He nodded. "Where did you learn to shoot like that?"

I shrugged. "Nowhere, sir. I've never used a rifle before."

"You did well. A perfect score." One side of his face flinched as if he had a disturbing thought, and then he pointed as his head dipped, like they were connected by an invisible string. "I don't know if I've ever seen a recruit shoot a perfect score the first time they picked up a mortal weapon. In fact, pretty sure it's unheard of. Does that have anything to do with it?"

At first I had no idea what he was talking about. Then it dawned on me. He was referring to Creed. My hand slipped protectively over the halberd's knob.

"I'm not sure, sir. It just came to me once I concentrated. In fact, wasn't really that hard."

I didn't think it was possible, but Sergeant Kelem laughed. The lines on his forehead didn't dissolve, but the dark shadows seemed to fade ever so slightly from under his eyes. "You truly are something, Sunstone." The smile faded, the light dimming in his expression. "Let me give you a bit of advice even though you didn't ask for it."

"Yes sir," I said with caution.

"Don't become reliant on that thing," he pointed at Creed once more. "It's a curse, but even curses can be bad. What I guess I'm saying is," he pressed his palm against his eyes. In that moment, Sergeant Kelem became very normal. "What I'm saying is, don't get lulled into some false sense of security. It's a wonderful curse, no doubt, but it can make you lazy. And if things in the Overworld are headed in the direction we're being told, all of you will find yourselves in some Lucifer forsaken country, surrounded by mortals wanting to kill each other. And kill you. You'll need to be sharp and aware and if you over-rely on that thing, you'll lose the advantage. None of you are trained well enough yet, but that's out of my hands. We've got to make do with what we have. So you cannot veer, son. Okay? Don't let that happen to you. Understand?"

The drill instructor's questions lacked the hardness I'd grown accustomed to in our weeks in boot camp. With the developments in the mortal realm, things were changing for all of us, apparently even this hard-as-brimstone drill instructor.

"Yes sir," I said in a careful, measured response.

"I know you have been to the Overworld a couple times," he continued, "but I still feel it's my responsibility to warn you away from getting comfortable with the mortals. I've seen it happen to other demons. I don't know if you remember or not, but a few decades ago, they had a nasty little fight called the Vietnam War, and we lost a lot of good demons in that one, let me tell you. I was a drill instructor then too. Had a few dozen boys I'd trained killed up there. And time and time again, one major reason bad shit happens to us is because we get too close to those blessed mortals. You're different, okay? You need to be extra careful, even more so than the rest of the boys. Before you all get out of here, I'm going to give everyone the same warning, so you better act surprised when you hear it again. But I mean it, Sunstone. Keep your head low and that thing," the message about Creed, harsh, "strapped away somewhere safe."

"I will, sir."

He measured me. "Do exactly like I tell you and you just might make it back home. I can't say the same for any of your friends in this platoon when you get deployed."

A dark thought fluttered across his face.

"How long before they graduate us?"

He tilted his head away from me. It was only then that I realized I hadn't used the formal and mandatory 'sir.' Sergeant Kelem seemed to forgive me; I think he had more important things on his mind.

"Soon, scum. Very soon."

7

UNDERWORLD/OVERWORLD

"I RECOMMEND you double-check the line or you might die," Charlie said in between gasps as we hid behind the fallen tree. His narrow face, like all ours, was painted in camouflage, but Charlie had taken the extra step of also covering his thick bottom lip. Sometimes, I think, Lucifer gets bored and simply creates interesting demons to entertain himself.

I shook my head, taking a swig of water from my canteen and screwing it closed. "I will when I get a second to think. You need to worry about dying long before me. That red hair of yours is like a freaking beacon."

Charlie pulled his cap down over the tips of his ears to cover his burning follicles before peeking his head over the log.

Day Four. The fourth day of our war games campaign. I was exhausted and trying to strategize through a thick mental fog. At fortune's blessing, deployed to a far corner of the installation isolated with a team of demons incapable of seeing how close we were to the end, Sergeant Kelem assigned me as squad Commander after firing Charlie. Charlie refused to let the meaningless personnel switch go, his attitude deteriorating each day. As Commander, I got to deal with it.

Lucky me.

It was my job to decide the next course of action, but doing so was impossible. We didn't have the information I needed to make an informed decision. Decide wrong and someone would die in the simulation, and I refused to get pseudo—blood on my hands, not least of all at the beginning of my command. Everyone rode Charlie hard after he was fired and I didn't want to follow his fate. Real or not, the war games reminded me of Sergeant Kelem's impromptu conversation about my overreliance on Creed and possible death in the Overworld, even almost three weeks later.

"We can't sit here all day," Charlie said, falling back to his rear.

I knew that, and he knew I knew that. But Charlie loved hearing himself talk.

"What did you see?"

"Nothing."

Where was our enemy and would they—the instructor staff—strategize their attack? What approach would they take? They were intimately familiar with this area, and we had only been out here for days. They were real Army personnel. We were children new to the service. Some of them had been in battle, with real bombs and bullets. The only battle I'd ever seen was on my video game console.

Yes, I'm being hyperbolic to draw on your sympathies, but the fact remains that we were facing a foe who had an advantage in every sense of the word. Caution and calculating maneuvers were required, not the ramshackle approach Charlie proposed. Throughout his short command and even in his impromptu role as self-assigned advisor, his strategic approach was like that of a lust-blinded teenager who hadn't yet noticed his date had left him for another incubus.

I grumbled out of frustration before spinning onto my knees and popping my head over the fallen tree.

Staring into the murky depths of the forest, I couldn't see a blessed thing that gave clues to the other team's location. If they were close, they hid well. As thick as the tree coverage and underbrush was, they could be on top of us, laughing over our naivety, and we'd be none the wiser.

I slinked away from the tree, still on my knees, to draw the forest layout in the mud. Plotting our location and that of the other two teams, I laid out the known battle space. Five instructors against twenty-eight trainees. This mock war was not a numbers game. This was about strategy, and I was smart enough to know that I was too dumb to out–strategize them. My small team crowded around.

"This is our location, and here are the two spots where the other squads should be," I said, pointing at the three Xs I'd drawn. "We know this is where the enemy entered the battlefield."

"Only if the instructor team was being honest," Charlie said.

"True, they could have come in anywhere, and we could sit here all day wondering and waiting. It's a great comment," I added when Charlie's face dragged at my correction. There is no sense in kicking a demon when he's down. "But we have to plan on the intel we have. This is a training environment, guys. They're preparing us for what happens after boot camp. Let's keep that in mind as we think about our response. They want us distracted; they want us to operate in confusion. The time we spend contemplating the whats and maybes, they're on the move."

One of the more promising squad members, Tantric was his name—a story I wanted to pursue before we left boot camp—placed his finger to the side of my impromptu map before looking at me. "Do you mind if I add some detail?"

Tantric had his shit together from Day One. Unlike Charlie, he excelled not because of the way he manipulated and politicked. Instead, Tantric was so highly regarded because he was one damn good soldier. I nodded.

Tantric's finger moved up the periphery of the map, drawing a squiggle up its length. "When they were busing us in the other day, I noticed a river running alongside the training field." He tapped his finger next to the line he'd drawn. "I can't be sure exactly how close we are to it right now, but it runs the length of this training area, forming a border."

"What's your point?" Charlie asked, his eyes on the squiggly line.

"My point is, either we outflank them or they're going to outflank us. That river forms a natural boundary that will limit the team who doesn't reach it first. I say we don't become that second-place team."

"If we move for the river, can we can squeeze them into a space to corral them?" I said, checking to make sure I was following Tantric's thinking.

He nodded. "You got it."

A broad grin spread across my face. "Let's do this, boys."

I crawled back to the edge of the tree, checking the clearing to ensure no instructor lay in wait. Clear, I scrambled to my feet, pinned my paintball rifle to my side to prevent it from bouncing against me, and sprinted across the expanse to a spot where the hillside dropped away. The height variance would provide a hiding spot for anyone at our current elevation. It would be a disadvantage for fighting, but fighting wasn't our priority. Getting to the river was.

Once the team gathered again, we set out for the next intermediary point, twenty yards up the slope. The brush, overgrown and thick, provided enough cover for a temporary check.

I sprinted across the gap uncontested, got to the new location, and checked once more for any sign of the enemy while waiting for the rest of my squad. I winced at the racket the team made, snapping branches and crunching dried underbrush. Thank Lucifer our mission wasn't to sneak into Heaven in the middle of the night.

"How far is the river?" I asked Tantric.

Huddled in a small clump, the excitement was audible through everyone's rapid breaths. Tantric was the only one who looked composed. He didn't respond verbally, tapping his earlobe. At first, I didn't get the gesture, but then he tugged the lobe, probably frustrated by my stupidity. And that's when I heard it. Moving water. The river was close.

Encouraged, I raised my hand, two fingers pointing forward, and waved twice; the signal for the squad to move out. Sixty yards of tall grass separated us from the next spot that would give us an opportunity to check our surroundings. Otherwise we were in the open. My skin burned, not with exertion but with excitement as I crossed the field of tall grass, checking behind me for the squad's position. They were close enough that I worried they'd be caught if an attack came to take me out, so I increased my pace and distanced myself.

The gurgling of the water grew louder, no longer muffled as the field sloped downward. Ahead, a grouping of trees offered intermediary cover. The trees were still a good forty yards away, so I slowed to allow the squad to close the distance.

Standing at the edge of the field, my skin warmed—and not from the heat of the Hellfire painting the dome above me blue.

I faced the squad, turning my back on our destination and frantically waving them backward. Tantric pulled up. I hoped he recognized the strain on my face for what it was. This wasn't part of the exercise. Something was wrong.

Someone was conjuring.

I dropped to my knees, using the tall grass as cover. From this vantage point I couldn't tell if the rest of the squad had retreated, but I had faith that Tantric was astute enough to pick up the urgency of the situation from my wild gesticulating.

Wind whipped across the field, rustling thousands of stalks. I scrunched lower, looking up and hoping for a hint to what I sensed and why. If this was one of the instructors, we were all dead. If it was one of my squad, I would make sure they were.

The grass whipped violently, shifting from one direction to another in a chaotic pattern. My skin flushed, heating, when the caster put more into their spell. The stalks responded.

All around me, they grew, extending into the sky, sprouting tendrils of smaller stalks along the lengths of each blade. Thousands of tall stalks of grass became tens of thousands as they multiplied upon themselves, as each grew dozens of arms.

And I was in the middle of it.

The blades swayed in a malicious dance, the smaller branches now growing longer, thicker. Stronger.

I hoped whatever was happening was isolated on me and that the squad was free. This was Manipulative magic, and someone was breaking the boot camp rules. I thought I could wait out the spell since there wasn't a clear and obvious purpose for it. But I was wrong on both points.

A sucking, as if the air around me was being vacuumed out of the field, came from far above. It ended with an ear-thudding *whoomp* before everything fell silent. I fell to the mud, waiting for something to happen.

Before I moved, the stalks swooped, bending in smooth arcs. My legs were snared first, stalks wrapping around them, their newly sprouted arms snaring my ankles, knees and thighs. As I reached to pull the blades off, other stalks dove and ensnared my wrists, elbows and biceps. I couldn't even reach for Creed. The one steadfast rule of boot camp was that we weren't allowed to conjure, but someone had. Not only had they cast, but they were using magic offensively, which in my book meant I was free to defend myself.

"Cree—"

A thick stalk shot around my neck, choking off the air and my call. Small tendrils that sprouted off the blade reached for the corners of my mouth, pulling it wide, preventing me from finishing.

But that wasn't necessary. I didn't need words to complete the action. I could do it silently, such was our connection.

Rattling, as if it could sense the danger, Creed vibrated loose, slicing through the air and smacking against my open palm. I gave it the best shake I could with my restricted range of motion. But Creed didn't need encouragement to activate, just that signal. It extended to its full length, the wavy blade at the butt end jutted out as the double axe head sprang to life.

I couldn't do much in this current position, but I could move it enough to slice some stalks. Each pass severed dozens of stalks from the ground, releasing small wispy gasps as if the grass itself was crying out.

My arms freed, I sliced through the ones holding my feet. I stabbed the blade end of Creed into the dirt and fought the last remaining tendril wrapped around my neck. It put up a fight, but I still yanked it out of the soil, cutting off its life.

My freedom didn't last. Standing in the small clearing I'd created, stalks began to regenerate. I wasn't interested in sticking around to see how quickly they grew back. I swung Creed in an arc along the ground, back and forth, back and forth, severing hundreds of stalks every few seconds and carving a path to my squad.

Their screaming and yells confirmed I hadn't been the

only one attacked. I extended my senses, feeling for other spells and finding nothing. I thrashed at the living field of grass, beads of sweat running down forehead, into my eyes. The skin on my arms itched from tiny slices I received.

I found the group pinned to the ground just as I had been. Without thought, I sprinted around them, swinging Creed and creating a clearing broad enough for everyone to stand. The wisps of dying magic grew louder the faster I ran. Once freed, the squad was on their feet, conjuring their specific type of magic. Every reaction, individual and combined, flooded my capacity to process what Abilities everyone was using.

"Halt!" A voice boomed through the chaos and the grass stopped swaying and growing, instead retreating to its waste–high height.

"What the heaven?" Charlie gasped.

I swallowed the lump in my throat, still holding Creed at the ready to sever any stalk looking for a fight. "I don't know. Just be ready."

Instead of a fight, we received a slow hand clap coming from the edge of the field. It was soon joined by another pair of hands, and then another. And then the instructor staff stepped into the open, Sergeant Kelem beaming a broad smile that brightened his dark face.

"Well done, Sunstone. Well done," he said as the group approached. When they joined the open circle I created, he flicked a hand at Creed. "You can put that away now. The fun and games are over, and you lost."

"But you used your Abilities," Charlie whined.

Sergeant Kelem's expression lost its humored overtones. But then the drill instructor laughed, a lighthearted sound of victory. "All is fair in love and war, boys."

I shook my head. "You only did it because we were going to outflank you. Sir." I added the last bit in a rush of thought.

"Every battle provides an opportunity to learn, to develop, to grow. Today, I hope this one did that for all of you. What did you sorry gaggle learn from this?"

The squad took turns looking at each other as if the answer was there, etched on someone else's face. It wasn't.

"That we're so good you had to cheat to win?" I said, a wry smile on my face.

Our leader shook his head, still half humored. "Hardly. If we'd wanted to, we could have decimated your squad, even though there's only five of us. No, I want you to take something else from this. Think boys. What was it?"

I tried to decipher his code but couldn't see through my frustration at them cheating. Frankly, I was pissed. It wasn't right. And then the answer came to me. "There are no rules in war, sir?"

Sergeant Kelem winked and made a gun with his pointer finger and thumb, snapping his thumb down. "Bam! Nice work, Sunstone." He extended his arms, waving his hands towards each other, encouraging us to move together. "Brief the platoon who are out there, somewhere, probably hiding. Teach them what happened when you're together again. This isn't about boot camp anymore, boys. This is about the real shit you're going to face. Too soon. When you go up there, the Overworld is going to tell you all sorts of things. You'll hear every lie mortals ever concocted, and some of the most egregious are the lies surrounding war. They'll say you must comply with their rules of conduct, which put you at a disadvantage when facing an enemy who doesn't play by them. The intellectuals will have debates about the ethics of war. But those who preach behind lecterns lack the courage to throw on a uniform and step into battle. If they ever found the guts to give it a go, they would burn every rule ever printed that they hold so dear. It's easy to assume the position of moral authority from behind a desk or in a classroom, but it's a different beast when you're hunkered down behind a collapsed wall with bullets flying over your head." Sergeant Kelem stepped forward, opening his hand. "Relinquish your weapon, Sunstone."

That was it. In front of my squad, right at the beginning of my command, I was being fired.

I pulled the strap from my shoulder and handed the paintball rifle to my drill instructor, the heat of shame burning my cheeks.

Sergeant Kelem lifted it above his head, looking very much like the war heroes in every mortal war movie ever made. "These are toys, nothing more, and yet you felt the exhilaration, the panic and anxiety of what it means to fight. Very soon, you might find yourself in a similar situation, and the things being shot at you will make a permanent mess of your uniform, not something your mommies will be able to wash out. Don't ever forget that we are vulnerable in the Overworld. Don't ever forget that angels will also be recruited to fight against us to maintain the Balance. This isn't about which mortal side is right or wrong. That doesn't matter. Never forget the square." His voice lowered at the mention of Gemini's failed execution and the angelic attack on Hell. His head dropped, as did his arm holding my paintball gun aloft. "No boys, there are no rules once the bullets fly. Never," he paused, a snarl forming, "ever forget."

He handed my paintball rifle back and gave me a nod. That was the end of that. Our lesson learned did not include my firing after all.

And we shared it with those who missed out. Over the next week and a half, we shared a lot of stories with each other. Behind each story, lesson, and words of encouragement was the unspoken realization that we were a single team, with a single purpose. We grew, as soldiers and as demons. We went into our war games as implings and came out as warriors.

WE DIDN'T STOP LEARNING AFTER OUR TIME IN THE FIELD. FOR weeks, the lessons continued, hot, heavy and intense when we returned to the main base.

Over that time, we'd become a well–oiled machine. We marched with precision. Everything we accomplished, we completed with snap and urgency. The entire platoon was effective and efficient, sharp and perfect in the first time of asking. Heaven, one of the greatest accomplishments was the fact that I could now make one nasty hospital corner on my bed sheet.

As we performed to higher and higher levels, Sergeant Kelem reduced his intensity and scrutiny, slowly becoming more of a peer than a dictator. He still held the title as our drill instructor, but what I noticed over the past few days was he was our leader because we wanted him to be, not because he told us he was.

So it wasn't any wonder that when Sergeant Kelem shattered our world three weeks after our war games, we knew, as scary as the future was, everything was going to be all right.

He ordered us to the dayroom, telling us to forgo sitting at attention—a shock—and wait for him. Charlie called us to attention and our leader walked in. His face was troubled.

"Relax boys," he said in an even tone. "We've got a lot to get through." He tossed his campaign hat on the desk. The manilla folder in his other hand was thick with paperwork. He grunted when he sat in the chair and let out a long breath. "I know you're sick of seeing me and I'm definitely sick of seeing your ugly faces, though they do look a lot better now that most of you have grown back your hair. Some of you," he looked over at one of the quieter trainees, "will never have back what you once had. Better get used to shaving that dome of yours if finding a young succubus who will accept your ugly ass is important to you."

We laughed at the incubus in the way no one outside the military could ever understand as a true sign of respect.

Sergeant Kelem flipped open the folder. He slapped his hand on the top sheet. "And that's why I'm happy to have received these earlier."

Everyone sat up straighter, trying to get a look at what was on his desk.

The drill instructor barked a laugh that sounded half dead. "You scum look like implings on your first day of kindergarten. Settle down. You will find out soon enough what this is. But before I get to that," he paused, swallowing before composing himself. "I wanted to let you know that as trying as this class has been, it has been a pleasure to be your drill instructor." Sergeant Kelem cleared his throat. "Now, we need to get to business. What I have here is your rank designation and your orders"

Boot camp or not, the incubi in the room burst with disbelieving chatter, me included, at the announcement.

Sergeant Kelem held up his hand. "There's been an official declaration of war by the majority of mortal nations involved in the tensions. Some of you will walk out of here with bigger paychecks than you deserve. Most of you will, in fact. But, in the wondrous omniscience of your Army leadership, some of you are going to leave as Privates and nothing more, as it should be."

We were graduating? Now? It was a moment I had looked forward to and one I had dreaded in equal measure.

"Don't let this lift you too high or sink you too low. It's administrative stuff, mostly, though I did have a little input. Trust the system and know that Lucifer has a reason for everything. Now, let's get you sorry excuses for soldiers out of my sight, shall we? Dasher?"

Dasher stood in the corner. "Yes, sir?"

"Private Second-Class. Stationed at Fort Leavenworth, Kansas. Stevens?"

Dasher nodded and sat even as Stevens jumped to his feet. "Yes, sir!"

"Private Second-Class, stationed at Fort Knox, Kentucky."

"Yes, sir!" Stevens shouted louder than necessary, obviously excited by his elevated rank and duty station. I didn't know anything about Kentucky, but based on his reaction, it must be a wonderful place.

And so this went on and on, through each one of us. Bilba was the first of my tiny group called.

"Private Second-Class, stationed at Joint Base Lewis McCord, Washington."

Bilba smiled. "Yes, sir!"

A few recruits later, Ralrek was called, receiving the same rank and assignment as Bilba. They would be together! My spirits rose, keeping my fingers crossed that I would soon join them.

"Sunstone."

I shot to my feet, my heart thumping in my chest. "Yes, sir?"

"Private, stationed at Joint Base Lewis McCord, Washington."

My mind buzzed. I didn't move. Sergeant Kelem must have sensed that something was amiss because he looked up from his paperwork without tilting his head. "Are you going to get your ass on the floor, Sunstone?"

I was flustered but did my best to hide it. "I'm sorry, sir. I think I misheard you, and I just wanted to check that I didn't."

"What was there to misunderstand?"

"Sit down, Zeke," Bilba mumbled beside me.

"It sounded like you said my rank was Private, sir."

"I did, Sunstone. Take your seat so we can get through the rest."

My face flushed. My platoon, a third of whom I had

commanded only weeks earlier in our war games, examined me. Only a handful of us had been designated the lowest enlisted rank. I'd taken leadership positions. I was a blessed commander. Bilba and Ralrek had not done either. Sure, they had responsibilities they'd performed throughout boot camp and they started quicker than I did, but did that necessitate my lower rank?

"I'm sorry, Zeke. I don't know why they did that," Bilba said when we packed. "But it doesn't really matter, right? This is just a temporary thing."

"Don't worry about me. It's nothing," I lied, shoving the last of my belongings into a bag.

I'd left one uniform out for the morning ride to the gateway that would take us home for a few days before we headed to the Overworld and our mortal military future. Everything else I'd haphazardly crammed into my bags, because I truly didn't care. The only thing I cared about now was getting away from boot camp and Sergeant Kelem.

WASHINGTON STATE IS GREEN. VERY GREEN. THIS WAS MY second time in the state. But last time, when chasing Aries, we'd been restricted to the city of Seattle. This time, near Tacoma, I was amazed by the endless open space on Joint Base Lewis McCord. Even though we were assigned to the dormitories on an installation crowded with nearly thirty thousand soldiers and their families, there was still so much space in every direction. One day I tried to walk the perimeter when I was bored and needed a break from my crowded living conditions and found myself lost. It took half a day to find my way back, and I missed mealtime. I was too tired to walk to the fast-food joint. That was a long night.

There were a lot of those nights once we reached the Overworld. Partly because we became mentors for the other demons secretly assigned to the unit, some from the Fifth Circle but many not. Adjustment periods can be wickedly cruel and this one was for a lot of incubi—most who outranked me, unfair as that was.

The job wasn't easy either, being in an infantry unit. Our Staff Sergeant was a cruel little man, I learned. He was the type of military person who hid his insecurities behind the chevrons on his chest, who didn't seem happy unless everyone around him was miserable. There were days, oh so many days, where I wanted to pull Creed out from the seam I'd sewn inside my utility uniform pants and whack Staff Sergeant Basker "Jake"—his self-assigned nickname he thought made him sound cooler—Rogers upside the head. But I'd been told that doing so was an excellent way to end up in mortal prison, so I refrained.

Instead, I did what I could do; I tolerated him and counted the days until I returned home. The only aspect of life here that I enjoyed was the fact that I was beyond the practical reach of the Council, though I dearly missed Dialphio and working in the bookstore. It brought a peace I had not had since leaving home. That peace, I embraced.

Time passed, and I settled into an unhappy routine, still struggling to accept the circumstances and trying to forget about the Underworld.

We hadn't been assigned to the infantry unit for more than a half year when the orders came down and we found ourselves on a mixture of military and civilian aircraft as we crossed the world to the Middle East—let me tell you, as a demon who spent six thousand years living in Hell, flying over the Overworld in a metal tube was not the proper way to be introduced to the miracle of flight. Heights are bad enough in Hell; they're a nightmare in the Overworld, when the endless expanse of the universe is within reach. I think my fingerprints are still etched in the seat handles on three different aircraft.

Qatar was its name and endlessly waiting for a flight into the war theater was its game. Day after day, we sat around, slept, sat, slept, and waited … and waited … and waited. I struggled to resist the urge to wish Lucifer would send the war here. This terrestrial purgatory was torture.

My life was going to heaven in a wheelbarrow.

8

OVERWORLD, QATAR/BAGHDAD

I REGRETTED EVEN THINKING about wishing.

It was our fourth morning in Qatar—it could have been our one hundred and fourth. Half the mortals I came across in the tent spent sixteen hours a day sleeping the days away; a quarter looked ready to shoot anything that moved; the last quarter moved, spoke, and interacted with the world like zombies. I sympathized with the latter, stayed away from the shooters, and envied the sleepers. The heat didn't help any of them. Six millennia in the Underworld and even I found this part of the Overworld toasty; I couldn't imagine the toll it took on the humans. I tried to ignore the hot, stale air by focusing on ignoring the sheer boredom of every passing minute. Trust me, that took quite the effort. I swear, the greatest struggle on a deployment is surviving the grueling nothingness of waiting for something to happen. And I did, day after day, until they bussed us to the passenger terminal for a flight into the theater.

Final destination: Baghdad.

"Get moving, girls" Sergeant Rogers shouted, even though we had a few females in the platoon, and I'd don't think they appreciated his using their gender as a slight.

Less disgusting but equally problematic was the fact we were moving to where killing was a thing humans wanted to be part of—side note, you'd think with such brief life spans, you humans would avoid rushing death as a visitor. I wanted out of this mortal purgatory, but I really, really was not in a hurry to get into Iraq.

Thankfully, the Army moved at a sloth's pace when moving troops, even in war. So many soldiers to move, but only so many aircraft to move us. It did not help that only two personnelists were available to process the outbound flights at the moment. As we sat and waited, they worked feverishly to get us on a plane to where bullets were flying, as anyone not named Rogers could easily see.

Over the next three hours they called chalks—a number assigned to a group of soldiers and their associated cargo. It was excruciating to think we were on our way at the beginning of the announcement, only to discover another chalk was headed out and we were left waiting again. Talk about toying with a covert demon's emotions. When the chalk before us was called, we had to report to a corner of the passenger terminal where we formed a line at the front of a caged door.

"What do you think this is about?" Bilba asked, trying to peer past the human and demon soldiers.

"No idea."

We found out soon enough. This line was another step in the process, just with darker overtones.

I looked at the young enlisted troop handing me the Kevlar vest. "What's this for?"

She was an Air Force member with three stripes on her sleeves—such a weird place for someone's rank, and for the life of me I couldn't remember the Air Force ranks.

She looked at me as if I'd grown a third eye. "For your rotator." She didn't wait for a response, turning to hand Bilba his.

The next station was where I picked up a heavy helmet that might as well have weighed fifty pounds for as heavy as it felt. Maybe the long hours of resting had exhausted me.

Stepping down the line, I wondered how in the heaven was I supposed to carry all of this plus my bag—don't get me started on the lack of overhead storage on military aircraft. I waited until we processed through to see if anyone else knew. Anyone else, that was, besides Sergeant Rogers.

He intervened anyway. "Are you dull, boy? We're flying smack into the middle of Baghdad." He stretched his hand up in the sky and flared out his fingers repeatedly, as if attempting to flick something off the ends of them. "They're gonna try to shoot our asses down. You'll need that equipment to save your sorry life and getcha back to Nebraska or wherever the hell you came from in one piece."

Shooting what, I wondered. And why did he have to blaspheme whatever a Nebraska was or my home? What did the Iraqis—I noticed the humans always added a spruce of hostility when they used that word—have that could bring down an aircraft? And if they had a weapon that could, how would a heavy vest that made me wobble when I walked save my life? And how long did it take to fall back to the Overworld? Would we skip when we hit the surface or just splat into a gooey mess? Questions upon unspeakable questions bounced around my skull. Bilba and Ralrek looked more bored than bothered and I needed to remind them we were vulnerable to injury and death here. We hadn't even gotten into the war zone!

Sergeant Rogers walked away, but not before ordering us to don the protective gear. We were outside the passenger terminal, sitting as close as possible around the building because the walls provided at least a little shade, which was twenty degrees cooler than standing in the direct sunlight. Fatigues, whatever they were made of, didn't allow airflow and were suffocating. Having to wear a heavy Kevlar vest and helmet didn't help. After twenty minutes of waiting, too many humans were blotchy and drinking water like it was a hot dog eating contest. One of the larger guys passed out and had to have the medics called. I imagined a mix of humans and covert demons stripping down to their undies and standing in front of anything that generated a breeze. Somehow, I think the Army would frown on that and the funny image did nothing to satiate my growing unease.

I don't know how long we waited, melting in the heat. The roar of the props of the C-130 approaching the building brought reprieve, and a sense of relief for the shooters. And me, I have to admit. As sweaty and miserable as I was, I'd walk straight into Heaven's front door if it meant getting out of this miserable day. The ride into Baghdad, if you ignored the fighting and killing, was our salvation.

The roar of the engines grew louder as the plane crept closer, cutting off our aimless conversation. As it neared, so did another Air Force troop, this one with a clipboard in hand. He waved for us to follow him, choosing not to shout over the noise of the roaring aircraft.

We loaded our last bags on pallets and then boarded. The air inside the plane was stale but markedly cooler than outside, for which I was grateful. Like farm chimera, we were herded into an impossibly narrow rows of seats where legs touched legs and arms connected to arms from elbow to wrist. Packed like this, if we were shot down, we'd probably land in one, amalgamated piece of flesh and bones. As the plane taxied away from the terminal, beginning our journey into the mortal's fight, I put in my earplugs and tried to sleep, because waiting to be shot out of the air just did not sound like a fun way to pass the time.

The flight was a bitterly cold, bumpy ride into Iraq. At least we hadn't been shot out of the sky by the time sleep came, and that was the highlight of my time in the war to that point.

I WAS YANKED OUT OF SLEEP WHEN THE WORLD TIPPED SIDEWAYS.

Instinctively, I grabbed for my armrest and found the thighs of my two neighbors. Ralrek squinted as if he thought I'd lost my mind. Bilba was fast asleep and didn't notice.

My best friend also didn't notice how severely the aircraft tilted. At this angle, I pictured us slicing the air sideways. That didn't make for good viewing. With nothing to hold on to, I gripped the arm holes of my Kevlar vest. Around me, soldiers woke with gasps. Metal—Lucifer, I hoped that was not the frame of the aircraft, rattled. Something, up toward the cockpit, fell with a thump that turned two dozen heads. If I listened closely enough, I swear I could hear the engines protesting. We didn't break out of the turn for minutes. Around and around, we spiraled toward the surface. The forces pulling on me were so fierce, I would have rather taken my chances with the Iraqi's anti-aircraft guns.

Once my panic subsided enough to think, I realized this was the tornado landing we'd been warned about back at the terminal, the evasive pattern pilots took to minimize risk of being shot out of the sky. My breathing slowed, and I did not panic myself into a blackout. This was not much different from the time I rode a firehorse into the sky of Hell to break into Taurus's house. The only thing that made this worse was my lack of control; at least with the firehorse, I had that— don't fight me on that, it's what I choose to believe.

The prolonged downward spiral brought on a bout of vertigo. A blackout lingered on my personal horizon. But before it rolled over me, the plane tipped back to a horizontal position, leveled out, and dropped in an aggressive descent. I sucked in my breath and heard—because I didn't dare try to turn to look—Ralrek do the same. Even Bilba shot into a sitting position from his slumber. We fell toward the surface.

I knew it! This was how the story of Hell's reject was going to end.

Plane met planet with a jarring impact.

We bounced on the runway. I didn't mean to, but the landing forced me to grab for anything solid, and my friend's legs were in the way again. Bilba yelped for a second time, but Ralrek also did, swatting my hand away even as we bounced our way to safety. Always so cool under pressure, that one.

Once we weren't going to die from crashing into the ground, the planed taxied at a speed that was ridiculous for something of this size. Everything metal rattled, barely covering the thudding from somewhere deep in its bowels. The entire plane was falling apart.

We slammed to a halt and, seemingly within seconds, the aircraft door shot open. Two young male Air Force personnel rushed on-board and ushered us off the plane in a panic.

"Move!" the blond one shouted once we were on the concrete taxiway, rotating his arm over his head in a vertical circle like he was trying to crank a giant, invisible wind-up toy.

A piercing screech split the dark night sky. I turned, looking for the source, and saw nothing in the blackness above. Someone from behind pushed me forward.

"Keep moving, Sunstone," a shaking voice demanded.

I did not need the encouragement.

Everyone ahead was running, and without thinking, I copied them. Five hundred yards of open concrete separated us from a tall metallic building when the air was pierced again. I swore it vibrated against my face. The Air Force personnel helping us disembark the aircraft fell flat on the ground if they didn't have barriers to drop behind. That's all I needed to understand we had walked into the middle of a shit storm. Shit stunk, no matter how it was dropped.

Bending as low as possible, I scurried toward the closest

building. Beside me, Bilba and Ralrek did the same. The last of the troops poured from our aircraft, dashing for safety as a third screech announced another attack.

The mortar hit concrete taxiway only thirty yards behind our plane. A six-wheeled cargo loader had been pulling up to the rear of the aircraft. The mortar exploded when it struck the vehicle, blasting the rear into shredded metal and rubber scraps and spraying a cloud of concrete and dust into the air. I couldn't see into the cab, but hoped the driver was jumping free before the next attack came.

Vulnerable. We were vulnerable here.

The thought spurred me forward. I am fast, faster than anyone I know or have ever fought—some would argue I'm faster than Angelfire, though I'll reserve judgment on that for now—and I cannot recall I time I squat-ran more rapidly than now, passing soldier after soldier until I was at the front of the line, even outpacing our escort. He gave me a curious look of shock. Military mores didn't mean a thing when death fell from the sky. In front of his lead, I guessed the tall metallic building was our destination, and I accelerated toward it, not really caring if I was wrong. If I got inside, that was what mattered. Dead demons can't apologize.

Two armored personnel sheltering inside the doors jumped to open them when they saw us coming. They remained low; I did too. I made eye contact with the one to my left; she could not have been more than twenty human years, yet she put herself at risk so we could get inside. I would thank her after this was over, if I survived it.

Inside, personnel hid under desks or squeezed into doorways. Whatever we found was better than standing out in the open and tempting chance.

Shouts for us to take cover rang across the building, which looked to be a mess hall, just a very nice one—the Air Force troops apparently lived better than us Army grunts. I ran to the closest open spot along the wall and cowered in the corner. We sat like that for another hour before silence fell over the night.

When it was apparent the attack was over, the permanent personnel resumed their routines, moving about and starting our platoon's processing as if nothing happened, almost like a switch was flipped and playtime had ended.

Bilba exhaled deeply. "Well, that was something, wasn't it?" His voice shook, and when he tried to laugh it off, even that vibrated with nerves. He wasn't alone.

"Oh, I don't know. I expected it to be worse here."

He looked at me like I lost my mind.

I winked. "Just messing with you."

He shook his head but smiled. "Not cool, Zeke. Not cool at all."

I laughed. "I don't know about that."

Sergeant Rogers was suddenly in our midst. "Something funny, girls?"

Would the deployment help him see how obtuse he was? I could try to work with him—after all, the Army was a temporary blip in my immortal life. But it would be more effective, and far more hilarious, when one of his own troops lost her mind at his provocation and let loose a string of heated insults that would rock his world. Plus, he wouldn't listen to me.

"Nothing funny, sir," Bilba replied, standing erect.

His eyes traveled across the three of us pressed against the wall, having not moved since the mortar attack ended.

"Good, you better not be," he lifted his chin. "This isn't some schoolyard shit and you're no longer in boot camp, playing boot camp games. So don't be acting like you are."

Reminding me of boot camp, I wondered how Sergeant Kelem would respond to the insult of his profession that Sergeant Rogers was. I had gotten over Sergeant Kelem's snub —getting promoted in the human Army helped—but part of me still wanted to understand where I'd failed him.

"Yes, sir."

His smug expression deepened. "Good. Here, take these." He handed out a single sheet of paper to each of us, moving down the line, repeating the gesture.

"What's this, sir?" I asked.

He scowled. "Processing paperwork. Stop asking questions and just fill it out. We've got to bed down for the night after we get the pallets unloaded. No time for fucking around." He turned away.

We spent the rest of that first long night disassembling baggage pallets and finding our personal bags, which is far more difficult than it might sound to the uninitiated. Piles of identical olive green bags, differentiated only by our stenciled last names in three-inch blocks, made a simple task exhaustive. Ninety minutes later, I'd finally found mine.

At that point, my body revolted from the cold, hunger, and ceaseless exertion. Baghdad seemed warm enough to the mortals, many of whom had stripped off their utility uniform tops and worked in their t-shirts. But pockets in our platoon and in the larger company remained fully dressed, giving me a hint they might be one of my kind— telling mortals and immortals apart is all about the subtle clues.

"All right, let's get your sorry asses bedded down!" Sergeant Rogers stood to the side of the front door of the tent that would serve as our temporary home until the personnel we were here to replace freed up our permanent trailers.

Groaning, I retrieved my bags and dragged them toward the tent. In six thousand years, I don't think I've ever been this tired. My body protested against further work as it crashed from the sustained adrenaline rush of our Iraq arrival.

"You're kidding me?" Ralrek said in a flat voice as we waited.

We shared unspoken apprehension as we looked at the tent, a long, tan Alaska shelter shaped like a half tube.

"I can't wait to see how we all fit in that," I said, not meaning any of it.

Little did I know that chance, Lucifer, Yahweh, One—it really didn't matter—revealed the answer much more quickly than I'd anticipated. One second, we were slowly unloading the bus, and the next we were running for cover when the piercing screech rang through the night.

"Down! Down!" someone shouted.

I fell flat to the cold gravel, covering my head. Each edged rock pressed against my uniformed body, making the terrifying wait annoying uncomfortable. Sometimes having supersensitivity to the world around you really sucks.

The whistling of the mortar flying overhead stretched out beyond us. A miss. But close. How many more chances would we get? We stayed in cover until after the explosion. Then we were on our feet, scrambling to get bags and ourselves into the shelter. We did our best to get settled while always keeping an ear out for the next attack.

"Don't worry about your damn bunk assignments," Sergeant Rogers barked. "Get your sorry asses bedded down and we'll figure all of this out tomorrow. And, goddammit everybody, keep your situational awareness. This shit might go on the rest of the night. Their aim is lousy, but they might get lucky."

Everyone claimed the nearest bunk without argument or complaint. Before I found my latrine bag—my breath was nasty by this point—another whistling harbinger of doom cut through the quiet. I dove under the bunk across the aisle without thinking, sharing the space with two unwelcome partners—misfortune and Sergeant Rogers.

The mortar slammed into the world like a fist behind a kidney punch. The tent sides and roof flapped as destruction rippled across the camp.

I cowered lower, accidentally slamming my head into the

floor and earning an instant headache. When I looked up, Sergeant Rogers looked at me, smiling.

"Having fun yet, Sunstone?"

Before I could even answer his rhetorical question, the distant whistle of yet another mortar approached. I covered my head, keeping my forehead pressed against the dirty tent floor.

"Not really, sir," I mumbled, trying not to breathe in the months' worth of accumulated dust and grime.

"Yeah, I didn't think so," he shouted before his voice was drowned out by the whistle of the death device. Everything stopped as we waited to see where it would strike.

It hit closer than the last one, rattling the bunk beds. Somewhere in the darkness, one platoon member cried for his mother.

Sergeant Rogers, the maniac, laughed. "Welcome to Hell, boys. Welcome to Hell."

I was too scared to tell him how wrong he was.

9

BAGHDAD

I NEVER THOUGHT it would be normal for mortals to lob bombs at each other, sometimes from miles away, to take over someone else's land and bend them to their will, putting so many at risk to control a dead slab of the planet. I don't get it, humans. So much space and plentiful resources, what's the point of fighting over any of it when you live as long as a mosquito in the Underworld?

I also didn't think it was normal to duck for cover in the middle of a meal or to watch the humans do so during a prayer to Yahweh—we'll talk about the utility of that some other time; sorry, but us demons are sensitive about the fact that none of you seem interested in having a conversation with Lucifer. And I didn't think it was normal to think of angels trying so hard to kill fellow immortals in a human war. Though I should have known better if recent history in Hell was evidence of their nature. Sending a death squad to kill hundreds of demons to rescue one angel, Gemini, was a disproportionate response to what were, admittedly, grotesque actions by the Council. Call me naïve, but I hoped they would be better than that. More like Cassie.

Cassie. There was a name that hadn't come up in a while. Best to keep her out of my mind too, if my immediate future included possibly squaring off with her kind in a life-and-death series of battles.

Two weeks into our new journey, months into faking being a mortal—which I admit was much easier than I anticipated, and I was settling into a routine. We finally relieved our predecessors to return to their lives and families. We were now fully responsible for our mission; no more babysitting.

To be honest, it was exciting. I could handle only so much sitting around and exchanging debriefs on areas of responsibility. Now, we had more tasks to complete in a day than time to complete them, and it was nice to have something to do, even if it was inherently dangerous. It made the time pass, and each second that did was another second closer to getting back home. Even if simply passing the time was my only purpose, at least I had one now.

"I don't know about you guys, but I'm pumped to be going out," I said as I shoveled another spoonful of delectable oatmeal into my maw. We don't have oatmeal in the Underworld, and I wasn't sure how, but when I left the Overworld, I'd smuggle this delicacy in—though I said that about chickens too and I hadn't figured that one out either.

Bilba nodded over his bowl of cereal, wiping his mouth before agreeing. "Me too."

Ralrek grimaced. "Just because you're in the Army doesn't mean you can act like an ogre," he told Bilba, looking away when Bilba turned, a flake of cereal caught in the corner of his mouth. "You're gross."

Bilba replied by shoveling in an oversized spoonful, some of it falling back out. He really was gross. Adorably gross.

Today, we were headed into the Khadra district, a neighborhood we'd patrolled a dozen times already, but never on our own. This was to be our first solo mission, and the entire squad carried virgin journey excitement in their faces. This was, after all, everything we'd trained for. At first I struggled to understand the urgency of these humans to head into something so perilous—I still disagreed with the need to fight at all—but I began to appreciate why they wanted to be part of this. These humans sacrificed so much to be in this moment and honestly, outside the patrols, it wasn't easy to find a purpose in anything we'd done in our time in the Army. But patrols were different. When we were out, we were doing something important, something that mattered. It was the only time in my entire service in Lucifer's Army I felt part of something; heavens, it was the only time in my life that I had —it helped that none of the demons could use their Abilities too. I belonged. So I learned to embrace it, and dare I say, even enjoy it. And now it was all on us, our responsibility. A heavy one, but one most of us excitedly accepted.

Fed and geared up, the three of us headed to our rally point. Most of the squad had gathered by the time we got there, though we were well ahead of schedule.

"You girls ready?" Sergeant Rogers asked as we approached the group.

"Yes, sir!" Bilba said, slamming down his backpack.

Sergeant Rogers pulled on his gloves, jamming the webbing of his opposite hands together to ensure a tight fit. "Good. We're heading over to the Khadra Bakery this morning."

"Hungry already, sir?" a demon everyone called Smitty said, slapping his partner on the back, proud of his exquisite joke, I guessed. For what it was worth, the guy standing next to him didn't seem impressed by the joke or the back slap. Smitty's smile slipped.

Sergeant Rogers didn't notice. "Don't know about that. Just know what I was told in this morning's mission brief. I figure there's got to be something happening in that part of the district. Mother Army, a bitch she may be, still knows what's best, boys."

Blatant sexism aside, we followed our NCO and finished preparations. The squad loaded into armored Humvees and set out to secure peace—at least that's what they kept telling us we were doing.

There's always something that happens in your head when you make the transition from peaceful existence to tense survival instinct. One minute, we were sitting on the post making vulgar jokes at each other's expense, and the next we were pulling out into unsecured territory. Each time my body tensed, feeling each muscle fire and flex, the heightened state of alertness that wore me out by lunch. In fairness, I was probably too alert for my own good, bordering on the edge of paranoia. But being sensitive to all stimuli wasn't something I could turn off, and Creed, hidden in a pocket sewn on the inside of my pant leg, wasn't calming me. The magical halberd was increasing my acute awareness if it was doing anything, and I was jittery from adrenaline long before we entered Airport Street.

The main thoroughfare was open ground, ripe for an attack. Smart anti-terrorism measures meant we would change our route from time to time, and we did, except for Airport Street. It was the only route in or out of the installation we ever used. The air in the humvee was electric, as if everyone felt the tension of the unspoken risk of using the popular route. I know I imagined all sorts of enemies hiding in supposedly vacated buildings across blocks of destroyed neighborhoods, watching and waiting for the right convoy to rip into. My breath came in rapid, short bursts until we were clear through.

Off the thoroughfare, we took a different exit today, heading past the Lahmacun Al Mosul restaurant, my favorite kebab place—even though our squad only ate there once after the owner insisted we try some of his meats. Like a lot of Overworld food, it was a little spicy, but I gratefully accepted the challenge of acclimating to its culinary intensity—Overworld food is so good. One day, I planned on talking Sergeant Rogers into patrolling that block again.

We turned off the street, zigzagging through neighborhoods to keep our route unpredictable.

We crossed Highway 11 to Salah Al-Din Street before entering Khadra, the area of Baghdad where the Americans held fragile control and shit got too real, too often. Nasty insurgency and counter-insurgency moves were played in the midst of real life for thousands of civilians, teaching me that war was grosser than the way Bilba ate.

My heart thumped as the convoy entered narrow neighborhood streets where brown, multi-story homes and businesses hovered, sometimes feeling as if they leaned over the sidewalk below. My claustrophobia was immediate; it always was when we were in these neighborhoods. Iraq's highways were bad enough because we had to be wary of buried roadside bombs and on alert for rocket-launched missiles from afar. The enemy, unseen, was braver out in the open, where they could kill while minimizing civilian casualties. But in the neighborhoods, the dynamic changed.

Long before we arrived in Baghdad, the Russians had set up camp in northern Khadra up to and across Highway 97, establishing an outpost to cut off the Americans from the northern areas of Baghdad.

The Baghdadis had little say about the standoff. The larger human nations treated them like implings forced to sit in the sandbox and watch two bullies fight over a toy they stole. I felt for the people of this city, trying to imagine what it would be like for warring contingents of angels to take over the Fifth Circle as if it was theirs. I mean, who do you root for when you don't want either side to win?

I kept that thought in the front of my mind when we were

amongst them on patrol. The Army might try to convince them that what we were doing was to the Iraqi's benefit, but I'm not sure they bought the message.

We turned left, heading down a road so packed with mortals and vehicles that it was impossible to squeeze the armored vehicles through. A dusty—everything in the city was—Toyota Camry parked with two wheels on the sidewalk, blocked half of one lane, and an old blue van stood, stopped, in the other. We idled until our sergeant got nervous about becoming easy targets.

"Disembark, boys," Sergeant Rogers' voice barked through the crackle of radio static from the lead vehicle.

The convoy pulled to the side of the street. When I exited the Humvee—not an easy thing to do, by the way—I double checked my vest, belt, and pockets to make sure I had everything, namely tons of rounds of ammunition. When we were safely on the installation, I'd already run through that mental checklist, but it didn't hurt to do it again, even through the discomfort of sweat trickling down my spine.

"Here we go," Charlie said through heavy breaths.

I felt his apprehension. We were on our own for the first time now, completely responsible for what happened. Before our predecessors redeployed home, I always felt vulnerable on patrol. But now I realized just how vulnerable we were, and part of me admitted it would have been nice if we were allowed to use our Abilities. Compared to Bilba and Ralrek, I was still crap at casting, but even half-baked spells were better than relying solely on my rifle, no matter how good of a shot I was. If I survived this year, it would happen only at the grace of Lucifer.

"You guys ready?" Sergeant Smith said while triple-checking his own equipment.

Hank Smith was our squad leader, a human, I was sure, since I could not detect any remnant of Abilities on him. He had a distinct twang to every word he said. His skin was whiter than the snow I'd seen in mortal movies. Thin as an Underworld lamppost, he somehow lasted long days on patrol, weighed down with a hundred pounds of equipment, but one thing he'd proven in our scant time in Iraq was that he was tough as overcooked meat.

"Yes, sir," we said, in automatic unison.

We were using the Humvee as a shield from any threat from the opposite side of the street, but we were still open to anything coming from either end or the buildings on our side. Sergeant Rogers gave us the mission brief back on post to prevent us from overexposing ourselves when the risk was high, like standing around in a circle on a sidewalk in the middle of a neighborhood where a healthy dose of residents saw us as aggressors and where our enemy hid insurgents in vacated homes.

Smith peered around our clump of four soldiers to check the status of the other squads behind us before nodding to Sergeant Rogers.

"K," he started, always efficient, "let's do this."

Bilba and I found each other's eyes. Shared fear was a powerful prohibitory device, I discovered in that moment. He had wanted to volunteer for Lucifer's Army to recover his financial status. He delayed because of me, and that delay caused him to be drafted into the very specialty he wanted to avoid all along. Bilba was now in a potentially life-threatening situation, and it was my fault. In Hell, we had been through a few scary situations together, and even though we came out of those with a lot of bruises and some awful memories, they did not compare to the reality that demons could die in the Overworld. A world without Bilba was not one I wanted to experience, so I would do everything I could to make sure he got home safe and sound.

"We're good, bud," I said, trying to sound confident. My dear friend pinched his lips and nodded.

We started up the tight street, one soldier behind the other, close enough to respond to and assist one another, but spaced out enough that we had room to maneuver and couldn't be taken out by a single attack.

The Iraqis did what they always did when we were in their neighborhood—they gave us wide birth. I didn't blame them. Families were not free to take a stroll and parents always ushered children inside at the sight of our Humvee convoy filled with soldiers armed to get through a long day of fighting. Weapons of destruction. Understanding the local's skepticism was easy.

The only Iraqis who remained out on the street went about their normal routines as best as they could with us around. Vendors littered the sidewalks. Some spread their wares along broad tables that crowded the sidewalks and curbs of the road. Others laid out goods and products on the ground, only a blanket separating their work from the unrelenting dust of desert living.

Many of them didn't bother with us when we passed; they knew we weren't buying. That didn't stop Sergeant Rogers from conversing through our squad's translator. It was always interesting when he did these informational interviews. It was our role to protect him while he engaged, but we also needed to ensure that we didn't crowd out the vendor's business or appear to intimidate anyone. The mortals, it seemed, had a balance to maintain as well.

After he got what he needed, we reconvened in a covered area where we weren't so susceptible to attack from above.

"From the sounds of it, we had some company in this neighborhood last night," Sergeant Rogers said, taking a long swig from his canteen before continuing. "Keep your eyes open for any insurgents."

"No Russians?" Sergeant Smith asked.

Rogers shook his head. "Came in and left without making much of a fuss. But they had to be up to something."

"Dumping arms probably," Private First Class Jenkins observed.

Rogers nodded. "A possibility. Boys, situational awareness. Eyes wide open. We have no idea what we could walk into. And we're in charge now. It's up to us to keep these people safe, and we can't do that if we're dead."

Say what you will about him, he knew how to motivate simple soldiers. At least, he knew how to motivate me. Dead was not a destination I wanted to visit.

We took turns stepping out of the covered area and back onto the street. A few Iraqis had trickled outside again until they saw us and retreated, trying to appear as if they hadn't been caught checking to see if the pesky American Army had left. I didn't mind. It was sort of funny. Playfulness wouldn't hurt international relations.

Ahead, the street opened at an intersection, broad enough for cross traffic but still suffocatingly narrow for my tastes. A group of boys and girls passed a soccer ball around, laughing as they competed. Life, normal.

"Look alive," Smith said, waving his hand above his head in a circular motion, his signal that we couldn't let our observation skills slip even the slightest.

No worries there. I never felt safe around the open spaces of intersections. Baghdad was very different from the two other Overworld cities I'd been to. This was the first where humans wanted to kill me.

Buildings were dangerous because insurgents could hide in them and attack from above, giving them clear advantages. But the structures also had difficult angles and narrow windows of opportunity to attack. There was no such challenge when it came to broad, open intersections.

A pharmacy occupied one corner. Its dirty windows plastered with advertisements for sweets, treats, and meats. Much more than the typical pharmacy in Hell. The signs did little to hide the dusty film coating the glass. I loved the Arabic script, much more fluid than what the mortals in America and Germany used. Hell didn't have diversity on this level.

On the opposite corner was a single story building with a line of cars parked in front and around the side. Most of those had seen better days.

On the other two corners each housed a multi-story building. Residences, I guessed, by the laundry draped over balcony railings. The building on the diagonal corner drew my attention because of the number of women standing around the open doorway.

"Should we check that out, Sergeant?" I asked Smith, pointing at the building.

His squint showed he shared my slight concern. "Yeah, let's pop in for a visit and see what's going on."

The squads split up, each crossing a different street of the intersection to approach from varied angles. Three pairs of eyes of Iraqi women wearing niqabs turned first toward our squad, then the other, noting us. Six women wearing open-faced hijabs did the same, but frowned or scowled openly. The girls playing around them kicked up dust, free from headgear or the oppressive full-length black outfits of the adult women.

"Tell them it's just a regular security patrol," Sergeant Smith told the interpreter, Muhammad, who did as ordered.

The women backed to the wall as we approached, not caring or not believing the explanation. I could not tell from the blank expressions I could see, but the fiery eyes, even from the niqab-wearing women, gave enough clues to their opinion of our presence.

We took our defensive positions, three soldiers to the sides of the door, backs-to-wall, rifles ready. The cluster of women shuffled away, upset by our actions.

Civilians were around, but this could also be a trap. We had been briefed on the rising number of 'civilian shield' attacks by insurgents over the past two weeks, and even though we had never experienced anything of the sort, we were not about to lower our guard simply because there were non-combatants just a few feet away.

"You two." Sergeant Smith used a horizontal v-shape with his pointer and middle finger, aiming it at me and Bilba. "Head inside.

I looked across the open doorway to Bilba, who had taken up the first position against the frame. We nodded together.

"I would advise against that, Sergeant," Muhammad said, shaking his head in fast, restricted jerks. "You will upset the women, and this is simply a medical practice. Nothing more."

He was correct, at least if you could believe the cracked metal sign tacked to the building's clay wall.

"I don't care," Smith replied. "Rather have upset ladies than dead solders. Wouldn't be the first cell of insurgents to hide behind a clinic."

"Those ladies have husbands," Muhammad said, his eyes rounding as he looked at me and Bilba. "If you are too aggressive, the husbands may feel you threatened them. That may lead them to seeking help from the insurgents or the Russians. Exercise caution."

"Enough," Smith snapped. "You two, get your assess in there and give me the clear signal."

"Yes sir," I said, and swallowed, my throat scratchy and rough.

The Iraqi women spoke unkind, even harsh words in quick Arabic—demons, as immortals, can understand all human languages—about our squad, and some of their comments were not very kind. Muhammad did not translate, and I had to stifle a smile when a short woman said Sergeant Smith was so thin he would break in a stiff desert breeze.

From across the doorway, Bilba stepped past Sergeant Smith.

We'd been best friends for thousands of years and knew each other's tendencies without speaking a word. That wasn't different now that we were in the human army. I've always been faster, stronger, and more agile than Bilba, but those assets had ballooned ever since Aries gifted Creed to me. Ancient magical halberd aside, I was still superior to Bilba in every important physical way—he was taller and weighed more, and those were the only attributes where he had me, so the lead would be mine.

I drew a deep breath and swiveled around the door frame and into the room, my gun lowered, just in case. The floor was a kaleidoscope of yellow and purple swirls embedded in tiles. The design could have tried to replicate a sun burst or it could have come from an artist on an amphetamine high. It was a small room, no more than three hundred square feet, but it was wide enough to hold hospital beds. Before the war, it might have been a foyer or someone's sitting room, but with the mortal international struggle, whatever life this place previously held was erased so it could serve as a place of care.

The women in the room were likely not the owners of the converted home, but that did not mean our sudden appearance did not startle and upset them.

Not if the screams that greeted me were any indication.

I jerked my gun back up and slung it around my shoulder, offering my empty hands in apology. Nearly a dozen children crowded around the four beds that filled the tiny room. The women rushed to cover their hair, their palpable panic causing the three youngest children to cry.

"Sorry. Sorry," I said in Arabic, low enough that my squad outside couldn't hear, and held my hands up further, as if that would convince them I really meant no harm.

Smith and Muhammad ran in, and a scowling woman stormed in from the back room.

Her hair was a mass of black curls, loose and frayed. Her youthful face betrayed stress, deep lines running underneath her eyes. Her brown skin was light enough to make it difficult to tell which part of the Overworld she was from. The blue smock and pants she wore were loose enough to convince me this was a standard issue uniform, not one she'd picked for herself.

A stethoscope hung in her hand, which she then wrapped around her neck as if it was the one thing preventing her from choking us with it. "What is the meaning of this? What are you doing in my clinic?"

My mouth dropped open, and I glanced at our sergeant. For a brief second, he looked too confused to speak. Her words held none of the dialect of the Iraqis. She spoke perfect English. She wasn't from this part of the world, but looked fierce enough to defend it as if it was her own.

"My apologies, ma'am," Sergeant Smith stepped forward. A small girl with big, round eyes whimpered and slid behind a woman who wrapped a protective arm around her. "We're just doing a routine patrol and noticed this crowd gathered here. We wanted to make sure everything was on the up and up."

The woman stepped forward to meet him. "This 'crowd' are civilians. Are these people not free to gather where they want?"

Smith looked at the interpreter as if the woman wasn't speaking his own language. That didn't slow her down.

She stabbed a finger at Smith like she fully intended on poking his eye out. "Because let me tell you, they are free to do what they want, regardless of what this place is and what it may not be in your own perspective."

Our sergeant grimaced, his hands flailing at his sides. "Ma'am, I didn't mean to upset you. We're on the same team here. Just trying to ensure the safety of the neighborhood. We did not mean to intrude on your work."

She crossed her arms. Smith was in trouble. "Yet that's exactly what you did. You know, I'm sick and tired of you Americans and Russians constantly invading my clinic. This is a place to treat people and help them recover, not for insecure military boys to attempt to get one over on the other."

"We're not Russians," Smith said as if he needed to avoid the tension with a response, useless as it was.

"Of course you're not," the woman screeched. "I'm an American and know damn well who you are. Just take word back to your commander that this clinic is off–limits. I don't want you here. I don't want the Russians here. The only thing I want is to be allowed to treat these poor people you keep making victims of. Leave us alone!"

Though I had only recently lowered my hands, I raised them to shoulder height again as I stepped forward. The words were falling out of my mouth before I thought through what I was going to say. "Aren't you," I paused to look around at the Iraqi women who were watching the conversation closely. I knew they wouldn't be able to understand me, most likely, so I figured I could check in with the American civilian. "Aren't you worried about your safety?"

Her folded arms tightened. Now, I was in trouble. "The only people who are a threat to my safety are soldiers like you. And you're also a hindrance to me being able to provide care for people who desperately need it. There aren't very many doctors left in Baghdad thanks to you either scaring them off or forcing them into service to care for the soldiers so they can keep killing the other soldiers."

This woman was tough as nails. She made a shooing gesture with her hands. "Out! All of you, get out!"

The children smiled at the woman's outrage. She strode toward us, still shooing, one intentional step at a time.

"Out! Out!"

"Out! Out! Out!" a boy of ten mimicked her. Two girls, maybe his younger sisters, watched until joy overtook them and they copied their brother copying the doctor.

"Back," Sergeant Smith said, his voice edged with anxiety. "Back outside now."

We did so without question, stepping into the heat of the day again, beyond the shadow of the building and the reach of this irate American.

In the open street on the outskirts of Baghdad, I felt safer than anywhere near her.

10

BAGHDAD

"LET'S GO, GIRLS," Sergeant Rogers shouted to the twenty–man strong platoon itching to hit the streets of Khadra once more.

"Arrogant ass," I grumbled to myself.

Bilba snickered. "Patience. We still have a long time to go with him."

"Don't remind me." I threw the two ammo buckets to Ralrek, who loaded them into the Humvee. I climbed into its cramped quarters.

Two weeks had passed since we were kicked out of the field hospital by the angry doctor and her pint-sized horde of bullies. During that time, we patrolled enough blocks of western Baghdad to put a nice wear pattern in the heel of my boot that ensured I walked with a slight tilt now. And since being scared by one-hundred-and-forty pounds of the meanest medical practitioner I'd ever met, we became intimately familiar with the city and her mortals. I'd learned a lot about the Baghdadis and saw how they struggled because of the military presence. My empathy grew by bounds.

Maybe it was the comfort I felt from my new knowledge about these humans and their home that I was looking forward to patrolling the doctor's neighborhood again.

Two weeks. That was all it took to open my eyes.

Two weeks and we were fully in our independent rhythm, enough to consistently be ahead of schedule. A well-oiled machine.

We waited for the human clock—I really wish we could get satellite signals through the Earth's bedrock so Hell could enjoy the pleasure of accurately synchronized time—to inch its way to our departure hour. Finally, it came, and we pulled away from the Baghdad international Airport safe zone and headed northwest, catching Highway 11 and heading east into the city.

"Remember to keep your heads on a swivel," Sergeant Smith said through his heavy southern accent. "Been some rumors that we might have friends in the neighborhood."

'Friends' meant the Russians, or one of their allies. Word around post was that they were leveraging relationships with a local terrorist cell who operated swiftly and secretly. Small but mobile, they could hit us and scamper away before we knew what was happening. Only once had that happened, not on a patrol I was on, and the damage was minimal. Minimal, but very real.

The Russian influence was growing, but until we saw something, I wasn't going to get myself spun up about it. We had a long deployment ahead, and I didn't want to wear myself out. Plus, thinking of the 'what ifs and maybes' led me straight into the possibility of angels fighting for the Russians. And that led me to thinking about the gorgeous angel Cassie and if she might be in the Overworld again. Then she would distract me, dull my edge, and put me at unnecessary risk.

Best not to think about Russians.

On our left, we passed a mosque. A group of men outside stopped chatting to watch our convoy. I watched them back, silently thanking them for not making any suspicious moves that necessitated evasive action on our part. Or something worse.

The street teed off at an intersection just before an elementary school. We took the left branch and circled the building, respecting the agreement with the local government. Mosques and schools were a no-goes, unless we wanted a hundred thousand pissed off Iraqis on our asses—my vocabulary was, admittedly, becoming a little limited and a lot racier in my time in the Army. Three blocks later, we disembarked from the Humvees and started our patrol.

"Damn, it's hot," I said as sweat trickled down my back after only a few minutes.

"You're telling me," Bilba replied, waving at himself in an up-and-down motion from shoulder to knee. "At this rate, I'm going to be half the size I was when we left the Underworld."

"You say that like it's a bad thing," Ralrek said, snickering behind us.

"You're just jealous about how good I look," Bilba said in jovial defense. "I understand. It's not easy, being this sexy."

"I think you look great," Ralrek laughed.

We joined him.

Bilba did look good, having dropped significant weight since the beginning of boot camp to now. He was fitter than when he'd returned from the Eighth Circle after wasting his time attempting to get his mother to love him, fitter than the months after that when he ate well and worked out, and fitter than the grueling first days of boot camp. But as incubi, we couldn't let him think we agreed, or it would go to his head.

"Too bad you can't reduce those big ass ears, or you'd really have the attention of the ladies," I laughed.

Our fun jibes were cut off by the distinct pop of a rifle. Five feet ahead of Sergeant Smith, the concrete exterior of a building puffed out smoke as shards fell to the sidewalk.

"Down! Down! Down!" Sergeant Smith dropped where he stood. We already were, even before his order.

"Shit," I shouted, looking around for cover. Like most of

the squad, I was out in the open. The lucky few fell behind parked vehicles when the shot came.

Three more distinct shots popped through the morning air.

"Zeke, crawl backward!" Bilba yelled.

I looked back under my arm toward him. He and Ralrek, along with Charlie, shared the cover provided by an old model sedan—I've watched enough television during my time in the Overworld and might be slightly obsessed with mortal vehicles to distinguish most makes and models, and can even tell old from new—that looked like it would take a bullet for us and keep chugging along as if nothing happened if we asked it to.

Keeping myself is low to the ground as possible, I scooted back along the rough sidewalk, which was more difficult than it sounds with the body armor, weapon, and supplies weighing me down. Months ago though, I wouldn't have been able to move further than one length of my body; at least the Army had done that much for me.

When I reached cover, I took a deep breath to calm my jagged nerves and oriented myself.

"We have to give cover to Smith," Ralrek said, nodding toward our squad leader's location.

Sergeant Smith was pinned down on the sidewalk, his rifle jutting out in front of him as he sent suppression fire back toward a building on our left.

"Over there!" I pointed to a two-story building with crumbling walls and missing windows. Small mountains of trash were piled along the base of it. Worse for the wear, it had probably been abandoned long before the current escalating tensions. Anyone interested in conducting attacks on convoys would consider this an effective location because I doubted locals even took note of it any longer.

We fired on the building, drowning out the shouts from down the street and the screams of frightened children. After a few rounds of suppression fire, Sergeant Smith scrambled ahead to hide behind a collection of busted pallets and other trash. It wasn't solid protection, but something was better than nothing.

"We've got to get him out of there!" Bilba whimpered during a pause.

"We're trying, buddy."

The call from Smith came over the radio. He was asking for reinforcements. The other squads would be here soon. We just had to hold our positions and keep the attack suppressed until they got here. "Let's keep them dancing for a couple more minutes."

My three counterparts nodded, and we took turns ensuring that whoever was in that building was busy ducking for cover of their own.

In between rounds of traded attacks, the low rumble of multiple Humvees approached. In seconds we would have the full advantage. I checked Smith one more time. He remained hunkered low behind the trash heap. Our assailants would have to know they had him trapped, but not that they were running out of time.

The Humvees racing toward us were now visible, and the attack ramped up. The trash pile in front of Smith popped and puffed under a hailstorm of bullets, bags exploded, pallets splintered. Bullets punctured the walls of the building past our NCO. The insurgents were not the only soldiers who were running out of time.

Instinctively, my hand slapped against my leg, where Creed was hidden. Before I could yank it out, though, Bilba's hand wrapped around my arm.

"Don't."

I growled. He was right. Smith was our leader; our job was to look out for him, but tipping the Balance to save a single human wasn't a smart move, no matter how right it felt. I conceded with a nod to Bilba, then without waiting to give instructions to my counterparts, I opened fire on the location, trying to keep track of how many rounds I'd spent.

The lead Humvee rounded the corner.

"Bilba, tell them to block that trash heap for Sergeant Smith," I shouted.

Another pop and then a scream came from up the sidewalk. From our squad leader's location. My head snapped in his direction and I saw Smith holding his leg, a pained grimace on his face.

"Smith has been hit!"

"We have to get to him," Bilba shouted and then, shaking, rose and popped four more rounds at the building.

I shook my head. "We can't. Got to stay undercover until the Humvees shield him."

Smith was now lying on his side, in danger of being exposed to the enemy. We couldn't get to him. There was too much space between our location and his. The first Humvee was almost on us; he was on his own until then.

I exhausted my clip, hoping I would get lucky, and fell behind my cover to reload.

"Please, Lucifer, make my aim true," Charlie muttered, holding his rifle against his chest.

Ralrek growled. "Just shoot the bastards, Charlie."

Bilba, Ralrek, and Charlie rose above the car enough to level their rifles and took shots through the building's windows.

Two more pops from above. Smith's vest puffed from the first strike. He was flung backward with the second.

Finally, the Humvee raced past and slammed to a halt alongside the trash pile that blocked off Smith. The door flew open and two soldiers jumped out and dragged him toward the vehicle. Once he was safely squared away, the vehicle backed to our location. A soldier popped into the turret and lit the day and our ears on fire by laying suppression fire to the building with the fifty-caliber machine gun.

We squat–crawled alongside the vehicle to get back to ours. Once inside, I climbed up in the turret, gripped the machine gun and let loose on the insurgents. The gun's roar of violence made my ears muffle against the explosive noise. There had been no time to don the double-hearing protection, and as sensitive to sights and sounds as I was becoming, I don't know if it would have helped. Ears were a luxury at this point. The vehicle absorbed the gun's recoil, so at least I'd still have my hands after this.

The walls of the building crumbled as our guns tore into it. It was a powerful feeling behind that weapon, blasting exterior walls apart in a spray of bullets, watching clay, concrete, and the last few slivers of glass splinter and fall back to the earth.

With a rumble, one half of the corner wall crumbled, exposing the interior and the pair of insurgents who had injured Sergeant Smith. The other gunner was still firing at the wall like he planned on taking the entire building down. But I was aiming for the pair of men. This attack felt so close to the angel's attack on the First Circle square that killed hundreds of innocent demons. A field of red rage filmed my eyes. I took aim at the pair even as they fled through a doorway in the back of the now exposed room, but the gun swiveled slower than they moved, and the pair disappeared before I could make them pay for what they had done.

Once I was sure they were gone, I took cover inside the Humvee, my chest pounding as adrenaline surged through every muscle. The world outside the vehicle had grown unnaturally quiet—probably because my ears were ringing— as happens during armed battles in the middle of a neigh- borhood.

"Smith needs urgent care," Sergeant Rogers' voice squawked over the radio. "Need to get him back to base fast, he's losing too much blood."

I snagged the handset. "How bad is it, Sergeant?"

"Bad."

"Think we can get back to the base?" The handset was slippery in my sweaty palm.

A long pause. Finally, Sergeant Rogers' answer crackled over the radio. "We need to be quick. He's out."

"There's a clinic nearby. We found it on patrol a couple weeks ago. We can take him there."

"Iraqis? Don't think so."

I gripped the handset tighter and waited for my scowl to slip from my face. "What if we get caught in traffic or another attack on the way back? Do we have that kind of time? Does Sergeant Smith? The clinic is two blocks away. We'll be there in a matter of minutes."

More silence. I shared a look with Bilba and could have chewed through a chimera's femur, so tense was my jaw as we waited to hear Sergeant Rogers' decision.

The radio crackled, voice incoming. "Okay. Swing around and take the lead."

I slapped Ralrek on the shoulder as he punched the Humvee forward, pulling out and speeding through the streets.

We rounded the corner and pulled alongside the field clinic. Unlike the last time, there wasn't a long line of patients waiting to access the clinic. We slammed to a stop, checked for threats, and jumped out of the vehicle. It was irresponsible, but the urgency of the matter called for some measured risk.

The squad in the other Humvee extracted Smith as I raced inside to find the doctor.

The front room only had a single occupant in a bed, the rest were free. The tone was much more subdued this time, at least until I rushed in, Bilba close on my heels.

"What do you need?" A short, ancient Iraqi woman asked, lifting her chin in open rebellion.

"I'm looking for the American doctor," I said quietly in Arabic. "We have an emergency."

The little old lady sniffed at me and gave no other response, but turned away and walked through the single door in the back corner of the room.

"Should we follow her?" Bilba asked.

I shook my head. "We're invasive enough. Let's give them their space. If she doesn't come back, then we'll go snooping."

Within seconds, the frazzle-haired American doctor stepped out. Her brown eyes sparked. I hoped she was in a better mood than last time.

"Didn't I already kick you out of my clinic?" she said as soon as she entered the room.

"A guy in our squad was shot. I think multiple times. He's bleeding out. Can you help?"

The little old Iraqi woman stood behind the doctor, shooting daggers with her eyes. "Serves him right," she grumbled in Arabic.

"Afra, be nice," the doctor said without turning. To me, she said, "Bring him in."

"Can you?" I asked Bilba, who scampered away. Turning back, I said, "Thank you for doing this, doctor. We weren't sure if we could get him back to the base in time."

She shook her head. "I'm not a doctor."

I raised my eyebrows.

She extended her hand. I took it tentatively. "Tamika Johnson, nurse."

"You run all this," I said as I gestured at the small room, "as a nurse? I didn't know you could do that."

"Well, there's a lot nurses can do. A lot we *do* do, and rarely get credit for. You'd be surprised what we're capable of."

I shook my head at my inept comment and tried to salvage the conversation. "I didn't mean anything by that. I just wasn't sure you'd be allowed to run this. That's all."

She wrinkled her nose at me. "Do yourself a favor and stop before I change my mind about helping your soldier."

Before I stumbled further into a backhanded apology, the squad carried Smith inside. His uniform trousers were now dark with blood and he was still unconscious. It wasn't until they carried him past that I noticed his sleeve was also soaked.

"Put him over there," Tamika said, pointing at the bed in the far corner. "Keep him away from that child."

They set Sergeant Smith down as carefully as expediency allowed. He didn't even groan.

"Now, get out of my way," Tamika said, firmly but not forcefully pushing a soldier away.

As the team stepped outside, leaving less than a handful of us in the room, she kneeled at Smith's leg, pulling a pair of shears out of her breast pocket and slicing open his pants with skill disguised as reckless abandon. When she had cut them up to his groin, Tamika carefully pulled the material away, exposing the damage done from the bullet. Bilba gagged, Sergeant Rogers bit on his bottom lip and grimaced, looking like he was challenging himself to watch. Ralrek immediately stepped outside. Our NCO's leg was a mess. The sunken flesh. Blood around and coming from the wound. The shredded meat of an appendage. The stench of trauma.

Tamika remained focus on her work. "If you can't be helpful, get out."

Sergeant Rogers, paler but finally pulling his eyes away from the wound, said, "We have to guard him."

Without looking up, she answered in a harsh tone. "And you can do that from outside. There is no other way into the building. He's as safe as any place in Baghdad. This one," she said, pointing at me, "can stay behind since he doesn't seem affected by a little blood. But the rest of you need to get out. Now go."

Sergeant Rogers did the right thing by not arguing. "Out,"

he ordered, and the small team spun and exited. The little old Iraqi lady made sure the squad complied, pushing them toward the door even though they were already moving. She was the one to fear.

"Thanks for letting me stay," I said. "Is there anything I can help with?"

Tamika's hands were on Smith's leg, around the wound. She did not even pause to shake her head. "Just stay out of my way. I can't be sure I can save him."

"Okay." I stepped back and watched her care for my squad leader. There was a tenderness in her work, in the way she moved, and how softly she rubbed down his skin with water to clean the blood around the wound; with the way she adjusted and wrapped him, constantly checking in to see if he'd woken. If anyone in Khadra could save him, we'd found her.

"I'm sorry about last time, about the way we barged in here," I said, trying to find something to fill the quiet. I should have let her concentrate, but it was awkward just standing around not doing anything helpful, especially with the way the old Iraqi human stared at me like a hellhound on a chain, waiting to break free.

"I understand," Tamika said. "Your unit just rotated in, hasn't it?"

"We've been here for almost three months now," I answered.

She kept working, not bothering to look my way. "So you don't really know your way around the city yet?"

"We know a lot of hot spots. But," I said after a pause when she stayed silent, "I guess we have a lot to learn still."

Resuming her work with swift movements that convinced me she could provide care like this in her sleep, she spoke, her voice trembling. "I don't fault you and I apologize if I came across too harshly. When you've been here as long as me, you get sick of the intrusions, sick of men pumped up on adrenaline walking around the city ready to kill the first thing that twitches. I can't tell you how many horrors I've seen." Tamika paused, eyes flicking to the little boy sleeping on the bed along the other wall. In that moment, I saw her age a hundred years. "His parents were killed last week, caught in the crossfire between Russians, their insurgents, and your side. It was a quick fight, not even fifteen minutes. And in less time than it takes to make a damn dinner, that little ... that little boy lost the rock in his world. Now he has to navigate life, this life," she emphasized, waving a bloody finger toward the street, "all by himself. How is he supposed to do that?"

I opened my mouth, but my throat was so tight it was a struggle to squeeze out a few words. "I don't know."

Her shoulders rose and fell. If she was trying to hide how they trembled, she didn't get it by me. "Afra, help me," she said, her voice edged in concern.

The older Iraqi woman scrambled to the bedside.

Smith's breaths were shallow now, ragged.

The nurse was sweating. "Listen, I know this is not your fault. This stuff happens way above your pay grade, above anybody's pay grade. You're just part of a bigger machine, one that doesn't seem to understand the ramifications of its actions. Heaven, for all I know, you might not even want to be here. I've seen that happen too many times, to too many soldiers. But that doesn't excuse people from not being empathetic. Especially to innocents."

"How long have you been here?"

"Almost twenty months now." She wavered, not taking her eyes off Sergeant Smith, pointing toward his bloody arm. "We need to get that opened, Afra. Cut the material carefully." She pried into his leg with forceps. I had to turn away.

"I have to get this out," she told the other woman in Arabic. "Cut as much of his shirt away as you can. See if you can find the entry and exit wounds. I need to know what I'm dealing with."

"Is he ..."

"I don't know," she snapped, before drawing a big breath, speaking less harshly. "Hard to believe that it's nearly been two years. Best years of my life."

I adjusted my rifle. "You sound happy with what you're doing."

"How can I not be?" Her response was immediate, emboldened with passion. "Look at that boy. It's quiet now, but it will pick up again. For every one of him, there are a dozen children out there, somewhere in the streets, who are suffering and I don't even know about them because the Iraqis don't trust me enough because I'm American. Even though I'm helping and have been for nearly two years. It's your presence that keeps them at guard, and the children suffer. They always suffer. So when I do have an opportunity to make a difference, I embrace it. It's the only way I know. So, yes. I have a purpose here. Even the longest, most trying days are still rewarding. There's nowhere else in the world where I get that feeling. Do you feel that way about your military service?"

Oh boy, that was a rabbit hole I didn't want to go down. I scrambled to think up a believable response. "Not really. I was sort of ... encouraged into service because I come from a small town. Not much going on, no jobs, no hope. The military was a way out."

Tamika glanced at the middle of my chest, at my solitary upside-down v-shaped chevron. Did she understand the rank structure of the American military? Had I made a mistake in my story? I was lax, and it might have cost me.

"And now you find yourself on the other side of the world, working long hours in a foreign city where someone wants to kill you every time you turn around," she said as she swiftly worked on my NCO.

I turned and saw Smith's skin now had an ashen tone. He

was breathing so fast I didn't know how he wasn't hyperventilating.

I swallowed. "Yeah, I guess so. But, on a positive note, if I don't wind up dead within the next nine months, I get to go home."

"And hope they don't turn around and redeploy you," she said heatedly.

"I hadn't thought about that," I admitted, eyeing the old Iraqi lady as she grimaced when she peeled away Smith's sleeve. Blood covered any signs of a bullet wound from where I was standing.

Afra said, "Look."

Her tone shared an understood meaning. Tamika's shoulders slumped. "Maybe you should think about that ... among other things about military service."

"Like what?"

"Like why you're here, for starters," she said simply enough.

"We are here because of the Russians. They invaded, not us."

She tilted her head to the side as she pulled the forceps out of Smith's leg, bullet pinched between them. She stood and moved around to Afra's side, and the Iraqi woman switched positions and began cleaning my NCO's leg. "Not accurate, but exactly what I expected an American soldier to say."

Smith's lips were a faded blue.

"What's that supposed to mean?" I had no actual dog in the fight, and it's not like I was even American. But things had changed in my time in the Overworld. This was the longest I'd ever been here, nearly nine months. Bonds and identities evolved in that time. No mortal was perfect. Heaven, no immortal except for Lucifer and Yaweh were supposed to be either—I was still reserving judgment on that. But my immortal friends and most of my new human ones in the Army were good souls, who believed their actions were just. No one was here out of malice. A civilian might not see that.

"Just means that you fell for the propaganda," Tamika said, feverishly sanitizing her forceps with alcohol pads and glancing at me with sad eyes. For Smith or for the lack of proper medical procedures, I couldn't be sure. "War isn't something you can slice open and tell rot from healthy muscle. It isn't like that at all; take it from someone who's been here as long as I have. Everything is gray. There is no black-and-white. No good guys. No bad guys." She leaned over Smith's shoulder, analyzing his wound. "Do me a favor."

"Sure. What?"

"I'm going to try and save your friend here." She pointed at my NCO. "I don't know if I can, but I'll do what I can to make him as comfortable as possible if I can't. But I want you to promise me you'll think about the nature of this war and your personal role in it."

"My role? You think I'm more important than I am."

Tamika glanced at me, her eyes crawling through me. "What's important is that none of us ever forget the truth."

"What truth?"

She lowered her head toward Smith's destroyed arm, grimacing. "A single person can make a monumental differ-ence in the lives of others."

11

BAGHDAD

SMITH BECAME our squad's first casualty. A somber cloud had hung over the entire team since his death. All the brashness and bravado wiped away, even from the younger, impervious troops, with his loss. I found out that he was twenty-seven.

Twenty-seven.

I had underwear that were nearly that old.

Since his passing, I reflected often on Tamika's last words before she kicked me out of her clinic to rejoin the rest of my crew. I think she knew what was coming and did not want me witnessing the last moments of my sergeant's young life. Maybe I did too much reflecting.

"You've got to let it go, Zeke. It's getting old." Bilba brushed off the toes of his cattlehide leather combat boots. Silly, since we were on the outskirts of Baghdad, a place of perpetual dust—I was never going to complain about the air quality in the Underworld ever again—but it kept him occupied. "Just relax."

"I don't know. What she said makes sense," I said with a shrug, thinking back to that lesson Tamika taught me a month ago. "Really, what difference are we actually making here?

What are we actually doing that makes the Overworld a better place for them? How is this keeping the Balance?"

They were hardly fair questions considering the fact we were sitting on bleachers watching a far–too competitive match of tug-of-war between rival units after a long day and longer wait at the mess hall for dinner. The Army team was struggling against their Air Force counterparts. Someone turned the field's lights on as night settled, as if they wanted to highlight the blasphemy of this humiliating loss for soldier-kind. Ralrek was on the Army team and, even in the middle of the desert, at this hour, pulling and being pulled in a tug-of-war, he looked put together with not even a single black hair out of place. The grimace on his face as he struggled to help his team recapture the lost advantage was the least composed I think I had ever seen him. How was this enjoyable?

Even in the middle of war, soldiers needed to relax. Even after losing fellow soldiers, relaxation was key to sustainabil-ity. I got that—an ugly truth of war no one wants to mention. Tug-of-war was ours—I didn't get that. But even in the middle of time I should use to let go of the demands of deployment, Tamika's question haunted me. It had for a month and showed no signs of giving me a break.

Bilba watched the tug-of-war struggle with only a passing interest. Even at his fittest, he could only dream of tests of strength like this. He was much more likely to be found reading the latest geek news than exerting himself in tests of masculine strength and bravado. Competition was not some-thing that interested either of us, but this sport was, by far, the least interesting of them all. It was like an explosion of testos-terone. Thankfully, we sat far enough away to not get any on us if it did decide to blow.

"We need to unwind too," he finally answered during a break between matches—the Air Force beat the Army team by the way, which resulted in serious shit talking. "We can't patrol all the time. These times are important for our sustainability."

"Oh yeah, I forgot about sustainability. About our need to be here for a year. Lucifer knows, it's unquestionable that our presence is necessary."

Bilba rotated on his rear, half cocked on the bleacher seat. "You don't think we need to be here? You don't think we're doing something important for the people of Baghdad? See? That nurse got in your head. She has you thinking all sorts of crazy stuff. What we're doing is important. The Russians and their angels ... allies," he said quickly, wiping his mouth with the back of his hands as he glanced around to make sure no one had overheard. No one could. The closest soldiers were in the smoking pit, busy taking seven minutes off their lives with each cancerous stick. "They're not backing down. Heavens, things are just starting to ramp up. Long after we've gone back home, these ..." he lowered his voice but only removed a portion of its heat, "these mortals will still be fighting."

"Over what?" It came out as a growl. I wasn't frustrated with my friend, just with the situation, my recent level of awareness, all of it Tamika's fault. She asked me to think about the nature of the conflict and the role each nation played. And that's all I had been doing, and it was seriously starting to annoy me. The fact I could not let it go only amplified my annoyance each time it crept into my mind.

This was a human struggle with human motivations and implications, and the only dog in the fight us immortals had was for the sake of the stupid Balance. But what Tamika couldn't know, what bothered me enough to keep me constantly thinking and agitated, was that I didn't see my personal role in this or how my presence made this better for anyone. What was I doing here? I surely wasn't keeping the Balance; I could not stop insurgents from attacking convoys or threatening locals; I could not stop little boys from having their parents killed. This all felt like such a waste.

A new tug-of-war match started, the opposing teams taking their places at each end of the rope, reviewing tactics and shooting verbal barbs to their opposition. A few chests were beat with fists. These mortals were so fresh-faced; babies, all of them. In relative terms, they were about my age, but I'd lived through thousands of their generations. And they were here, happy to die for a ridiculous aim. Lucifer and Yahweh, pulling strings and moving chess pieces and making the mortals dance for their eternal entertainment. My gut filled with sympathetic grief for them and disgust at our role.

Damn Tamika for making me think.

Three months in Iraq and I still didn't feel I'd done anything of significance. A part of me wondered if I ever would.

"I hope you know that I truly appreciate your friendship," I said, placing a hand on Bilba's shoulder, rubbing it. "Without you here, I don't know if I'd make it."

His cheeks puffed when he smiled. "You would."

I shook my head. "Don't be so sure. You're good for me."

"And you are for me."

"Why don't you make out already?" A new voice said, followed by a gruff laugh. Looking into Bilba's eyes, I smiled and leaned closer. He jerked back, almost falling off the back of the bleacher. I broke out into a hearty laugh, as did our new visitor, Ralrek. Having just finished an intense tug-of-war, he looked as fresh as if he had just stepped out of the shower, not a grain of sand to be seen.

"What's up, asshole?" I stood and grasped his hand, thumb around thumb, palms meeting in a harsh slap. We hugged in the quick way guys do while in public.

Bilba, now recovered, stepped down the rows to welcome Ralrek. "Where have you been?"

"Before the match? Inside, watching the movie."

"Well, Zeke and I are going to chow soon. Feel like going with us?"

Ralrek's lips pinched. "Not sure."

"Why, do you have other plans?"

"Something like that," Ralrek said in a flat tone.

I watched Ralrek's face. Things had regressed in our time in Baghdad once we fell into a smooth rhythm. The daily patrols off-post and mortar attacks on-post prevented Bilba and Ralrek from talking through the taboo subject that was Ralrek's experience in Germany. The tall demon making out with a mortal seemed resolved back home, though there was always a little underlying tension about the subject, but that was attributable to the incubi not being fully open and raw. Given enough time, things left to simmer boiled. The Army had solved that by turning our lives upside down. But now that we were operating in a flow, we had more time. More time led to us being around mortals in a more relaxed atmosphere. More time around mortals brought back all the unaddressed issues Bilba had with Ralrek's attraction to them. I always attributed it to the handsome incubus being a slut, but Bilba had hangups over the issue and seemed to suspect the taller demon of slinking away to make out with any male who happened by the portable toilet.

This blessed deployment made me lose focus on important things like this, maybe a warning sign that I needed to pay attention again. Wasn't that what Tamika meant when she told me to think about the impact a single person can have on others? Her comment wasn't only aimed at some grand, global perspective because I was an American soldier. She may have meant I needed to think about times like these, when I could make things better, even between just two friends I'd known for a few thousand years who needed to heal their relationship.

"Oh, okay," Bilba said. "We haven't chilled together in a while. I miss our conversations."

"Me too," Ralrek answered, sounding less invested than Bilba.

I changed the topic because I'd failed them both and had no idea how to rescue them from themselves. "Heard we're going back into Khadra tomorrow."

"Supposedly," Bilba said curtly, his eyes lingering on our tall, handsome friend.

"You're just hoping to see that nurse again, aren't you?" Ralrek said through squinty eyes as he examined me. I saw the playfulness on his lips, a playfulness he had not displayed to Bilba.

"You guys make it sound like I have a thing for any female who crosses my path."

"You do!" The pair said, synchronized.

I didn't appreciate their instantaneous agreement when they typically could not agree on the color of the sky. We shared a laugh just the same, a moment that nearly covered the whistle of a mortar through the air.

"Shit," I said, climbing down from the bleachers and walking to the overhang a few feet away. The tug-of-war stopped, and the players moved behind the closest T-wall barriers.

Bilba laughed when we were underneath cover.

"What's so funny?"

He pointed up. "Remember when an inbound mortar made us scramble and dive for cover? Now look at us. We can barely be bothered to stop a tug-of-war session."

I snorted and nodded.

"I think they're called matches, not sessions," Ralrek said.

"And I think that proves his point," I said, sitting at one of the picnic tables under the overhang. We waited. The mortar struck, somewhere in the black night, on the other side of the runway. None of us flinched, then, or when the shock wave sailed across the volleyball court, rippling the net.

Silence followed. A solitary attack.

"Probably some drunk Russian getting off a volley when his NCO wasn't watching," Ralrek said with a smirk.

I snorted, imagining him do something similar if the Army ever gave us access to mortars.

Bilba exhaled slowly.

"What's on your mind, bud?"

He grimaced. "Do you think we'll get so lax about these attacks that we'll get ourselves in trouble one time? Look at us; they could kill us if the Russians get lucky, and we're just hanging out near picnic tables. What will we be like in another month? What if we are in the path of the next one?"

Ralrek and I looked at each other. I considered the question. We still had so long to go. Bilba was right. I was completely relaxed on the picnic table. The attack interrupted a meaningless tug-of-war match, and some players grumbled. Yesterday, the soldiers in the recreation tent bitched because the power went out after an attack, cutting off the air conditioning and the movie marathon. Most soldiers only took cover out of automated responses and peer pressure now, but even the NCOs gave lazy commands when they demanded hustle. What was it going to be like in the next months or as we neared the end of our rotation?

I tilted my head. "I used to think how weird it would be to go back to the Underworld and not worry about death raining from the sky. You know, until you asked that, I can't remember the last time I even thought about that."

"Yeah, weird," Ralrek said in a flat voice.

Damn Tamika. It seemed like all of us had something to think about.

WE TOOK THE LONG WAY INTO KHADRA FOR THE NEXT PATROL, heading north on Highway 1 and looping back once we reached Highway 97.

The convoys were more enjoyable as things around the city settled after the United States and its allies gained a stronger foothold, pushing the Russians across the Tigris. It also helped that Smith had been our last casualty. Time had passed, giving us time to numb, but not forget—I would never forget.

Progress manifest when we passed a busy market and no one shot us a dirty look. As we rolled by the police station, a pair of officers actually waved in greeting. I waved back, possibly too enthusiastically by the way they yanked their arms down, but the spirit of positivity encouraged me. However, even as tensions eased around the western half of the city at the pull back, rumors of insurgents using mosques as recruiting grounds and observation posts lingered. I never felt comfortable whenever we were near one—and it had nothing to do with Yahweh getting so many gorgeous buildings while Lucifer didn't have a single one dedicated to him.

The convoy stopped a few blocks deeper into Khadra and emptied. We might be cocky and comfortable while on the Baghdad International Airport complex of Army posts, but out here, we followed the rules and protocols.

"Jones, take your squad back down that street," Sergeant Rogers told our squad leader, newly installed after Sergeant Smith's passing. It wasn't the same with Jones. He had a harsher, rougher accent that made his words sound different, yet similar. I didn't know anything about Massachusetts, but if everyone there sounded like he did, even my immortal nature wouldn't help me understand a blessed thing anyone from there said.

"Stay smart," Jones said as we broke off and began our patrol.

I had a spring in my step as we rounded the corner. Tamika's clinic was only a block ahead. We would pass right by it during the patrol, and I was looking forward to possibly crossing paths with her again. "Sergeant Jones, can we check in on the clinic and thank the doctor? See if she needs anything from us?" Jones didn't need to know that Tamika wasn't a doctor, and he did not need to know I wanted to thank her for challenging me to think; he just needed to grant my request.

"When we get to it, sure," he said curtly. "But focus on your surroundings right now. Situational awareness. This is war."

Bilba covered my groan with a fabricated cough. Jones sounded like he tried to memorize all of Sergeant Smith's one-liners so he could build an air of authority, even though the military already awarded him with the formal variety.

As we neared Tamika's clinic, activity buzzed outside the front door. My instincts spurred me forward, but we were in formation and were not allowed to break it. Still, the urge to break and run was strong. Each step seemed intentionally slow.

We were close enough to overhear the conversation of the small cluster of women gathered by the door. Those whose faces I could see appeared upset. The one in a niqab was crying. I checked with Bilba and Ralrek. They heard too.

"Stay calm," Bilba whispered carefully.

I focused on the crowd to keep my face straight and avoid drawing attention from the humans because still, after all this time, I had not come up with an explanation for how I could speak Arabic.

"What are they saying?" Sergeant Jones asked Muhammad.

"They are upset. They have," Muhammad said, stopping abruptly to listen. Then he nodded when he had the gist of the conversation. Heat flushed up my neck at what the crowd was discussing. "There is an adolescent boy in the clinic. A car bomb went off in his neighborhood about half an hour ago and he is severely injured."

Sergeant Jones spun, raising a balled fist, palm forward, our sign to a halt. "Be on your toes, soldiers. We've got possible heat."

He radioed Sergeant Rogers to relay the details. The rising adrenaline from the squad was palpable as rifles were pulled from shoulders and heads jerked to scan the street ahead, behind, and above. I almost didn't recognize my hand slipping to my hip, feeling for Creed. Secured in the pocket inside my pants, I played it off by checking my ammo.

We hustled to the clinic now that Jones knew something serious went down, telling Muhammad to check in with the women to see if they needed help. I couldn't see Tamika fast enough. She had to be okay, because the crowd was here. It had to be Tamika who was treating him; I hoped.

As Muhammad approached the crowd, many of whom eyed us with suspicion, I drifted closer to Jones, feeling that if I kept the conversation between the two of us, I wouldn't put him in an awkward spot. "Sir, do you mind if I check in with a doctor?"

"She's tending to a patient," he said sternly, not pulling his eyes from our interpreter and the group of women.

"I understand that, sir. But we need to maintain relations in the neighborhood if we want good intel. I figure a couple seconds of her time will do that. She's an American, sir. We need to do right by her."

He considered my argument. "Make it quick. Don't disrupt her. Don't need these Iraqis turning on us."

I dashed past the cluster as a woman with a youthful voice mentioned a small group of insurgents holed up in a building down the street. I figured Muhammad would pass along the message to Sergeant Jones. Time was imperative here. I yanked open the door and bolted inside.

Wailing greeted me as I entered the room. A weary man desperately held a woman about his age, presumably his wife. She was crumbled in his arms, the source of the wailing. Tears left trails on his dirty face.

They stood next to the bed in the corner of the room where a small boy lay. Tamika and Afra, her aged dagger-shooting eyes turned down, tended to him on bed sheets soaked in blood and smeared dirt. The boy only had one leg; the remains of the other in ragged shreds just below the knee.

Afra was assisting Tamika, holding a towel. She took the one, heavy with blood, from Tamika and handed the nurse a clean towel.

I rushed to them. "Can I help?"

Tamika looked up, her brows pinched together and mouth opened in response until she saw who I was. Her scowl shook before softening and disappearing. She wiped a forearm across her forehead, leaving behind a trail of pink in her loosely-curled hair. "Grab more towels from the back room."

I raced into the back, scanning the room. Medical equipment, generic bottles of prescription drugs, the aforementioned towels, and even a small refrigerator crowded every inch of wall. I grabbed a stack of towels and dashed into the front room.

"What should I do with these?"

Tamika looked up, her eyes welling with tears as she frantically worked to staunch the blood flow from the boy's missing leg. "Give me a clean one and hold the rest until I need you."

I did as she ordered and stepped out of the way, glancing at the terrified family just a few feet away. I wanted to reach out, to comfort them. I hadn't noticed when I first entered, but the family had another child with them. A girl of no more than four years, her wide eyes watched.

I turned to Afra. "Where did this happen?" I said in Arabic.

Tamika's head flicked in my direction and then returned to the boy. The little old woman, not bothering to cover her graying hair, answered while keeping her eyes on the patient.

"I'm not sure. They say it was near the butcher's shop. Three blocks south," she said in her native tongue, pointing with a bent finger as if I could see the building.

"Insurgents?"

She gave a succession of head shakes, as if trying to loosen the thoughts from a clouded mind. "I don't know. We've been busy trying to save this young boy's life. God willing, we will."

"See? This is what happens when you blessed soldiers can't put down your guns for more than a day," Tamika said through a shaking voice as she applied pressure to the boy's leg. Sweating, she pressed. "Afra, hold this. I need to elevate it."

The older woman dropped the bloody towel on the floor, where it splunked, and went to the bed. She leaned over the boy, taking over for Tamika. Spinning on her stool, the nurse snagged a pillow from the empty bed behind her and carefully, but expediently, elevated the boy's leg.

No matter how quickly she moved, no matter what she did, he was losing more blood. Her eyes were locked on the leg even as she said, "If you just let these people live in peace, none of this would happen. This boy's life, if I can save it, has changed forever because of men playing God."

I knew she was not personally attacking me. Standing in her clinic, I represented everything she was working against because I wore a military uniform. I hadn't even shared her ideological impact, and I would not get to it today, but I wanted to tell her how deeply I understood why she was so upset. To be honest, this upset me too. The boy looked tiny on the bed, his face beaded in sweat, the bleeding was the only real sign he was still alive judging from his pallid complexion. I sent a thought of gratitude to Lucifer that the boy was unconscious, hoping he wasn't able to recognize what was happening. That time would come soon enough.

"I'm sorry, Tamika," I said in a hoarse voice.

More water. More pressure. More blood. This was a losing fight.

"Sorrys don't save lives," she growled.

I stepped back.

Sweat dripped from Tamika's forehead as she worked feverishly. The leg looked worse with each passing second. Without looking at Afra, Tamika ordered, "We need to get a new IV and blood bag. You," she said to me, "take the family out of here. Say anything you have to since it's obvious you speak Arabic. Just get them out."

I swallowed and removed my helmet and set my rifle by the bed. Sergeant Jones would kill me if he saw what I was doing. But reducing the amount of body armor I was wearing would make me appear as normal to humans as a demon with white skin in the middle of Baghdad could. I took a few tentative steps toward the family, careful to not scare them. I softened my expression and tried to hide my worry.

I put my hands out to show them I wasn't a threat. "I'm so sorry about your child. The doctor is working very hard, but she needs to concentrate. She asked me to have you step outside so she can help your son."

The wife crumbled against her husband. He almost fell as he tried to hold her upright. The little girl scooted closer to him. Once he had a secure grip on his wife, he wrapped his arm around his daughter. "We're not leaving him," he said in a voice that shook like an earthquake was rolling through it.

"I understand," I said softly. "But she needs to focus. Please help her do that. She understands how difficult of a request this is, but she pleads with you to honor it so she can help him."

The father's eyes searched mine, examining me to see if I was trustworthy. Without a word, he guided his grieving wife and frightened daughter outside.

I exhaled deeply and started to turn around when I froze in mid-step at an icy feeling creeping over my neck and face, the only exposed areas of skin. My hand slapped against my leg, sliding into the cargo pocket for Creed.

Someone was conjuring.

I spun, still clumsily trying to yank Creed free. If I didn't die in this moment, I would need to rethink where I hid it.

Afra was crying in the back room, mournfully calling out in prayer to Yahweh.

Tamika was over the boy. And she was conjuring.

Water magic. Tamika was a demon!

I moved to the end of the bed and watched the nurse's hands move over the boy's knees in opposite circular motions. Water poured over his leg, and then she reversed the direction and the stream dulled to a bluish–white. With his leg set in ice, stopping the flow of blood, Tamika took a deep breath and wrapped it with the only clean bandages she had left. I stood by speechless, willing Lucifer to keep my squad busy gathering intel about the insurgents. When she finished, Tamika looked at me, her eyes unblinking as she measured my reaction.

I released Creed and pulled my hand out of my pocket.

"Afra, please bring the next IV," Tamika said, her eyes still locked on mine. She had been sitting rigidly in the chair, but now stood and crossed her arms. "I imagine you don't understand what just happened, but I need you to promise me something."

I didn't know who she was or what her Abilities were. Her magic was relatively low level, definitely a minor demon, and most likely why I did not sense she was one of my kind before. I needed to play this tightly. "Of course. Name it."

"What you saw," she said carefully, "Tell no one about it. If I … if I hadn't done that, he would have definitely died, and I can't lose him. It might be hard to understand, but I need you to believe me. There isn't an explanation for what I did, but it needed to be done. For him."

The boy's breaths were slower now, the sweat beads evaporating from his forehead. Rest had come.

For the first time, Tamika sounded vulnerable.

Glancing toward the back room where Afra was retrieving

the IV and blood bags, I asked, "Does she know that you're a demon?"

Tamika stepped backward, placing her hand on her chest. "What are you talking about?" She tried to laugh.

Thank Lucifer she was a great health care provider, because she was a lousy actor. I pointed at the boy as if he provided the evidence to solidify my opinion. "That was Water magic. Only a demon can use it."

I sensed the icy tingle of a new spell long before her hands moved. I stepped to her, grabbing her wrists and pinning her arms to her side. She flinched at my sudden touch. I leaned in, smelling her sweat, the payment for a saving a mortal's life.

"Listen, I'm not going to hurt you. And I won't tell anyone your secret." I pulled back, relaxing my grip on her wrist but not completely letting go. I needed to make her believe that or everything would change. And there was only way to do that; a secret for a secret. "I want to show you something. But I need you to relax and trust me. Can you do that?"

Her eyes had grown big. She nodded slowly.

I released my hold, and slowly slid my hand into my cargo pants, gripping Creed's knob. "I know your secret, and I want to show you mine so that you trust me. But I need you to not say a thing to anyone, not even the guys out there." I jerked my head backward, toward the squad outside.

Her eyebrows flattened, and her eyes drooped in skepticism. "Do something gross and I'll freeze you where you stand. I don't care who sees."

I moved my hand like I was bouncing a basketball. "I promise, this is nothing weird. I just ... I can't let the mortals know or see."

I reached into my cargo pocket and pulled Creed out.

"A stick. Impressive."

Checking over my shoulder, hearing Sergeant Jones still engaging the anxious crowd, I activated Creed with a shake.

Tamika jumped back, a small yelp escaping her lips as the halberd extended, the wavy single blade at the bottom and the double ax head at the top, burning blue with the Hellfire. "Creed, meet Tamika. Tamika, this is Creed, a magical halberd gifted to me by Aries, a first of his name. He gave it to me during a mission the Third Council sent me on about two years ago. As I said, your secret is safe with me, because now you know mine."

"You're a ... a ..."

"Demon." I gave her the warmest smile I could under the circumstances.

Now it was her turn to shock me. Her face crumbled, and she collapsed into me, crying. I wrapped my arms around her in an awkward hug while attempting to collapse Creed.

"Thank Lucifer," she said in between quiet sniffles. "You don't know how trying this has been. I've been alone this entire time, and I'm so exhausted." She pulled back, her eyes returning to the soft vulnerability of before. "Are you the only one?"

Before I answered, I checked over my shoulder to ensure we were still alone. Whatever Afra was doing in the back room, she was taking her time.

"No, the Council started a draft and selected thousands of us. There's two guys out there right now, lifelong friends, who are also one of our kind."

Tamika stepped away, running a hand through her chaotic hair. "This is good. Good. Really good."

She was more mumbling to yourself than talking to me.

"I can imagine, especially if you've been the only one in the city."

She turned to me, her hands dropping to her side. "Not just that. I need help."

I looked around at the empty beds. "I'm not sure what we can help you with. I mean, there's a few medics I can ask questions of or maybe have them sneak supplies to you, but beyond—"

"Not here, not healthcare."

"Then what do you need help with?"

"Removing a curse."

12

BAGHDAD

"WHY DOES she need to talk to the three of you?" Sergeant Jones snapped.

I wanted to spew the truth, that the fate of an immortal was in the balance and we were compelled, if not obligated, to help. That the freaking state of the Balance was at risk. But I stopped myself because I don't know where the Army puts crazy soldiers, but I'll bet it's worse than Iraq. Even pausing would raise suspicions and put everything at risk.

"I told you, sir," I started my lie over again. "She needs help to rearrange beds, but she doesn't want too many soldiers in there because that will break the trust the locals have with her. And we're the lowest ranking in the squad, so she'll feel less threatened if it's just us. Plus," I lowered my voice and added a spruce of conspiracy notes to make it enticing to Sergeant Jones, "Sergeant Smith might not have had the chance to tell you this, but this nurse is the major source of intel for our patrols. He kept her out of the reports to keep her safe. She's an important source and we can't lose out on what she might have to say." I backed away, resuming my normal level and cadence of speech. "I promise, sir. It won't take long."

His eyes narrowed. "Is that so?" His voice rose. Loud. Haughtiness mixed with the heat of embarrassment of one of his soldiers knowing more than he did—though it was not true. "Well, this one is too lazy, and this one is too pretty to be effective securing the perimeter," he continued with pompous confidence after insulting Bilba and Ralrek equally. "We need to report in, so don't screw around. Get in, get the job done, and let's get out of here."

Permission granted, I waved for Ralrek and Bilba to join me inside the makeshift clinic where Tamika waited to meet the two demons.

She was pacing when we entered, spinning as if we surprised her.

"These are the two I was telling you about," I said carefully. "They're good guys, though they can be asshats from time to time. We're from the same Circle. I know them like I know the back of my hand."

"You mean, the palm," Bilba quipped and blushed when Tamika's head snapped toward him.

I cleared my throat. "If you need help, these are the only two I trust fully. They won't betray you."

She nodded and shook their hands, then turned away and waved for us to follow her into the cramped back room. When we were together, she explained. "I'd rather do this in here. If anyone in your squad gets curious about what's taking you so long, at least this will give us a few seconds to cover our conversation. It will still be awkward, but I'll take that chance. I'm more interested in getting your help. Plus, Afra can be quite the bulldog if anyone, even your commander, tries to barge in here. Trust me, she knows how to manipulate your rules of engagement."

I smiled. "We don't have a commander on patrol, so we're safe there. And, honestly, part of me would like to see Sergeant Jones put in his place by her. She's scary."

But she wasn't in the mood for humor. "My name isn't

Tamika. That's the name I use for the mortals, but my actual name is Cancer Nijal."

Cancer. It didn't fit her. I wondered if she would allow me to continue using her human name.

"Nice to meet you, Cancer," Bilba said, fumbling with his rifle which clunked against the small medication refrigerator, leaving a small dent as a sign of his presence.

"Careful doofus," Ralrek said playfully, even though I imagined taking a swipe at Bilba helped balance the unresolved tension between them.

I peeked around the open door into the patient area. "This attack that hurt the boy will get a quick response and Sergeant Jones won't fall for the lie I gave him for long. I'm not sure how much time they'll give us, so let us know how we can help or it might have to wait, and I have no idea when we'll be back."

Cancer wrung her hands, biting the corner of her lip. "I understand. I hate it, but I understand. I'm just happy that we met each other, even if it was by accident. Like I told you, I need help with a curse."

"I'm not sure what we can do about curses, except listen and maybe find someone who can." She didn't need any false hope, especially since the Army kept us restricted to the post when not on patrol.

Cancer leaned against a shelf holding bandages, medical tape, and linens. "I have to be careful who I involve because ... well, that doesn't matter. To understand the curse, you need details about my family, because I'm not the only one it affects."

"It affects everyone in your family?" I asked.

Cancer shook her head, her mass of loose curls swaying back and forth even after she stopped. "Not everyone. Sometimes it skips entire generations. But it affects too many of us. For one demon to be cursed, it's bad enough, but when so many in your family are, it becomes everything."

"I imagine," Bilba said, trying to take a seat on a stool and almost toppling over. "Curses are no joke."

"What do you know about them?" Ralrek looked down at Bilba with a hint of disbelief in his expression.

Bilba's eyes narrowed, focusing on Ralrek like he was the only other demon in the room. "I know they're real. I know demons can cast them with Hex magic for anything like giving someone back luck, making animals sick or causing crops to fail. And I also know that major demons can curse other demons and even mortals. What do you know? Do you know that Celio Darviolos was the first demon to cast a curse?"

Ralrek snickered. He didn't sound humored. "Don't know that name."

"Oh, but you try to call me out?"

"Guys, we're on a time crunch here," I reminded them. "Who is this Celio?"

"You wouldn't know him," Bilba said, his voice losing the heat he responded to Ralrek with. "An ancient. Just someone I did some reading about."

"Never heard of him."

"You wouldn't, Zeke," Bilba said. "He lived more than five hundred thousand years ago."

I jerked my head back. "Hex magic goes back that long?"

"Probably longer. It's an ancient Ability; maybe even one of the first created after the Fall. According to what I've read, there are a small percentage of demons who still have it, though it's mostly a weak Ability now, for some reason. I don't even know if there is a single major demon with it anymore."

Cancer gave my seated friend a sad smile, likely finding his clumsiness adorable. "My family's experience with it started with my great-grandfather and a feud with a rival. He was an accountant."

"I never thought of accountants having beefs with each other," I said.

Cancer shook her head. "Not with another accountant. His was with one his customers. He supposedly filed a report on the customer's finances that got the customer in trouble with tax authorities. Going to jail type of trouble."

"I can see how that would upset somebody. Jail isn't fun," Ralrek said with a quick sideways glance at me over our shared experience.

Cancer registered his reaction but continued without prying. "He was justified in what he did, because he would have been liable if he didn't report the inaccuracies. His customer's family saw his actions as antagonistic. His customer wasn't in jail for more than a few days before his family started harassing my great-grandfather. And that's when it happened."

"The curse?" I concluded.

Cancer nodded a few times in stunted dips of her head, making her loose curls bob beyond her face. "The customer's wife was a renowned witch in the Second Circle. That's where my family is from."

"Oh, I'm familiar with the Second Circle," I said with only a hint of humor to cover my immediate thoughts of Cassie, the spy who had been part of the angelic attack at Gemini's failed execution. She was also the one who helped me see more of my nature than anyone in the Underworld bar Dialphio, so she was not all that bad.

"You've been there?" Cancer said, straightening.

Ralrek answered before I could. "The Council had a job for us there."

Cancer blinked, her shoulders dropping and lifting as her full lips spread out in a impressed smile. It looked like an invisible weight had been lifted from her. "Imagine my luck tripping across demons who have done work for the Council."

"It's not as glamorous as it seems," I said with a laugh I didn't feel. Jitters were setting in. This was supposed to be a quick furniture-arranging mission to cover as an intel run that would elevate our squad leader's impression of himself. Much longer and he would start suspecting something else was going on. "We're running out of time, Cancer."

"This customer's wife, Adadi Vicu, visited great-grandfather to confront him, and slipped a powder into his tea, setting the curse in motion."

I shook my head. "He never knew what hit him?"

Cancer's shoulders sagged. "No. And they did that to him, to our family, because he'd done his job. He wasn't the one who falsified records or tried to hide coin from the Council. He just did what was right."

"And they cursed him for it," Bilba said in a raspy voice.

"And the curse is perpetual, genetic. It is a powerful spell; passed down through our genes."

"That's gross," Ralrek complained. "If you've got a problem with somebody you take it up with them, directly. You don't beat around the bush, or get others involved. You handle it like an adult."

His outburst cast silent speculation over the room. The heat in his comments was grounded in something much deeper to him than Cancer's familial curse. His barbed comments were intended for Bilba, whose issues with Ralrek's attraction to mortals still hadn't been addressed.

I rubbed my face, frustrated at keeping this focused so she could share what she needed to about this supposed curse. "And it was passed on to you?"

Cancer gazed at the floor, giving us a tiny nod of her head.

"What happens?"

She looked around the back room with an air of nostalgia, her eyes disconnecting from the here and now, drifting off to another place and time. "The curse is a rot that slowly eats away at its victims. The infected demon doesn't even notice it until long after it has taken hold and started breaking them down. Tortuously. It's terrible. I've seen so many of my family …"

"That's barbaric," Ralrek snapped. "Who does that to another demon?"

"The Vicu family," Cancer said the familial name as if it was the most blasphemous curse someone could pronounce.

Bilba got up from his seat and walked to her, whispering. "Has anyone tried to break the curse?"

Cancer reached out, wiggling her fingers for Bilba to give her his hand. When he did, she took it in both of hers. "Believe me, we have tried, even long before I was born. My mother and aunt looked for ways to break it too. No one has been able to. The Circle's Council isn't interested. We've met with the Vicu family, but the talks constantly break down. And as far as countering it? Nothing."

"Out! Get out!" Afra yelled from the front room. "No more soldiers! No more!"

Bilba jumped. I peeked around the corner and saw Cancer's elderly assistant blocking Sergeant Jones and Muhammad in the doorway.

I turned back to our small group, urgency pushing bluntness. "We have to go. Tell us how can we help, because you might not see us for a long time."

"There is a way to remove it," she said. "But it has to come from the family. Only a Vicu can break it, and it has to be voluntary. Coerced if necessary, but the choice still has to be theirs."

I cocked my head. "Coercion isn't voluntary."

"Semantics. Take this," she said, handing me a slip of paper. "One of them just has to recite this counter-spell. Word-for-word. That will end the curse."

I took the paper and tucked it into my pocket. "We want to help, and I'll try, but we're obligated to the mortal Army for our entire year. It'll be months before we return home. We can't do anything until then."

Her soft eyes locked on mine. "You don't need to go back to the Underworld to break the curse."

Footsteps stomped in our direction.

"Privates," Sergeant Jones yelled. "Where in the hell are you? Get your sorry asses in gear."

"There is a member of the Vicu family here in Baghdad," Cancer smiled.

At least there was someone in the family in the immediate vicinity, meaning we might be able to help after all. Maybe.

"I have no idea how we could get to an Iraqi even if they lived across the street. The Army watches us too closely. They control everything we do, especially around locals."

Cancer's smile spread. "You don't have to worry about that, because he isn't an Iraqi. He's serving in the American Army."

13

BAGHDAD

"WHY IS it so hard to creep?" Bilba said as he slumped against the aluminum picnic table, almost dropping his tray that held three slices of pizza and a super-sized soda.

My eyes grew as large as his stomach would when he ingested that meal. "I thought you were serious about taking better care of yourself?"

"I'll care about that when I'm allowed to paint my finger-nails black again. Plus, I am," he said defensively, and then looked at the content of his tray. "I just haven't eaten in a few hours and I'm starving. Plus, we're burning tons of calories every day. I'm basically just trying to maintain now."

"With that much food you won't need to eat for another day," Ralrek said, spreading strawberry cream cheese over his bagel and taking a huge bite. He smiled behind the bagel.

"You guys are jerks," Bilba said as he sprinkled pepper flakes over the pizza. Anyone caught in the shit trailer with him after that meal would regret their timing.

"But you're right, it's harder than heaven to find a single soldier in a sea of them," I said as I watched a squad hurry past to reach the coffee stand line before another group.

Even in Baghdad, Americans excelled at over-consuming

unhealthy diets, something Bilba was becoming too comfortable with as our deployment stretched on. Pizza stands, hamburger vendors, coffee shops, exquisite bagels, a bakery; you name it and this single food area, one of many around the compound of Army posts and Air Force bases, had it all. Though I'd never been to the Third Circle, I imagined it looking a lot like this, which was fine until the mountain of useless calories started catching up. These young soldiers didn't seem to mind because deploying to the desert was doing wonders for everyone's waist band, mine included. With nothing to do when we were not working, nowhere we could go, and only so many films to watch in the recreation tent, the food court was a popular stop for those tired of mess hall food.

So I, too, felt justified eating this crap food. It would undo all my hard work in getting a rippled stomach, but it was a glorious way to pass the time on this recon mission to find Chax Vicu, the soldier who Cancer claimed was stationed on the compound. The problem was, there were over seventy-five thousand soldiers around six different posts, and that didn't include a few thousand fortunate enough to be with the Air Force at the two smaller air bases. Cancer had said she saw him on patrol. That meant he had to be embedded with an Army unit, not the pampered flyboys—I have no idea how female mortals in the Air Force feel about that moniker. Chax was around here, somewhere.

In the ten days since our visit with Cancer, we'd spent every non-working, waking minute searching for her family's enemy. Our boot camp in the Underworld taught us how to blend in, which was great for survival, but a pain in the ass when it prevented us from finding a single soldier among a small city's population of them. Name tags blurred together, becoming an amalgamation of names the more of them I sneaked glances at. Recreation tents, volleyball courts, outdoor movie area, swimming pools, the outdoor tracks, too many food courts to count; we'd searched them all, over and over.

"I have no idea how we're going to find him or *if* we ever can," Bilba said between huge bites of the greasy pizza, which added a shine to the corners of his mouth.

"We keep looking," Ralrek said around a mouthful of creamy bagel.

Three more soldiers passed, two of them smoking. If they weren't dodging bullets or bombs, they taunted death with those stinking pollutant sticks. What was it with mortals doing everything they could to accelerate their own demise? None of their name tags read Vicu.

"It might be easier if we spend more time trying to catch everyone's name then staring at food menus or swimsuit calendars over at the PX," I said, knowing I was as guilty as any of us—hey, deployments are long and boring, and there are not a lot of females on them.

"Ouch," Ralrek laughed.

"I'm talking about you too. If you looked at name tags of every single guy who walked by instead of their asses, we could have eliminated half the post by now. I thought you hated them? One guy in Germany changes your entire outlook? Must have been a great kisser."

"Don't be jealous of the buffet the Army has laid out for me, Zeke. I can still not be a fan of them while enjoying the aesthetic beauty of His creation, can't I? Plus, you're wrong. I've been looking as hard as you."

"The only thing hard you've been looking at is—"

A pair of female soldiers walked by. Bilba's head followed.

"Definitely not named Chax," I said. "Seriously, come on, guys. How are we going to find him if you both can't stay focused?"

"Because it's not our issue?" Ralrek said with a shrug.

"That's disgusting," I said, crumbling the paper wrapper

from my sub sandwich into a ball, throwing it on my tray and getting up.

Bilba set his slice of pizza down, but still held it. "Where are you going?"

"To do the right thing," I said over my shoulder, walking to the trashcan, dumping my tray and turning to look at the open food court area.

Surrounded by fifteen foot high concrete walls, hundred soldiers filled the enclosed area, sitting at dozens of picnic tables. Food trailers lined the perimeter. The layout made it difficult to navigate while appearing casually interested in the various food offerings. We came here because the layout corralled hungry soldiers and was an excellent observational opportunity. Conversations were abundant, insightful, and often entertaining, but were rarely helpful. Time was ticking away, and we were no closer to finding Chax than when we left Cancer. She said she'd seen him weeks before we discovered each other's secret. It was possible Chax arrived in the theater before us, which meant he would rotate out earlier too. That could happen soon, or already had. Each second we wasted was another closer to him potentially stepping on the rotator plane back to the Underworld via Qatar and America.

It didn't help that the only thing we had on him was his name and Cancer's description. She said he was tall, but not as tall as Ralrek, and white. That he had rounded cheekbones and his upper lip always looked like it was being pulled up toward his nose. A tall, thin, white guy in the military—why did I ever think this would be a simple task? Besides gender and skin tone, every single blessed soldier looked like the other. While my hair had grown out, the humans preferred the uniform close shave approach.

There had to be an easier way to find him.

I kept moving because standing still was ineffective and ridiculous. After making a pass around the court, Ralrek and Bilba still hadn't left the table. At least they watched me until

I made eye contact, then looked away each time I caught them. The tips of Bilba's ears turned pink.

I grumbled under my breath. Ninety-nine percent of these soldiers were fit, white males. Chax could be any or none of them.

Ten days of public spaces visits had turned up nothing, and hanging around the food court was hopeless, so I decided to head toward the unprotected road on the other side of the T-wall barriers. A two-directional gap in the cement slabs forced foot traffic leaving the court to pass through in a single-file. It was the only vantage point that narrowed the mass to a manageable level.

Not thirty seconds after taking a position outside the walls, Ralrek and Bilba joined me.

"What are you doing? You didn't have to leave," Ralrek said, still holding a half-moon of bagel.

I pointed at the T-wall gap. "If Chax is in there, he has to come out this way."

"You can't watch both."

"Nope, you're going to take that side," I answered. "Both of you, since this doesn't seem urgent for you, it will take twice your effort to match mine. I can handle this side alone. Just …" I took the heat out of my voice, "just *try* to keep your eyes open for him."

"Sure thing, boss," Ralrek said, walking away while stuffing the bagel in his mouth. Part of me hoped he choked on it. This was the old Ralrek, the one I didn't like. Why wasn't this more important to him?

An hour passed with no sign of the demon Cancer needed us to find, unless we missed him during the few times inbound soldiers met outgoing and the jumbled mess made reading name tags impossible. The meal I'd shared with Bilba and Ralrek along with the setting Iraqi sun sapped my energy and did little to reduce the funk of being out in the heat for so long. It wasn't helping anyone's temperament either.

"This is stupid," Ralrek grumbled from fifteen feet away outside the opposite exit from the food court. He sat on the aluminum picnic table reserved for smokers, given away by two brown cigarette butt cans underneath each end of the table.

Bilba shuffled between looking at him and me. "Yeah, come on, Zeke. How long do you expect to wait for him? There's no guarantee he's in there or even headed this way. We can be out here for a month and never see him. We've been looking for over a week now."

"You don't think I don't know that?" I snapped. Maybe it was the digested food working its way through my system or the unbearable heat, but my patience was exhausted. I ignored the fact it might be attributable to my negligent agreement to this impossible task.

I wanted to help Cancer. She was everything I hoped to see in my fellow demons, those who constantly disappointed me. She hadn't, giving of herself to so many, even humans. She put herself at risk by living in a war-torn city to provide medical care for locals they wouldn't have without her. It wasn't pretentious or self-centered. Anyone who doubted her only had to look in her face while she served the Iraqis to see her passion for what she was doing. In so many ways, Cancer was a lot like Aries. I could help her, and hopefully, in a way, make up for failing Aries.

"You guys can head back out if you want to."

Bilba shuffled his feet. Ralrek held a handful of small pebbles and was picking one at a time, tossing them against the base of the T–wall.

"Seriously guys, head back to the trailer, the rec tent … whatever. I'm fine and I'm staying because I have no idea what else to do. It's really either this or the mess halls."

Ralrek jumped off the picnic table, his feet crunching the rock. "If you say so. Try not to stay out too late or you'll miss chow in the morning. But, seriously, you have to do what you want to do, but I don't get the whole point of this."

I risked missing Chax by dropping my gaze to between my feet. "I don't expect you to. Cancer can't get on any of the posts, and it's not like she can confront him in the middle of a patrol. Some of these gung-ho bastards would shoot her just to help fill their day. We are her only hope of finding him."

Bilba looked beyond me, along the T-wall barrier wall. "Come here," he whispered, like an impling who had discovered a secret stash of cookies and didn't want his parents to know.

"What is it?"

Bilba waved his hand aggressively, mouthing silently for me to move to him. I did.

"Try to be casual, but turn around and look at that guy against the T-wall. He's smoking. Tall, thin."

I tried to act as nonchalant as possible, bending to one knee to untie and then re-tie my boot. Three soldiers exited the food court, providing cover for me to spy. The soldier was a thin, white male who could have been a few years older than my relative age. He was half-turned away, smoking—of course.

"What about him?"

"You can be so frustrating sometimes."

"We share that."

"Whatever." Bilba moved closer, lowering his voice. "I'm going to take it you didn't see his name tag?"

I hadn't, and he took my nonresponse as a response.

"If you were paying attention instead of pouting—" Ouch! "You would have. Anyway. It says Vicu."

I spun. So much for subtlety. My eyes honed in on the soldier's name tag as he turned forward and blew out a white puff of carcinogens. Bilba was right. After ten long days of searching we'd stumbled into our incubus, who'd been here long enough to pick up the nasty human habit of polluting his lungs.

His eyes flicked in our direction, probably because of my awkward movement.

"Do you think that's him?" Bilba asked.

"There's only one way to find out." Before he could ask how, I called out. "Hey! Chax! How have you been?"

At the mention of his name, Chax Vicu, Cancer's Curse Bringer, looked our way, the cigarette hand dangling at his waist. We made eye contact before he flicked the cigarette to the gravel and bolted, disappearing around the corner of the T-wall.

"Bless it!" I snarled, giving chase.

"Where are you going?" Bilba shouted as I raced around the T-wall.

I didn't waste time. This might be the only chance to confront Chax. Lose it and we might never cross paths again.

Around the corner, he was thirty yards ahead of me and breaking into a sprint. I stretched my stride to overtake him. This had to happen quickly. Two soldiers sprinting in the Iraqi heat wasn't normal. In a war zone it would only raise paranoia, even for this jaded populace. I gained momentum. Within fifty yards, I was on him, grabbing him by the bottom flap of his uniform top and spinning him around.

"What do you want?" he spat. "Leave me alone!"

I slammed him against the T-wall, snarling into his face. "Don't make a scene."

Chax's hand went to my wrist and tried to pull it away. He couldn't match my strength, even with the advantage of leverage from superior height. "Let go of me, asshole."

"Not a chance. We need to have a conversation. And that's not a request."

He looked at my single, lonely chevron, and laughed. It was full of cockiness and privilege. "Private, you better get your hands off me. I'm an NCO."

I moved my face close enough to smell the remnants of his cigarette. "I know what you are."

His brow furrowed at the implication. "What are you talking about? I will report your ass, Private ..." He searched for my name tag that was partially covered by my rifle strap. He huffed, "Let go of me and show me your name tag. You're going to pay for this."

"The only one paying is you," I said. "Now, I will let go. Be a smart little soldier boy and don't run. I'll just catch you again and I won't be so kind next time."

Bilba and Ralrek joined us. Chax tensed. "Who in the heaven do you think you are? A bunch of junior enlisted who think they can bully an NCO? I'll have your heads."

"No, you won't, Chax," I said, gripping his utility top in a fist. I flicked my head to the side toward a covered smoking area—yes, there are a lot of those provided to military personnel, especially in deployed locations. "What you'll do is join us over there and smile the whole way so everyone will think you couldn't be happier than in this moment."

Chax looked to the smoking pit. His voice shook. "Why?"

I pulled him off the wall, spinning him and encouraging him along with a shove. "Get moving."

Chax grunted as he caught his balance. Fortunately, this part of the post was empty. The T-wall barriers hid us from the food court, and only a trickle of soldiers walked down the road toward the showers and personal trailers. They were too far away to notice. This was a safe place as any for a conversation.

"Sit." I pointed at a bench. Chax huffed but did.

He dug into his pocket and pulled out a box of cigarettes. He flipped the top open, gave the box a sharp flick, popping up an uneven strand of cigarettes, and put one in between his lips, lighting it. "One thing I sure as fuck know is that you have no idea who I am."

I gave my head a quick shake. "Actually, we're quite familiar with you."

His eyes turned to a sneer. "You have no fucking clue."

"Don't be so quick to be that confident," Ralrek said with a sarcastic laugh.

"Why?"

"We have a mutual ... friend," Ralrek said, climbing on the picnic table just out of reach of Chax but close enough to make the other demon uncomfortable. I appreciated the gesture.

Chax slowly clapped his hands. "Good for you. Losers like you have friends." He pushed himself to his feet. "But I'm an NCO and I've got a million things to do, so unless you have something specific you needed, I need to report your pathetic asses. Your deployment will get nastier by the time I'm done."

He took a step forward, but I blocked his path.

"Get out of my way," he growled.

"I won't tell you again," I said in a voice so low he had to listen carefully. "Sit down, shut up and listen. You're not leaving until we're done talking to you about a problem you're going to clear up."

Chax read my expression. I met his eyes but covertly released a breath when he crept backward and re-took his seat.

I said, "It seems your family has a problem with a friend of ours and has caused her some headaches."

"What problem? I haven't done shit to no one," Chax said so confidently he could be telling the truth.

"If I said our friend's family name is Nijal, what would you say to that?"

I didn't have to watch Chax's reaction carefully. His understanding and associated panic was immediate. He couldn't hide it if he'd been trained to.

"Wha-who ... who are you guys?"

With a cocky smirk, I crossed my arms. "Let's focus on what we're here to talk about."

Chax laughed. It was fake and grating.

"I don't see what's so funny."

He answered by leaning against the picnic table, raising his elbows to rest on it, the cigarette dangling between lazy fingers. It vibrated with a shake he was trying to hide. "Did they put you up to this? Want to bully me, huh? I don't tolerate bullies."

"No one ... no one is bullying you." Bilba said.

"That's exactly what you're trying to do, and it won't work!" Chax's disposition didn't match his words. He was trying to look composed, unruffled. But hearing Cancer's family's name bothered him. His eyes flicked with clarity and he leaned forward now, resting his elbows on his knees and pointing with a two fingered swivel motion. "You're demons. You can't do a blessed thing about this here without getting your asses in serious trouble. So drop this adorable tough guy act. I promise, if you push me, you're not going to like my reaction."

Bilba swallowed slowly enough that I could easily track his Adam's apple bobbing. In truth, Chax's bravado bothered me, but if I couldn't show similar confidence, this chance, likely our only one, would go to waste. I watched him. His confidence was building again, washing away the anxiety we had briefly introduced. Demons who shifted like that made me nervous because it usually meant they had an advantage others couldn't see or they were delusional. Chax Vicu looked like a dick, but he didn't look crazy.

What was I missing?

He sneered. "Let me guess. Whoever sent you is claiming to be a victim, that they're somehow oppressed by my family? Is that right?"

"Something like that," I said, not nearly as confident as I'd been only a minute ago. I needed to keep as much information close–hold as possible.

"And I'm assuming that this poor victim of yours told you exactly how they were victimized?"

"Your family put a curse on her great-grandfather that has spread to other family members," Bilba said before I could stop him, handing the advantage to Chax. I wanted to palm-slap my face.

"Cancer? You losers know Cancer?" None of us responded, answering the question for him. "Oh, this is rich. How is that petty bitch doing nowadays? She obviously hasn't changed much, since she continues to send her boyfriends to take care of her business. If she thinks the likes of you will bully me into submission, she's wrong."

A pebble trickled across the concrete slab. It had come from Ralrek. "No one is bullying you, you little twat."

Chax looked like Ralrek had called the entire Vicu family cherubs. "You ... you can't call me that. I'm an NCO and we're in the Overworld. I'll make sure you three rot in jail for this."

"All you are is a weak demon from a conniving family who likes to torture others," I said. If Chax thought he could raise his voice and intimidate us, I wanted to send clear signals that he wasn't the only one who could. Sometimes when cornered by a snarling hellhound, your only defense was to snarl back.

"Weak? Weak?" His voice raised each time he repeated the word.

"I'm pretty sure that's what I said," I said, adrenaline making me tense.

Burning around the rims of my eyes distracted me. I smelled ... *onions*. Discernment magic!

In a flash, so rapid even Ralrek jumped, I was on Chax, grabbing his throat. His hands shot up, spinning the cigarette through the air. The lit end landed on the back of my hand. I flinched but didn't release him. The burning in my eyes ceased, the onions, gone.

"Zeke!" Bilba shouted in disbelief.

"What are you doing?" Ralrek couldn't disguise his panic either. He was on his feet beside me.

I squeezed Chax's throat. His eyes widened.

"He was casting," I said with a snarl.

"Dumbass," Ralrek snorted at the demon I was choking, and sat on the bench again as if Chax's predicament was as interesting as a chess match.

"You shouldn't do that. Zeke can tell." Bilba smirked.

"Don't try that again, you idiot," I said in a low hiss, inching my hand from Chax's throat before a human tripped across our confrontation.

"Who … who are you guys?"

"You're going to make right with her and her family, and you'll do it while you're in Baghdad. You're not waiting until you get home, under the protection of your family. This gets done now."

Chax straightened his collar, trying to compose himself. After a moment of useless uniform manipulation, he ran his hand over his head. "What the heaven can I do? I got drafted just like you guys. Plus, I'm not the one who started this. This whole feud thing goes way back, long before me. Long before her."

He said that last word like it was the most disgusting thing he would ever have to say.

"It doesn't matter. You're *going* to stop it."

Chax looked up, the fire of defiance burning in his eyes. "Oh yeah, genius? Exactly how am I supposed to do that?"

"Well." I stopped, patting my pocket for the note—the note I had left on my nightstand, back in the trailer I shared with Bilba. Shit. "I know how. I just don't have it on me right now, but I'll find you again and then you'll remove the curse. After that, your family swears to hers that this stupid feud is over and that you're deeply sorry for the harm you caused them. I don't care what you need to do. Stop the blessed curse."

"Or?"

"There isn't an option."

Chax chuckled and dug into his pocket for a fresh cigarette. "You'd risk upsetting the Balance for scum like her? Oh, that's pathetic."

I slapped him across the cheek; I don't know what overcame me. He reeled, half spinning toward the picnic table, leaning on it with an elbow and whimpering. I hadn't even used a quarter of my strength.

Bilba's mouth hung open. Ralrek just smiled and bounced a pebble off the back of Chax's shoulders.

My sensitivity to my surroundings told me what I would see before I turned. The empty road confirmed. No pedestrians or vehicles. We were still okay. For now.

"You just tried to cast, so don't act like you're concerned with upsetting the Balance. I'm not playing around. Tonight, I'm grabbing the note and then we'll meet up for chow in the morning and I'll get it to you. And if that doesn't work, then whatever you have to do; write a letter to your mommy and daddy, beg your auntie to stop this silliness, make an elixir, whatever. Stop the curse before it causes more harm."

He turned to face me, which must have been difficult. Shame filled his eyes behind crocodile tears.

"You're a damn fool for believing everything the Nijal scum tell you."

"Seems like he is itching for another beat down," Ralrek mocked. "Maybe you should slap him again?"

Chax flinched without me making a move.

"No. But I will do much worse if he doesn't fix this."

Hand still pressed against his cheek, Chax whined. "She's got you eating out of her hand, believing every word. Her family aren't the victims, let me tell you. They've been putting curses on us just as long as we've been cursing them. This didn't start with some stupid spat, like they lie about. It goes back longer than that. You don't want to get involved in this, Private ... Sunstone." He read my name tag that was exposed when I slapped him and my rifle strap shifted. Well, bless it. "Trust me."

I swatted away his threat. "Don't tell me what I want to do, Chax." I refused to refer to him by his mortal sergeant rank, no matter how much he embraced it. "I'll get involved until you take care of this. All you have to do is put an end to it. You do that and we're good. You don't, and—"

"I know, I know. You're going to make my life a living heaven." Chax paused, holding up a single finger. "But what you don't understand is that you'll never be able to do that before I crush you. You have no idea who my family is, but trust me, they're more powerful than an army of yours. If you're screwing with me to protect precious little Cancer, you're going to regret it for the rest of your life."

There's something to be said for confidence. Doubt fell around me like a blanket. What had we stepped into? Demons rarely acted like he was now unless they had good justification. I couldn't deny that I might have agreed too quickly to take Cancer's side. Just because she was a giving and caring nurse to the mortals didn't mean that back in the Underworld she and her family were free of guilt. I mean, really, I didn't know her from Shiva. Had I made a wrong and regrettable miscalculation? Had I just ruined not only my life, but Bilba and Ralrek's as well?

"Chow." I snarled. "That's when you stop this."

As we made him hand over his security card to get his unit's information to find him whenever we needed, I stuffed my hands in my pockets to prevent him from seeing them shake.

Ralrek tapped him on the head. "Be a good boy and don't let us down."

"Yeah, Zeke is small, but he's as vicious as a hellhound

when he wants to be," Bilba grinned dumbly, obviously enjoying the pile-on. Unfortunately for me, in his exuberance, he'd also just given Chax my nickname, after the incubus already had my last name.

Great. Would that come back to bite me?

After getting the information we needed, we walked away. Ralrek and Bilba's humored reflection of how scared Chax looked faded into a blur of noise. I reflected on the incubus's confident statement that I would regret this for the rest of my life. We hadn't made it back to our trailer before I believed Chax was telling the truth.

14

BAGHDAD

CHAX DIDN'T SHOW up for chow, and avoided us throughout the three weeks since our confrontation under the overhang. I did everything I could to get him alone, but he kept himself surrounded by others. Making him recite the counter-spell had proven impossible. On some level, it probably qualified as stalking, but I stopped caring about Chax's priorities from the moment he opened his arrogant mouth and dropped his first threat.

Despite our efforts, the issue of a curse had not been resolved, at least by Cancer's prescribed method. Bilba said he thought he remembered there being other ways to break spells, but without guide books, all of which were back in Hell, he could not be sure. We couldn't be sure if Cancer had found another way, or even tried to find another solution, because we had not patrolled her neighborhood since the fateful day she revealed herself to be a succubus before sharing her family's struggle.

Until I could see Cancer again, I was going to stick to Chax like the pages of a young imp's succubi magazine. I caught him leaving the rec tent one night with three other soldiers, and I followed them back to his unit's housing area.

We already knew his unit, so I knew the general area of where he bedded down, but not the exact trailer. Now I did. And I made sure he was aware I knew where he lived and used that to keep the pressure on. He reminded me, carefully, since there were three clueless mortal witnesses, that I would pay. We maintained a mutually hostile relationship. Working toward resolution with him wasn't a priority until I confirmed that Cancer and her family were free of the curse, which wasn't possible from my current position, flat on my back, listening to a podcast.

Bilba burst into the trailer he and I shared, one hundred square feet of intimacy. "Oh my Lucifer, Zeke. Did you hear?"

I sat on my bed, listening. "I don't hear anything."

"Ha, ha, funny," Bilba said, his back to me as he closed the door and began stripping off his uniform.

"No, seriously," I said, closing my eyes and ready to push the earbud back in my ear to resume the podcast I'd been trying to enjoy, "what am I supposed to be hearing?"

"Not literally," Bilba corrected. "I'm talking about the rumors." When I didn't respond, he clarified. "About our next patrol?"

"What about it?"

He collapsed to his bed with a frustrated grunt. "We're heading back into Cancer's part of Khadra! Maybe we can finally get this business of the curse over with."

At the news, I sat up, podcast forgotten. "Don't screw with me."

"I'm not. That's what I heard."

Finally. Cancer would hear our news about Chax, if the curse wasn't already lifted. We could put this behind us or keeping looking for a way to isolate Chax. Either way, we'd have clarity on the situation, and that beat this ambiguity every day of the week.

"This is the first time I'm looking forward to going to work after chow," I said, a sly smile spreading across my face.

"I thought you would like that."

"I do, my friend. For the first time since we got to this horrible place I feel like we're doing something worthwhile, if that makes sense?"

Bilba laid back on his bed. "It does." He wrapped his hands behind his head and stared up at the ceiling. "But it isn't the only thing we've done, Zeke. The picture may be too big to see the entire thing, but our time here hasn't been wasted. We've done good for the mortals."

"I think the Russians and insurgents would disagree." I rolled onto my side and looked at my best friend. "Do you really believe we're making a difference with what we're doing? Do you really think anything is going to change for any of them by the time we leave? Honestly, sometimes it feels like we're just pushing the cyclops down the road, hoping someone else will deal with it."

He turned his head, hands still locked behind it. "What else can we do?"

I rolled onto my back, sighing. "I don't know. Something." Thoughts rolled through my mind of all the things I would do if I was Lucifer, all of them more active than the role us demons in the Overworld were serving now. "Instead of sending us to pass the time until we go home or died, maybe we could do something that would change the course of this situation."

"That's not how it works, Zeke. Politics are tricky. You can't just force change."

"There won't be change if no one does anything more than dance around the subject, hoping they don't flinch when the other side says boo."

Bilba's bed creaked when he spun and sat up, facing me. "You would want an all-out war?"

I looked at my best friend, whose eyes had grown wide. "What?" I laughed, short. "No. I want to go home, and prefer-ably not in a coffin. I'm talking about real progress. Look at how these mortals live. This was happening to them before we got here and it will after we leave. Heavens, it has for generations now. What life is this for them? And all along, right under their noses, there are demons and angels being pulled by Lucifer and Yahweh, positioned and counter-positioned. For what? Nothing changes."

Bilba put his hands on his knees, his shoulders slumping like a father trying to be patient with a stubborn child. "Maybe that's all the Balance is? Maybe it doesn't move. Think of it like a metal ball braced between two blocks of wood. You hold one and I hold the other. We have to push against each other's block to keep the ball steady in the middle. Too much tension and one of us will shift the ball and it will spurt right out. Too little tension and the ball just drops to the ground. Maybe that's what this, the Balance, is? Maybe this is all it will ever be?"

Bless him and his insight. How did you argue against something like that and how could anyone be satisfied with a reality like the one my friend proposed? What was the purpose of our existence, the angels, heavens, even the mortals, if Bilba were close to pinning the nature of the Balance?

"Hey, if nothing else, it gave us something to think about to pass the time until we can get out of here."

"A little callous, but I get where you're coming from." I swung my feet over the edge of my bunk. He might have moved on easily, but I wouldn't. I couldn't. So, I needed to force a break before my thought train took me down a trail I didn't want to walk. The podcast wouldn't do, but food would, because there are few things incubi enjoyed more than food. "Want to grab chow before we report in? I am absolutely starving."

Bilba rocketed out of the bed at the mention of food. "Me too. Let's go."

It was one of the best meals I'd had yet during this deployment, something I really needed to shut up my dark thoughts. Before long, we were cutting our way through the side streets of Khadra.

We turned the corner to Cancer's clinic, and I nearly stumbled. Something was wrong. Not one person hung around the building. The street was quiet, but some locals were out, at least until we came around. But the small clinic was different than ever before, as if everyone had abandoned the building.

"Sir," I said, and Sergeant Jones stopped the patrol.

"What, Sunstone?"

I nodded at the building. "Can we check in?"

"Again?" he sighed. "Is she really that cute to you?"

I shook my head, the gravity of the situation blocking any thoughts, true or not, about how attractive Cancer was. "It's not that, sir. I think something is wrong."

He turned, looking at the building. "I don't see anything. We keep going."

He didn't notice the quiet; he couldn't have. He didn't notice the way the door wasn't fully closed even though no one waited outside; he should have. He didn't notice the marks in the door that hadn't been there before and signaled that it had been forced open from the outside.

I drew a deep breath through my nose, stopping from calling him out in front of the entire squad. Jones seemed to sense my frustration.

"Jesus H. Christ, Sunstone. Go ahead."

I raced into the building without waiting for him to change his mind or to assign any of the other squad members. Delay was not an option.

Pushing the door open, I halted in the doorway. Sniffing, I gagged and turned from the wrecked room when the pungent, rotten rust smell hit me. The clinic was empty, of people, medical equipment, and beds. Blood-stained sheets were coiled on the floor. The cabinet was smashed like someone had beaten it with a bat and tipped it over. The privacy curtains hung in shreds, as if someone had taken a sword to them.

My hand slipped to my leg. My rifle wasn't appropriate in these small confines with concrete walls that could ricochet a bullet if I fired. But Creed's magic would work, and I was willing to chance upsetting the Balance to save Cancer, even though my more rational part of my brain said this destruction happened well before today.

Inching Creed up so that the knob poked out of the flap of my pocket, gripped in my fist, I made my way to the rear room, extending my senses for any sight, sound, or spell that might be waiting.

The rotten rust smell was worse back here. Empty shelving greeted me. The refrigerator and single stool were gone, along with every blanket and bottle of medication. The floor was covered in dried blood, the source of the funk. Violence.

Everything, all of Cancer's work, ruined.

I moved to the front room in a daze, not sure what to do. Too many thoughts buzzed, too many ways to respond and no way of knowing how to do them or who to do them to. The rot and decay told me we'd abandoned Cancer to this.

"Chax," I growled. This wasn't about a curse. This was demon–made, done out of vengeance.

I stepped out into the day, and Sergeant Jones' gaze hardened when he saw my face. Bilba and Ralrek raced to me.

"Something happened. An attack," I said in an exasperated voice. "There's blood. Cancer."

The squad moved in my direction before Jones instructed two guys to head inside to confirm what I saw, while the rest secured our surroundings. "Go see what they know," he said to Muhammad, pointing at a pair of locals who sat at a small table outside a closed bakery.

"What happened?" Bilba asked.

"Is she ...?" Ralrek followed up.

I pointed back toward the empty doorway. "I don't know. Someone robbed her and destroyed the clinic, and there is blood everywhere. At best, she's injured. At worst ..."

"We'll find her," Ralrek said, grabbing my rifle strap and giving it a tug. "Head up, Zeke. Focus."

My eyes flickered. He was right; we would find Cancer. And then I was going to find Chax Vicu. I rubbed my face. "Let's go."

"How?" Bilba turned, looking around the street as if it would answer.

The dusty road became my focal point. The swirling thoughts clouded my mind. The urge to run in every direction at once, invading every home regardless of how dangerous, safe, unethical, or taboo pulled at me. My skin prickled with the burning desire to whip Creed out of its hiding place, activate it, and go looking for Chax, even if I had to walk all the way back to the post. Right now, even an entire company of mortals could not stop me from putting an end to this.

"Zeke? Are you okay" Bilba's voice drifted in through my fog. I tried to reach back out to him, feeling myself falling toward the emotional tumult raging inside.

A sturdy hand on my shoulder pulled me further from the doorway. In my clouded state I didn't recognize who it was. It wasn't until the vice grip led me around the corner of the building, away from the rest of the squad, that I looked into the eyes of Sergeant Jones.

"Snap out of it, Sunstone," Jones ordered, holding me by both shoulders and leaning his head in towards mine. "What's going on? Give me a status."

I recapped what I found in the clinic.

I saw something in his eyes, something beyond the Army, mortal and beautifully human. "We'll find her," was all he said, before straightening and allowing the harshness to return to his face. "Now, get yourself together. We've got a job to do."

He disappeared around the corner, leaving me to follow. After a few seconds, reassured, I felt better, my head clearer, and rejoined the squad. Just before I reached the front of the building, something scraped behind me. I expected a stray dog, hoping for a precious meal, or a rodent trying to avoid the hot Iraq sun. The small boy was neither.

"Soldier?" said the tiny, frail voice in Arabic.

I looked into the eyes of a familiar young boy. He stood on one leg, using makeshift crutches to navigate.

I rushed to him and got down on a knee. "Hi," I said awkwardly, careful to not betray my ability to speak the native language to my squad. I gestured to the boy's missing leg. "How are you feeling?"

He smiled. "It doesn't hurt anymore. It aches sometimes, but Miss Cancer said that's normal. She told me I'm so brave and strong that it will keep getting better."

Cancer? The boy she'd saved talked about her as if they'd just had a conversation. I wanted to hug this kid.

"Is Miss Cancer okay?" I tilted my head back toward the clinic. "Do you know what happened?"

The boy's big, round eyes drifted to the building. He nodded so subtlety it looked like he was fearful of being watched and didn't want to give anything away.

"What? What happened?"

His eyes locked on mine, defying his age. His cheeks held the robustness of youth, round and smooth, but in that moment, when his lips pinched, they took on a solid defiance, a sort of internal rebellion of someone three times as old. "Mean men came a couple days ago and took everything. They hurt Miss Cancer, soldier. Hurt her bad."

My throat seized. "How bad? Is she okay? Do you know where she is?"

This time the boy nodded viciously, a wicked smile of victory spreading across his lips. I liked this kid's attitude.

"Yes, soldier. I know where she is, and she is okay. She sleeps too much, though."

Without thinking. I rubbed the boy's arm. He hobbled backward at my touch and almost toppled.

"I'm so sorry. Please forgive me?"

The boy still smiled, trust unbroken.

I smiled back at him graciously. "I would like to see Miss Cancer. Can you take me to her?"

He nodded and turned, hobbling down the street. I shot to my feet, spinning to find Sergeant Jones and ask for permission to follow. But Jones was right in front of me, his eyes wide.

"How long have you been able to speak Arabic?" he asked cautiously.

Busted.

Wanting to avoid further questioning and the dangerous territory those answers would lead to, I answered with more information than he'd asked for. "The entire time, sir. I didn't tell you because I didn't report it during my recruitment process, and I wasn't sure how the Army would treat that, sir. I promise, we were just talking about Cancer. She's hurt, but alive. The boy will take us to her."

Sergeant Jones didn't react initially, dragging out the torture. Then he glanced at the interpreter and smirked. "I know. Muhammad conveyed the entire conversation while you were having it. You were so engrossed asking about your girlfriend that you didn't even hear us come up behind you, soldier. You'll need to be more careful in the future."

My chest released the stress at his accommodating attitude.

Then he snapped at me. "What are you doing standing here? We've got to go find this American."

The squad followed the one–leg boy for blocks. It was slow-going and drew the attention of locals.

"Wave and smile, boys. Wave and smile," Sergeant Jones ordered and modeled the behavior he wanted us to copy.

So we did. Some of the men who had stopped to watch us waved back. Most didn't. None smiled. A boy kicked a soccer ball to Bilba, who tried to stop it by placing his foot on top of it when it rolled up to him. Except Bilba is clumsy on the best of days. His foot slipped over the top and his leg splayed forward, pulling away from his plant leg. He crashed to the ground, landing on his ass and a melody of rattling gear. The boys laughed. So did we. Just below the rim of his helmet, Bilba's ears turned pink.

"How far away is she?" I asked the boy after we'd stopped laughing at my best friend.

He pulled up and leaned on his crutch to point down the street. "She's there."

"Is she in a hospital?" An Iraqi hospital might not even allow us in their front door. I had no idea if it was legal under the terms of military operations. That was way above my pay grade.

The boy shook his head. "She is with friends."

We headed deeper into the Khadra neighborhood, a long and empty lot bordered the street to our left.

"I don't like this," Sergeant Jones mumbled, looking at the lot that stretched for the entire block.

I agreed. Exposure created vulnerabilities. Insurgents in an abandoned building could attack while we were stuck in the middle of the street without cover. But the one-legged boy was setting our pace, and he was hobbling as fast as possible. I needed to keep Sergeant Jones focused on the good he was doing, and distraction would help achieve that.

"Can I ask your name?" I asked the boy.

"Yasin," he said comfortably.

"Thank you for your help, Yasin. But we need to go home soon. Are we close?"

He nodded, his small head angled at the sidewalk as he

scoped for obstacles while swinging the crutches. His thin body swiveled from back to front.

I smiled at his determination and turned to Sergeant Jones. "We're almost there."

We turned the corner, away from the empty lot.

"There it is, soldier. That big building over there," Yasin said with a jerk of his head.

Across and down the street, a three-story building towered over the single-story homes surrounding it.

"Is that somebody's home?"

Yasin nodded. "Miss Cancer's friend's. She's a very important person. Miss Cancer is lucky."

That was debatable, but I wasn't going to deflate the hopes of such a courageous boy. We reached the home, a modest but clean structure that dominated this side of the street. Yasin hopped up the steps with ease even after the long walk.

About to follow him in, Jones stopped me by grabbing my arm. "Let Muhammad go in first. We need to handle this with tact."

I nodded, and Muhammad walked into the home with Yasin. We waited.

I paced.

"You're going to wear a hole in the dirt," Ralrek commented with a wry smile.

"Anxious," I replied, looking up and down the street for anyone who might be a threat.

"She's being taken care of, Zeke," Bilba said.

I knew he was trying to be helpful, but I did not want to hear any of it right now. I could not ignore the convenience of the attack on her and her clinic after she asked for our help and we confronted Chax. Two years. Nearly two years in Iraq and Cancer had not been assaulted before. Within three weeks of talking to us, less actually, she had been. She was not a victim of a senseless crime; the attack was deliberate.

Muhammad's re-appearance settled my building tension a

few minutes later. "Only one may come in," Muhammad said in his typically tight style.

I turned to Sergeant Jones, begging him to allow me to be the one. "No one can get what I can. Plus ..." *I want to see her*, I finished silently.

He sighed. "Go ahead, private. But be watchful."

"I will, sir," I said and hurried inside before he changed his mind.

"Whistle if anything is wrong, Sunstone." He called after me. "We'll light this fucker to the sky if they look at you wrong."

Yasin waited for me in the cramped entry. Next to him was a middle-aged woman as round as she was tall. Her hands were clasped, as if she was trying to keep them from shooting in the air. Noting her caution, I kept my mouth shut.

"Come with me," she said in a way of greeting and ascended the stairs.

I followed, taking a second to check the front room for potential threats. If one came from the three middle-aged women sitting there, it wasn't obvious. One of them gave me a flitting smile before returning to her chai tea.

The stairs creaked as we ascended. The house smelled of fresh bread and my stomach growled, reminding me that wonderful culinary work transcends international borders and those between mortals and immortals—though it definitely favored the species with the shorter lifespan.

We reached the landing. The woman raised her arm to a doorway with a silk purple and gold curtain drawn across it.

"She is in there. She has been resting. Do not stay long or I will pull you out by your ear."

I nodded, failing to keep the smile off my face. "Yes, of course. Thank you."

She gave me a strange look before rocking slowly down the stairs. I pulled the curtain aside. Cancer was laid in a bed, a compress across her forehead. Her brown skin was paler than normal and there was a bandage wrapped from her elbow to wrist on one arm. One cheekbone shone purple with a healing bruise. Her loose curls were as chaotic as ever. For some reason, it lifted my spirits.

Her eyes slid over to me. The corners of her mouth curled up in a weak smile. "About time you showed up."

"Hey." I smiled, walking over to the bed, having no idea what I was doing with my hands, awkwardly going to shake her hand, rub her arm, or move the hair out of her face all at the same time. Instead of making a creepy ass out of myself, I intertwined my fingers and clamped down on them. "How are you feeling?"

Her head lolled to one side. "I've been better." Her eyes narrowed. "Not to sound ungrateful, but how did you find me?"

"I don't give up my sources, but he's about this," I said, raising my hand to just above my waist, "tall."

Cancer struggled to keep the smile off her face. "Yasin is such a brat. When I get better, I'm going to—"

"You're going to hug him," I said over top of Cancer's insincere criticism. "If he *hadn't* helped me find you, do you know what that would have done to me, heading back to the base without an idea of whether you were injured, missing, back in the United States, or dead?"

"The States," Cancer replied weakly.

"What?"

"Mortal soldiers don't call it the 'United States.' They just use the single word. You'll give yourself away if you're always that sloppy." Her smile spread now. "Speaking of, how did you convince your NCO to allow you to come see me."

"We're all here," I replied. "They're waiting outside, so I don't have long."

Cancer's eyes grew wider. "Your entire squad came?"

I nodded. "Of course."

"Good," she said, all humor wiped away.

"What's that?"

"What?"

I wiggled my finger at her face. "That. Something happened there when you asked that. You didn't want me here alone."

"Of course not," she answered. I noticed an edge to her voice. "This is still Baghdad and you're still, for all intents and purposes, an American soldier. Not exactly someone who can walk around the streets of the city freely. Plus ... there are other reasons."

"Like the people who destroyed your clinic?"

She nodded, not offering anything more.

"Who did it, Cancer?"

Her head turned, scrunching the poof of black curls to the pillow. "It was the curse, Zeke. I told you, it reaches my family here just as it does in the Second Circle. And with that family—" She couldn't use Chax's family name "—having someone in the Overworld, they have easy access to me. I sent word of what he did to my family, and who knows how they will respond. For all I know, for all I expect, they would have no problem putting these mortals in harm's way." She looked away, her chest rising in a deep, mournful breath. "I'm tired, Zeke. So tired. The curse ... it's wearing me down. I don't have the energy to fight him or, Lucifer forbid, any of his family who might also be here. There's already so much tragedy here. These mortals don't need more."

Even in suffering, Cancer thought of others. Remarkable.

"Chax acts like he doesn't know what's going on, denying having anything to do with a curse. In fact, he was pretty frustrating to deal with."

Her nostrils widened as she snorted. "He's like that. Enjoys playing stupid. Does it quite well. Did you get him the paper?"

I moved closer. We were speaking English, because that's what anyone within hearing range would expect. But I couldn't be sure that the women in the home weren't eavesdropping or able to speak the language. It wasn't worth the risk.

"I threatened him with his safety if he didn't end the curse," I admitted with a guilty smirk.

Cancer laughed heartily at first, and then, wincing, she coughed before catching her breath. Seeing her like this made me want to drag Chax Vicu into this modest room by the throat and hold him accountable for the toll this ridiculous family feud took on its victims.

"Sorry," she said when she'd recovered enough to speak. "But that was funny. I wish I could have seen his face. I don't imagine he took it well?"

"I can't get him alone, but we're not giving up," I said and shrugged. "We're always on the look out for him. When he wasn't denying this whole situation, he was telling us we needed to be careful."

"Really?"

I nodded. "Yep. Said his family was powerful, and that I had no idea who I was messing with and that we needed to mind our business or his family would make our lives miserable. Not exactly in those words, but in that spirit, for sure."

Cancer ripped the compress from her forehead and slapped it on the bed.

"What is it?"

Her eyes were filling with tears. "I'm so sick of this. I'm so tired of his family bullying us, of doing things like this to us. And they're never held accountable. They just use their connections and do whatever they want. No one cares because everyone is afraid of them."

"Is it true that your family has done things to his?"

Cancer's eyes shot to me. "What do you mean?"

"Chax said your family started this entire feud thing, that it predates the story you told me about your great-grandfather."

"That isn't a *story*." Cancer's thick lips twitched. "It's the truth. What? Are you going to believe what he told you? His family is the one cursing mine. The family that *has* been cursing mine. *He* is behind the attack on me and my clinic. The one that served thousands in Khadra. Where are they supposed to go now? Between the Americans and the Russians and all their Lucifer-blessed allies, the actual hospitals are being used for *their* needs, and those needs don't include serving the victims of this war."

"I get that, Cancer," I said in the calmest voice I could muster. "I'm just trying to understand the context of this entire situation."

"The context is that the Vicus have terrorized my family for thousands of years and Chax Vicu tried to have me killed," she said in a biting tone. The room felt hotter. "That's the only context needed. Honestly, I thought I could rely on you."

"You can," I said, hurt.

Cancer's voice grew quieter, still holding some heat. "Yet after you spoke to Chax, I'm attacked, and my clinic destroyed."

"That has nothing to do with being able to rely on me."

"What have you done about him then? What are you going to do when you get back behind your walls on the post? Are you going to help me stop him?"

Her conviction was substantial, but I needed facts. "Did you see him do it? Was he one of the men who attacked the clinic; who attacked you?"

"Of course not," she said, shaking her head. "He couldn't put himself at risk. You know that. No, he is working with the insurgents through his family's connections. That's who did the actual attacking, but Chax and his family were behind it. And ..." she trailed off.

"And what?" I asked after a while, not sure that having this conversation now was worth either of our time. Cancer was emotional, and that was blinding her. Her clinic, an extension of who she was, had been attacked by unknown men. She had not seen Chax. I did not know anyone with Hex magic and believed Bilba knew what he was talking about in terms of curses, but men attacking a nurse and destroying her clinic was not a spell. It was a violent display of manipulation to instill fear. Chax could still be—and probably was—guilty. If he was, I would help her. But I needed more than a lifetime of animosity to justify anything I did to the incubus. Heavens, I'd enjoy putting a good scare into him for what she was suffering through, I simply needed Cancer to give me something solid.

I wasn't going to be like the rest of demonkind and decide to act based purely on emotions.

"And I'm worried he'll do it again," Cancer said. "You don't know what it's like to live in constant paranoia and worry, that any time you turn around you might face another incident. These ... these deliberate acts to terrorize. Do you know how exhausting that is? I don't think you do."

I stopped myself from grabbing her hand, to show I still stood by her.

But I didn't. I stood where I stood, making no move to calm her beyond my words. "What do you want me to do, Cancer? If I can help, I will."

Cancer's head was turned toward the wall. She was quiet for so long I thought she fell asleep. I waited her out.

"Do you really want to know what you can do?"

"Yes. I want to help."

Turning to lie flat on her back, Cancer stared at the ceiling. Thick tears trailed down her cheek. She didn't bother to wipe them away.

"The next time you see him, if he doesn't recite the counter-spell, I want you to kill him, Zeke," she finally answered. "Kill Chax Vicu. While he's in the Overworld; kill him. That will send a clear signal to his family that the curse must end. Help my family, Zeke. Please help them. Then, we can live in peace, and I can focus on serving the mortals."

In a million years, I never expected someone like Cancer to ask for the death of another. She was supposed to be different from other demons.

"I can't do that," I said through a scratchy throat, memories of Taurus's death never far removed. Even the memory of Creed obliterating the Kaiserslautern assassin still haunted me. "I can't kill him, Cancer."

She huffed. "Then why did you even come see me? If you can't give me that, what can you give me that's worth anything?"

She didn't mean it; she couldn't. She was injured, angry, and probably scared. But I wasn't going to abandon her. I just had to prove it first.

"Justice," I said firmly. "I can give you justice."

15

BAGHDAD

I LEFT the demonic notepad open on the small nightstand next to my bed. The scratching woke me. I pushed myself up on my elbows and squinted against the bright desert sunlight prying itself into our trailer. My eyes were pulled away as the scratching continued, just underneath the constant whir of the small air conditioning unit.

Words scribbled out with big, reckless loops. No pen, no hand guided the writing, at least one not in the Overworld.

"You're getting a letter, Zeke," Bilba observed from his bed.

It was good I shared the hundred square foot Conex trailer with another demon. The magical appearance of letters on the demonic notebook paper would freak out a mortal. But since my roommate was Bilba, I could afford to leave it out on my nightstand.

The words formed. The letter was from Dialphio. It was the first time I heard from her, or anyone in the Underworld, in weeks. I wasn't the only one. Mortal and immortal, our loved ones at home seemed to worry at the beginning of the deployment, but that tailed off as everyone fell into a routine. Months into our Baghdad-based lives, and Bilba was the only one who had constant communication with anyone from home. His father checked in weekly.

Watching the words take form, it was nice to see something from Dialphio. I'd been missing her. I didn't pick up the notepad until the words stopped.

"What's it say?" Bilba asked, sitting on his bed, his legs crisscrossed as he wrote to his father.

It was the end of the week, a chance for us to catch our breath and prepare for the next six workdays, a time to catch up on everything we didn't have time for during the workweek. Laundry, cleaning up our living space, rest, and, yes, connection with those who were important to us were crammed into the single day in the week we had for ourselves.

"She's telling me how things are with the store. Sounds like it's going well. But she hired a part-timer. She told me I'm going to have to compete to get my job back, and I'm not sure if she's joking or not."

Bilba, his head bent as he wrote, jerked with a laugh. "I'm sure you're fine. She needs the help and will keep that demon on until we get home. You'll have your job back and be complaining that you do in no time. Don't worry."

"I hope you're right because I don't want to think about how I'm going to pay the rent."

"Maybe you'll have to move back in with your parents."

I hefted the notebook. "If this wasn't a demonic notepad, I'd bash your brains in with it."

Bilba smiled at my empty threat. So did I.

"Well, look at it this way. I'm not sure what we're supposed to do with the mortal bank account, but we've been paid the entire time in Lucifer's Army and we haven't been able to spend a single copper. By the time we get home, your account will be fat enough to take your time and decide what you want to do."

That was true. I hadn't given consideration to it, because I was busy trying to not die or being dulled by the daily routine of nothingness whenever we weren't outside the fence, patrolling Baghdad. The only change we saw, the only excitement we had, were those times ducking mortar attacks or dealing with Cancer, Chax, and the curse—an excellent argument for removing 'C' from the alphabet. But our Army-restricted lives saved a mountain of coin. Maybe there were actually no worries awaiting me in the Underworld.

I set Dialphio's letter on the nightstand, promising myself to get back to her. My thoughts were now fully on Cancer and the never-ending curse.

I hadn't seen her in over a month. I didn't know if she was still recovering or if she'd even left Iraq, an unattractive thought. That was one of the greatest struggles of being a deployed soldier, the disconnection from the entire world except fellow soldiers and the locals we sporadically inter-acted with.

But I thought about her and the curse at least a few times every day. Obsessive? Possibly. I thought about how I left her, less than thrilled with my offer. I knew she wanted more from me than a platitude promising justice. Her call for Chax's death was driven by emotion and turmoil, not a desire for blood. Cancer wasn't that type of demon, I was convinced of that. By now, I was sure she would be more agreeable to a less aggressive approach.

In that time, I'd only seen Chax once. It was in passing, at a commander's call, when our Central Command General came for a morale visit. With over three thousand soldiers in attendance, it wasn't like I could corner him and force an end to this situation.

He saw me too, giving me a smirk, like he wanted to remind me he had one up on me. I never got an answer from him.

Rumor had it we would be back in Cancer's neighborhood on our next patrol. I would get my answer soon enough.

For now, on this solitary day of relative freedom, I wanted, needed, nothing more than to enjoy the peace of not worrying about drama and strife. Tomorrow would deliver both. Refreshing my system, to allow myself to think about home and all those things in Hell I missed, like the bookshop and getting a bite of familiar bland demonic food at an expensive restaurant in Old Towne whenever I had the money, and a food stand when I didn't. The scent of sulfur on the manufactured wind. To be back where it didn't get so cursedly cold —who knew a place in the desert, like Baghdad, could get cold?

Thinking of home, I stood and pulled Creed out, going through my warm-up exercises. Using the weapon kept my rustiness at bay, but also kept the connection with what it meant to be a demon. Our accelerated training taught us how to blend in with mortals, but not how to sustain that act for so long. No offense to mortal soldiers, having served with them for a year now, I understood how amazing most of them were, but this role play had run its course.

"Watch out," Bilba said with a frown, scooting back against the wall.

The confines of the trailer were tight, and Creed was a long weapon, but I was proficient with it—if more than a little rusty. My best friend would be safe even on my worst day, unless I had a really bad one.

Running through my forms always felt good, making these Sundays the highlight of my week. Time with the halberd made me forget the past week, through the endless patrols and exhausting days. It was the only time I felt like me, and I soon lost myself in the forms. I'd even started naming them.

First, there was *Rising Dawn*, my basic warm-up form.

Then came *High Sun*, which I named a week after arriving in Iraq and understanding exactly why mortals complained about it so much.

There was *Silencer, Frigid Bite,* and *Endless Dream.* And, lastly, *Shadows Fall.*

By the time I finished the forms, the connection to the halberd and my true self was strengthened. I was my old self again. It was a wonderful reconnection on a transcendent level. My forms guided me, centered me, helped me wash away the stain of doubt, and the lack of confidence.

I ate, then I slept—because I could, and that was good enough of a reason. I only woke to watch a movie in the rec tent in the late afternoon. One thing about the Overworld I'd miss when I finally did return to Hell was the timely access to mortal movies, being able to watch them as soon as they're released instead of having to wait months before they showed up in the Underworld through market runners. Mortals had no idea how good their lives were.

Fed, rested, reconnected; I fell into a peaceful sleep as night fell on the desert.

POUNDING ON THE DOOR WOKE ME. EVEN AS I WAS COMING OUT of my slumber, the fist struck the door in rapid succession again.

Bilba grumbled, waking slowly. "What is it?"

"Someone with a death wish," I said.

I pulled on my PT shorts and T-shirt—sorry for that mental image, but I sleep in as little clothing as I can, a remnant of spending six thousand years in Hell and choosing comfort over warmth in the Overworld. Now dressed, I went to confront the source of commotion.

Charlie stood outside the trailer in his utility uniform. He stepped back when I swung the door open. "Hey guys, sorry to bother you."

By the expression on his face and tone in his voice, he was a reluctant messenger.

"What's up, Charlie?" I said as I rubbed the sleep from my eyes.

"We've got orders to head out within the hour," he said, taking a chance to check his surroundings. "Seems like there's been trouble in Khadra, something about a missing soldier, and patrols are being dispatched. We're one of them."

Nothing like starting the work week early.

"Thanks," I said and closed the door without waiting for a reply. Rudeness aside, Charlie could be loquacious and if we were leaving within the hour, that didn't give us much time.

Before long, we were rolling off the Baghdad International Airport compound we controlled and headed back into the suburb of Khadra.

"Supposedly the Russians are kicking up some trouble through the damn insurgents," Sergeant Jones shouted over the roar of the rattling Humvee. "Bunch of civilian casualties and, worse, I guess they're setting up a sleeper cell headquarters in and around Khadra. That's how the soldier was abducted, apparently. About two weeks ago. I remember hearing rumors, but that shit got squashed quickly. Now, guess it was true, and they're sure he's in our old stomping grounds. Keep your ear to the ground and eyes open. Last name was, *is*, Vicu. We need to shake them out if we can find them. I need you to work your charms on that doctor and see what you can find out."

I only half heard him. Chax was the missing soldier? That explained why I'd only seen him once in the past month. I had to run it over in my mind a few times. If this was true, it had so many dangerous and troublesome implications.

We started our patrol from the pharmacy that had become one of our checkpoints. It looked vacated. In fact, more homes and buildings than ever looked abandoned. There was a chill in the air, and it had nothing to do with the time of year. Even before Jones warned us to be ready, I already was, sensing hidden danger lurking in between buildings, hanging from the rooftops, and just about any other hiding hole in the section of the city.

Life, minimal, was still happening in this part of Khadra, but it was noticeably muted, as if those who hadn't yet fled had the joy of life sucked out of them.

As always in situations where I expected things to turn to crap in the blink of an eye, I felt for Creed, ensuring it was still strapped in. I needed the confirmation; I just hoped Creed didn't recognize my dependence on it. Thank Lucifer it was not sentient.

We walked towards Cancer's clinic without a problem, though I sensed eyes on us the entire way. Hidden. Secreted behind the blackened walls that scarred a few buildings. But watching. We moved carefully, deliberately, but it was hard to resist the urge to run.

We rounded the corner at the bakery where our translator leveraged his friendship with the owner to get intel. The glass windows had been shattered since our last visit, the glass cases that used to be filled with Iraqi delicacies, now lay empty.

"Be on your best, boys," Sergeant Jones said, noticeably tense. "You've got the lead on this, Sunstone. If she's there, get us every bit of information you can."

"Yes sir," I said.

The neighborhood held no hope or promise. Only despair resided here. Residents, the few we saw, scurried at our approach. Once they fled inside, nothing moved except the chilling desert breeze.

As I crossed the street, I found hope underneath the silence. Noise, life, came from the bottom floor of the building that used to serve as Cancer's clinic. I ran into the building even before Sergeant Jones gave the command.

Breathing a sigh of relief, I smiled at the succubus who tended to Khadra's injured for nearly three years.

If she was angry or frustrated, she hid it well. She dropped the towel she held and hurried toward me, unable to hide the exertion required. When she embraced me I felt how weak her grip was. I hugged her back.

"Bet you never hear this from succubi, but it's so good to see you," she said, pulling away and grinning.

"You'd be surprised how often the ladies miss me." I laughed.

So did she. "Sure. Keep telling yourself that. But, seriously," she said, her voice turning sober, "I am glad to see you."

Cancer, and her clinic, were an encouraging sight. Gone were the bruises and cuts from when she was attacked. The clinic had two hospital beds, instead of the four she used to have, each accompanied by a table. A cabinet in the corner held a few, not many, packages of bandages and splints. No blood stained the floor. The clinic was not fully recovered—yet—but Cancer appeared to be.

I cocked my arm, thumb thrown toward the door and street beyond. "What happened around here? The entire neighborhood feels deserted."

She tugged on the stethoscope hanging around her neck. "Oh Zeke, it's been horrible. One group of insurgents fighting another group, fighting another, and so on, and so on. It seems like every day there's a new faction fighting the old ones they're trying to replace."

"All Iraqis?"

Cancer shook her head. "With the war expanding like it is between the Russians and their allies, the Americans and theirs, it's getting worse. They're trying everything imaginable except for bombing this region of the city from the map. I don't doubt angels are getting involved now. That's why I opened the clinic again, hoping to help. There's just so much death and harm; I'm not sure I'm even making a difference. But I've got to try because I don't know what else to do."

"I get it. It was creepy getting through the neighborhood to you."

"Imagine what it's like for the people living here. Most of them don't even have access to clean water and electricity now. The food lines are getting longer each day."

I took comfort in knowing that she was well enough to have resumed her clinic operations. Now I needed to know the truth.

"Where's Chax?"

She straightened. Her hands dropped, and she stared as if I was speaking a language she didn't understand.

"What did you do with him?"

Her eyes narrowed in that dangerous way succubi did when incubi pushed them too far. "What are you talking about?"

"Listen, this can stay between us. I won't implicate you. The Army is looking for him. It's too obvious, and it's only going to get worse if we don't find him. Where is he?"

"I don't know what you're talking about and don't appreciate you thinking I am involved in anything to do with him. If something happened, it wasn't me. He probably pissed off the wrong person, or maybe another demon. The Vicu family is good at that."

I searched her eyes. She was being honest. Well, maybe our dilemma was solved for us.

I closed the distance between us, checking over my shoulder to ensure no one from the crew was within hearing distance, including Bilba and Ralrek. I lowered my voice. "I swear, if you tell me you don't know anything, I'll believe. But if you're covering for someone, I swear, I won't say a word. You can blame it on whoever. But if the Army can't find him tonight, they'll start doing house-to-house searches and no one wants that. Help me help them."

"I said I don't know anything," she said each word as sharp as a razor's edge. Her hands gripped her stethoscope like she was trying to choke herself with it. "This is more proof that you believe him over me."

Her voice rose, nearing a level that would draw attention. "No, it's not. And I don't. I believe you. I'm on your side, Cancer."

"It sure as heaven doesn't feel like it."

"I'm sorry."

She spun, stomping away, disappearing around the corner. Clanking came from the back room seconds later and she reappeared as quickly as she was gone, holding a piece of bent and twisted black metal in her hand. She shoved it at me. "You see that? Take it. Take it," she said more forcefully when I didn't. "There's your proof he's still terrorizing me. So if he's gone, I say good riddance."

I studied the blackened metal. It was rough and twisted, heavy. A tube ran down the center, filled with dirt. At one end, four fins were twisted in a design that rivaled modern art. The other end was ripped open, the thick, shredded metal bent back on itself. A homemade bomb.

"Where's it from?"

Cancer shuddered. "That was planted under garbage along the route I take to the clinic. It went off as I was walking to work. He tried to kill me. Chax tried to kill me."

"That would explain the blackened walls on the buildings," I said. "When did it happen?"

Cancer's eyes rolled up as she thought. "Last week. I'm still shaken, Zeke. Every day has been a blur."

Chax could not have done it because he was already missing by that time. Someone else was responsible, and in the middle of a war zone, everyone was a suspect. The attack possibly was not even targeting her, but the general populace, to strike fear into their hearts. Toying with civilians for military aims was a favored tactic of militaries for thousands of years.

"Zeke?" Cancer said. "Are you okay? You look ... confused."

I nodded slowly.

"Please," she said, emphasizing the word the second time around, "please find out if he's truly gone. I won't be able to focus on my patients until I know. I don't care about this stupid feud. I just want it to stop. And I want to be left alone. Does that make sense?"

Again, another nod. "I'll do what I can. I promise."

She reached to grab my hand that held the remains of the bomb. "Thank you more than you know. Please find out if he's gone for good."

"I will. Listen, use this," I said, reaching into my cargo pocket and pulling out a few sheets of paper from my demonic notebook, handing them to her.

She took them, staring down. "Is this one of ours?"

I nodded. Relief washed over her face. "I can't tell you how much I appreciate this. I don't know if I could wait another week or two, or a month, to hear from you again. This really means a lot. Do I need to be careful?"

"No. I leave it at my bedside, and Bilba is my roommate. Any message you need to send will be safe."

She hugged me one more time, and I left, waiting until we were away to brief Sergeant Jones. We finished our shift patrolling the neighborhood until the sun hugged the tops of buildings and darkness started its creep over the world—yes, I still hate looking up at that expanse. Darkness stripped us of safety, and all patrols had to be back on post long before it became unsafe.

Back on post, we debriefed and went our separate ways to prepare for the next day.

"I'm hungry. Want to grab chow?" Bilba patted his stomach.

"Sure thing," Ralrek answered. "I'm starving."

"What about you, Zeke? Hungry? Zeke? Hello?"

"Huh? Oh, sorry. What?"

"Man, what happened back there?" Bilba asked.

I stared at the gravel pathway. "I'll tell you when it's safer. Not out here in the open."

They both understood.

"So, food?" Bilba prodded.

"I'm going to hit the showers before the rush," I said. "I'll grab food later. Save some carrot cake though, in case I miss out."

"Again?" Ralrek snorted. "Aren't you tired of it yet?"

"We're almost halfway done with this deployment and you know our cake tastes like paste. I'm eating as much of it as I can before we head home."

"Deal," Bilba said with a chuckle, and they bounded off toward the mess hall.

I headed back to the trailer, lost in thoughts of Chax and where he might be and who was behind his disappearance if it wasn't Cancer. He was gone, and I had a gut feeling his disappearance had nothing to do with insurgents, Russians, or any aspect of this mortal war.

I had no energy left to think about the increased tensions around the city, especially Khadra, that might force Cancer to flee. If that happened, I might not be able to help her anymore.

At least she now had pages from my demonic notebook and could send a message if she needed. No matter where she went, somewhere in the Overworld or back to her Circle, she could reach out, and that gave me a rare moment of peace.

I was so distracted I almost bumped into a grouchy officer, dodging him right before we collided. Apologizing as I saluted, I watched him stomp away as I unlocked my trailer door, making sure I had not inspired him to come back and chew me out for my inattention. He didn't. But that did not prevent me from stepping inside my trailer and failing to notice the demon sitting inside, bundled against the cool air of the Overworld. I froze in my tracks when she spoke.

"About time you got back. I was beginning to worry I'd

have to go look for you myself," Seraph said, seated in the only chair in the living space I shared with Bilba.

"What are you doing here?" I said, looking over my shoulder to make sure no one saw her, and locked the door.

She was as beautiful as ever. Her long blonde hair was pulled back into a ponytail, making her icy blue eyes pop even more. She lifted her hand and languidly waved it back and forth. The murky sliminess of the listening ward crawled over my skin. I shivered.

"We need to talk."

I drifted to my bed and sat, unlacing my boots. I had not heard from the Council in nearly a year and now a Founder was sitting in my trailer. How? How was she here? Had they assigned our trailer to be a sanctuary? Thoughts buzzed my already clouded mind. The boots gave me a delay to antici-pate what was coming.

"Okay. What's up?" I finally asked.

Seraph sat back, crossing a leg over her knee, and wrap-ping her hands around the bent leg. "You can't seem to stay out of trouble, Mr. Sunstone," she said with a smile devoid of joy.

I sighed. What now? The Overworld had been my home during my forced military service. I had not seen Hell in so long I was starting to forget the names of streets in Old Towne. What problem could she have with me when I hadn't been around to cause any? What? Did Gemini show up again or Taurus come back from the dead? After they imprisoned me, I swore I would never have anything to do with the Council again, and I meant it. This bordered on harassment.

"How?" I said.

"Even here, you can't stay out of things you shouldn't be getting into," she said with the calmness of someone explaining the ingredients to a recipe.

I stopped unlacing my boots to look at her. "Seraph, I have no idea what you're talking about and I'm exhausted. We've been out in the field again today. I haven't eaten in over ten hours. I just want to get clean and dive headfirst into anything that looks halfway edible. Can we speed this up? Obviously it has to be something important if it brought one of you here. So what is it?"

Seraph's face was stoic, unbothered by my aggressive attitude. As smooth and as beautiful as ever, it was still the face of the Council, the entity I despised more than anything in Hell and Overworld combined. Then she shot forward, planting both feet on the floor with a slapping sound and jabbing her elbows onto her knees. Her lips curled back, baring her teeth. "This entire situation between Chax and Cancer Nijal!"

Her tone rocked me almost as much as the names she dropped. I wasn't ready for her fiery temperament. And I sure as heaven wasn't ready for her to name-drop two minor demons. Stunned, I noticed Cancer received the full-name formal treatment, but the Founder only referred to Chax by his first. An intimate connection?

I pushed back against the wall, realizing the truth. "No."

One corner of Seraph's mouth curled up as I understood. "You're going to stop meddling in this business between Cancer's family and mine."

You've got to be kidding me. Trying to cover my panic with false bravery, I pushed the discussion back. "Who is he, specifically, to you? A little brother? Nephew? A cousin?"

"Be very careful, Sunstone." Her eyes flashed. I suddenly felt like a fairy being pinned to a board while an adolescent tyrant burned my wings with a magnifying glass. "He's my nephew. My family. My sister's son."

"You have family in Hell?"

"Plenty of family," she said through clenched teeth. "You don't think I would suffer that realm on my own, do you? Everyone needs family. Even a Founder. I love my family, Mr. Sunstone. Dearly. I would do anything for them. Anything."

Apparently, I had inadvertently stepped in an enormous pile of chimera dung.

"Up until Gemini, I expected you to be the one member of the Council with integrity. Maybe that was my first mistake and I should have realized none of you are above contamination." It would have been best to stop there, but I didn't. I was on a roll. "Why doesn't it shock me then that not a single member of Lucifer's Council has an ounce of integrity? It can't be any wonder why the Underworld is as dysfunctional as it is. Hard to paint us as the victims of angelic totalitarianism when our leaders suffocate us, isn't it? I imagine you're fine with the fact that Chax, your family, launches attacks against Cancer, an innocent who is trying to help mortals and the Balance? If that's the case, you, the Council, Lucifer Himself can kiss my ass."

Seraph sat back, lifting that leg and wrapping her hands around her knee again. I didn't trust the smile she wore. "I'm pleased with the way this conversation unfolded. It is unfortunate for you, as you will discover, but you've given me what I needed."

With that, Seraph waved her hand, and the listening ward disappeared. The rift roared to life like she was trying to make a statement with its ferocity, and she stepped through, back to Hell and out of my life for now.

Shockingly, I was no longer in a hurry to end this deployment.

16

BAGHDAD

THE OFFICIAL SEAL OF LUCIFER, an upside down triangular shape encasing two diagonal lines that curled above a small v-shape in the center, burned blue with the light of the Hell-fire on the cover of my demonic notebook just hours after Seraph threatened me. I was getting a letter from home.

I cracked open the notebook to find the letter was not from Dialphio or my parents—not that I expected to hear from them since it had been so long since they had written.

Sitting up in my bed, I pulled the notebook onto my bent legs and watched as the words were seared into the magic paper. My brain refused to process what I was seeing.

"What is it, Zeke? Is everything okay?" Bilba asked, his voice a dull sound in the background of my world.

"I ... I don't know."

I held the notepad in shaking hands. I heard Bilba scramble off his bed and walk the few feet to me, but his movements were muffled, like he shuffled in another dimension.

My eyes scanned the length of the letter, jumping back to the top once I'd finished reading it. My throat no longer worked.

Gently, Bilba took it from my hand, and I was too deep in shock to stop him.

"This can't be right," he said, holding it up. "What are they talking about?"

"Seraph," I said through a constructive throat, my gaze locked on my combat boots on the floor.

"This is a joke. It's ... it's not possible. This just doesn't happen." His voice rose to a higher pitch, his cadence galloping. "They're charging you with blasphemy, Zeke. *Blasphemy*. No one has been charged with that in ... I can't even remember. The last case I remember hearing about was well before our lifetime. Heavens, even our parents' lifetimes. It just doesn't happen. What is this based on?"

Blasphemy was the crime of crimes in the Underworld; a demon couldn't commit a greater offense. To blaspheme Lucifer was unthinkable. Demons knew that, we were taught from our earliest years, even before we started our schooling. Showing or acting with contempt or lack of reverence toward Him was so taboo, the fact I was being charged for doing exactly that when I had done nothing of the sort made my throat swell with bile. The Council? Sure, I would blaspheme the heaven out of them; but Lucifer? No way.

I turned to my best friend and fought to keep tears from showing. "She was here, in our trailer, when we came back from patrol. You and Ralrek were at chow, and I came here to shower. She was waiting for me and we got in an argument."

"An argument? About what?"

The name tasted like bitter lemon oil. "Chax."

A few seconds passed. Bilba set the notebook down on my nightstand. "What about him? Was she upset that he is lost or something? What does that have to do with you, or blasphemy, for Lucifer's sake?"

I raked a hand through my hair. A sour laugh escaped my lips. "We never got around to where he is. She didn't look worried about that either."

Bilba grabbed my shoulders. "I need you to focus so I can help. Why would Seraph come to the Overworld, especially to see you in the middle of a war? What in the world do you have to do with Chax?"

My vision cleared, my friend pronounced in the foreground. "Remember when we confronted him?"

"Of course, Zeke." Concern flickered across Bilba's face.

"He told us to not mess with him. That he has a powerful family. Well, guess who that family is?"

Bilba rocked back, swallowing hard. "You've got to be kidding me?"

"I wish I was."

Now Bilba ran a hand through his, much shorter—because I think he was digging the standard Army haircut—hair. "Oh, this is bad. Bad."

"She told me to stay out of it. To stay away from all this business between Cancer and him."

"The curse?"

I nodded.

"But she's ... she's a Council member, Zeke. She's a Founder. If Chax is her ... what is he to her?"

"Nephew," I answered, fingering Lucifer's seal on my closed notebook. I could not look at that blessed notification any longer.

"Well, at least he's not her son or something," Bilba said with a quiver I think he meant as a laugh. "That would be worse. Who knew she had family in the Underworld. Regardless, this is bad. Blasphemy is no joke. What did you two argue about? Specifics, Zeke. Be honest, even if you said something stupid. You know your temper can get the best of your tongue sometimes. Tell me everything."

So I did, recalling my earlier conversation with Seraph, leaving nothing out. When I was finished, Bilba sat back against the wall, still on my bed, looking across the tiny shared space.

"There's nothing blasphemous in that," he said, finally breaking his reflection. "Are you sure that is everything?"

"Yes. I'm not lying, Bilba. Why would I?"

He was already shaking his head. "I don't think you are. But they're still charging you, so either you're forgetting something, which I don't think you are," he said in a rushed tone, looking at me, "or …"

"Or what?"

He swallowed and looked around. "Or they're fabricating, making up details of the conversation. Embellishing."

"Lying."

"Yes." The word came out as a whisper.

"But why would they do that?" I slammed the notebook on my nightstand.

Bilba winced. "I don't know, Zeke. I really don't. Maybe because you, we, maybe because we are involved in this curse thing and Cancer was telling the truth. Maybe this thing goes way back between their families. Think about it; it would make sense that, if it were a real feud, the tension would be such that one flick of the string could cause the entire thing to explode. The hatred must run so deep, generation after generation. Hate piling on hate."

"And we stepped in the middle of it."

"Right in the middle," he said.

"Lucifer, she did us no favors," I said, leaning back against the wall.

"Careful with using His name like that," Bilba said.

Usually, a comment like that, at a time like this, would have been sent with a flavor of good-natured ribbing. But there was no hint of that in my friend's comment, because this time was like no other. Charged with blasphemy. What in the heaven was I going to do?

Bilba sniffed sharply. "Well, this isn't going to just happen. We will fight this. They can't just do this to you."

His determination did nothing for me. I'm sure he meant it

to be encouraging, but I couldn't find encouragement in the hottest Hellfire at the moment. "There's nothing we can do," I replied quietly.

"The heaven there isn't!" Bilba raised his arms above his head and waved them back and forth. "Hello? Zeke? It's your friend, me. Trying to help you see your options. We'll fight this."

I shook my head. "You can't fight the Council when they trump up charges like this. It'll only get worse for me and my mother, and I can't do that to her again. She doesn't deserve to be run through the wringers by the Council if I make trouble for them. My father? I'm sure he'd help them however they asked."

"Stir up things? You're defending yourself against false charges, aren't you?"

The conversation with one of Lucifer's Council members flashed through my mind, and I started spiraling down the funnel of despair again. Hours ago, I was focused on helping Cancer; now, in the span of a single chat with an irate Founder, I felt like I was sitting in the prison cell with Ralrek again, waiting for Hell's rulers to pluck me apart, bit by bit. It was as if no time at all had passed.

A fog of exhaustion shrouded my mind, my spirt, my will to care. I was never going to get any peace.

"I never thought of you as a quitter," Bilba said, walking back to his bed and dropping on it. "Never you. Between the three of us, you were the one who would fight until the bitter end. Where is the demon who stood in the face of Beelzebub and told him no? The incubus who wouldn't attack a demon who wanted to remain in the Overworld to live out the last years of his life? Ralrek and I sure as heaven didn't have the courage to do that. You did. And you were punished. When I was deluded into thinking I could change my mother and stayed in the Eighth Circle, you and Ralrek got blamed for bringing an angel to the Underworld, even though it was the Council who put you on the task. You've been shamed and humiliated, treated unfairly from the beginning with the Council. Heavens, Zeke, you're the Segregate! Demons still think of you like that even though you have Creed." His voice softened. "You've been fighting all your life, so why won't you now?"

Bilba had a point. He always had good points when he wasn't acting like a doofus. But it was easy to get riled up about being treated unfairly when it wasn't you who was being abused. He was asking me to stick my head in the guillotine.

"Because I can't," I countered weakly. "There's nothing I can do. They'll destroy me, make me look like a fool, *more* foolish than they've already made me appear. And this time, my family will suffer. You weren't there, bud. You didn't hear what Apopis said he would do to my parents if I didn't admit to bringing Gemini and Cassie into Hell. What do you think they'll do to my family, to everyone I care about, if I'm screwing with Seraph's family? That's too much of a threat to them. Too personal. They'll make those I care about pay. I can't fight one against five, especially when those five are the demons who control everything."

He wagged a finger. "Ah, but you won't have to."

My eyes slid over to him. Bilba was grinning like he'd just snuck an entire baked chicken into Hell for me to enjoy. "What do you mean?"

He shrugged, both his hands out to the sides. "One of the first laws Lucifer ever instituted was that all demons are allowed to defend themselves against charges by calling witnesses. His infinite wisdom or whatever; He knew that ethics could become an issue at some point, so He established a law of self-defense by allowing character witnesses, one for each Council member. We have five Council members, so you get five witnesses to testify for you."

I shook my head. "There aren't five demons who would do that."

Bilba made a fist and then pulled up each of his fingers as he named who would stand up for me. "Me. Ralrek. Dialphio. Cancer."

"That's four."

He gripped that last finger, his pinky, allocated to Cancer, and wiggled it. "Four strong witnesses. Especially Cancer. The Council would expect us to say anything for you, even to lie. But they won't expect her. She could turn the case in your favor."

"I don't know."

"Stop quitting on me, Zeke," Bilba said firmly. "If you don't stand up to them, who will?"

"I didn't realize I was Hell's counterbalance to the Council."

"Don't be like that, not right now. This is serious."

"I am being serious. Did you ever stop to think I might be sick and tired of fighting them, of always having to defend myself against their ridiculous claims, their suspicions? It's exhausting. Absolutely exhausting."

"Then let us do this for you. Let us help. You deserve that much."

I pressed both hands against my face and pressed, rubbed, gripped skin.

Bilba stood. "Why are you thinking about this? Why are you torturing yourself? I'll tell you what, I'll talk to Ralrek, and you write a note to Cancer. You said you gave her the notebook, right?"

"Yeah," I said as I tucked my hands behind my head—still gripping my hair, just unseen by my friend—and stared up at the ceiling, trying to ignore the swarm of hopelessness descending on me. I didn't watch Bilba leave, I only heard the click of the lock as the door swung shut.

He was a really good friend. Everything we'd been

through, we had grown and become better demons for it. Without him by my side, I would have been lost long ago. As it stood, I now was.

Could I really lie around and pout, sulking like an impling while Bilba was out working for me? The Council was moving forward either way, whether I participated or not. I could care about it happening, or ignore it, hoping it went away, knowing it never would. If Bilba believed in my case, then shouldn't I as well?

Plus, deep in my soul, the last thing I wanted to do was to look in the mirror one day and recognize that I willfully allowed the Council to push me around. A blasphemy charge was the be-all, end-all. A demon could only take so much before being pushed too far. I allowed the Council to push me around after Beelzebub killed Aries because I couldn't distinguish my head from the Hellfire blue dome. I let them do it again after Gemini's trial and before his attempted execution. I allowed them to make me their fall-incubus. Was I okay standing by while they pushed me around because of Seraph's need to protect a relative and a family secret she wanted to keep under wraps because feuding should be beneath a Founder's station? Blasphemy was grave. A line had been drawn.

Slapping the bed, I swung my feet off to the cool floor, snatched the notebook from my nightstand and scribbled out a note to Cancer.

I wished I could do this in person instead of depending on her to read my jumbled mess of thoughts without a filter. But I wrote it anyway, because it was my only option to save myself.

Done, I rolled over to face the wall and waited for Bilba to return with news of Ralrek's decision.

I tossed and turned and was asleep before I heard from him or Cancer.

———◆

I don't know if I can, Zeke. I'm sorry.

THAT WAS THE ONLY REPLY FROM CANCER.

I pushed the notebook away.

"You're going to write her back, right?"

I stared at the ceiling, tired from a fitful nap.

"You're not just going to stop there," Bilba said, continuing his motivational machinations. "I'm in. Ralrek is in. You and I both know Dialphio will be. By the way, you need to write her," he said, almost as an afterthought. "But you have to get Cancer. She is the key. You did what you thought was right, for the benefit of others. There was no selfishness in any of this for you. Heavens, this time you didn't even have a crush to blame your actions on. Write her back, or I will."

"And what would you say?"

"I'd tell her she doesn't have a choice after everything you've done for her," Bilba replied. I don't think I have ever heard him sound so resolute.

"I can't make her do that. That's not right."

"Right or not, it's true," Bilba said, flipping another page of his demonic notebook.

"What are you doing?" Changing the subject might help get the focus off me and my struggles. I was wrong.

"I'm writing my father, telling him what's happening and asking him to coordinate on that side," Bilba said, not looking up as he scribbled away.

"I wish you wouldn't do that."

He slapped his pen on the paper. "I'm sure there are a lot of things you wished I wouldn't do. But I'm doing this. I'm tired of you not sticking up for yourself, so if you won't do it, I'll do it for you. It's that simple. Now, instead of worrying about me, why don't you write Cancer again?" He paused, watching me. "Well?"

I smirked. "You won't let this rest until I write her again, will you?"

"Nope."

Groaning, I sat up and grabbed the notepad, scribbling out a quick note, about as safe and bland as possible. It would turn her off and give me an excuse to not carry out this ruse.

Are you there?

A few seconds later, a reply came in.

Yes.

"She's busy," I said. Bilba was off his bed and hovering over my notebook before I could put it away.

"No, she's not." He poked my page. "Tell her what you need. Ask for help, Lucifer, bless it."

I stared at him. He stared at me, refusing to back down. "Okay, okay. Leave me alone so I can concentrate."

Unsmiling, he retreated to his bed.

Remember that favor?

Of course.

I need you, Cancer. The Council is serious.

I waited, hoping she would tell me no, and I could prove to Bilba that this had been an immense waste of time. She replied within seconds.

*That's asking a lot. Don't know if I can. I would have to leave the
Overworld.*

I WAS ABOUT TO SET MY PEN DOWN WHEN BILBA INTONED, WITH
emphasis, "Zeke." I put the pen back to the paper.

*I really need you. They're charging me with blasphemy, but it
directly relates to Chax.*

What do you mean?

Chax is the nephew of Seraph.

The Council member?

The one and only.

*Then this is more than a blasphemy charge. They're trying to
suppress what they've been doing.*

And they'll get away with it if I don't have your help.

THE NOTEBOOK STAYED BLANK.

I waited. And waited.

"I think she's gone," I said to Bilba.

"Did you say something offensive again?"

"When do I *ever* say anything offensive?"

Scratched words formed. Two words.

I'm coming.

RELIEF MIXED WITH TREPIDATION. SHE WOULD BE THERE FOR ME. If this family feud was as serious as it appeared, if the curse was true, and there was bad blood between the families, Cancer would be within reach of Seraph. And I didn't trust the rest of the Council enough to fool myself into thinking they'd ensure her safety. My relief at her being willing to help was immediately diluted by the knowledge that she was putting herself in danger. For me.

"And?" Bilba said, elongating the word.

"And she's coming," I answered, feeling like garbage while he fist-pumped from the other side of the room.

17

UNDERWORLD, UNDISCLOSED

THE RIFT OPENED at the scheduled time in the middle of our small Conex trailer. My bags were already packed, laying at the foot of my bed. There was no sense in resisting or delaying. Bilba's bags were as well, and so were Ralrek's. Both incubi sat on Bilba's bed, waiting, which was going to be a splendid ambush for Seraph, assuming my best friend was correct about Lucifer's laws.

Admittedly, I was still reeling from the whirlwind of events that led to this moment. As shocking as the experience was up to this point, it still held one last surprise.

The rift hissed and Azazel stepped through tentatively, a stale look on his face. "Good day, young Ezekial. I apologize for my tardiness. Traveling isn't as easy as it used to be."

"Azazel," Bilba yelped, shooting to his feet.

The Founder rotated as if his neck and chest were connected to the same pulley system. His goatee, nearing touching mid-chest, was still tipped with the same faded orange that streaked his long gray hair. "Hello, Mr. Ravenous. How are you doing this fine day?"

Bilba seemed confused. "Oh, I'm fine ... sir. Can I ..." he looked around our trailer, dashed to the refrigerator and pulled it open. "Can I offer you something to drink? We only have milk. Um." He straightened. "It's from a mortal farm, but you're welcome to it."

Azazel laughed heartily before coughing into a fist. "No, no. That's fine. My stomach doesn't cope well with mortal cuisine, and I'm only here to collect Mr. Sunstone. We've finished expunging your service to the mortal Army. Those in your unit will miss you, but the official record is already gone. To the Army, you never existed, so it's best if we move along. Are you ready to leave?"

I looked at my two friends. Bilba gave me an encouraging nod. Facing the Founder, I lifted my chin, forcing myself to manifest the confidence I didn't feel. "They will be joining me." Azazel blinked as if he'd been slapped. "They're my character witnesses. You'll also need to open a rift at the clinic where Cancer is assigned. I can give you the coordinates if you need them. She'll be coming too."

My statement hung in the air. Of the Council members assigned to babysit me back to the Underworld, Azazel was the least confrontational. Never once did I think he was a pushover, but he also would not drag out the torture of debating the legitimacy—if it was legitimate—of my claim. But in a way, it was a stranger experience having him selected, because it was as if I was hurting the ancient demon's feelings.

"Most interesting proposition, Mr. Sunstone," he said, his upper torso stiffly bending. "As is your right. I will open the rift for Cancer Nijal as soon as we are back in the Council chamber."

I breathed a sigh of relief and mouthed a 'thank you' to Bilba for knowing the obscure things he knew. When I went to retrieve my bags, my best friend stopped me. "Hang on." He turned to the Council member. "Sir, we request that the rift be sent to Cancer now, before Zeke attends the trial."

Azazel's cheeks wobbled. "That's highly unconventional."

"It needs to become conventional."

I didn't move for my bags, pausing to see how this power struggle played out. Bilba's courage in the face of a Founder lifted my deadened heart. This was for me.

"With all due respect," Bilba continued, "Zeke is entitled to character witnesses, one for each Council member, as you know. And with the Council's history of ... interactions with him, I think it's well within reason for him to ask this of you."

Azazel mumbled to himself. "Highly unconventional. Highly unconventional. The rest of the Council won't like this. But alas, the imp is right." He shook his cheeks, his eyes becoming clear as he addressed me and Bilba. "So it shall be."

He extended his arms straight and clapped loudly. "There, young ones." When he read our expressions, he clarified. "The rift has opened for Cancer. Now if you three young ones will join me."

Azazel didn't say another word as he turned and walked into the rift. This was it. We were saying goodbye to the Overworld once more, to the human army who had become an extended family, and to the mortal struggle for power that was killing more of their species each day.

I took stuttering steps toward Bilba and Ralrek, and in the small confines of what was nothing more than a metal box in the middle of the desert, we hugged. Three incubi sharing a solitary moment of togetherness. "Thank you, guys."

Ralrek slapped me on the back before pulling away and grabbing his bags. Within seconds, he was back in Hell.

Bilba lingered. "You deserve demons standing beside you. That and so much more. Now, let's go kick the Council's ass."

———⟶

RALREK PACED THE ATRIUM OUTSIDE THE COUNCIL CHAMBER. The serious look on his face lifted slightly whenever he looked my way as we waited. "We've got your back, Zeke. I'm done with this shit."

"Thank you," I said, hearing the truth in his fervor.

Another sizzle from a rift a few feet away and Cancer joined us, stepping tentatively onto the smooth brimstone tile. "Zeke," she rushed into my open arms, her mass of curls enveloping my head. "I'm so sorry about this. It's all my fault."

"No," I said firmly, "it's not. Don't blame yourself. This isn't on you; it's squarely on the Vicu family's shoulders."

"The Council too," Bilba said from the side.

"The Council too," I agreed.

We stood there awkwardly looking at each other while Bilba and Ralrek played spectator.

Bilba was the first to break the silence. "Awfully nice to be back in the Underworld. I want to conjure a few snakes just to see if I remember how to use my Abilities. I really got tired of relying on a rifle to save my ass."

Ralrek snickered. "That ass would need more than a rifle to save it. Plus, you could have conjured in your trailer. Zeke was your roommate; I had a mortal, so I couldn't practice unless he was at chow or in the shitter."

Bilba straightened. "You conjured there?"

"Of course," Ralrek said. "No way I was going to go that long without touching my Ability. Can you imagine how rusty I'd be?"

"B—but, I didn't," my best friend said.

"Your own fault, dumbass," Ralrek said with a brief chuckle. "I'm sure it will only take you a year or so to get back to where you were. If you can touch your powers at all."

Bilba looked from him to me and back again. Each time he looked away from Ralrek, the tall incubus would wink at me. "I—I can't lose my Abilities. That's not possible ... I don't think. I'll have to check the—"

"He's screwing with you." I slapped Bilba's shoulder.

The tips of my friend's ears turned pink. "You jerk."

Smiles were shared around the small circle, but no one laughed at their good-natured sparring. No one felt like laughing. The ominous air dampened any joy.

"Can I tell you guys a secret?" I asked, immersing myself in the conversation because I wasn't sure if this was the last one I would have with my best friends. They were the only demons in the Underworld who mattered besides my boss, and to a lesser extent, my parents. "That was my third trip to the Overworld and I sort of liked it there."

"Even in the middle of a war?" Bilba asked.

I found Cancer's big, soft eyes. "Weird, right? But it's the truth. I mean, I didn't like the war and could do without the Army controlling every aspect of my life. There's something liberating about just existing, not worrying about who is more powerful than the other. Not watching your back at every turn. In the Overworld, I'm just Zeke, not the Segregate. It's weird; I only ever wanted to come back home, but ... I'm not sure I'll ever be welcomed again. I guess I never was."

Bilba stared at me. Ralrek nodded sadly. Cancer's eyes held mine as she bit her bottom lip. We became a silent friendship circle until the two incubi looked at each other and chuckled.

"I don't know what Overworld you went to, but I want a ticket there next time," Ralrek said with a fading grin. "Because the one I just spent a year in was terrible."

"You almost had me with that one," Bilba punched me softly on the shoulder.

I was serious and let the laughter slowly die, feeding into the uncomfortable knowledge of the event looming over us.

"No matter what happens, I want you all to know how much I appreciate you coming here and being willing to put yourself in front of the Council for me. I know it's risky, and none of you asked for this. So it means the world to me that you're taking this on. I just hope that—"

The air buzzed as a gateway opened a few feet away, cutting me off. I knew who was coming before she stepped through.

"Dialphio!" I hugged her before she oriented herself. "You came. Thank you so much!"

"Did you think I would miss this for anything? Don't be silly. If this is the only way I can get you to come back to work, then I'll do it. You've been slacking for too long. And might I say, you look dashing in uniform, Ezekial."

As we hugged, the Underworld felt slightly more like home again.

The other three approached as the gateway disappeared behind my boss.

"Well, that makes four of us," Ralrek observed. "Did you invite a fifth, Zeke?"

I shook my head without putting words to the fact I could depend on no one else to represent me truthfully and accurately, no one who would stand bravely in the Council's face. Everyone understood, because it passed over their expressions. Bilba took it the hardest, I imagine, knowing he could rely on his father for anything but still relating on a deeper level because of his heartbreaking troubles with his own mother. Ralrek's family had been plagued by divorce and toxic relationships for so long I don't even think he knew what a healthy family looked like. And in all the time I worked for Dialphio, we didn't delve into her family history, but it wasn't healthy enough for her to spend the Samhain feast with them. Familial blood ties were lacking for a number of demons, apparently, in my circles. But family could be anything and I had mine here, standing beside me to face the five Founders.

Behind us, the chamber doors creaked open. Dressed in his formal black robes, lined with red hems, Azazel stepped through. Two guards in black armor pulled the doors closed again, but not before I noticed the virtually empty room behind them. That was surprising. When Gemini was tried, the Council chamber was full of demons ready to slay him there and then if Hell's leaders allowed. I figured I would have the same humiliation before they found me guilty for something I didn't do ... again.

Azazel approached cautiously, without the cockiness of Apopis or the aggression of Beelzebub. He moved as slow as a lava flow. "Young Mr. Sunstone, are you and your witnesses ready to proceed?"

I checked with the four demons who moved closer, protectively. This was happening so fast. I wanted more time with the most important demons in Hell. But I couldn't deny the Council any longer. They were going to do what they were going to do and the longer I made them wait, the harsher they would be. The four friends gave me silent reassurances. None of them were backing down, even as they stood feet away from one of the five who might change the course of their own journey, if not mine.

What if they were punished? What if Bilba and Ralrek lost everything they had worked so hard for? What if the Council forced Dialphio to close The Book Abyss? What if Cancer didn't survive this face-to-face with Seraph?

"Come on," Dialphio said, placing her hand on my back.

I nodded to Azazel. "Yes."

He turned and began the slow flow back to the chamber. The doors opened as he approached, their timing so exact Azazel did not have to break stride. I followed next, with the four demons who might be able to change my fate close behind. Inside, I confirmed no raucous crowd waited to witness my downfall. Creed warmed against my leg.

Adorned in their black and red formal robes, the four Council members—Azazel would make it five as soon as he got to the table—which might take another millennia at his pace—were the room's only occupants besides the door guards and two dozen more guards lining the walls. Was the

Council expecting trouble? I guess they didn't understand how beat down I was from their constant harassment. But they were not going to see that side of me. The way Apopis sneered and Beelzebub snarled, I refused to give them that.

But my heightened senses didn't miss the singular oddity in the room, though they'd been tucked into a far, darkened corner. My parents. The Council placed them off in the far corner, shadowed beyond the Hellfire torchlight coming from the evenly spaced sconces.

Of course they would be here too, summoned by the Council to witness my humiliation. Even in this moment, all energy focused on fighting this bogus claim, I couldn't help but ache for what they must have went through when the Council's merlin showed up, delivering their summons to appear today.

Hell's rulers were trying to break me, again.

Not again. Not this time. No more. Their calculated tactic of using my parents as pawns wouldn't serve their cause. Instead of weakening before their examination, I took a deep breath, swelled my chest and threw my shoulders back, and strode forward. Filled with defiance, I felt like an ancient and powerful demon, maybe even more powerful than Lucifer Himself. The faces of the three Council members beside Apopis and Beelzebub gave nothing away. No one spoke until I stopped thirty feet in front of them, centered on the table.

"Ezekial Sunstone, you are hereby called to the Third Council of Lucifer to face charges of blasphemy," Beelzebub announced loudly enough that I figured he was aiming for every angel in Heaven to hear him. His muscular arms filled the sleeves of his robe. His dark head shaven, the Prince of Demons still wore matching blonde sideburns. "How do you plead?"

How did I plead? I didn't do anything—and these five Founders knew that too. This was a trumped up charge to protect Seraph's family secret, along with her, likely, culpability. Blasphemy was a serious charge, but one they had no proof for. If they thought I would sit by without me raising a single question, like I'd beg for their forgiveness, they were clueless. They might as well have charged me with existing, for as good as this farce sounded.

"I request the Council tell me specifically what I've done," I said instead.

Beelzebub's mouth opened as if he was going to snap a response and then he clamped it shut, deferring to Michael.

The lanky lead Council member's eyes tried to bore into my head. This was their chamber, the one place in Hell where even thoughts were not safe. I needed to be careful but not completely protective; my thoughts would reveal the absolute truth to combat their subjective one.

A warmth against my leg distracted me, the pant leg inside the mortal military uniform where Creed was sewn. The distraction pulled me away from worrying about how deep the Founder's could extend into my mind. I tried to concentrate, feeling Michael rooting around in the folds of gray matter inside my skull—something I felt but never distinguished during my previous visits. The heat coming from the halberd increased. Burning. Like Creed was lit afire. Michael's prying slipped, regained a hold. Creed burned hotter, making me fidget to pull the heated material away from my skin. Michael's grasp slipped again, this time completely.

His squinting eyes widened, and his mustache and beard twitched, but he straightened, covering his loss. Creed had blocked his access to my mind.

"It has come to our attention that during a recent ..." he paused, and his eyes flicked, less than pleased, in Seraph's direction. He continued, "A recent discussion you had with a Council member, in which you made blasphemous statements against Lucifer."

My mind scrambled back to that conversation, attempting to decipher the connections between what I said to Seraph in the heat of the moment when she threatened me under a listening ward. What happened then that matched Michael's claims?

Nothing. There was nothing blasphemous—Lucifer, how I hated giving credence to such a ridiculous concept—about what I said. If anything criminal happened, it came from the Founder, not me.

"I wasn't blasphemous," I said, allowing the heat to rise in my voice. "And considering the context of the conversation—"

Before I said another word, I was cut off again, this time by Seraph herself. Her aqua blue eyes as hard as stone. "I have already provided testimony to the Council about your statements and they have been accepted. The contents of our conversation aren't what is being put on trial, Mr. Sunstone. Your blasphemy is."

Convenient, I thought. With an icy tone, I said, "I didn't blaspheme."

"So you plead not guilty?" Apopis said, the 's' remnant of his words elongated. He wore a stupid smirk on his slender, half-tattooed face.

"You still haven't told me what real charges you have against me, so I refuse to enter a plea."

Michael's voice was flat, calm. "Unfortunately, Mr. Sunstone, you cannot refuse to enter a plea. If you don't enter one, the Council will enter one for you. You remember Gemini's trial?"

Was that a threat? Veiled though it seemed, threats were threats no matter how they were dressed.

"How is this justice?" The harsh question came from behind me. Bilba.

Beelzebub sat back, crossing his muscular arms. His thick lips pulled up in a snarl. "Mr. Ravenous, let me remind you that, as a character witness, you are denied from contributing to these proceedings until we call you. If you cannot comply, a silencing spell will be cast to assist you in the matter."

Light shuffling of feet from behind faded. Bilba acquiesced. I loosed a shaking breath; there was no reason for any of my friends to go down with me.

"Then I enter a plea of not guilty, since nothing I said was blasphemous, because we did not even discuss Lucifer. And, as far as the Council is concerned, what I said about you was accurate."

Michael nodded. Apopis and Beelzebub smirked.

"Seraph has already provided her testimony," Michael replied as if it explained everything.

"I wasn't there for it. How do I know what she claimed," I said.

"She is a member of Lucifer's Third Council," Apopis hissed, leaning forward. "It is inappropriate for someone of your station to hear her testimony. Besides, we do not need to recall the things you said about our Lord. Consider yourself cursed to even be given this chance by the Council. It proves His graciousness that He has allowed this, after the words you have spoken against him."

"I didn't say anything!" My voice echoed around the chamber.

"This petulance and disregard for Council proceedings will not be tolerated," Apopis spat.

Five pairs of hard eyes stared down from the large jade table atop the riser. There were no friends in this room beside the four behind me and the two demons relegated to watching from the far corner.

"Call your character witnesses, Mr. Sunstone," Azazel said.

So I did, and the proceedings continued. One after another, starting with Ralrek, then Bilba, with Dialphio following him, and ending with Cancer. The group of demons who rallied to my side each stepped forward and defended my case—defended *me*—to the Council. Never had I felt valued like this.

The most intriguing was when Cancer stood before the Council. Her eyes, though she spoke to every Founder, firmly locked on Seraph. She defended me and my actions with grace and an air of confidence I would have never found myself. She was courageous in the face of covert hostility from one of the most powerful demons in Hell. And she was here because of that courage and the fact that Bilba pushed me to defend myself and ask for her help.

Everything the four of them said in testimony was the truth, without embellishment or hyperbole. They described me, my attributes, complements, and blemishes, without apology or rationalization. The Council listened. I expected no favors, and they afforded none. There was no sign or reaction, no change of perception after my four character witnesses gave their last testimony.

After that stage, Michael conferred quietly with the other four members before sitting straighter and facing me. "The evidence presented, the defendant has had his character witnesses attest for him. We will now move on to the verdict."

The verdict? Was this done now, so quickly? Was this the end of it? The Council moved so slowly on other matters, yet they were dispensing with this case within a lunch meal?

I looked over to my parents. My mother wrang her hands, her lips pressed together but her jaw moving as if she was speaking to herself. My father leaned against the wall, his hands clasped in front of him. He was as unreadable as ever.

"Lucifer's First Council established the punishment for blasphemy," Michael announced in solid formality to the nearly empty room. "And that punishment is Abandonment in the Overworld."

I could have heard a fairy drop across the chamber as still as the room was at the announcement.

They were moving forward with this charge of blasphemy,

set to determine my fate for a crime I did not commit. How could justice come by taking the word of Seraph over my testimony and that of four other demons—two of whom who had served this very Council's mission numerous times? It was as if the words of my four friends did not matter, as if I'd wasted their time, so unheard was their testimony. As if the Council had decided my fate before we stepped into Hell.

A yelp, like a small animal crying, sounded from the side of the room. My mother.

Abandonment in the Overworld.

"We will now vote on the verdict," Michael continued as if reading instructions on how to assemble a desk. "The verdict will be determined by a simple majority. Members, you will vote with either an aye or nay. Ayes for Abandonment. Nays against Abandonment." Michael's eyes fell from mine to my hip where I hid Creed. Something flashed in his eyes. Fear? Desire? "My vote is nay."

I nodded, not sure if the gesture was appropriate or not, and not caring. I was just grateful for it.

"Beelzebub?"

"Aye," he said simply, too simply, like he'd put no thought into my condemnation. I wasn't shocked, not from someone who still held a grudge because I didn't help him kill an innocent demon trying to bring joy and happiness to mortals.

One to one.

The room got hotter, and not from Creed burning in my pocket.

"Apopis?"

Shock is not something I expected or experienced when Apopis said, "Aye."

One to two.

I was losing my fight to stay in Hell, losing my right to be a demon. Thankfully, two votes remained, and I was confident Azazel would come through. Azazel was levelheaded. Seraph was a mystery. She was protecting her family. This all started because of her selfish desires. But she was also the Founder who made sure I had a few moments with Cassie before the angel disappeared back to wherever angels go when they're not in Heaven. If not for Seraph's efforts, I would not have had angelic confirmation about the nature of Creed and One.

Still, she had pushed for this. She had provided testimony in secret to the rest of the Council that pushed proceedings forward. Friend or foe?

Abandonment in the Overworld was as serious an issue for a demon as any. When was the last time anyone was Abandoned? It was a tale of terror parents used to straighten out wayward imps. Abandonment had been my father's soapbox, not a legitimate punishment. It was something Beelzebub said in frustration during my first mission, not a reality.

"Azazel, how do you vote?"

The oldest scowled. I couldn't swallow until he answered. "This is a travesty. I vote nay."

I released a deep, trembling breath.

Tied again. Two to two.

"Come on," Dialphio growled just loud enough for me to hear.

The vote, my fate, came down to Seraph. Would she put fairness before this outlandish rivalry and mutual hatred between the Vicus and Nijals? Would she see that I'd been trying to help the situation, not instigate anything or even act as the aggressor? Seraph worked with us during the Taurus mission; she knew I had a low flash point at times, but I would have never hurt her nephew unless it was in self-defense, or to defend an innocent. Recent evidence aside, wasn't she rational enough to see past her emotional bias? I was about to find out.

Michael leaned forward to look down the length of the table. "And last, Seraph. Your vote will break the tie. A reminder to everyone; a simple majority dictates the Council's decision. We will not tolerate displays of mortification or outrage. With that being said, your vote, please."

Seraph folded her hands atop the jade table. She leaned in my direction even though five body lengths separated us. The air was sucked from my lungs. My heartbeat thudded in my ears. Her mouth opened, and a single word echoed around the chamber for eternity.

18

UNDERWORLD/OVERWORLD

BILBA SAT at the foot of my bed. Ralrek at the head. Out in my kitchen, dishes clanked, a haunting, solitary background ambience.

"This isn't the end, Zeke," Bilba pounded a fist into my innocent mattress. "I promise you, everything I do, from now on, will be aimed at fighting this."

"It's not like we can go back to the Army and get distracted by all those hunks," Ralrek said with a wink.

"Being expunged makes you a figment of their imagination," Bilba said. I think it was supposed to be a joke, but it was too level to sound like one. Maybe now that the Overworld was destined to be my future home, forcing these two together, they would work out this issue of Ralrek's attraction to mortals.

I nodded, my head dipped toward my suitcase to hide my shame. I shoved another shirt into its open gullet. How many was I going to need in the Overworld? How was I going to get new clothes up there? A job. I would have to work for a living in the Overworld—which I wasn't afraid of—but how did I start? The money I'd made in the mortal Army wouldn't last long—did I even still have my bank account back in

Tacoma now that the Council expunged my existence from that realm?

"This isn't right," Ralrek growled. "But I'm with Bilba. Whatever you need, we'll do it. Even if you don't hear from us for a while, know that we're working on it. I don't quit on friends."

My throat constricted so tight I was surprised air passed through. It took every ounce of energy I had to not cry out. But if there was one thing Kanthor Sunstone taught me, it was that incubi didn't cry. Yet, that's all I wanted to do.

Deciding to test Kanthor's theory, I opened my mouth, hoping to not make a fool of myself. "I appreciate it, guys. But there's nothing you can do. The Council made their decision. The only thing I can do is hope that, after a while at least, they'll reverse it. But I do know one thing," I said, turning and finally facing them. "I don't want you two getting involved and making trouble for yourselves. This isn't your fight. It's mine. And the last thing either of you need, the last thing I need when I'm up there and can't help, is for you to start a fight you'll never win. Please promise me you won't do that."

Bilba and Ralrek shared a look.

"I can't," Bilba announced.

Ralrek was nodding before Bilba finished. "Me either, Zeke. This isn't just your fight."

I gave him a quizzical look.

"Gemini?" Ralrek said in a harsh bark. "I rotted in that prison cell alongside you. I was shamed publicly, standing right by your side. That doesn't sit right with me, it hasn't. How many others have they treated like that over the last thousand years, never mind the last fifty thousand? Do you think we're the first to be used by the Council? We weren't the first and we won't be the last. You're naïve if you think that."

"I don't," I said in a croaking response.

Bilba was off the bed and by my side in an instant. "You're not alone. We can't do anything right now, but we will figure what we *can* do. Be strong. Be focused. And, I mean this, do not give up hope. We're not abandoning you."

Ralrek slid to my other side, tapping my suitcase. "Did you pack all the demonic notebooks?"

I snorted through the sobs threatening to burst out of my chest. "Yeah. Tons of them."

"Good," he nodded. "You'll need them. We're staying in touch throughout this, so make sure you keep one with you at all times." I smiled and didn't need to be a clairvoyant to know that he recognized it as fake. He rubbed my shoulder. "It's going to be okay, Zeke."

I closed my suitcase lid and latched it. Maybe I was being too sentimental, but closing it was a significant gesture, the severing of a tie.

The three of us looked at it as if it could give insightful guidance. After a long and awkward silence, I said, "You guys want to walk me out?"

"We're walking you to the rift," Ralrek said.

Bilba nodded.

I shook my head. "You don't have to do that. There is no sense in putting yourself in front of the Council if they're there, which wouldn't surprise me."

Ralrek opened my door and headed out, speaking to Bilba. "Can you believe this guy? Thinking he's got a choice in the matter?"

Bilba hefted the suitcase as if showing me some secret prize he'd just won. A comical light in his eyes, he said, "You coming?" And then he left too.

I shook my head, looking around my bedroom one last time. The rush to get rid of me deprived me from seeing my landlord, and that brought a smile to my face. Someone from the Council having to deal with Manes Mezess about my broken lease would be the only form of justice I could ask for.

I joined Bilba and Ralrek at the front entryway. They were trying to be strong, their jaws set. "Let me say goodbye," I said, and they gestured with head tilts that they would wait outside.

"Hey, Mother," I said as I walked into the kitchen. She stood at the sink, her back to the door, washing my dishes. "You don't have to do that."

Without turning, she said, "You can't leave the apartment like this, Ezekial. Let me help."

"The guys are going to take care of everything."

My mother clutched the dishtowel. She spun, and I saw the toll this was taking on her. Red-rimmed eyes, strained veins protruding along her temple, the quivering lips. She looked like the ghost of the demon I knew before I began my service to the Council.

"Please let me do this for you," she said in a voice so frail it was as if she'd aged three millennia overnight. "It's a mother's duty to care for her child. I need to do this. Please let me."

"Okay," I said in a soft voice and held her.

She collapsed against me, sobbing. We stood there as time stood still, mother and son, saying goodbye without speaking a word.

I tried to pull away numerous times, to break the agony of goodbye. A dragged out farewell with my mother was an unfair additional punishment. Pain didn't subside as long as the instrument causing it remained. I was that instrument. The quicker I disappeared for my Abandonment, the better for everyone. It was the only way forward. Plus, the longer we carried this goodbye out, the more I thought. The more I thought, the more it solidified my rising doubt about ever being allowed to come back. And I couldn't lose hope now; it was all I had left.

She held on to me. Clutched. Gripped. I moved my hands to hers, and gently, but firmly removed them. "Mother, I have to go."

"I know," she said in a weak voice, those two words trembling so severely they were almost unrecognizable. "I had hoped you would have made peace with your father. We can't change that now, but it is something I will struggle with forever. I love you, Ezekial."

"I love you too," I spun, not wanting to think about my father, and definitely not wanting to see my mother break down. I scrambled for the front door, my throat almost exploding in pain.

There was a thump and the rattling of dishes behind me. I paused long enough to look back into the kitchen to see my mother collapsed against the sink, her shoulders heaving as she sobbed. At least she'd waited for me to walk away before revealing the true state of the pain I'd caused.

Bilba and Ralrek waited for me at the street, just as they did outside the one stop I had to make before heading for the rift. I had to say goodbye to the demon who always believed in me, without question or fault; the succubus who never wavered and who helped me see the potential I had.

"Closed?" I asked Dialphio.

She nodded, her hair unkempt, her cheeks flushed, which was easier to see now that she wasn't wearing her typical rose-colored blush. "Call me crazy, but I'm not in the mood to deal with customers today."

"Even book lovers?"

"Even book lovers," she answered without offering at least a sad smile.

"I need to go. If they haven't already, I imagine the Council will send patrols if I'm not at the rift soon. They can be like that."

Dialphio's unsteady chirp was the sweetest sound. She sniffed back tears. "Before you go, hang on. I have something for you."

"Okay."

I waited as she disappeared around the corner of stacks of books that formed a wall to hide her desk. Within seconds, she came back holding a burlap-wrapped package in one hand. It was small and rectangular.

"What's this?"

Dialphio stared at what she held, finally releasing it to my hands. "It's a gift, one I want you to protect. But," she said firmly, still not relinquishing full control of the gift, "Make me a promise before I hand this over?"

"Of course," I said, more curious than ever. "I hope you know I would do anything for you. If I promise it, it'll happen."

Her expression turned serious, wiping away the sadness and sorrow that haunted her from the moment I walked into The Book Abyss. "You will not open this until you're in the Overworld. The second you step through and that rift closes, you can, but not a minute before that. Understand?"

I knew enough about Dialphio to know when she truly meant something and truly meant to kick my ass if I violated that something. This was another one of those moments.

"I promise." And she released the gift. "Thank you for this … whatever. I'm sure it's awesome."

We shared a soft, sad laugh. It was time for me to leave.

Before I made it to the door, Dialphio grabbed my hand. Her eyes steady as she spoke one last promise. "None of us know what will come of this, Ezekial, but others don't determine your fate unless you allow it. Remain true to your course, to who you are, and don't doubt your path."

"Thank you. Thank you for everything, Dialphio. I'm a better demon because of you."

"Oh, I know," she said with a laugh–cry. "Now do me the favor of repaying that by staying true. You'll understand what I mean one day. At least I hope your bonehead does."

We hugged one last time, and I cranked the door open.

"And stay away from mortal women," Dialphio shouted after me. "They're nothing but trouble!"

I didn't care to hide the tears flowing freely, nor my

heaving chest, as I stepped into the pedestrian zone of Old Towne. True to their word, Ralrek and Bilba wrapped themselves around me, escorting me all the way to the rift. The whispered words and stares of the demons enjoying another day in their innocent existence barely registered. The cobblestone gave way to smooth brimstone streets, which my eyes never left until we were at my final Underworld destination.

None of the Founders bothered to ensure I left. Only a small cadre of guards stood by the rift to ensure the mission to rid Hell of Zeke was complete. Ten guards, no less.

"Here," a tall one said, stepping forward and dropping a hefty sack at my feet. It thumped on the brimstone.

"What is this?"

"From a friend," he said, his back to me as he rejoined the squad.

A friend? I hefted it; it was lighter than I expected for as full as it was. It didn't make much noise. Before saying my last goodbyes, I crammed the sack into my solitary suitcase—I learned from my Army debacle.

"Well, I guess this is it," Bilba said, hugging me one last time. I'd lost count of how many hugs I'd received in a single morning. As we embraced, Bilba whispered, "I meant what I said. You are not alone, and we're not letting this go. Don't forget that." And then he pushed me away playfully.

Ralrek took his place. "We've got your six." We slapped each other's backs and then let go, me appreciating him using a mortal military colloquialism on my send-off.

The rift sizzled with the blue flame of the Hellfire. It was the first time I thought about my father since the sentence was passed. Right now, he was probably at work, maintaining that eternal fire, the flame of annihilation, the very thing that would separate us from each other forever. I wondered if he was bothered by knowing he would never see me again.

I paused at the mouth of the rift, aware of the guards watching. The Council and their armed thugs could kiss my ass. These last few seconds with my best friends were mine to enjoy.

"You guys take care of each other," I said, gulping down what would be a seemingly endless string of sobs. "I love you both like brothers."

They had their arms around each other, and I hoped they would be all right. As I turned, they shouted the same in return.

As the blinding flash of light obliterated Hell for the last time, I finally released my boiling pain. No more time for goodbyes.

"SEATTLE, HUH? WHY?"

From the roof of the hotel that would be my home for the immediate future, I looked at the streets below, across the blocks stretching away toward Elliott Bay. The Colman Dock was abuzz with mortal activity. Mortals. My new tribe.

The city was the location of my first visit to the Overworld and being back, I felt a certain connection spark to life. I felt energized, as if my connection to the city had been severed too early. There was only one answer to why I selected Seattle as my Abandonment—one of the few favors the Council did for me. Bilba told me sending me to a destination of my choosing was required, not a favor. The only favor I received from them was the sack full of mortal money at my departure, more than I could spend in the next year. Them, or the mysterious friend it had come from in a sack, delivered by a guard.

I faced Cancer, thinking of the wonderful things she taught me about servitude during our shared time in Iraq. She'd never met Aries, but something told me she would have gotten along with him. They were one and the same.

"You chose it too," I reminded her.

"Because of you," she laughed.

After her own Abandonment, a punishment dished out within an hour of them doing the same to me, I was honored that she accepted my invite to join me in Seattle. More than that, I was grateful she hadn't been killed by Seraph—though I doubt she would be so bold in the Council chamber, around her peers. Getting Cancer to the Overworld was the one way to ensure her safety. Accepting her Abandonment was the only safe solution, Cancer realized. But I knew it was not only about that. Leaving her family had to be difficult, but she also felt horrible about what happened with me. The price I paid was too steep, she said, and she could not let me suffer alone.

I fought her, not wanting Abandonment, and the price it required, but she made me see the sense of giving up her Abilities forever for the chance to live a life where she did not have to look over her shoulders at every turn, waiting for a Seraph-shaped threat. After everything that happened in Baghdad and with the Council, I couldn't blame her if she'd wanted to stay as far away from me, and the trouble that seemed permanently attached to my side, as possible. But she hadn't rejected me. In fact, she jumped at the chance, telling me we would find plenty of opportunities to continue serving the mortals. I think Aries would have liked that.

"We can have a lot of fun here, I think," I said, staring out over Elliott Bay, the water below rippling in the constant wind, the backdrop of mountain peaks and valleys off in the far distance. "It's a beautiful place."

"It is," she said, turning away from me to take in the natural beauty unlike anything we have—had—in Hell. "I imagine the Council will track us."

I tried not to think about the Council or anything related to that realm, except for the handful of demons who held a special place in my heart. I didn't want to think about the Council—except to wish for its self-destruction—or my powerlessness to affect change for the innocent demons who would suffer. It was too painful. To survive without breaking my mind, I needed to focus on my reality—living as a mortal in Seattle.

"No matter where we go, they'll track us, likely for the rest of our lives. I don't expect any peace."

Next to me, Cancer nodded, still staring out over the water.

I drew a deep breath. "This is home now. And there are mortals in need. We can do a lot of good for others here."

"We can," Cancer said with a satisfied exhale. I wish I felt as calm. "We will. By the way, can you still use your magic stick?"

"Are you hitting on me?"

She slapped my arm, but with a broad smile across her face. "You're gross."

I winked at her. "I haven't used Creed yet. I'm not really ready to call any Council attention to myself. I'd rather we start our good works project."

Thoughts of Aries flooded my mind. If he could see me, what would he think? Was I, at least, making headway in correcting my wrongs against him? Now was my chance. The Council might have accidentally given me a gift.

My hand went to the satchel at my side.

"Guess I can open this now," I said. I wanted to wait until I had privacy, but looking down at the streets of Seattle, my new home, and out over the water, the compulsion to unveil Dialphio's gift was strong.

I had carried the package to the roof just in case the desire to open it came over me. It sat at my feet as Cancer and I talked about the mortal future we would share. Now, as our conversation was winding down, and the sun was starting its descent out of the endless sea of blue—that I no longer feared floating off into, still not understanding gravity—the time had come.

Cancer watched as I untied the strings binding the burlap together.

She watched as my hands shook as I pulled the burlap back.

She smiled at my shock when I read the title on the book cover.

The Histories of the Balance.

I slid the note tucked into the fold of the cover from the book. It was in my boss's—ex-boss's—handwriting.

"What does it say?" Cancer asked, searching my face.

When I pulled my head up and roared with laughter, Cancer stepped back, eyes wide, and then laughed herself. "I hope that's a good sign and not one that you've lost your mind?"

"Not at all," I said, showing her the note.

Cancer read it. "She's giving you homework assignments, all the way from the Underworld."

"That's Dialphio," I said, a film of grief falling over me. "You would have liked her."

Cancer was there, rubbing my shoulder, handing the note back to me. "I'm sure I would have."

As my finger and thumb pinched it, Creed warmed against my hip. "No sense dwelling on it, right?" I said, turning to enjoy the sight of the descending sun and the way it lit her radiant cheeks. She still stared out over the water, its reddening light dancing in her brown eyes. "Plus, I have a legacy to fulfill."

THE END

WHAT'S NEXT IN THE ZODIAC?

Abandoned in the Overworld. Left to fend for himself. What does Zeke do without Bilba and Ralrek in the only place where demons can be killed?

Find out in "The Pride of Leo," book 5 of The Zodiac, out now!

REVIEWS HELP

If you enjoyed this book, I would appreciate your review.

Your time is valuable, but reviews not only help other readers find something they might like, but they help me as an author. They are important to me because they allow me to see what readers like you enjoyed about the book and what I could have done better.

Thank you to every one of you who takes the time to leave a review!

ARE YOU MISSING OUT?

Get the latest news, special deals, exclusive stories, first looks at book covers, and more by signing up for Paul Sating's newsletter!

Sign up for Paul's newsletter to follow all the news and special deals for upcoming novels, and to catch up on the latest regarding his podcast at http://www.paulsating.com.

GET EXCLUSIVES!

Get free ebooks, chances to win autographed books, exclusive stories, "first looks," have input on Paul's future books, and more, by supporting him on Patreon.More stories on-the-go! Get exclusive access to Paul Sating's fiction, including free audio books, in podcast form!

Get more stories each month by becoming a Patron! New exclusive fiction each month!

Become a Patron, for as little as $1/month at patreon.com/paulsating!

ACKNOWLEDGMENTS

This book's Acknowledgments section will be different that anything I have done before.

None of the *Zodiac* books would happen if it weren't for those immediate loved ones; my wife, Madeline; daughters, Nikki and Alex; and my best friend, Kevin Baker. Cindy Niespodzianski, my editor, is such a key to these stories, someone who honors me with her talents. J. Caleb, the visual might behind bringing Zeke to life on these covers. I am forever grateful to all of my Patrons on Patreon; the cast of *Paul's Epic Peeps* who beta and advance read these books so you don't have to slog through garbage; all of my newsletter subscribers; my *Audio Fiction* podcast fans; the friends and family who support and encourage me. Writing these books to take you on fun adventures with Zeke and the gang takes a lot to pull off.

But this book's Acknowledgments, though I love the aforementioned people, is all about Adam Burke.

On the weekend of July 18th 2020, Adam lost his long battle with cancer (yes, I realize how surreal it may seem that I'm dedicating this acknowledgment to him, considering the disease he died from and the name of the Zodiac sign for this book). I'm not being insensitive; we simply hoped this would not have happened, at all, though he knew it was coming, but for many years yet. This was never how it was supposed to be.

I dedicated *The Gemini Paradox* to Adam, but never told him, because I wanted it to be a surprise. You see, Adam came into my life when Jon Grilz of the *Small Town Horror* podcast (and now of *Creepy* podcast), promoted my *Subject: Found* podcast. Right away, Adam became a Patron, a fan who donates money to the show every month. He did that for years. Not only did he contribute to help pay podcasting bills so I could continue creating art for free for everyone, but he bought every one of my books, and as we became friends, he became even more supportive, in more important ways.

Ask any writer friend you have; writing is tough and lonely. No matter how many people you have on your team, you never really know if the story you're putting out into the world is good. Yes, there will always be things that can be fixed. Internet trolls are everywhere, and writers aren't free from them. And authors have to put a lot more than just blood, sweat, and tears into our stories. Each book an author writes is a peek into the person's life, not only at that moment, but all the paths they've taken to get where they are. No matter how numb we may seem to sensitive topics and situations (we're not), publishing books is a very intimate event in an author's life—each and every time we do it. We treasure those supportive people in our lives. People just like Adam. They're very good for us.

When a book doesn't do as well as we think it will/can/should, when it flops and is received with silence. That hurts. A lot. We put ourselves out to the world in the form of fictional characters, settings, and even worlds. We open our minds and hearts to build the stories readers enjoy.

We are open for analysis, by every single reader holding or listening to our book.

Laying ourselves open for (literally, if we're lucky, the world) strangers is an incredibly vulnerable thing to do. And rejection can get us spiraling into the center of a mental and emotional storm.

Adam routinely checked in with me. Every time we chatted, regardless of what the conversation was about, his courage and strength reminded me to stop being a baby, and to get to work on making the next book better than the one I had just finished. He would playfully—sort of—yell at me when he felt I was giving too much away for free. He would get on his Facebook and repost my book and podcast posts so his friends knew about my creations.

Adam and I were in discussions about me telling his story through a character in a future series. We never got to finish those discussions as cancer took more and more of his strength. But Adam's sharing of his life's stories has given me enough that I will be able to immortalize him in that character. I just hope I do him and his memory justice.

He did all this and more while fighting cancer; a ravaging beast that tortured him for years. There were times when he suffered greatly, and times when remission gave him hope. There were times when chemo kicked his ass, but those times never lasted, because Adam always told me he was going to "kick *cancer's* fucking ass."

Adam did not lose in the end, he just wore out. Along the way, he taught a lot of people a lot of things. He encouraged everyone with his "no quit" attitude. He made people laugh. He reminded everyone who came into contact with him that the world can be healed if we all simply loved one another. He taught us what courage looked like. He embodied what it means to never quit.

To him, I will forever be grateful, and though I am very

aware that this tiny acknowledgment does not make up for my failure to tell him about his *Gemini* dedication, I hope, in some way, it solidifies the legacy he left behind.

Remembered always; Adam Burke, warrior.

ALSO BY PAUL SATING

Fantasy

The Zodiac Series

The Fall of Aries (Free for newsletter subscribers)

Bitter Aries

The Horn of Taurus

The Gemini Paradox

Cancer's Curse

The Pride of Leo

Virgo's Vigilantes

Libra's Liberation (Coming 2022)

Battleborn Series

Bloodborn (Free for newsletter subscribers)

Battleborn Trilogy

Fireborn (Coming 2022)

Rageborn (Coming 2022)

Battleborn (Coming 2022)

BoneBreaker Trilogy

King of Bones (Coming 2022)

War of Bones (Coming 2022)

Breaker of Bones (Coming 2022)

Crown of Thieves

Birth of a Thief (Free for newsletter subscribers)

Horror

The Plant

The Scales

12 Deaths of Christmas

Suspense

RIP

Chasing the Demon

Nonfiction

Novel Idea to Podcast: How to Sell More Books Through Podcasting

Nonfiction

Audio Fiction with Paul Sating

(Free for Patreon supporters!)

Urban Fantasy Author Podcast

(Available on all major podcast apps)

ABOUT THE AUTHOR

Paul Sating is an author, podcaster, and self-professed coolest dad on the planet, hailing from the Pacific Northwest of the United States. At the end of his military career, he decided to reconnect with his first love (that wouldn't get him in trouble with his wife) and once again picked up the pen. Years on, he has published eight novels and he hasn't even screwed up his podcasts, which have garnered over a million downloads.

When he's not working on stories, you can find him talking to himself in his backyard working on failed landscaping projects or hiking around the gorgeous Olympic Peninsula. He is married to the patient and wonderful, Madeline, and has two daughters—thus the reason for his follicle challenges.

Find out more about his other books and free podcasts from his website: paulsating.com.

HOW TO CONTACT PAUL

How to Contact Paul Sating

Published by Paul Sating Productions
    P.O. Box 15166
    Tumwater, WA 98511
    paul@paulsating.com

Follow Paul:
    Facebook: www.facebook.com/authorpaulsating
    Bookbub: bookbub.com/paul-sating
    Goodreads:
goodreads.com/author/show/16982359.Paul_Sating
    Instagram: @paulsating
    Pinterest: pinterest.com/paulsating
    Twitter: @paulsating

THE PRIDE OF LEO CHAPTER 1

BOOK 5 OF THE ZODIAC SERIES

(Click Here To Order Your Copy)

1 - Olympia

Months After Cancer

"HEY, FREAK."

My stride hitched, assuming someone was talking to me. Throughout my six-thousand-year life, nicknames stuck to me like statically charged lint sticks to socks, so why would this one not be included in my litany of titles?

But I wasn't the target of the felonious name. The taunt had come from a tall human, on the desirable side of six feet tall. His long appendages dangled, his fingers nearly reaching to his knees. Gangly, but not awkward.

Sunglasses obscured the gangly man's identity, along with a hoodie, pulled up to cover his head. I doubted I knew him; I didn't know many people in Olympia, having only lived here after moving from Seattle just over a month ago. That larger city was too expensive, so Cancer and I tried our luck in the state's Capital. I knew less than a dozen mortals, and they all came into my life at the soup kitchen where I volunteered.

I had just stepped off the bus and was walking toward the soup kitchen in downtown, passing the Red Lion that was once the Governor Hotel. The new ownership's banner hung at an angle as if hastily erected during an overnight hospitality siege.

I had planned on crossing over to Legion Way through Sylvester Park, but the park's grass glistened with the sheen of sprinkler systems and sun, and I didn't feel like getting my new sneakers wet. Half a week's salary went into obtaining them, and without a vehicle, my feet were my primary mode of transportation. I had a long day ahead and wet socks made for cold feet, and as a demon, Abandoned though I may have been, the Overworld was already could enough. This realm did not need my help. The sidewalk suited my purpose, even if it added thirty seconds to my walk commute. This route also gave me an excellent observation point to watch this aggressive guy.

The gangly man who drew my attention to the park wasn't alone. Five others stood behind him in a v–formation. After my time in the mortal army, I couldn't help notice how slack their formation was.

I scanned the park to a bench on the other side of a large gazebo clinging to a few spots of white paint. A slim man looked up toward the group from his seat on the bench. Squinting, he took in the gangly, hooded man. As I continued along the sidewalk, I pulled my bag closer. I didn't know much about the city yet, but I didn't need to be a native, nor a genius, to recognize this first sign of trouble.

The slim man on the park bench had the same sense. His hand slid to the side of his leg, where it wrapped around the sling of his backpack. Slowing my gait, I paused behind a big-leaf maple tree, whose branches spread a shadow. At this time of day, my presence could not be hidden from the group, but at least I would be obscured.

The four–lane street to my left streamed with cars and busses, normal for work week midday. Traffic crowding Capitol Way was a constant of this small Pacific Northwest city. Vehicles filled the lanes, and pedestrians filled its side-walks. My presence wouldn't stand out to this group, so I hung by the tree, interested in seeing how this played out. No one else seemed to notice.

"Yeah, I'm talking to you," the gangly man said, strutting forward. He and his entourage approached the gazebo, less than fifty yards away.

"I thought I told you I didn't want to see you around here anymore. You stupid or something?" gangly barked at the man on the bench.

The slim man rose slowly, slipping his backpack on in a fluid motion that neither hinted nor displayed aggression.

"Shit," I whispered.

I did not like this. The slim man moved with the caution of cornered prey, buying time while figuring a way out. I didn't know him from anyone in the group, but I knew six-on-one spelled peril. This had the potential to be a serious crime, and every indication around Sylvester Park signaled I was the only one aware of it.

"Leave me alone," the slim man said. His voice was soft, but direct, higher-pitched than I expected. It reminded me of Taurus's voice, one of the last incubi I wanted to be reminded of at this point. I was questioning a lot about myself and my recent history of decisions that led to my Abandonment, and the memory of Taurus right before I killed him in self-defense was still too vivid. A raw reminder of my troubles.

The slim man moved laterally along the bench.

The trees lining Capitol Way provided enough cover for the group. A hill ran the length of the park on Seventh Avenue, rising fifteen feet to meet the street and topped with a row of bushes and trees that made great cover for nefarious activities.

When the gang saw the slim man sliding along the bench, they moved to cut him off.

"Shit. Shit. Shit."

I stepped off the sidewalk and down the slight slope to the nearest tree. Turning sideways, I peeked around it and watched as the group shepherded their victim toward Seventh. His escape route cut off, he was probably unaware of the danger he was putting himself in. I glanced up and down the road, not seeing a police vehicle or anyone who passed as an authority figure. On sidewalks crowded with government administrators, elderly shoppers, artists, and hipsters, not a single uniform made an appearance. In the Underworld, Lucifer's Council has armed demons everywhere. Not so much in the Overworld, as if those who ruled it trusted the populace. What a concept.

"Where are the Lucifer-blessed police when you need one?" I grumbled.

"Come here!" a rough voice yelled.

The slim man tried to pull away. A burly brute, desperately in need of a shave, dove for his target's backpack and snagged a pocket. Slim attempted to bolt, but the other man's size prevented him from moving further than the backpack strap's reach. The brute gave it a yank as the slim victim slid his arms out of the strap and sprinted away.

"Grab him!" the gangly leader snarled, giving chase along with his cadre.

While keeping my eyes on the situation, I dropped to a knee behind the tree, hurriedly unzipping my backpack. The zipper caught halfway—snagged.

"Shit!" I repeated. Look, after spending the better part of two years around the American Army personnel, I can hardly be blamed for the complete disintegration of my vocabulary.

Slim sprinted across the green. He was fast, putting distance between himself and most of the group within a few strides. Unfortunately for him, one younger man, his hair split by a shaved zigzag pattern, measured him step-for-step.

Lunging, Zigzag sprawled out, swinging his arm in a sharp scissoring movement that took the slim man's feet out. He went down with a scream, landing and rolling through the wet grass.

Wet sneakers were in my immediate future.

The rest of the gang caught up. One, his hair a mass of loose curls like an overused shower poof coming out of a month-long heroin binge, lifted one of the forest-green garbage cans and slammed it down on the slim man before he could raise a protective arm. A metallic clank rang out as trash met human.

Glancing away from the unfolding scene, I searched inside my backpack for my halberd.

Creed, being a magical halberd of mysterious origins, was as stubborn as my father's perspective on unquestioning obedience to Lucifer and His Council. A long time ago, I learned the halberd had a mind of its own any time we were physically separated. According to Aries, the ancient Founder who gifted it to me, I was the only one who could wield it. Somehow, it knew if someone other than me touched it. Proof came in a few unfortunate—not for me—incidents. I did not have to fear anyone stealing it, but I sure as heaven needed to worry about mortals seeing it. Thus, the backpack.

The park was empty except for this group, their intended victim, and a few stragglers who navigated the bordering sidewalks. Even if the pedestrians noticed, which I suspected a few did from their quick sideways glances, none intervened. I had to help this human, and I needed Creed.

Beyond the gazebo, underneath a tall tree, the group surrounded the fallen victim, who shielded his face with his hands.

I glanced down the street again, gripping Creed and hoping for a lucky law-enforcement break. The foot-long, four-inch circumference truncheon appeared to be nothing more than a solid piece of dark, petrified cherry to the uninitiated. With a flick of my wrist, I could transform it into a six-foot halberd.

Creed was power. More importantly for this situation, I was dangerous.

The slim man stood and raised his fists, a scowl coloring his face. He didn't look like a victim or someone who would accept what this group aimed to dish out.

They circled slowly, their steps, careful.

"I told you what would happen if I saw you out around the city, didn't I?" the gangly, hooded bully snarled.

"I don't care what you want," the slim man said. "I have as much of a right to be here as anyone."

Gangly flicked his hand. "No, you don't. You're a freak. Told you last time, I better never see your freaky face again, or I was going to fix that ugly mug."

A sly smirk undercut the slim man's high cheekbones. He wiggled his fingers. "Come and try then."

The others *oooh'ed* and *ahhh'ed*.

"Shut up!" the group's leader ordered. Most refused, still snickering behind balled fists. He turned on the slim man. "I'm going to break you, freak."

"I'm still waiting for you to try," came the response. Their target inched backward.

I pressed Creed against my thigh, inching from behind my cover. I wanted to give the target the opportunity to hold his own. Plus, if this resolved before I needed to get involved, I wouldn't have to use Creed. During the day. In public.

Gangly snarled and lunged.

So much for that plan.

I stepped into the park, still trying to keep a low profile.

Gangly swung and the slim man ducked, sending his sunglasses–wearing enemy swirling away. He spun to counter his aggressor's momentum. The move only drew more laughter from the gang, enraging the man behind the sunglasses.

"You fucking freak. You're gonna pay for that!"

He lunged again and the slim man dodged once more, swinging a fist into the hooded figure's back as he passed. The smack was sharp, a solid connection.

Raising both fists, the attacker half-cocked his head at the gang. "What are you waiting for, idiots? Jump her ass."

Her?

Then the context of this confrontation hit me. If I despise anything more than Lucifer's Third Council, it's bullies. After six thousand years of being ostracized because I was the Segregate, the only demon ever born without magic, I understood what it felt like to be treated differently. And I despised demons—and people—who did that to others.

The group cinched their loop around the slim man. Zigzag moved to the left, Worn Out Shower Poof to the right. The burly man and the other spread out, circling as the instigator moved in.

"This ain't ending good for you," he spat. "If you're not smart enough to stay holed up in your freak house or stay out of town, we'll make sure you can't walk back into it."

The slim man didn't wait for the group to corral him. He sprang, his fist connecting so hard with the bully's face I could hear the splintering of the plastic sunglasses from three dozen yards away. The bully's head rocketed, and he stumbled backward.

Burly Boy moved in for the attack. The target spun and thrust a kick into his thigh, kicking his leg out from underneath him. He screamed in a voice too high-pitched for someone his size.

"I'm done!" Burly Boy whined, holding his leg and limping at an impressive speed toward the intersection in the opposite corner of the park, where a handful of window shoppers gawked at goods through glass.

Though it gave him a temporary advantage, the move threw the slim man off-balance as the others neared.

The slim man might be able to hold his own for a while, but he would have to be seriously bad ass to last more than a half dozen minutes against a half dozen pieces of trash.

I lifted Creed. "You ready?"

The halberd-in-truncheon-form warmed in my hand.

I sprinted forward, giving Creed a shake. The truncheon extended. A six-foot weapon of destruction, its double-ax head sprang to life, the asymmetrical and half-moon axes promising violence from the top, while a wavy dagger jutted from the bottom.

"Please don't make me regret this," I whispered to the halberd, knowing full-well it would do whatever it wanted.

I never cast magic with Creed because I couldn't control its spells. The weapon had once shown me its full promise in an apartment in Kaiserslautern, Germany, when an assassin attempted to, well, assassinate me and an angel named Cassie. Since that time, Creed's magic had only shown itself on a few sessions where I practiced in privacy, and always of its own accord. I wasn't even sure how to engage its magic, stubborn as that halberd was. Magic happened when Creed wanted it to, and not a moment before. The only gifts I partially controlled were my heightened inherent senses.

The haft vibrated. Was Creed laughing at me?

One man with a fluffy beard partially covering a long scar on his cheek, turned as I approached. His eyes widened almost comically when he saw me sprinting at him with the three-bladed weapon.

I lowered Creed and swung before Scar Boy figured out his next move. The haft of Creed connected with the man's ankles as he attempted to leap over my strike. Wood cracked on bone, the halberd using the man's momentum and lack of grounding to send him flying. He landed in a heap behind me as I continued toward the next bully.

This one had close cropped hair, the sides shaved in a military style. He tried to jump out of my way, but I thrust Creed to my side, looking like a marching band baton twirler. Creed clothes lined Military Man. The air sucked from his lungs at contact, and I left him behind, gasping and clutching his throat.

I didn't want to use too much force, but like I said, Creed has a mind of its own. Taking care of Military Man was something he decided, not me. I was just the halberd's executor.

I stopped, raced back to check on the human to make sure Creed had not done too much harm, and received a nasty surprise for my consideration. Scar Boy had grabbed the discarded garbage can during my distraction and sent it crashing down against the back of my head, knocking me flat on the ground. The world exploded in brilliant white light, and my mouth filled with the musky combination of dew and city water sprinkling systems. I tried to roll over but he was on my back, sending punches into my kidneys, shoulders, and skull. I kicked and scrambled, hoping to knock him off-balance and get to my feet before he knocked me out. I couldn't get myself free. After a few rounds of punches, he made the mistake of mistakes. His hand slid along my arm to where I held Creed in a weakening fist.

"Don't." The word came out as a croak.

Either he couldn't hear me or he was too stupid to heed my warning. His hand continued past my own to the haft of Creed. As soon as his skin contacted the weapon, energy bound in the fires of Hell surged through Creed. First forming a blue light at the point of skin and petrified cherry, the flame of the Hellfire spread rapidly in a ball around the man's hand, heating to a brilliant white. There was nothing I could do. He was on his own as Creed extolled the punishment.

At the zenith of its brilliance, Creed's energy sent the man flying backwards into the large white gazebo fifty yards away that hadn't had a paint job since the Ford Pinto was popular. The man crashed through its shingled roof and to the floor in a cloud of dust.

I steadied myself and surveyed the scene, trying to ignore the splitting headache and sore ribs.

These were much better odds.

The intended victim had Gangly in a headlock. The bully was bleeding from a spot between his eyes, presumably where his sunglasses had snapped. With their leader corralled, the others were all mine.

Shower Poof and Zigzag glanced at each other as I neared. I read their silent exchange. Neither looked confident about the outcome, and that's exactly where I wanted them.

"You two have a choice. I'll let you walk away, but you go now. You don't help the idiot back there, and you never bother this man again. Sound like a deal?"

Zigzag glanced once more at Shower Poof before nodding and turning to a full-out sprint toward the popular coffee shop across the park. Shower Poof hitched his pants and growled, his nose wrinkling as his lip curled. He was about to make a terrible decision.

"And let that bitch prance around the city? Getting away with everything at the job? Carl ain't going to put up with that anymore. No way. That chick needs to know her place." The confidence in his voice shook me. No one could be this stupid.

"Wrong answer," I said.

I shifted Creed from hand-to-hand, despite its length. It was a tall weapon, taller than me by almost half a foot, but sometimes it felt as light as a demonic notebook, only with far more balance. The haft slapped against my palms each time I caught it. Shower Poof's eyes traversed the gap along with the halberd. Mesmerized like most people who witnessed the weapon's charm, he was too intimidated to realize how stupid of a decision he just made.

"You were saying?" I asked with a wicked grin.

Instead of doing the right thing, the smart thing, Shower Poof made his move. I ducked under his fist and smacked him across the back with Creed. He arched, his arms flinging out to the sides. The strike had hurt, Creed hardly in a forgiving mood.

He turned.

I raised an eyebrow. "You sure?"

Doubt skittered across the man's face. But he still came at me. As I raced forward I saw a flicker of regret. Planting the wavy dagger into the ground five inches deep, I grabbed the haft with both hands and jumped. Rotating laterally, I spun, my feet crunching into the man's back. He fell into the wet grass, and this time I did not give him an opportunity to decide on how this fight went.

I grimaced. "This is going to hurt you more than it will hurt me." With a quick shake of my hand, I collapsed Creed into the truncheon form and brought it crashing against the back of the man's head, knocking him unconscious. I stood and wiped off my pants. "Dumbass."

The fight was almost over. The last thing I had to do was pull the slim man off Carl the Bully.

The intended victim was allowing his pain and anger to get the better of his judgment. He now had Carl pinned underneath him, his knees pressing down on the other man's arms. The slim man slammed his fist into the bully's face, over and over. Even at this distance I could hear the pinned man grunt with each strike. He was defeated.

I wanted to stop the slim man from doing something he

would regret for the rest of his life. I knew what it was like to be a killer, after all.

I moved alongside the pair, out of arm's reach. I did not want him seeing me as an enemy. Tucking Creed against my leg so it was out of view, I raised my other hand in the universal sign of friendship.

The slim man did a double take, recognition flickering in his eyes.

"I'm a friend," I breathed, nodding my head to the side toward the fifteen-foot statue at the back edge of the park. Scattered around it, limp bodies of the group lay. He looked at what remained of the gang, holding his fist in the air, but not bringing it down.

He said, "You did that?"

I nodded. "How about ending this? I think he got," I said with a dip of my head toward the bully, "what he deserved. If he's an idiot, he'll come back. But I don't think that's going to happen." I straightened and looked around the park. Whereas no one got involved before, dozens of people had stopped along the sidewalk to watch. Some had their mouths covered. Many were on their phones.

"Shit."

"What?" the slim man asked.

"I think we're going to have a visit by Olympia's finest pretty soon," I said. "I'd get up if I was you."

There are few things in life I'm ever correct about, but predicting the arrival of police at this scene was one of them—of course. Bad luck and all that. Olympia's entire police force showed up—I'm being hyperbolic, I know, but there were a *lot* of them. When all was said and done, they were kind enough to only cite us for the incident, though it took an hour-long interview to get to that point. One of the conveniently interested witnesses mentioned my use of a weapon, but when the cop saw Creed—in its truncheon form—he was satisfied.

I was grateful they didn't attempt to take it, even for hasty examination. The snub might have been a shot to Creed's ego, but the halberd's cockiness needed to be checked.

"You promise no more trouble?" the cop asked.

I nodded at the beat up old model Mustang idling at curbside and the beautiful soul of a demon behind the steering wheel, her halo of brown hair glistening in the sun. "Nope. I was going to head into work, but I missed the start of my shift because of this. They wouldn't be happy about me walking in looking like this." Cupping my hand, I made an up-and-down motion at the blood and mud that stained my pants and shirt.

The cop jutted his chin at the gang. "Those guys are idiots, but they're not going to stay locked up forever. Keep yourself and your friend away from them."

I nodded. "Will do. Thanks."

Once the slim man finished his interview, we took a second to commiserate.

"I'm sorry about this," he said.

Rarely do I see eye to eye with someone, literally, not metaphorically. The slim man was my height with short, sandy hair and some light stubble along his rounded jaw. For the life of me all I saw was a human being. Nothing more. Certainly nothing to hate.

I waved away the apology. "Don't worry about it. It's no trouble."

He shrugged. "I heard that you missed your shift. I hope this doesn't get you in trouble with your boss."

"Nah, they're pretty cool. Plus," I said coolly flipping my hand, "it's not like they pay me much. If they've got a big problem with it, I can always find someone else to pay me too little for too much work. Anyway, the cop said he would stop by and let them know what happened. So that should help." I looked at him. "What about you? Are you okay? This won't get you in trouble with anyone?"

"Not anyone new," he replied.

"These guys been giving you trouble for a long time?"

He snapped his eyes shut, holding them like that for a few, long seconds. There was a long story hidden in there.

"Sorry. My name is Zeke. Ezekial really, but I prefer Zeke. Well, that's what my friends are allowed to call me. I figure, you and I connected over a brawl with bullies, so you're more than welcome to call me Zeke." I tried to laugh and lighten the moment a little, feeling wholly inadequate for the crap this man had to deal with. "And... I'm sorry this even happened."

The man smiled, but it held sadness. "It's not yours to apologize for, but I appreciate it. I'm Steve, by the way."

"Nice to meet you."

He shook my hand. "Likewise. Thanks again. Hope to see you around sometime."

Cancer smirked when I approached her car. The window rolled down, she cat-called me before I reached for the door handle.

Bending, I smiled. "You sexist. I'm not a piece of meat to drool over."

One eye widened, a playful look dancing across her smooth, brown skin. "Don't worry; I like more meat on my ... meat. Get in."

As we made our way back to the apartment, Cancer tapped on the steering wheel. "So, what was that all about?"

"You would think with a world war kicking off, humans would have better things to do than hate one another. Apparently, I'm just a dreamer," I said bitterly before explaining how the day unfolded.

At a few points, Cancer scowled. "I've heard and seen some dumb crap ever since we were Abandoned. I'm not surprised."

I sat forward. "What do you mean? Things that happened to you? Stuff like this?"

"Of course, Zeke. I'm a black woman to these mortals.

That makes me prime real estate for ignorance and stupid comments. It's nice, what you did for that man. But it's hardly isolated; don't fool yourself."

"It's bullshit."

"I know."

I slapped my leg. "I mean, no one bothered to help or get involved, not until we had the upper-hand. Then, all of a sudden, everyone cares. I got cited by the cops. Me! All I was doing was helping someone, and I got cited. Where is the fairness in that? It's just like everything else."

She cast me a sideways glance. "Are you comparing your situation to what that mortal goes through?"

It was a dangerous question. In terms of intelligence, I might be a butter knife in a drawer full of steak knives, but I was smart enough to know to be deliberate in answering. Our Abandonment had changed a lot, but one thing it had not altered was Cancer's outlook on life. She was still thoughtful of others, always considerate and giving. She helped the people of Baghdad, nursing untold scores through a war that ravaged their city. She faced down a familial enemy, the most powerful succubus in Hell, to ensure justice would not fail me. Ultimately, it did, but Cancer did not. When she spoke, it was best to shut up and listen, because her words always came from the right place.

"Absolutely not," I said in a rush. "What he went through … what he *is and will* go through is bullshit. Everything is. It's just unfair."

She shook her head.

"What's that about?"

"What?"

"You. Shaking your head. You've got something to say. Just say it."

Her shoulders rose and fell. "One of these days you're going to have to let go of what happened. You're not the only one who got screwed by the Council. I did too."

"I know. I didn't say you hadn't been."

One finger uncurled from the steering wheel, pointing at the sky as she made her point. "Yet, you don't hear me complaining about them as often as you do. Why is that?"

We passed a few city blocks before I could comment. "Doesn't it bother you that Chax got away with ... everything? That Seraph hid him so he could avoid accountability for what he did to you and your family?"

I met Cancer in Baghdad, where she was serving as a nurse in a neighborhood in the Khadra district. She had asked for help with a terrible curse she believed had been placed on her family that affected all of her relatives across generations, breaking them down, killing them long before their natural course. I helped—at least I tried—to get it removed by someone from the rival family by attempting to get them to recite a counter spell. Chax Vicu was in that rival family and served in a different brigade of the Army. With Bilba and Ralrek's help, we almost got to him, but the incubus escaped back to the Underworld. Making matters worse, his threat of being connected to a powerful family was true. Seraph, the most powerful succubus in Hell, was his aunt. She cast the deciding vote for my Abandonment.

"Of course it does. How could it not?" Her voice was level, but her hands gripped and rotated around the steering wheel. When she spoke again, the edge was gone. "But Zeke, I can't let that drive my actions. Talk about exhausting... and I'm already exhausted enough from... our Abandonment. Chax isn't worth it."

I wanted to confront her on that. Chax and what he got away with *did* matter. I wanted to remind her that she was in the Overworld amongst mortals, and growing weaker through her newfound mortality caused by being dispatched to this unnatural—for us—realm, while he was living it up large somewhere in the Underworld. Fat, dumb, and happy all because he had a powerful aunt.

Her furrowed brow told me to keep my big mouth shut. This was stressful enough. The war overseas was growing larger, and she was not there to help. She did not need me reminding her of the unfairness of how her life was panning out, especially now that the toll Abandonment was already wearing her down. I had never seen Cancer look so exhausted. Not even back in Baghdad, when she was the only care-provider for an entire suburb of Iraqis. Not even when she was saving a young boy's leg that had been shredded by a bomb. Not even when all Heaven was breaking loose around her. She was stressed enough about this situation, even if she was too stubbornly positive to admit it.

So instead of putting it on her, I focused it on myself. "I hate it Cancer. I swear, if I ever get the chance to make the Council pay, I will."

A nasally sigh later, she replied softly, "I know, Zeke. I know."

No matter how much I adored and respected her, I was not convinced Cancer truly knew how much I meant it.

Keep Going With Book 5 of The Zodiac!